MY SOUL IMMORTAL

Ashley Lauren Mitchell

The imagination of a boy is healthy, and the mature imagination of a man is healthy; but there is a space of life between, in which the soul is in a ferment, the character undecided, the way of life uncertain, the ambition thick-sighted: thence proceeds mawkishness, and all the thousand bitters which those men I speak of must necessarily taste in going over the following pages.

--John Keats, April 10, 1818 (in the Preface to Endymion)

May, 2005

Call me Lamia.

At least that is what I tell people to call me. However, many of them don't last long enough after hearing it to repeat it. I live at Désirs Cachés, an adult entertainment facility, or strip club to be more...colloquial. It is a house of salacious sin. The prurient members of society that end up in my private room at this particular strip club are very, 'exclusive'. They get the type of treatment they only dream about. But not pleasant dreams. Actually they would call them nightmares. These degenerates hear this name and don't think twice about its meaning. The girls that work here think it's a pretty name. How can I blame them? It is indeed a pretty name. But that is not why it is my name.

I own Désirs Cachés with two other...people. It is located on the corner of St. Ann Street and Bourbon in New Orleans,

Louisiana. We opened it in late October, 2003. It is not fancy and it's usually overlooked because of all the other more flashy and lavish ones that surround it. It provides fewer amenities than the others as well. Also, I think it sends a bad vibe. I believe I am that bad vibe. It probably can be blamed on a number of things however, but not my girls. I've never had a problem with any of the girls that work here. Many of them never get to see me anyway. I don't want them too spooked to work for us. I think, perhaps, I have a sort of sympathy, even empathy for these young ingénues. Of course, only to a certain extent. These girls are not my peers or my victims. If anything, they are my children under my aegis for as long as they are here. And they don't even realize it. They think it's Uncle Tony that does all the protecting behind his badge. And that's okay with me.

Uncle Tony is here every night, *protecting*. Apparently, he really is my uncle and he's also one of the owners of this club. Supposedly, my dead mother's brother, and the only surviving member of my family that I know of, or care to know of. He makes a good living and doesn't have to be here; but he is here, every night. He's not in this for the money or the girls. No, he's different. Like me. No, he is not like me. He is in this business because of me. Besides the fact that I'm his niece, he does this because he sees me as somewhat of a vigilante, ridding the earth of licentious banes one by one. I am a bane. No, I am Lamia. Call me Lamia.

　　　　　　　　　　Ashley Lauren Mitchell

"Lamia."

"Yeah?"

"You ready, honey?"

"Almost Diamond."

If I were a human, Diamond would most likely be my best friend. I believe that before this curse happened to me, we were best friends. I was told we met ten years ago through my Uncle Tony. She is the third owner of this strip club and the only other person besides Uncle Tony that knows my secret; and somehow she thinks it's the coolest thing in the world. I believe she's deranged for thinking that, but she's a sweet mortal. Her alias is as generic as they come, but she is not. She was rescued from a horrible situation by my Uncle Tony years ago. I know she's in love with him but is too afraid to ever tell him. Instead, I believe she expresses her love for him by helping me.

Tonight she's wearing a white, evenly cut wig, with sparkles throughout many of the strands, over her long brunette hair. The bangs of the wig are cut just above her eyes and the rest stops short of touching her shoulders. Everything else on her is just as white and sparkled, including her white eyeliner and sparkled eyelashes.

　Ashley Lauren Mitchell

She resembles a go-go dancer with her silver knee-high boots, short white skirt and silver bra like top that barely covers her breasts. The strings of her thong are showing just above the skirt. She is wearing a diamond bracelet that I have never seen absent from her left wrist for the eighteen months that I've known her. She looks like a bright angel that had been picked apart and sent to earth to work in a strip club. But she is not an angel. Angel is leaving the stage now which means it's almost feeding time.

Désirs Cachés was Diamond's idea, and a great one. Unlike the unfortunate girls who are forced by family members, significant others, or maybe just the need or want of money to be here. No, I do this for Charles and for men like him. He is the one that will satiate my thirst tonight. It's been the three days that Uncle Tony and I have agreed on and tonight Charles will be mine. Somewhere I remember reading that having sex at least every three days is healthy for humans. Since I do not have sex, cannot have sex, I interpret that bit of information to mean anything one enjoys doing which has a psychologically calming effect, done every three days would be just as efficacious. So, every third night, I collect my psychologically calming effect, and tonight it is Charles.

"Is he sitting out there?" I asked Diamond, who's leaning against the doorway of my private dressing room and looking at me with eyes that carry the weight of pity in their gaze. I stare at the mirror. I hate pity. I hate mirrors more.

"Of course gorgeous. You knew he would be. Uncle Tony wouldn't let us down. If he had to drag him in here himself, he'd be here. He wants this fucker just as bad as you do." Her words thick with deviousness.

"Doubtful," I respond, with a grin just as devious.

Diamond. The only other human besides Uncle Tony I know I can trust. The only other one who knows what I am and is still alive. It's not her fault I'm this way, and she wouldn't dare tell a soul about me. Who would believe her anyway? She knows that any such claims being distributed by a person like her would only prove that those in this line of work are just as stupid as people think. But she is not stupid. She is clever, like me. And she is avaricious, like me. And she is...No, she is not like me. She doesn't want the same things out of this as me. Diamond is in this for the money, and Uncle Tony and I make sure she has plenty of it to keep this joint open.

Ashley Lauren Mitchell

I have no need for money, so she and Uncle Tony divide it and take care of everything. Diamond loves the money, and tonight I love Charles.

    I hate that name.
    Charles.

I've been waiting to entertain Charles for three nights now. Uncle Tony did his background checks on this depraved individual, Charles, and has decided he's the chosen one. Charles will be brought to me and I will ease his suffering. He will no longer have to think about the pain he's caused, or will cause, anyone again. I will be his savior, providing his retribution and he will be mine. Charles is 44 years old; 6'2, maybe 280 lbs. He has no wife, no children, and no strings attached to anyone that would miss him when I send him to hell tonight. I like that. I don't need anyone wasting time searching for this man. If he's going to be in my private room, he deserves it. And I can't wait to give him what he deserves.

I'm almost finished preparing to receive Charles. I'm wearing...nothing at all. I believe that's best because I don't want any blood getting on my clothes. The business of blood is a messy one, but I prefer to keep it as unsoiled as possible. Charles will appreciate my naked form, especially since it will be the last tangible thing he sees.

                                           Ashley Lauren Mitchell

I often wish I could see myself in a mirror so that I can see what these men see before they close their eyes, forever. I envy them for being able to see their horrible images staring back at them in the glass. As if they deserve it. As if I deserve it. I can only look down and see my hands and arms, my breasts, my stomach and everything else below. But what I want to see most are my eyes. I have a photograph of what I look like, but I'm sure it's not the same as looking in a mirror and seeing my own reflection. To be able to look at myself and say, this is me, this is what I look like, this is who I am. I don't have that luxury so I'm forced to find out who I am by watching others look, or rather, stare, at me.

It's different with Uncle Tony and Diamond. They don't fear me when they look at me like the others do. But they also don't allow me to go downstairs and mingle with the humans. I understand that. What if someone noticed I don't have a reflection in one of the many mirrors that we have in the club? Or that I have two long, pointed incisors. It wouldn't matter how drunk they are or how much they may forget what they see. It could still mean that they wouldn't leave out through the same entrance they came in.

Diamond is the one that 'dresses' me for dinner. I put on my robe and she comes in to adjust my hair and Mardi Gras mask. Since it's the only thing I wear to dinner, she takes great

Ashley Lauren Mitchell

pleasure in choosing a different mask for me every time. Tonight my mask is designed with black and red sequins with feathers at the top. If it were up to me I wouldn't wear the mask. But Diamond likes all the girls to wear Mardi Gras masks; and because she does so much for me, I submit to her desires. The masks do seem to add more mystery to faces. On rare occasions, I'm allowed to step out of my room, but I must have on a vizard. I could, of course, do anything I want, but for Uncle Tony's and for Diamond's sake, I comply with the rules they've established. I guess they have kind of grown on me. Uncle Tony and Diamond. Not the rules.

My number one, and really only rule, is that none of the girls are allowed to work here when they are menstruating. I thought that would be a tacit understanding, but I guess these poor girls need money so much they're willing to work here during their time. I don't have that rule because I care about how the girls are feeling on their cycles. I have that rule because I can smell the blood seeping out of their bodies. One night when we first opened the club one of the girls, Sable, I believe, was menstruating. She was putting on her make-up in the mirror when I appeared like a shadow behind her. She couldn't see me standing there, watching her in the mirror, wondering what it was about this girl that made me want to devour her. I bent over to smell her and I breathed on her neck. I saw the chill bumps rise on her skin and her nipples instantly

                    Ashley Lauren Mitchell

became hard. I watched her eyes shift in the mirror to the vent on the ceiling, probably thinking it was the air conditioner that was making her shiver, and not knowing she was only inches away from drawing her last breath. I closed my eyes and opened my mouth...

"Lamia?" Diamond shrieked as she burst through the door. "What are you doing in here?"

Sable immediately turned around in her chair. When she caught sight of me, she froze, like a statue. Her brown eyes wide and curious. I smiled at her shocked appearance.

"I smelled something in this room, and, I, wanted to see what it was." I replied trying not to sound irritated for having been interrupted.

Diamond looked at Sable then back at me, hoping Sable would believe what I'd just said. "Okay, well, I'll find out what it is and take care of it. You go back to your dressing room and wait for me." She demanded.

I calmed down; realizing Diamond was only doing what she knew was best for me, and for Sable. I gave a quizzical last look at Sable, turned, and walked out of the room. Moments

               Ashley Lauren Mitchell

Ashley Lauren Mitchell

later Diamond and Uncle Tony came into my dressing room asking me what I was thinking. I told them that Sable had a strong bloodlike scent emanating from her body and I couldn't resist her. The two of them looked at each other and then back to me.

"Lamia, she's having her period right now." Diamond said.

I wanted to believe her but I wasn't sure. I'd done my fair share of reading about when females go through that phase. Something that I had never, would never, experience; and because of an operation years ago, Diamond won't ever experience again either. "Oh, well, I don't think it's a good idea for her or any of the girls to be here during that time." I said.

I watched Diamond and Uncle Tony as they pondered how they would handle the situation. "We make enough money." Diamond finally said, "We'll just pay the girls to stay home during that time of the month or find another option for them so they can work here and not be in danger. Birth control perhaps?"

"Good idea," agreed Uncle Tony.

                    Ashley Lauren Mitchell

"I'll go talk to the girls," said Diamond.

"What about patrons? There are females that frequent strip clubs. Can we refuse their entrance because of that and get away with it?" I queried.

"Maybe not *because* of that, but we can find some kind of excuse. We'll have to. You just let Diamond know if you ever have that feeling again and she or I will take care of it, okay?" said Uncle Tony, awaiting my response.

"Okay." I said, hoping it would work out the way they wanted. They'd already taken so many precautions for me. Why should I think they would fail at this? They cared for me and were trying to protect me and this whole morbid operation. The least I could do was understand and try to work with them as much as possible. But, back to tonight...and Charles.

"You look...drop dead gorgeous." Diamond says as she finishes adjusting my mask. Then we laugh. When she says things like that, I know she doesn't fear me or take what I am as seriously as I think she should. I feel I'm like a wild animal, or maybe a pit bull. Once I've tasted blood it's time to get rid of me. Instead, she and

Uncle Tony pamper me like a helpless feist that needs protection and grooming. It's something I don't understand but I'm grateful for, I suppose, like any pet.

I stand and face her. She steps closer to me and I can hear her heartbeat quicken slightly. She loves me, not like she loves Uncle Tony, but I know she loves me. She places one of my curly tendrils over the top of my mask. Then she uses her same hand to softly caress my face and trail down my neck and chest as she'd done so many times before. I watch the chill bumps rise on her arms from touching my flesh and we smile at each other. Not many people get to touch me, and definitely not how she's doing. It would freak them out, but not her. She likes to feel my cold skin. And sometimes she's audacious enough to rub her thumb over my long, slender, dagger-like teeth. She loosens the belt from my robe, glides it off of my shoulders and lets it fall to the ground. I'm standing naked in front of her without shame from either one of us.

I know that certain erogenous parts on the human body are sensitive, and when stimulated they have an explosive effect. I've tried feeling those reactions by touching myself on my breasts

          Ashley Lauren Mitchell

and my vagina. But I don't feel anything...ever. Rubbing my finger on my clitoris is the same as rubbing my finger on my knee. I'm unfeeling, un-stimulated, except when I feed. That is my, sex, I suppose. I love how it makes me feel and I want it over and over. I've never seen humans have sex because I wouldn't want them watching me feed. It's a private matter. But I can tell humans crave sex, crave it like I crave blood.

Diamond looks at my body and I know she wishes it were her own. At least she could do something with it. I wonder if she ever feels like it's a complete waste to have a body like this and not be able to enjoy it as humans are supposed to enjoy their bodies. Or, maybe it's just me imagining it. Time had not been the best to her body, even though she looks better than most women at the age of thirty-six.

"Now you're ready." She says. "Tony will have the car waiting out back."

"Okay."

Her eyes, her lovely deep blue eyes stare into mine until we are sure. "My beautiful Lamia," Then she turns away, then I turn away.

                    Ashley Lauren Mitchell

When she leaves my room she walks down the stairs to Uncle Tony who's standing at the entrance of the club. They exchange a few words and his eyes move to Charles, sitting alone at his VIP table. Diamond walks over to Slate, the disc jockey, and tells him, in ten minutes turn the music up louder. This is so no one will hear any screaming that may come from my room. But I rarely ever have any screaming from my visitors. Also, hearing the music start to blare from the speakers will let me know everything is going according to plan, and in a few moments my dinner guest will be arriving at my door.

Diamond walks over to Charles and sits at his table. "Bonjour Monsieur. Would you like another drink?" she asks politely. "It's on the house."

His bloodshot eyes slowly drift to Diamond. His face is vague and he looks like he hasn't smiled in decades. "Why?" He retorts.

"Because...you...look...great tonight. I bet you look great every night." She says laughing flirtatiously.

     Ashley Lauren Mitchell

"Yeah," He says without sounding the least bit benevolent.

Diamond is never appalled by attitudes like his and motions to Kitty, the bartender to bring him another drink. "Weren't you here last night?"

"Yeah, I was. That a crime?"

"Not at all, I was just wondering if you had a chance to see our, I guess, secret house special we have upstairs."

"No," Charles said.

"Well, I think you should check it out. It's free the first night because we know once you've had it you will definitely come back to have it again."

Kitty brings his drink and sets it on the table. "There you go sugar," she says in her thick Texas country accent.

"Thanks Kitty," Diamond says looking up at her briefly before looking back at Charles, who wastes no time downing the drink. She waits until the liquor passes through him and he can feel the pungent corollary. "So what do you say? Free lap dance maybe?"

"Another time, I have a previous engagement I need to get to." He said and started getting up to leave.

She could sense the impatience growing in him, like a child that can't wait to play with his new toy; but she kept persisting. "So what do I have to do to get you alone and all to myself?"

By this time the special drink that Kitty had made for him had started working. His eyes became heavy and he sat back down. "Whoa, I guess I didn't realize how much I had to drink."

"Why don't we go upstairs and let some of that wear off then?" said Diamond. She grabbed his hand without waiting for an answer and began leading him upstairs. She looked at Uncle Tony and nodded, and he exited the club.

I can feel them coming up the stairs and I am...excited. I go behind the curtain and wait for Diamond to bring Charles in the room, leave, and lock the door behind her. The door locks on both sides just in case someone ever tries to come in...or leave out. Either way no one gets in or out without mutual consent on both sides of that door. The door opens and Diamond walks in with Charles only steps behind her.

          Ashley Lauren Mitchell

"Why don't you have a seat?" she says and leaves the room.

Charles turns around to follow her out but the door is already locked. He turns the knob and tries pulling it. "What the fuck?" I hear him say to himself.

"Bonjour, Monsieur. Why don't you have a seat?" I say. He turns around to see where the portentous, resonating voice came from. I can sense no fear in him, only annoyance. Men like Charles don't fear anything, not even of being caught.

"Who's there?" He asks, sounding aggravated. "Why don't you show yourself?"

"As you wish," I reply, pulling back the curtain to reveal myself. I wait for his reaction. It's the same as all the others. They breathe in deeply and stand motionless. Their eyes admire my body, and revel in the sight of the nude goddess that has appeared before them. Like all humans, his eyes go first to my breasts and travel down to my pubic area before returning back to my breasts. My nipples are hard because I'm cold and hungry, but he probably thinks it's from excitement. I touch them knowing this will get

Ashley Lauren Mitchell

him aroused.

"Now, why don't you have a seat?" I repeat again and this time he obeys. I slowly walk toward him. My eyes veiled by the Mardi Gras mask I have on. He searches for them anyway, when he can finally take his eyes off my breasts.

"Take off the mask." He commands, and I can tell he's used to people doing what he says.

I pretend not to hear him. He won't get to see my eyes until I want him to. Instead I get his eyes back on my breasts by cupping them and squeezing them together. I have the bad habit of playing with my food, making it hot and writhing; barely able to sit still. I sit down on a chair facing him, open my legs and arch my back. I'm sitting perfectly straight, displaying my alluring body for his astonished eyes. I began talking to him while he's taking this all in, in total disbelief.

"So, what do I call you?" I ask.

"What? Oh, my name is Charles. Call me Charles." He can't lie to me, even if he wanted to.

"Do you like my body…Charles?"

"Yes I do, um, uh. What do I call you?" He asks watching my lips.

"Call me Lamia."

"Lamia, huh? So Lamia, are you gonna take off that mask?"

I hate being questioned by my food. "You already have so much to look at Charles. Why are you worried about seeing my eyes?"

"You're just so beautiful; I want to see all of you." He says like he's talking to an incredulous little girl.

"As you wish." Slowly, I take my hands and rub them on the insides of thighs, to my hips, my torso, my breasts, my neck, my face, until they are on the mask. He doesn't know once I take this off, he might as well be dead already. I hesitate so that I can play with him a little longer.

His patience is wearing thin. "C'mon girl, let me see those beautiful eyes, I don't got all night."

This fucking bastard has no idea that I'm giving him a minute longer to live, to be able to deny the actions he's performed to get himself here with me tonight. This is my foreplay, and I am enjoying it. "Oh Charles, you are so impatient, just like a child. Do you like children?" I give him a moment to consider answering before I take off the mask. The rest of my body fades away and all he sees are my eyes; my eyes that are as empty as his soul. I repeat, "Do you like children, Charles? You know, a lot of the women you've hurt had children? Did you hurt the children after you were done hurting their mothers?"

He can't answer. He doesn't have to. I know the answers to these questions already. He wouldn't be here if the answers were *no*. His mouth is open and his eyes are as wide as an owl's. This is the initial shock of seeing an apparition, a ghost, a moving dead...thing. I stand up and walk toward him. I put my legs on either side of his legs. I grab his wrists and put his arms by his sides in the chair. I place my knees on top of his hands restraining his movement, not that he's trying to go anywhere. Now I'm straddling him and close enough to his face that he can feel the icy breath of death on his lips and tongue. His mouth and eyes are still wide open.

"I know you don't like children, Charles. I know you like killing their mothers while they watch, and then, you kill them. But now, Charles, I have to kill you." I say this all with a devilish smile on my cold, uncaring face. "Charles, can you hear me?" His eyes are staring into mine and I know what he sees. He sees the same thing I'm seeing. All of the repulsive things he's done and the lives that he's taken and destroyed. All those flashing images rushing through his brain, like a fusillade of bullets, sends his body into slight convulsions. But I'm able to hold him still, transfixed on my eyes. Then, he's suddenly, completely placid. I have administered my poison.

I rub his face with my chilly fingers. "I know that you've done some vile things, things you feel you can't stop doing. I know you were going to do some of those things again tonight. But, I'm here to help you with that problem Charles. I understand you can't stop it on your own, but I can ease your affliction by making it stop for you." I put my right hand over his heart and my left one on the nape of his neck. I run my fingers through his hair, grab it and gently pull his head back. His heartbeat is slow. He feels sleepy but his

                    Ashley Lauren Mitchell

dreary eyes are still on mine. He cannot speak, he cannot move. I finally blink and look at his neck allowing him to close his eyes. No more shock, no more feeling. He is numb, paralyzed. He is an animal that needs to be euthanized. I am the lethal drug that will do that for him.

I'm so hungry. I pierce through the skin of his neck. My teeth sink into the flesh so easily. The first delicious drops touch my tongue. The blood is so warm and thick. I can feel the warmth move through my esophagus and reach my viscera. At first I gulp it down. I'm so hungry. Then I slow down and loosen my grip on his head. Ten minutes later I'm finished. Poor human Charles. I lay his head on my chest and listen for the last beat of his heart. He won't hurt anyone again.

I put on my gown and my robe. There's a back door that leads to the alley. Uncle Tony will be there with his NOPD car, trunk open. Although he's unnaturally strong for a human he can't carry this cadaver as fast as I can. I lift the body over my shoulder and take it out to the car. After I toss him in, Uncle Tony closes the trunk and looks at me. I'm radiating heat. My skin is no longer its pallid hue. My teeth are so sharp after feeding that when I try hiding them I only end up puncturing my own bottom lip. He smiles. He knows there's nothing to be afraid of with me. Uncle Tony is the one that brought Charles and the ones before him to me. These men do things Uncle Tony doesn't think they deserve to live for, but somehow always get away with. He provides me with victuals that will not be missed and I am his mercenary, for the blood of serial killers in New Orleans. It is a 'win-win' in his eyes.

"Thank you, Uncle Tony."

"Thank *you* Baby Girl," He always replies so lovingly. "I can sleep a little better tonight, and so can the people you saved." He put his gentle hand on my face. "I'll move the car and see you inside."

I watch him drive away. I look up at the night sky. I can see the stars so vividly, as if I'm viewing them through a telescope. It makes me think of being back at the house in Donaldsonville. I close my eyes for a brief moment and suddenly feel a rush of cold air on my face. It's the middle of summer here in Louisiana, which means any mortal would be drowning in heat; even at night. I just ate so I'm not abnormally frigid. I sense a presence somewhere around me. I look, but see no one standing near me or paying any attention to me. I have felt this before, many times. I ignore it and go inside.

I head back to my private room which is also my bedroom. I sit down in front of the mirror knowing I won't see myself, but that never stops me from looking. Damn, sometimes, especially after feeding, I wish I could see the way I look. I feel warm and my skin looks darker, like Diamond's after she comes from the tanning spa. I want to be able to see my face and my eyes after I feed. Did they look different too?

Diamond comes through the door. "All done?"

"Yeah, Uncle Tony is moving the car now."

"Good. I sure hope Charlie boy has more money in his wallet and a car we can hock." She says laughing. Diamond is always looking for an opportunity to make more money. "What's wrong?" She asks. "You sick?" She walks up to me and puts her palm on my forehead. No chill bumps rise on her skin. "Well, you do feel a little warm," she says.

                    Ashley Lauren Mitchell

We're both amused by this knowing the only reason I'm warm is because I just fed. I'll be back to being preternaturally freezing tomorrow. Tonight, I'm satisfied and full. Tonight, on night three, thanks to Charles, or Charlie boy as Diamond just called him, I can manage living another night as an animal. At least she and Uncle Tony think I'm an animal worth letting live, unlike Charles and the others before him. I am grateful.

Uncle Tony walks in. "Here Diamond. The fool actually had more cash on him."

"Yeah, but does he have a car I can sell?"

"I'll look into it tomorrow girl, damn. Wit' ya greedy ass."

"Shut up boy. I'll slap the little bit of black right off you, you keep talkin' to me like that."

They go back and forth like this for a minute or so and I love that they are so inherently human in front of me. It humors me. Diamond's heart is racing because she's so near to Uncle Tony. He does love her, but not in the amorous way she loves him. Uncle Tony never has a girlfriend, has never been married and doesn't

                    Ashley Lauren Mitchell

have any children. I think he is like me. No, he is not like me. He doesn't drink blood from human bodies, like me. But, he has taken lives with a gun. Maybe he is like me. A killer, like me. No, he is not like me.

Here we are having our nightly meeting before locking me up in my coffin. I tried sleeping on a bed, but they're so soft that my hard body sinks right through.

"Lamia! Girl you don't hear me talking to you?" asked Uncle Tony.

I shake my head, waking myself from my reverie, "No, sorry, I..."

"It's okay Baby girl, you're probably tired. C'mon, I'll tuck you in and we'll talk about the next one tomorrow night." He brushes my hair from my forehead and kisses it.

"Alright Uncle Tony," I say and get into my coffin. He closes it and I lock it from the inside. I heard them both leave and lock the door still bantering back and forth. I'm a lucky animal to have them. No, I'm not an animal. I am Lamia.

Call me Lamia.

                              Ashley Lauren Mitchell

<u>Chapter 2</u>

1964-1979

Anthony Leduff was born in Jérémie, Haiti in 1964. His father, Antoine, and older brother Jean were killed defending their family during a massacre. His mother, LaJean, weak from childbirth, sent him and his older sister, Nahdia, to live with their aunt in a small village, miles outside the city. Nahdia was only fourteen years old at the time. She was a beautiful, brown girl with long curly black hair. She packed all the supplies they'd need and promised their mother she would take good care of her precious, newborn baby brother. She didn't know if she would ever see her mother again, but she'd do anything to keep her brother alive, and keep her promise to their mother.

Nahdia and Anthony's grandfather, Robert Leduff, was a marine from New Orleans. When Robert was eighteen years old, he was deployed to Haiti. After a year of being on the island, he fell in love with a lovely dark skinned woman named Annabelle.

                    Ashley Lauren Mitchell

He pursued Annabelle for another six months, before she finally fell in love with Robert too. They married and soon had two babies, twins; a boy and a girl. Robert named them Antoine and Antoinette. Annabelle died shortly after giving birth leaving Robert with two biracial babies and no mother. Knowing he couldn't return home with the children and not be shunned, he left them with their Aunt Naitana and returned brokenhearted and alone to New Orleans. He never saw his children again.

Years passed and Antoine grew strong and healthy, but Antoinette was feeble and fell ill often. One day while playing with her brother, Antoinette fell face down in the dirt and didn't get back up. Her aunt Naitana put the young girl in bed. Antoinette slept for days. Naitana used all her resources trying to find a cure for whatever was keeping the child so close to death. She'd heard of a man in Haiti that could help her but many people had warned her against it. They said that the man was strange because he never aged and people that visited him never returned. Naitana sold everything she owned attempting to save the little girl, but Antoinette's health got worse. Naitana knew she had no choice but to

Ashley Lauren Mitchell

go to this man if she was to save her niece's life.

She and the small children traveled for three days to find the man. At the end of the third day, when the moon was high, they finally reached their destination. Naitana was told that his house was a deserted plantation, big enough to have a hundred people living in it. When she saw the house, she knew they were right. It was an enormous structure that looked like no one had lived there for many years.

Although Naitana was afraid, she would not let the children know it. She walked up to the door and before she could knock, it opened. No one was standing there to greet her in. She poked her head inside, "Hello," she called out, "is anyone here?" She stepped inside. "I have a very sick child and I was told I could find help here." There was no reply. Naitana, carrying Antoinette and holding Antoine's hand tightly, cautiously walked into the house. She looked up at the grand staircase covered in leaves and dirt. After a few minutes, she figured no one was there and turned to leave.

Standing at the door blocking her exit was a

tall, handsome man with long brown hair pulled into a sleek ponytail. His eyes were as black as night, and his skin was pale and nearly transparent. "Hello, Naitana," he said with a strong, foreign accent. "You have come to the right place. Give me the child."

Naitana gasped and squeezed Antoinette tighter to her. She moved Antoine behind her. She tried thinking of how he knew her name even though she hadn't introduced herself. She became tense, but managed to speak, "Are you the one that can help me?" she said trying not to show the panic that was clearly taking over her.

"Yes. I am. You may call me Nathaniel. I am a doctor from Italy. I've been here a long time. I can help you." He walked closer to her, "Now, give me the child."

Naitana started backing away from him when before her eyes, he vanished like a vapor. "You do not need to fear me," he whispered in her ear.

She felt chills all over her body as she quickly turned around to face him. "How did you..." Naitana could barely get the words to leave her mouth. She looked up, into his eyes

     Ashley Lauren Mitchell

and was frozen with terror. He stared back at her before taking the child from her arms without struggle. Antoine grabbed the leg of the man and began shaking it, trying to get him to let go of his sister.

"Don't worry little boy, I'll bring your sister back to you shortly," he said before turning to walk behind the staircase and disappearing into a room. Naitana was standing there, still frozen, while Antoine sat on the floor crying.

An hour passed before Nathaniel went back to Naitana. He led her and Antoine to a sitting area. "She will be fine. No need to worry. She'll never be sick again. She'll possess immunity to every disease and illness known to man. Now," he said sitting down and crossing his legs, "we must discuss payment."

"I do not have much money, sir," she said.

"That's okay, I don't require money. I'd like you to do something else for me." Naitana squeezed Antoine close to her, covering herself with him. Nathaniel smiled, "I want you to bring me strong, young men. You're an attractive woman. Men would hearken to you. You can use your looks to get them here."

                    Ashley Lauren Mitchell

"What will happen to them when I bring them to you?" asked Naitana; not sure if she was being too presumptuous.

Nathaniel smiled at her concern. "I...will...put them to work on my dilapidated home here. It needs a lot of restoring and many times the men leave before their tasks are completed." He gave her a moment to consider the excuse he'd given her. "So, do we have an agreement?" He extended his hand to her.

"Yes," she said after a long pause, "we have an agreement." She took his hand in hers. It was as cold as ice and she immediately pulled her hand back and stared at his.

He stifled a smile and drew his hand back. "Good. Now, I own another derelict house only a few miles from here. No one has lived there for a long time. I would like you and your children to live there now. It will make your job of bringing the men here a whole lot faster and easier." He said, smiling devilishly the entire time. He didn't wait for a response from her. This was his command and Naitana must obey. "I'll bring the child back to you now." He said and turned to walk away, then remembered the most important thing and turned back. "But, there is one more thing. I need you to make sure she never tastes blood, other than her own. It's an odd request, I know, but she could die instantly. Do you understand?"

Naitana wasn't sure whether or not she understood but she knew she didn't want Antoinette to die. "Yes, I understand."

Naitana left the house with both of the children walking by her side, and instructions for when she was to bring the men to meet Nathaniel. She was so happy that Antoinette was feeling better that she said she'd bring as many men as it took to pay Nathaniel back. And she did.

Like the doctor had said, Antoinette didn't get sick again. But she did seem to age much slower than Antoine. They'd stopped looking coeval when they reached age eight. After whatever the doctor had done, Antoinette's eyes weren't dark brown anymore, but a light hazel. Antoinette, being the girl, was assumed to be the smaller, weaker one. She was smaller, but was much stronger than Antoine. She could lift things significantly heavier than herself. She and

Antoine would compete to see who was stronger and Antoinette would always win.

By age eighteen, Antoine had grown big and muscular. He began working with other boys his age and going out with girls. Antoinette still looked like she was fourteen years old, even though she was just as healthy as Antoine. The girls her age were already getting married and having children. Antoinette liked being inside with her aunt most of the time, at least until her aunt would leave the house on her secret missions that she'd never taken the twins on.

Antoinette knew Antoine would be leaving the house soon to become a man and raise his own family. She decided to stay and take care of their aunt when he did. In another year he left, with his wife LaJean and their infant son Jean. Antoinette watched over Naitana until she died, leaving Antoinette the house. Before dying Naitana told Antoinette about her mother and father, and how, when she was really little she was saved by a doctor named Nathaniel. She told her if she ever needed help saving the life of someone she loved she was to go to this man. Antoinette thanked Naitana for everything that she had done, especially giving up so much to save her life as a child.

                    Ashley Lauren Mitchell

"You are my blood Antoinette. Nothing is more sacred than that."

Fifteen years passed and Antoinette never left the house. She would gather food and go right back inside. She aged so slowly that when she turned thirty she finally looked like she was eighteen. She had wondered about what happened to Antoine and his wife and son, and hoped to see them all again one day. At night she often felt a strange presence watching her. She was never afraid. She hoped it was the soul of her aunt watching over her. She did feel lonely after all that time, however.

Then one night she heard a knock on her door.

A young girl was standing on her doorstep holding a newborn baby boy. Antoinette knew the baby couldn't be for this slender young girl, who somehow looked very familiar. The girl was so frightened it took a long time for her to speak, but she finally did.

"I'm looking for Antoinette Leduff?" she said. "My name is Nahdia and this is my brother Anthony. I

Ashley Lauren Mitchell

was sent here by Antoine and LaJean Leduff. They're probably both dead by now along with my older brother Jean. My mother..."

Before Nahdia could finish Antoinette began sobbing and hugged the young girl. "I am your Aunt Antoinette!" She kissed girl and the baby and said, "You will be with me now. I will take care of you. Everything will be alright." Nahdia began weeping too.

***

Three years passed and Antoinette, or Aunt Nette, as Nahdia and Anthony started calling her, was happy taking care of her niece and nephew. She wasn't alone anymore. She oftentimes felt the strange presence watching her at night, but it didn't bother her.

Nahdia was growing beautifully and she was hardly ever apart from her little brother. Antoinette still never left her house and she was glad she had Nahdia to run all her errands for her. They were a family and they did whatever they could to take care of each other.

                    Ashley Lauren Mitchell

Antoinette never had children of her own and never had the desire to try as most women do. She had her niece and nephew and that was enough for her.

One afternoon, Nahdia and Anthony were in the yard. Nahdia was hanging clothes on the line to dry while Anthony ran around playfully. When Nahdia looked over to check on Anthony she saw that he had fallen face down. She waited for him to get back up but he would not. She rushed over to him and her heart felt like it'd stopped. Anthony wasn't moving and barely breathing. Nahdia picked up her brother and ran screaming into the house, her heart racing with fear. She would gladly give her life for Anthony's. She remembered the promise she'd made to their mother and knew she must do whatever it took in order to keep him alive.

"Aunt Nette," she cried, "Something's the matter with Anthony! He's not moving!" She held her brother's small, limp body in her arms and tears streamed down her face.

Antoinette ran into the room. When she saw Anthony's little body her heart sank. It was the first time in over fifty years she felt weak. Then

                    Ashley Lauren Mitchell

she remembered what her Aunt Naitana had told her before she died. She thought hard to remember his name. "Nahdia, I know a doctor that can help him but you must go now!" She said taking Anthony into her arms. She gave Nahdia directions and the girl ran out the door.

Nahdia rode her bicycle two or three miles to what looked like a mansion. She threw her bicycle to the ground and ran up the steps to the giant doors. She began banging on them as hard as she could. "Please, you must help my brother!" Nahdia yelled. "Help me, please someone help me!" She banged her fist so hard on the door that it opened and Nahdia ran inside. She didn't see anyone. It looked as if no one had been there for years.

She started panicking and screamed, "Help me!" over and over. Sweat was beading down her face. After a while she was gasping for air. A man appeared from behind the staircase. He was tall, with dark hair and even darker eyes. "Help me please," she begged. My brother he's, he's...I am looking for a doctor named..." for a moment she couldn't remember his name, "Nathaniel!" She blacked out.

When she woke she felt dizzy and confused. She was back at home but had no idea how she'd gotten there. She looked over and saw Anthony lying in the bed next to hers. She quickly jumped up to check on him. He was breathing but he had a needle in his arm. The needle was connected to a tube and the tube was connected to a bag of what appeared to be blood. She gently touched his cool forehead as tears ran down her face.

"I'm so sorry mother. I've failed you," she whispered.

Anthony's eyes opened. He looked at Nahdia and smiled. "Hey Dia," He said in his young, sweet voice.

Nahdia looked at Anthony and noticed his eyes were no longer a lovely dark brown but were a light shade of green. "Anthony? Oh, Anthony! I thought I'd lost you! How do you feel? Are you okay?"

"I'm ok Dia. Don't cry."

Antoinette walked in the room. "I thought I heard voices. Are you children alright?" she asked.

"Aunt Nette, what happened? All I remember is arriving at the doctor's house and then I can't remember anything. What happened to Anthony? What was wrong with him?"

"Calm down child." Antoinette said. "Everything is okay now." She looked at Anthony and smiled. "Anthony won't ever be sick again."

***

Another year passed. Antoinette was right, Anthony didn't get sick again, but he didn't seem to grow either. He was just as small as he was when he fell ill. Nahdia was now eighteen and wanted so badly to have a more exciting and adventurous life. She loved her Aunt Nette and was so grateful for the years of help. But now she wanted to live somewhere else. Somewhere entirely different. Even so, she would not leave Anthony.

Antoinette knew she couldn't keep Nahdia with her forever. She was a young woman and needed her independence. Antoinette was scared of losing Anthony. Although he was strong, he was still very young and very small. He would need constant supervision and she wasn't sure if Nahdia could handle all it would take. She remembered Nahdia at fourteen when she first showed up on the doorstep. She was much younger then and she still took care of her infant brother. Antoinette knew she had to let them go. She also knew Nahdia would die before she let anything happen to Anthony.

After months of talking and planning, Antoinette decided they were ready to leave the nest. She gave Nahdia everything of value to be traded for food and money. One night when they were talking, Antoinette told Nahdia about her family and how her grandfather, Robert, was from a place called New Orleans. "It's in the United States," she said. "I have dreamed many times of going there. I think that is where you and Anthony should go. You're very good at speaking English and Anthony is so smart he will pick up on it fast. He'll grow slowly but he still needs to go to school. You may need to put him in a lower grade so that he won't feel too different from the other children, you know, because of his size. And remember Nahdia, he can never taste blood other than his

        Ashley Lauren Mitchell

own. He could die instantly, do you understand?"

Nahdia knew that already. It was one of the most serious rules of the house, repeated per diem. "Yes, I understand Aunt Nette."

In another month Nahdia and Anthony were hugging their Aunt Nette goodbye.

"But I don't want to go Auntie Nette, I want to stay here with you!" cried young Anthony.

"You're going to be fine," she said fighting back tears. "There's nothing to worry about. Nahdia will take really good care of you Baby boy."

Antoinette and Nahdia looked at each other and started crying. They didn't want to admit having any doubts about what they were doing. The three of them hugged each other tighter than they did the first day they met. Precious minutes passed. They let go of each other. Nahdia picked Anthony up and put him on her hip. Antoinette kissed them on their tear-stained cheeks and walked with them to the door. "Alright, you guys get on out of here or you'll miss the boat." She told them. There was a cart

cart drawn by a man on a bike waiting outside to take her niece and nephew away. "Remember," she said as they stepped outside, "you are my blood, and nothing is more sacred than that."

With a final wave goodbye Antoinette watched the most important things in her life ride away. Once they were out of sight she fell to her knees and put her face in her hands. She thought of the first day they'd met. Nahdia was so young and scared just like she is now. And little Anthony, she knew him nearly since his birth. The son and daughter she will never have, given to her by her twin brother. She thought of all the loved ones she didn't have anymore. They were all...gone. She was alone again.

Nights passed and Antoinette wouldn't get out of her bed. She would sleep then cry, and cry then sleep. 'How could I let them leave?' she thought. She put her face into her soaked pillow and continued weeping. After a few minutes she felt a cold chill down her spine. She lifted her face from the pillow and wiped her tears. She sat up, looked around her room, but saw no one. She was feeling the strange presence she'd felt so many times before and she knew what it was now. When Anthony got sick and the doctor came to her door carrying Nahdia like a baby, she saw his eyes and felt this same chill all over her body.

"Nathaniel, please show yourself," she begged. Her breathing became heavier. She felt so cold. "Nathaniel, I know it's you." She heard the wind outside her window and nothing else. She started crying again. "Please Nathaniel. I'm so lonely." She pulled her knees to her chest and buried her face in them. Suddenly, she felt a hard, heavy hand on her shoulder. She looked up and stared into those marvelous dark eyes.

"Hello Antoinette," said Nathaniel.

***

Nahdia and Anthony traveled for two weeks. When they docked in a New Orleans port, Nahdia couldn't believe her eyes. The city was so vibrant and filled with a myriad of people. She'd never seen so many well-dressed people in her life. There were colorful, shining beads hanging in the trees and on lamp posts. They were everywhere. The buildings were so beautifully designed.

The closest thing she'd seen to anything like it was when Anthony fell ill and she'd gone to fetch the doctor. 'Anthony,' she thought. She picked little Anthony up and kissed his cheek. "Isn't this great Anthony?" She pointed at a streetcar. "Look Anthony! Can you say streetcar?"

Anthony put his head on her shoulder and said, "I miss Auntie Nette."

"I know, Baby boy. I do too. Come on, let's go get some food and find a place to stay. Okay?"

"Okay."

By the end of that first year Nahdia had used all the money she'd gotten from selling the items her aunt Antoinette had given her. Even if she wanted to go back to Haiti she didn't have enough. She was glad that Anthony couldn't get sick but that didn't mean he couldn't get hungry. She tried for weeks to find a job. Every place she went turned her down. She became desperate. She remembered that her grandfather was from New Orleans. Would he be alive? Did she have any other relatives living here? Would they recognize her? Would they accept her? 'It's worth a shot,' she thought. She looked up Robert Leduff. There were so many. She didn't have time to check them all. She needed to take care of Anthony. That was her only family now. She'd thought about giving Anthony to an orphanage until she could support them both. 'No, I won't fail you, Mother. I will take care of Anthony.'

Nahdia found a job at a small café in the French Quarter. There was an older woman that lived next door to Nahdia and Anthony for the past year. They all had spoken to each other in passing but never held a conversation. Nahdia asked her to watch Anthony at night while she went to work. She told her she would pay her what she could and that he would be asleep most of the time. They came to an agreement and the woman started babysitting Anthony when Nahdia went to work. After working at the café for a while she still wasn't earning enough to take care of all the expenses. One night before going home she found herself walking up Bourbon Street. All of the lights and music and people made her sad. She had wanted so much more for herself and for Anthony.

A woman in a gold satin dress and matching high heels walked up to her. "Where

    Ashley Lauren Mitchell

ya headed lil girl?" she asked. Nahdia tried to get passed her but the woman kept stepping in front of her. "Ya look like ya in need of a lil fun." She pulled a wad of folded dollar bills out of her cleavage. "I ca' show ya some fun, and you ca' earn ya'self some cash too."

Nahdia thought about Anthony. She'd told herself a long time ago that she would gladly die to save him. She would not die physically, but morally she may have to. Before she found the job at the café she'd already pilfered a few items from some local grocery stores for her and Anthony. 'I have to do what I have to do,' she thought. She followed the woman into the door of a club.

Girls even younger than her were on the stage nearly nude. Men were throwing money at them, whistling, and shouting. Nahdia felt overwhelmed but kept following the woman in the gold dress. They walked to the back of the club and entered a room with a portly, white man sitting at a desk counting money.

"Billy, this is...," She turned around to Nahdia. "What's ya name sweetheart?" asked the woman.

"Nahdia."

"...is Nahdia," she continued while lighting a cigarette and blowing the smoke into Nahdia's face. "Ain't she cute? Nah, I won't her to work for us. What'chu thank?" said the woman.

Billy peeked around his money he had held up like playing cards in his hands. "Take off ya clothes."

"Excuse me?" asked Nahdia in surprise.

"Well suga, you goin' work in a strip joint, you goin have ta be comf'table takin' off ya clothes." He said apathetically.

"I, I..." Nadia couldn't speak. She wanted to get out of there as fast as possible.

"Look, I tell ya what baby," began the woman in the gold dress, "why ont you go on home and thank on it. If ya decide ya wont to, we'll be here. Mm'k?" She took a twenty dollar bill from Billy's hand and gave it to Nahdia. "Goin on home, nah," she said.

Nahdia took the money, bowed her head and walked as fast as she could back the way she came in. After she picked up Anthony from the babysitter, she laid him down in the bed that they shared. She laid down beside him and watched him sleep. She thought about what had happened earlier, all the money she had seen Billy and that woman in the gold dress flaunting. "I'll do anything for you Anthony," she whispered and kissed his forehead. That night while she slept, she had nightmares about losing Anthony because she couldn't support him. She woke with sweat covering her face. She felt the visions had been put in her head by the devil himself. She'd never had dreams that bad. The next night she went back to the club, and almost every night afterwards.

She eventually bought a two bed room apartment. Anthony began getting a little bigger but a lot older. Nahdia paid for all of his schooling and sports, which he excelled at. He started making friends that called him Tony instead of Anthony, and Nahdia believed he was a normal, happy little boy. She'd considered what her Aunt Nette said about putting Anthony in a grade lower but decided against it. She'd rather he be seen as a young genius. He may have been the smallest in all of his classes but he was definitely the smartest. She was happy she was taking such good care of him. He was such a docile boy that she didn't even have to leave him with a babysitter by the time he was ten. He never caused trouble and never disobeyed his elders.

Although Nahdia was proud of Anthony, she felt jaded by the path she'd taken in order to take care of him. What started off as a couple shots of liquor a night to 'loosen her up' turned into a couple of bottles to completely numb the pain. Because she was comfortable leaving Anthony home alone, she stayed out all night, and sometimes went home with different men. She'd decided that no matter how much money she'd make she would never go back to her Aunt Nette and tell her how low she'd stooped for money. 'No! This for Anthony,' she drunkenly said to herself.

She met a man named Louis. He was a mulatto, like her father and aunt, with hair and eyes as dark as her own. His skin was whiter than most white peoples' skin. She would go home with Louis several times a week, for weeks. Some nights she didn't go home to Anthony at all. She thought she was in love until the day she found out she was pregnant. She told Louis and he told her to get rid of it. She slapped him in his face and ran home crying.

"I'll kill him!" Anthony raged.

"Oh, no *you* won't either! Don't worry about it Tony, he's not worth it," she said through her tears. "He'll get what he deserves one day. But for now, we need to take care of this baby."

Anthony took a minute to calm down. "I promise to help you and my little nephew or neice as much as I can," he said. "You took care of me for so long, what better way to repay you than by helping you take care of this munchkin."

"I know, Baby boy. I know."

Months passed and Nahdia's belly got bigger. She quit drinking and quit working at the strip club. By this time, Anthony was in high school and was hoping to go to the police academy when he graduated in a few years. He barely slept anymore. When he was not at school he was working odd jobs to help take care of his pregnant sister.

The year was 1979. It was cold outside and the stars were shining so brightly, they could be seen past all the city lights. Anthony was studying

Ashley Lauren Mitchell

for a test he had the next morning.

"Tony, I think it's time," said Nahdia as she walked out of the bathroom.

His face flashed a eager smile, "Okay, let's get you to the hospital," he said.

Hours rolled by. Anthony sat, nervously waiting in the hospital lobby for word about his sister and the baby. Half an hour later the doctor came out to speak with him. She told him that his sister had complications during labor but was sedated and would be fine after some much needed rest.

"What about the baby? He asked.

"The baby is on the way to emergency surgery. I'm sorry but she..."

"She? It's a girl?" Anthony said, surprised.

"Yes," continued the doctor, "but she's having trouble breathing. We may need to do a blood transfusion."

"A blood transfusion? Is there anything I can do to help?"

"Well," said the doctor, "Do you know your

blood type?"

"No, I don't."

"If you like we can get you tested to make sure you have matching blood types and you can donate the blood that could possibly save her life," said the doctor.

"Yes of course," said Anthony. "Anything I can do, I'll do it," and he followed the doctor.

When Nahdia opened her eyes she saw Anthony in the chair next to her bed. He was holding the baby and talking to it. "Pink blanket? It must be a girl." She said.

"Hey there you. How are you feeling?" asked Anthony.

"Like I got run over by a streetcar." She said. They both laughed.

"Yes, ma'am. It's a girl. She has the most beautiful eyes too. She's a lil too white if you ask me."

"Well, I didn't ask you. Now give me my baby." Nahdia giggled. She gazed at her daughter's eyes in amazement. The magnificent

Ashley Lauren Mitchell

irises seemed to be every color imaginable. "Wow! She is gorgeous! Are you sure this is my baby?"

"Oh, I'm sure alright. I even added an extra dose of my blood so she's definitely for us."

"What do you mean?" asked Nahdia.

"The doctor said she had trouble breathing and needed a blood transfusion. I told them I would give her my blood if it would help. They got me tested and it was a match. They stuck a needle in me, drained some blood and put it in rugrat here."

"What?" Nahdia shrieked.

"It's okay though. The doctor said that she recovered faster than expected and is perfectly healthy now."

Nahdia thought back to when Anthony was three years old. He'd had a needle and tube in his arm and it was hooked to a bag of blood. "But, Anthony, your condition? You know you are... special. Now, she may not grow normally. And what about the blood thing?"

"I'm sorry Nahdia. I thought I was doing the

right thing."

Nahdia was remorseful for what she'd said to him. She'd forgotten that even though he was smaller than other boys his age, he was stronger and smarter. She looked into his lovely green eyes and said, "No, I'm sorry for saying that Tony. I'm glad it was your blood. At least my baby won't ever get sick."

Anthony looked at the baby and then to Nahdia and smiled. "True. And, the whole, never tasting blood thing? I think that was just meant to scare us. But I know I won't ever want to taste no blood anyways." Anthony saying that, made Nahdia think about their Aunt Nette. "So, what are we going to call her?" He asked.

"I was thinking about calling her Lily, like the flower. Lily Antoinette." Anthony thought for a moment. "I like it. No, I love it. Lily Antoinette Leduff. Perfect. Hey, Little Lily. It's your Uncle Tony. I promise to always take real good care of you." He put his finger in the baby's hand and she squeezed it. "Whoa, strong grip there Baby girl, we might have to watch out for you, wit'cha strong ass." "Tony?" Nahdia exclaimed.

"What?" He said laughing.

Chapter 3

June, 2005

Call me Lamia.

Uncle Tony has done something great for me. He's informed me that I'm to host two guests tonight.

"They work as a team so they should die as a team," he said.

I am happy to oblige.

"You can handle this, right, Baby Girl?" asked Uncle Tony.

"Yes, Uncle Tony. I can handle it." I said, trying not to sound too anxious. I have been thinking of it incessantly since he told me a couple of nights ago. "If I need help I'll sound the reveille." I say mockingly.

"Do you think this is a joke? These men are no joke. They are dangerous." He says. He was actually upset with me.

 Ashley Lauren Mitchell

"I apologize. I understand Uncle Tony." I say stifling a smile because I know he's serious and very concerned. I am not. He has no idea the alacrity I have to perform this task for him tonight. My mouth is salivating just thinking about having those two men in my room. Ménage à Trois. This opportunity has not presented itself before. It's like I'll be killing two birds with one stone. I know I'll be able to handle it but Uncle Tony has his human doubts. "Don't worry Uncle Tony. I can do this."

After a long pause he says, "Alright. I'll send Diamond up here in a minute. If you need any help you scream and I will come running up here. You hear me?"

"Yes, Uncle Tony. I hear you." I feel like a child having this conversation with him. Uncle Tony. He's been there for me since I was born, or at least since I was reborn as whatever it is I am now. A killer, like the men he brings to me. No, I am not a killer. I'm a savior. I am Lamia, the serpent that waits in the grass, ready to strike those that are worthy to perish. I wonder what I'd ever do without Uncle Tony. He walks out the room and a minute later Diamond walks in.

 Ashley Lauren Mitchell

"He's worried about you, you know?" She says.

"I know that. He shouldn't be."

"But he is. And I am too a little. You've never had two up here at one time. I can stand outside the door if you like." She said while doing something to my hair. I never pay attention to the styles she does. I can't see them anyway. It makes no difference how I look. I only care about one thing. Blood!

"Diamond, it's fine. I understand you and Uncle Tony are worried, but trust me, I can handle this."

Honestly, I feel their doubt is insulting, but they mean no harm.

When Diamond goes downstairs she sees Derek and Michael sitting at the VIP table we had arranged for them. The two of them were conversing and drinking and barely paying attention to the exotic dancers. Diamond went to Uncle Tony first and he left the club, then to Slate; her usual routine on night three. It's best Uncle Tony leaves the club before Diamond goes to talk to the soon to be corpses, so that they don't feel the need to be on their best behavior. We don't want that.

"Bonjour gentlemen," she said. "Would you like another drink? It's on the house." When Diamond asks this question, it's always rhetorical. She's not really giving an option. She's already signaling Kitty to bring the drinks over.

"How bout it Mike?" Derek says as he sits back in his seat. "Should we let this bitch get us another round?"

"Why not? This shitty ass club. Who the hell invited us here anyway? What's so special about this place, darlin?" Michael said, grabbing Diamond's thigh.

Diamond had a huge smile on her face. She's so glad these two will be dead soon. "Well, we have a surprise upstairs. You know, *a secret desire.* You boys need to check it out. You can go one at a time, but I think she can handle you both."

Now Derek and Michael have huge sinister smiles on their faces. They looked at each other and gulped down the drinks that Kitty brought them. Soon the drinks will be taking effect and without reluctance they will follow Diamond. She leads them to me. One after the other they make their way up the steps. I'm growing more and more eager with each step they take. I listen for the doorknob to turn; the scuffle of shoes on the floor. I peep through an opening in the curtain. They're in my room now and I can smell them. Their scent is strong. I need to collect myself so that this won't be over too quickly. I plan on savoring this moment. They're looking around the room curiously.

"Bonjour Monsieurs." I say. They pause and look at each other again. "Why don't you both have a seat?"

"It would be nice if we could see ya, baby," said Michael.

"Call me Lamia."

"Lamia. Well Lamia, why don't you come on out here and play with us?"

"As you wish." I say and slide the curtain back. The reaction I adore so much. I wait for them to speak. I believe all humans will have the same expression on their faces from seeing an enticing silhouette. Where do they look first? At

Ashley Lauren Mitchell

my breasts, always. Why don't they look at my mask? I saw it before Diamond put it over my eyes. Tonight it is purple and red with rhinestones. I like red. She even put lipstick and nail polish on me. I am a doll for her. I believe these men think I'm one too, so back to them.

"Oh shit! Damn girl. You don't waste no time do ya?" Derek said laughing.

I have dark meat tonight, I thought. They're circling me like predators taunting their prey. How odd considering I'm the predator. This makes me snicker. I could snap them both in half if I wanted to, but I don't want blood on this rug. I happen to like this rug. "You boys are whetting my appetite," I say flirtatiously.

"We'll make sure other parts of you are wet too," says Michael.

"You promise?" I would like to stick the toothpick he's chewing on, in his pupil. Maybe later, I will. I can't help myself. We're all having so much fun right now. The pernicious things we are all imagining doing to each other. I'm titillated beyond measure. They must be also because one of them is rubbing his hand back and forth over his erection under his jeans. "Are you boys

  Ashley Lauren Mitchell

going to let me perform for you first or what?"

"Perform for us? Shit girl, you already butt naked," says Michael. "What kind of performance you goin do, backflips or sum'n?"

"Please have a seat," I say attempting not to sound authoritative. These *are* my guests.

"We don't need *your* performance baby. We already have one picked out for you." says Derek.

I can tell they need to be sedated quickly if I want this to go my way. "Ok, well, then, why don't I do one of you while the other one watches for a while?" Now that's what they want to hear. I have them.

"Now we're talkin'," says Derek.

"Yeah, I'm first," says Michael.

"Nah man, I'm first," says Derek.

"No, you went first last time," says Michael.

"Man, no I didn't. You did." says Derek.

What the hell. It's so irrelevant who goes first. "How about I chose?" I say to end their annoying argument. I sit down in my chair hoping they will follow suit and sit in the two chairs I have facing me. They do. "How about...you?" I say pointing to Michael. And he laughs. Is he laughing because he gets to die first? I join him in laughter. "You must do this often if you are going first this time?" I ask, putting emphasis on *this time*. The question silences them. They look at me stunned.

"What are you talking about?" asks Michael.

"I heard you say that he," I say pointing to Derek, "went first last time." I still have a grin on my face. I'm getting really hungry.

"So?" he says.

"So...how many times have you boys done this?" I ask.

They take a long pause, look at each other, and then back at me. "Look bitch," says Derek leaning toward me, "that won't matter much soon."

"You despicable humans," I say and abruptly take off my mask.

　　　　　　　　　Ashley Lauren Mitchell

I wonder if the stares are because I'm aesthetically pleasing or because I'm grotesque. In their eyes, I see the vicious acts they've performed together. Their bodies are trembling from shock. They're under my complete control.

"Ah, but it does matter *now*. You boys have done a lot together I see. Those innocent lives you've taken. I see them. I see them all. Did you really think you could get away with it forever?" Their faces are blank, their eyes, captivated. "You know, I take that back. You are absolutely right, it won't matter soon." I stand and tower over them. "I'm here to give you redemption from the sins you've committed and send you both to hell. Now, who did I say was first? Right. Michael. Come, here."

He rises from the chair and slowly walks to me. "Turn around and kneel," I command. He obeys. I kneel down behind him. I rub my hands up his arms and shoulders. I gently tilt his head to the side and lock eyes with Derek who is watching, hypnotized. "That's it. Keep watching my eyes Derek." I open my mouth and ease my fangs slowly into Michael's neck. My eyes shudder and I fight to keep them from rolling back in my head as the first drops of blood saturate my tongue. It's so warm. No, keep looking at Derek, who still has the same stunned look on his face. I continue to drink Michael until he's depleted. I remove my teeth and feel streams of blood run down my chin and neck. I push him to the side like a ragdoll. I stand and walk toward Derek. "Now, it is your turn." I place his arms by his sides and straddle him like I'd done with Charles and many others before him. I imbibed his blood and held his head to my breast. I love listening to their last heartbeat. There is something soothing about it.

I carried them like full trash bags out the backdoor. Uncle Tony is waiting by the trunk of the car.

"Looks like you handled it." He said. "I

told you not to worry."

"I guess I just can't help myself, Baby girl. How you feelin?"

"I'm spent Uncle Tony. I think I'm going to go straight to sleep."

"Okay, I understand."

"Will you let Diamond know I'll talk with her

 Ashley Lauren Mitchell

tomorrow?"

"Sure. Get some rest baby."

"Thanks Uncle Tony."

"Thank *you* Baby Girl."

I watched him drive away. I looked up at the night sky. The stars were glowing brightly again. I'd never had two victims in one night. I felt invigorated and wanted to walk the streets with all the drunk, wayward souls of Bourbon Street. Uncle Tony wouldn't like that. I didn't even have on my mask. I shouldn't risk it.

Before I turned to go inside, an image appeared out the corner of my eye. Standing on the other side of Bourbon Street was a tall pale figure staring directly at me. He was mystique and luminous as if surrounded by a nimbus. As fast as I noticed him, he disappeared. Astonished, I started walking toward the spot I saw the figure standing in. Two giant horses, one piebald and the other dark brown, stopped in front of me. They had police mounted atop. The horses turned their heads to look at me and we all gazed at each other. The horses reared back knocking the police officers into a pile of horse excrement on the ground. People ran frantically away from the massive beasts. The horses walked toward me and I put my hands out to touch them. I watched their nostrils flare as they sniffed my fingers. I caressed the long bridge of one of their noses and laid my head against the animals' powerful jawbone. I closed my eyes. It was just as warm as I was, and I could hear its heartbeat pounding in its chest. The police officers scrambled to their feet and began staggering to recover their horses. I can't let him see me. I gave a final pat on the horses' heads and backed away, toward the door of the club. Perhaps it was the animal connection that drew them to me. No, I'm not an animal. Once I'm inside and close the door I remember the reason I wanted to cross the street. Something had noticed me tonight other than the horses.

When I entered my room Diamond was already sitting at my dressing table tousling her hair in the mirror. "So how'd it go?" She asked pertly. Even though she can't see me entering the room in the mirror she knows without a doubt it's me.

"I think I enjoyed it more than they did," I respond facetiously.

"Yeah, I bet you did." She turns to look at me and I notice a slight change in her reaction. Her face becomes flushed as she carefully makes her way toward me. She places her hand on my forearm and gasps. "You are so...warm," she says as she moves her hand up and down my arm. "Almost hot. I know this may sound weird but I like seeing your skin after you," she paused, "do what you do."

"Oh really?" I asked curiously.

"Yeah, it's so dark and shiny. You're almost the same color as your Uncle Tony. And your eyes..."

That's right, Diamond loves everything about Uncle Tony. She probably dreams about touching his skin the way she's touching mine. I guess I can tell that my complexion is a little darker this time than it usually is after feeding. It must have something to do with the fact that I had two victims tonight.

"What about my eyes?" I ask, just as curiously.

"They are so...bright and colorful."

I hate that I can't see what she is

                        Ashley Lauren Mitchell

witnessing. "Diamond, I'm pretty tired. Do you mind if I..."

"Sure baby, not a problem," she says blinking her eyelids rapidly as if waking herself from a trance. "I'm sorry. I'm just all in your hair. I'm headed downstairs to talk to Tony. I'll see you tomorrow, ok pumpkin?"

"Ok."

When I'm alone I inhale and think about the night I'd just had. It seemed more eventful than any I'd had in a long time. I feel more satisfied tonight as well. My *bedroom* and my *dining room* are separated by the curtain I stand behind and watch my guests before making my entrance. There is softly glowing light from the candles I lit in the dining room. It looks almost like a shrine. I blow out the flames and enter my bedroom. I have a five shelf bookcase, a much smaller version than the enormous one at the house in Donaldsonville. I like reading. These books are not didactic but I still like them. I like that I can go to different places and be different people when I read them. Especially since I never get to leave this room.

I reach for a book that I've read more than any

Ashley Lauren Mitchell

of them. It was sitting on Lily's dressing table. It contains a poem that is named after me. Well, not exactly after me. But it does speak to me. This poem, written beautifully, artistically, is a fantasy. The immortal, who becomes a mortal. It only seems possible in this work. I step inside my coffin and close the lid. My eyes adjust to the darkness and I flip through the pages until I find the book marked page; *Lamia* by John Keats. *UPON a time, before the faery broods...*

 Ashley Lauren Mitchell

<u>Chapter 4</u>

1979-1994

Lily Antoinette Leduff was a serene baby. She rarely cried. The pigmentation of her pale skin didn't get any darker than it was the day she was born. Her hair was curly and black, like her mother's and father's. Her eyes were like none that her mother or uncle had ever seen. They were splotched with multifarious colors. They were like two prisms of light cast from a chandelier. Lily was small and beautiful.

Anthony took great delight in caring for his niece, and she took great delight in him. However, Lily didn't like to be held. Instead she enjoyed playing in her crib by herself. Nahdia loved her daughter more than anything and decided not to go back to doing the degrading things for money that she'd done before. She found another café job and worked there at night while Anthony went to the police academy during the day. The three of them made a happy home together.

As Nahdia had predicted, Lily grew slowly.

 Ashley Lauren Mitchell

By the time the child was two, she had only just begun crawling. The doctors were baffled. They found no diseases or deformities in the child. In fact, she was one of the healthiest babies they'd ever examined. She had no allergies and she never got sick. They assumed her stunted growth was merely a coincidence.

Nahdia knew the reason, and she didn't want her baby to go through unnecessary tests to prove it. She knew that the baby would grow slowly like Anthony. This didn't bother her; as long as her baby was healthy. What did bother her was that Lily didn't like to be around other babies.

One afternoon, Nahdia took Lily to the neighborhood park. She put Lily by the other children and sat on a bench where she could observe her child. Lily crawled away from the other children and sat alone, watching them. When a child came by her she moved again and kept watching. Every day Nahdia took her out to the playground and every day she did the same thing. Lily seemed content sitting there watching the other children. She didn't cry or laugh or smile. She simply sat there and watched. After a couple weeks Nahdia decided to talk with Anthony about it.

"She just sits there. She doesn't do anything but sit there. Do you think there's something wrong with her?"

"No, Nahdia. If she doesn't want to play, then she doesn't want to play. That don't mean anything's wrong with her. I mean, c'mon. Do you know anyone who doesn't like going around anyone else or avoids everyone their whole life? She'll grow out of it." Anthony said indifferently.

His question made Nahdia remember someone who didn't like going around anyone and always stayed in their house. "Aunt Nette."

"Who?"

"Aunt Nette." Nahdia repeated.

"Oh yeah, I'd almost forgotten about her."

"You're probably too young to remember this, but Aunt Nette hated to leave her house. She'd make me run all her errands for her and she never had any guests. It was so quiet and lonely. I guess that's one of the reasons I wanted to get away from there. That and because sometimes at night it felt like something was watching me and it creeped me out." Her revelation had made her shiver.

"So, what? You think Lily is going to be like that?" inquired Anthony.

"I don't know. Maybe you're right. She'll grow out of it. I mean it isn't like Aunt Nette had any neighbors. Lily will be surrounded by peers. Yeah. She'll grow out of it."

Shortly after Lily's fourth birthday, Nahdia enrolled her in preschool. The teacher, Mrs. Johnson, told her that Lily was very precocious but that she isolates herself from the other students. "She looks at books at watches the other children play." said Mrs. Johnson.

"Does she cause trouble?" Nahdia asked nervously.

"No, no, nothing like that. I just thought you would want to know that she's just a little different from other children. I also believe she is colorblind."

"Colorblind?"

"Yes. She has a problem deciphering colors. I noticed this when we were having color

                    Ashley Lauren Mitchell

time. She was drawing a picture and I asked her what color she was using. She said she didn't know. I held up more colors and she kept saying she didn't know. If I may suggest, when you get home try to quiz her a little on her colors and make sure I'm not jumping to conclusions."

"Yes, of course."

At home, Nahdia took out Lily's color box. "This is green, Lily. Can you say green?"

"Green," said Lily.

"And this is purple. Can you say purple?"

"Purr...pull."

Nahdia help up each color and asked her to repeat the colors. Then she put the colors behind her back and switched them. She pulled out both colors and held them in front of Lily.

"Okay Lily. Now which color is purple?"

Lily pointed to the green color. Nahdia said "No. Let's try it again." She grabbed a third color and switched them behind her back.

"Okay Lily. Now which color is purple?"

"I don't know," Lily said.

"Just guess, honey. Which one?"

Lily took the red color out of her mother's hand. "Purr...pull."

Nahdia was shocked. She tried nearly all the colors in the box before succumbing to the fact that her daughter was colorblind. Anthony assured her that Lily's being colorblind wasn't something to obsess over. She could see and that was all that mattered.

At school, Lily continued to stay to herself. She'd watch the other children but never played with them. By the time Lily was in first grade, her self-alienation had worsened. Children began teasing her about being colorblind and not having any friends. One night while Lily and Nahdia were eating dinner Lily asked, "Mama, why do I have to go to school? Why can't I stay at home with you?"

"Why Baby? You don't like school?"

"I like the books and learning, and stuff, but I don't like the other kids." Lily said, pushing her peas around on the plate with her fork.

　　　　　　　Ashley Lauren Mitchell

"Well, what's wrong with the other kids?"

"They make fun of me. I don't want to be around them."

"That's nonsense. You should try being friends with them. Tomorrow, how about you try to make a friend for mama, ok?

"Yes ma'am." Lily said, huffing.

The next day Lily approached a group of children at school. She glanced up at each one of them before attempting to speak. She was as least a foot shorter than all of them. She stood biting her lip thinking of something to say.

"Well, what do you want?" asked a little boy in the group.

"Yeah, what do you want?" repeated a second child. The children started laughing.

"Um, I..." Lily was absent words.

"Get outta here," one of the children shouted while pushing Lily.

"You're so weird," said another. They all began pushing Lily and she fell to the ground. She immediately got up and punched the little

     Ashley Lauren Mitchell

boy in the face. The other she swung to the ground. Another child she pushed on the side and he ran into a pole. The other children ran away in terror.

"She did what?" Nahdia screamed through the telephone receiver.

"I'm sorry Ms. Leduff but you have to come and pick her up. We won't allow that kind of behavior. She broke one child's nose and fractured another's rib. The parents are outraged. I just don't think she belongs at this school."

Nahdia picked Lily up from school. "What were you thinking?" She asked as she paced back and forth in the living room.

"I tried to talk to them but they were mean and started pushin on me." Lily had tears welling in her eyes.

"You can't do that Lily. And you won't do that at the next school either."

"I don't want to go to a next school." Lily cried.

"You have to go to school Lily!"

                    Ashley Lauren Mitchell

"I don't wanna!"

"What's going on?" Anthony said walking through the door in his NOPD uniform.

"Lily got into a fight today at school."

"Really?" He asked smiling.

"Yes. She really hurt some kids and now she's expelled."

"What?" He asked bewildered.

"I don't want to go to school anymore Uncle Tony."

"Why did you hurt those other kids, Baby girl?" He asked lovingly.

"They were teasing me and started pushing me." Lily said with tears in her rainbow speckled eyes.

"Pushing you? Well I'd say they got what was coming to 'em. Nobody pushes my Lily and gets away with it. That's my girl!" Anthony said giving Lily a high five.

"She broke a kid's nose, damnit!" Nahdia screamed.

　　　　　　　　　　Ashley Lauren Mitchell

"I'll break all their noses if you make me go to school again, Mama!" Lily shouted back. Her arms were around Anthony's legs. After her outburst she buried her head in his calves, hiding her face from her mother.

"We gotta find another way." Anthony said picking up Lily, sitting on the couch, and putting her on his lap.

"Like what?" asked Nahdia.

"Nahdia, you know Lily never liked being around other kids. She needs more space. She needs to be able to go outside and not be surrounded by people. It's too crowded and too dangerous in New Orleans anyways."

"Well, what do you suggest, Tony?" Nahdia asked, standing akimbo.

"What if you guys got a house in the country somewhere. That way Lily can go outside and explore and be the kid she wants to be."

This was music to Lily's ears. Her face lit up and her eyes shone brighter than ever. Her smile revealed her large front teeth that had just grown in. She imagined her Uncle Tony was a knight in black and blue armor rescuing her from her

Ashley Lauren Mitchell

fire breathing mother.

"What about school?" Nahdia persisted.

"She can be home schooled. She can have one teacher that can teach her all subjects. Just let her stay home. You know I'd pay for it."

"Are you serious Anthony?"

"Yes."

"Where are we going to live?" asked Nahdia.

"Let me take care of it." Anthony brushed a shiny black curl from Lily's forehead and kissed it.

"So what's going to happen to the apartment?" Nahdia antagonized.

"I'll keep the apartment. I'll live and work in New Orleans and I'll come to visit you girls every chance I get." He said. "I promise."

"You're not just doing this to get away from us, are you?" Nahdia asked jokingly.

"From you girls? Never! You girls are my

                    Ashley Lauren Mitchell

blood," he said hugging Lily to his chest, "and nothing is more sacred than that."

***

Donaldsonville, Louisiana seemed like a whole other world to Lily. She was in awe at the open spaces of land. It was the perfect place for an introverted little girl like Lily. Her face beamed as they drove over the Sunshine Bridge. She'd never looked happier a day in all the six years she'd been alive. Nahdia turned around in the passenger seat and saw Lily gazing in amazement out the window. "I think someone is excited." She said to Anthony.

He looked in the rearview mirror at Lily. "Baby Girl, the house is coming up." After forty-five minutes of driving they reached the end of their journey. "Here we are."

Lily jumped out of the car and ran into a field of sugarcane. "Look Uncle Tony! Wow! They're taller than you!" She exclaimed. She ran around the house and in between the sugar cane stalks. "What are these?" She finally slowed down to ask.

"This is sugarcane, sugar," said Anthony. He walked to a stalk and snapped it. He pulled back the chaff and bit into the sweet, juicy cane.

Lily tasted the sugarcane. "Eww, it's too sweet!"

"What? Girl, this is good. What you talkin bout?" Anthony said laughing at the grimace on Lily's face.

"You know Lily only likes to eat meat," said Nahdia taking the boxes of clothes into the house.

"Oh yeah. She is weird like that." He said. Lily hit his leg and he chased after her. When he caught her, he threw her into the air. Lily laughed.

The house that Anthony had found for them was being sold at a reduced price by the owners; an older couple Anthony knew. It was an old house with high ceilings that looked like they had been made for people that were ten feet tall. The floors were made of wood and they creaked with every step the three of them made. The house had two bedrooms separated by a thin wall. The bathroom was across from Lily's room. There was no shower, only a large tub.

The house was quaint and cozy. Nahdia lit an old gas fireplace on the floor. Lily ran to warm herself by the fire.

"She likes it here, don't you think?" Nahdia asked Anthony.

"Yep. You were right. I guess she's more like Aunt Nette than I thought." He replied.

"Yeah, she'll be fine out here. Thank you Anthony. We love you so much." They gave each other a hug, and they both sighed with relief. They had come so far together. Nahdia was so thankful to have Anthony for a little brother, and that he cared so much for Lily. They pulled apart and Nahdia wiped a tear from her eye. "So, when did you say the teacher is coming?" she asked.

"On Wednesday. She has to take care of some things with her daughter first. She said she can be here every weekday morning, excluding holidays."

"That's perfect," said Nahdia.

"I'm sure they'll get along just fine."

                    Ashley Lauren Mitchell

"Yeah," agreed Nahdia.

That first night at the house in Donaldsonville, Lily couldn't sleep. She was still excited from the wondrous day she'd had. Her mother was sleeping in the room on the other side of the wall. Lily climbed out of her bed and slowly crept passed her mother's bedroom until she was at the front door. Each little footstep made a small noise, that seemed magnified to Lily as she giggled and walked on her tiptoes. She opened the door and looked out at the night through the screen door. She held her breath. She'd never seen anything so tranquil. The apartment complex in New Orleans was crowded and everywhere Lily went she was surrounded by people. Here it was quiet and deserted, just as Lily liked it. She stepped out on the front steps. The moon was full and low. She imagined she could reach up and touch it. The stars shone like a million jewels in the midnight sky. The house was nearly surrounded by sugarcane fields. She looked up at the night sky and closed her eyes. Suddenly she felt a cold breeze whip past her face and filled her small lungs. She trembled and opened her eyes. In the distance she saw a glowing bright light. She

          Ashley Lauren Mitchell

squinted and saw a sylphlike figure approaching. It glided through the field with ease. It kept moving closer to her.

"Lily!" Nahdia shouted. "What are you doing out here?"

"Hey mama. Look, it's so peaceful. I never knew a place like this existed."

Nahdia looked at her surroundings. She realized it was just as calm as it was in Haiti when she lived with her Aunt Nette. For Aunt Nette and Lily it was the ideal atmosphere. This time Nahdia wouldn't leave. If Lily liked being here, this is where they would live, for the rest of Nahdia's life if she must. "It's beautiful, love." She took Lily's hand and they walked inside together. "Have I ever told you about your great-aunt Antoinette?" She asked Lily.

"No. She has a name like mine."

"That's right. That's where you got your middle name from."

"Cool," cooed Lily.

"Well, your great-aunt Antoinette was your grandfather, Antoine's twin sister." Nahdia told

                                    Ashley Lauren Mitchell

Lily the story of her family history, and lulled her to sleep.

***

Lily's homeschool teacher was Mrs. Monroe, a widow from New Orleans. She taught high school for twelve years. She was the kind of woman that went to church faithfully every Sunday morning. When her husband died, she and her daughter Celeste moved to Donaldsonville. Anthony was one of the first police officers at her house after her husband's heart attack. He knew before the paramedics arrived that Mr. Monroe had died. He distracted Mrs. Monroe by talking about her daughter, the other light in her life. He told her that no matter what happened she had to be strong for her daughter.

When her husband was pronounced dead she fainted. Anthony caught her and moved her to the couch. When she woke Anthony was there talking her through her grief. When her daughter walked in the door she embraced her mother and they both started weeping. Mrs. Monroe looked at Anthony and remembered what he'd said, that she had to be strong for her daughter. She hugged and thanked Anthony. He made sure the mother and daughter found a house in Donaldsonville and secured Mrs. Monroe the job as Lily's homeschool teacher.

"Anthony, why do you care what happens to us?" asked Mrs. Monroe.

"If something ever happened to me, I would want someone to look out for my girls." He answered, thinking of Nahdia and Lily.

"Oh, God bless you Baby."

On Wednesday, Mrs. Monroe dropped her daughter off at Tulane University in New Orleans.

"I love you mom. I'll come home every weekend and we'll talk on the phone every day."

"I love you too, honey. Don't worry about me. You just enjoy yourself. You deserve some fun after all you've been through with...you just have a good time, okay?

"I will mom. I'll miss you."

                                    Ashley Lauren Mitchell

"I miss you already Baby. God bless you."

With tears clouding her eyes every two minutes, Mrs. Monroe drove back to Donaldsonville to begin her new job. "Oh God, give me strength and please watch over my baby girl," she prayed to subside her tears.

"Hello, Lily. I'm Mrs. Monroe. That is such a pretty name, Lily. You're named after a beautiful flower, did you know that?"

"Yes ma'am. And my middle name is like my great-auntie."

"Well, you are a special and smart little girl. And look at those eyes. My heavens, I've never seen such eyes before. You must have every color in the rainbow in your eyes."

"Mama says that too, but, I can't see colors. I'm colorblind."

"Aw, baby, that's nothin' to fret over. You just be happy you can see."

"Yes ma'am."

"Do you know how to read Lily?"

"Yes ma'am. I love to read."

"Well that's great! I have a whole heap of books you can read at my house. I also have magazines like National Geographic's that have pictures from all over the world. I can bring them and you can have a time."

"Yes ma'am!" exclaimed Lily excitedly.

For the next ten years, Mrs. Monroe homeschooled Lily. Although she missed her daughter, Lily was a sweet girl and she and Lily developed their own mother-daughter bond. Mrs. Monroe would take Lily and Nahdia to church with her on Sunday mornings. She and Nahdia grew close. Nahdia worked at a neighborhood grocery store, but on her days off from work the two ladies would go on picnics and walks with Lily. They enjoyed each other's company. When Anthony came to visit, which was as often as he promised, he always had a hearty, home cooked meal waiting for him. They all loved Anthony, and Anthony loved them too.

Chapter 5

July, 2005

Call me Lamia.

I can't stop thinking about three nights ago; the night I killed Derek and Michael. That following night, I still felt warmer than I'd usually feel. My skin retained its darker complexion, and Diamond and Uncle Tony were also surprised. I thought about asking Uncle Tony if more nights like that could be arranged, but I think I have an idea what he'd say. He'd say it's too risky and it's hard enough disposing of the corpses I create already. He'd say it in his affectionate way, of course, but I'd still feel like a greedy monster. I don't want them to see me that way, even if it is how I am.

I'm starting to enjoy this more than I should perhaps. I wish I could tell that to someone and not be judged; and not feel like an animal. There's no one that understands what it's like to be like this. I care for Diamond and Uncle Tony, but they can't possibly imagine what I'm feeling. I guess I should feel heroic for helping to save innocent

Ashley Lauren Mitchell

lives, but sometimes I feel I only do this for my pleasure, my desideratum, and my sustenance...the blood.

After discarding Marcus, the chosen one for tonight, in the back of Uncle Tony's car I return to my living quarters. I have no desire to do anything or be bothered by anyone. I feel empty and unsatisfied. I sit in the chair I just finished my meal in and look at the ceiling. I think about what my future could be like. Wasting away at a strip club, feeding off one human every three nights, and pouches of blood on the others. Damn this! No one understands the loneliness I am experiencing. I'm a freak of nature. I don't even believe nature had much to do with this either. I cannot, no one can, explain what I am or what I'm supposed to do. Will I be eternally trapped in this body? In this insufferable existence? I have no choice but to be cynical. I can see into human's souls. I can see all of their past actions and future intentions just by gazing into their eyes. I know before they speak the ulterior motives and deceptions they possess. Other than Uncle Tony and Diamond, the only other humans I see are those that I kill, the murderers and rapists.

                    Ashley Lauren Mitchell

I want to leave this place but there's nowhere for me to go. The sunlight is harmful to my susceptible skin, restricting me from being able to travel anywhere during the day. I'm trapped in so many ways. I don't think Death wants me either, and yet I cannot evade it. It's everywhere around me. I'm standing on the doorstep to perdition but I'm refused entrance. I can only wonder why the devil doesn't want me. I too, am a killer. Am I not? But then again I can't die. Can I? And my body is immune and impenetrable to pain and sickness. I am a wraith, a specter, an unwanted vagrant soul. What will happen when I can't depend on Uncle Tony and Diamond any longer? What happens to *me* when their mortal bodies die?

I shouldn't think such things. I don't want to think at all. I want the quiet to inundate my thoughts. I want...more blood. Damnit! I can't stop thinking about it! I continue to stare at the ceiling, then I close my eyes; hoping peace will soon quiet my thoughts. It doesn't.

I get up and lazily walk to the bookshelf. I've read every book on this bookshelf; some more than once. But perhaps a book will distract me. I rummaged through the pages of an

Ashley Lauren Mitchell

arbitrarily chosen book before throwing it to the floor. I grabbed another and then threw it down, then more books and threw them all to the floor. I continued to break things and knock them to the ground. In my rage I punched the mirror to my dressing table, shattering the glass I'd stared in so often, and never did it gratify me with a reflection. I fell to my knees and closed my eyes attempting to control myself. What is wrong with me?

Then I heard it.

My eyes instantly opened and I listened attentively for the sound again, making certain it wasn't my imagination. There it is again. A lovely, desperate... scream. I slowly, strategically rise from the floor. I close my eyes again and listen for where it's coming from. Over the music bursting through the speakers, I hear it once more. I look down. It's coming from right below me. The screams are strained but I can interpret the kind of cry it is. It's a cry for help. Someone is screaming for their life. I close my eyes again. When I open them a second later, I am miraculously in the room below me.

It's another private dressing room. The door

is closed and locked. Diamond once told me the girls aren't supposed to lock these doors, precautionary measures. So this was another's doing. On the ground in front of me is a man on his knees. He's on top of one of the girls and is strangling her. I notice small specks of blood on the floor next to the girls head. I quickly, quietly step closer. His back is to me. The girl's hands are wrapped tightly around the man's wrists. I remember this girl. Sable, I believe. She's struggling and kicking her feet wildly. She sees me. In her eyes, I saw something more than 'help me,' but it's fading because she's too near death.

I reach down and grab the man by the back of his skull. His grip around Sable's neck is instantly released. My fingernails break through the bone and I tighten my fingers fiercely through the hard, smooth holes they've made. I can feel chunks of brain underneath my fingertips. I bring his trembling body up slowly. His blood is running in streams down my hand, dripping to the floor. Sable is gasping for air, and her breathing is rapid, but the color is rushing back to her face. She stands without taking her eyes off of me. Her hands cupped around her bruised neck. I watch drops of

Ashley Lauren Mitchell

the man's blood splatter to the floor, before returning my gaze to Sable. Holding my victim's squirming body like a bowling ball I step closer to her. She steps closer to me. I can't understand what I'm seeing in her eyes. We continue walking closer to each other, she in a trance, and I in curious wonder.

A loud noise comes from behind me. Uncle Tony's voice is on the other side of the door. He's banging on it and commanding that it be opened, this second. The music has stopped. He's now kicking the door forcing it to open. Diamond is calling to Sable repeatedly but Sable is still staring at me... and I am still staring at Sable. I realize that in a few seconds Uncle Tony will be bursting through the door with a crowd of nosy, scantily clad women behind him, and I shouldn't be seen standing here in a puddle of blood, and especially not with a convulsing body clutched in my right hand. I give one last quizzical look to Sable, the same one I'd given to her less than a year ago. I can only assume that this time it holds a different meaning, one that I've yet to ascertain. Still, I want to devour her. I reluctantly close my eyes.

When I open them I am once again miraculously back in my room upstairs. What is more miraculous is that I'm still carrying the body of the perpetrator at my fingertips. He somehow travelled with me. But he's dying and dripping blood...on my rug. But, I can't let this meal go to waste. I bring him to my mouth and drink the remaining blood from his veins, listening to the last heartbeat. My fingers release his skull and I let the carcass fall to the floor.

I can only imagine that by now Uncle Tony and Diamond are in the room below and see the sanguine fluid spreading throughout the cracks in the floor. They'll be here shortly so I should rehearse what I *should* say. Anything I say will sound like a lie though. I'll just leave the door unlocked so Uncle Tony won't feel the need to kick it down. I believe he's still in that excited, kick the door down, mood. To my surprise, when Uncle Tony entered my room he first glanced at the body on the floor next to my feet, and then to me. All he said was, "Meet me out back in two minutes." I lifted the body over my shoulder. I looked down at the rug. I'll clean it when I return.

After I'd laid the body in the trunk, next to Marcus's, Uncle Tony spoke, "You know, you saved that girl in there."

                    Ashley Lauren Mitchell

I remain speechless. I was expecting a harangue, but he doesn't even look angry.

"Lamia,"

Here it comes I thought.

"I'm very proud of you."

"What?" I felt my jaw hang desperately in astonishment.

"You have a good heart, Baby Girl," he said. He licks his thumb and wiped dry blood from my face. He looks at it, pretends to taste it, laughs, and wipes the finger on his pant leg.

I can't believe how nonchalant he is about the situation. I manage a smile through my dubiety. I'd convinced myself that he would yell at me and start seeing me for what I really am. I wanted to tell him that I didn't give a shit about saving anyone's life, and that I only killed that man because I wanted more blood. But why ruin this moment of pride for him? I looked at the ground in shame, shame that I was being glorified by Uncle Tony for saving human lives, when all I really wanted was to kill them. I feel like a...a...No. I am not, whatever I was about to think. I am Lamia. Uncle Tony only thinks of me as Lamia.

Uncle Tony walks to the driver's side door, "Get back up there and go to bed," he said before disappearing into the car.

I watched him drive away. I looked up at the night sky. This night was almost as eventful as the night I had three nights ago. Then I recalled something about that night that had made it so eventful. I looked across the street, to the other side of Bourbon. Standing there was the same figure I'd seen three nights ago. Once we'd made eye contact he vanished. I wanted to go search for him but decided instead to retreat to my room. I had blood to clean off the rug.

When I had finished scrubbing the rug and tidying the mess I'd made of my room earlier, I decided to take a shower. Although I'd done a stellar job of cleaning the blood, the pungent odor lingered. I thought about how irate I was when I wrecked my room and how only more blood could appease me. In retrospect, I don't believe it was a good idea to have had both Derek and Michael that night. What if now, my body is expecting more blood than usual? Who was that figure standing on the opposite side of

     Ashley Lauren Mitchell

Bourbon Street? What was it about Sable that confused me so? Why is it that I wanted to crush her again? She didn't smell like she was menstruating. Is that the reason I wanted her? Sable.

I step into my small shower in the corner of my room. I let the lukewarm water beat on my face. I run my hands over my face and through my hair. I'm so warm and full, satiated from the two portions I had again tonight. Just like three nights ago. Ahh. I can still smell the blood in the room.

But, wait, that's not possible. I know that I cleaned the room well enough. There's no way that the scent is still that strong, unless...unless there's fresh blood in my room. Perhaps it's somewhere I missed. I have to clean it.

I turn the water off and reach for the towel through the opening in the shower curtain. I reach, and reach. It isn't there! It's not where I left it? No way! I'm too fastidious and methodical. There is no way I'm losing my idiosyncrasies now. I angrily pull back the shower curtain and look for the towel that I should have had waiting for me on the counter, where I always put it. Fuck, am I losing my

                    Ashley Lauren Mitchell

mind? And then I look up...

There, standing only a few feet away from me is a fragile, temporal being. My towel is extended to me from the creature's hand and I carefully move to take it. Our eyes are locked on one another's. The confusion I experienced earlier is back. I stare at those dark brown eyes as the being steps toward me. The towel is in my hand but I don't want the towel anymore. Beads of water are dripping from my warm body. She is so close to me now. I can see the open cuts above her eye where she'd been hit. I can feel her swarthy, smooth fingers touching the towel. Sable.

"How did you get in here?" I ask her. Our eyes remained captivated on each other's.

"The door wasn't locked, and I heard the water running so I knew you wouldn't hear me knock," she responds. Her voice is soft. It's hard for me to imagine it was this small voice that screamed so loudly not too long ago.

"You shouldn't be here," I admonish.

"I wanted to thank you for...what you did earlier," she says. She's shivering, but not because

Ashley Lauren Mitchell

I am cold, I'm far from it. She is shivering because, she is nervous. I make her nervous. She should be nervous. I still haven't decided if I'll let her live.

"You shouldn't thank me for that."

"But I should. You didn't have to save me." "If I

didn't Uncle Tony would have."

"But he didn't. You did."

"I didn't do it for you."

"But I think you did." Her statement shocked me, but I kept looking at her. She continued, "That time you came to me, do you remember that?"

Poor girl, she doesn't even realize. "Yes," I said, "I remember. But it's not what you think."

"I have thought about you ever since then. You are so...beautiful."

"What?" I asked perplexed. I can hardly believe what I'm hearing.

"I mean, look at you," her eyes left mine and looked down at my body. She returned to my eyes, and said, "And your eyes. Your eyes are

                                    Ashley Lauren Mitchell

gorgeous. They're the most beautiful eyes I've ever seen." She gazed. I gazed...

And then I saw it. I saw what it was that made me want to destroy this girl. "Sable, you've killed someone." It wasn't a question. I knew the answer already. She can't deny it.

"How do you know that?" she asked. The expression on her face wasn't what I'd expect after revealing something like that. She didn't look surprised or frightened. She looked, relieved.

"I can see it. I can see it in your eyes. You've taken a life."

"Yes. I did and I feel awful for it." Her face wasn't one of remorse. She's gazing at me in a familiar way but I can't put my finger on it.

"What happened?" I asked. I needed to know her explanation before I took her life. Why? I'm not sure. I guess out of habit from working with Uncle Tony.

"The man you...took care of tonight," she swallows and licks her lips, "he was coming to kill me because I killed his brother."

"Sable," I breathed, "why did you kill his

                                   Ashley Lauren Mitchell

brother?"

"He used to beat on me. He put me in the hospital for weeks one time. He wanted to kill me when he found out I was leaving him. So, I beat him to the punch, is all."

She wasn't lying. Damnit! Why wasn't she lying? Why couldn't she be just as guilty as the others? Why do I care if she is? I can just as easily take her life as I did the others'? No one is here to stop me. "Oh," was the only response I could rouse.

"He had it coming, don't you think?" she asked me. Her eyes are so pretty. They're begging me to keep looking.

I licked my lips. I'm not sure why. What is this feeling I'm having? "It seems that way." I finally answer.

My breathing is getting heavier. I can hear her heartbeat. It's racing in quick, rhythmic, cadences. Her eyes are jumping back and forth on mine. She begins to elevate herself on the balls of her feet until her lips are even with mine. She breathes soft words from them that force me to close my eyes. "I am...innocent." She gently

                    Ashley Lauren Mitchell

places her hands on my hips before she slowly glides them up my wet, warm body. Her lips are so close to mine I can taste them. I open my mouth.

"No, I can't," I say and open my eyes.

"What do you mean, No?" she asks in amazement.

"I can't do this with you Sable. I'm sorry." I'm not sure where 'I'm sorry' came from. Why should I be sorry to her, or for her for that matter? She lives, she should be grateful for that.

"I thought you wanted me?" "I

do, in a way, it's just..."

Her eyes are looking at me. They are so fucking...innocent. "Then take me." She says as she grips my waist tighter and tries to kiss me again.

I cock my head back slightly putting it just out of her lips' reach. "I just, can't." Great Lamia, what kind of explanation was that? Then, I see something else in her eyes. Something I don't want to see. For God's sake, she's in love with me. I shouldn't have made her feel so desired back then.

 Ashley Lauren Mitchell

She hasn't even discovered *my* secret. She doesn't know I am a...

"Lamia, please. Take me!" She begged.

I want to take her so badly. I want to wrap my dripping arms around her tiny body and squeeze it. I want to hold her motionless in my grasp and smell her before sinking my teeth into her thin, bruised neck. But she's immune to my gaze because she is...innocent. Innocent? I hate that word.

"Sable, you should go."

She takes a step away from me but her eyes remain on mine. Her expression has changed. She looks, hurt, I think. "I thought, that, you...," her eyes gloss over as if she wants to cry, "I'm sorry."

She started to turn and walk away. A conviction came over me. I made her feel like Diamond feels with Uncle Tony. She loves him but he doesn't love her. Sable loves me but I don't love her. Not the way she wants me to. She doesn't know why I made her feel wanted. I do want her, but not the way she wants me. I should let her leave but I can't. "Wait," I say, grabbing her arm a

     Ashley Lauren Mitchell

little tighter than I should have. She looks at my hand on her arm and then looks at my face. She's searching for a reason. "I didn't mean to hurt you Sable."

"Why don't you want me?"

I moved close to her again and placed my hand over her heart. I take my other hand and put it on the nape of her neck and run my fingers through her hair. I grip it and pull her head to mine. Gently, I lean into her face and smell her, closing my eyes for a moment and basking in the tantalizing scent. Then I kiss her. Her mouth welcomes the pleasure. Her lips are soft, supple. This is my first kiss. It is a human; a delicate, innocent, human. She kisses me back, and slides her tongue into my mouth. For a brief moment I am hers. Her hands are roaming my body and she grips my breasts. I let her think that that makes me feel, something, as she lightly pinches my nipples and rubs her fingers back and forth over them. Her hands, my body, our...blood, I taste blood, sapid, delicious blood. Should I taste blood?

My eyes are closed but I can feel a difference in her embrace. Her hands are now on

                    Ashley Lauren Mitchell

my shoulders. It feels as though she's pushing them backwards. Why would she be pushing my shoulders? I'm not sure how much time has passed before she starts moaning softly, then a little louder. She is pushing me harder but I'm holding her close to me. Her hands, she has one on either side of my head and is gripping my hair. Perhaps she wants more. I suck on her tongue. I still taste blood but I don't want to stop kissing her. I feel her feet kicking my legs. Her hands are slapping my face. Why are her hands slapping my face? I open my eyes and see hers, wide, panicked. Tears are streaming down the sides of her face. The passion I had felt in the heat of the moment had trapped me. I didn't realize my teeth were deep in Sable's tongue and I was drinking her.

When I pulled from her she clapped her hands over her mouth. She looked dizzy. She stumbled back, trying to right herself using her elbows on the dressing table. She eventually found my gaze again. The blood on my chin slid down my neck and chest. I cautiously walked to her. She swiftly stood to her feet and backed against the dressing table. I stopped.

"That is why I cannot want you Sable. Do

you understand?"

Her demeanor slowly changed from fear to compassion. She took her hands from her mouth. The needle point puncture wounds should've stopped bleeding by now. "Yes," she said, "I understand."

"I also need to know that you won't tell anyone what you've discovered here tonight. Do you understand?"

"Yes, Lamia, I understand."

Lamia. She called me Lamia. She called me by my name, the name I call myself. She didn't call me monster, or animal, she called me Lamia. My name. I stepped closer to her.

"You have to promise you won't tell anyone my secret either," she said.

Her secret? What secret? Oh, her *secret*, the secret that led her to my room in the first place. "Sable, you *are* innocent in my eyes."

"They are such beautiful eyes, Lamia. I wish I could see them more often."

"That's not a good idea Sable. But know

that these eyes are always watching you."

She stepped close to me and brushed a tendril from my face. She kissed my cheek and winked at me. "I'll gladly keep that in mind."

When she exited my room I stood, paralyzed by what had just happened. Another mortal knows my secret, and I let her live. In retrospect, it may not have been wise to trust her and let her walk out of here. It's too late now. I believed her when she'd said she wouldn't tell anyone what she knows. I better be able to believe her. Divulging this esoteric knowledge will kill her. I will kill her. But there is still someone else that knows.

The figure on the other side of Bourbon Street. I saw him, he saw me. That doesn't necessarily mean he knows. How did he vanish so quickly? Who is that man? That mystery being? I put on a night gown and settled in my coffin for much needed rest. My head is disoriented and burdened with questions. None will be answered tonight. I must rest. I close my coffin, I close my eyes.

Then I hear fingernails tapping on my coffin.

I open my eyes. No way. I locked the door. I locked all of the doors. No one can be in my room. *That* is impossible! I open my coffin lid. I sit up and feel a cold breeze blow across my warm face. I look around but see no one. "Sable, is that you?" No answer. "Sable?" No answer. I hear no heartbeats. I smell no blood. No one is in this room with me. But someone *was* in this room with me. They were here. I heard it. I sensed it. I know it. What is wrong with me? Come on Lamia, snap out of it. I close my coffin, I close my eyes.

Chapter 6

1984-2003

Celeste Monroe walked through the doors of Tulane University apprehensively. She watched the other students leisurely walking past her. She felt lonely. She missed her mother. She missed her father. She nervously fiddled with the diamond bracelet on her left wrist before finding the courage to ask someone for help finding her first class.

Weeks went by and she settled comfortably in her dormitory. She met a few friends through her roommate, Dana, and began having a real social life again, something she'd dismissed when her father died, along with going to church. She called her mother every night and went to Donaldsonville on the weekends, just as she'd promised. For her entire first semester in college, life seemed normal and good.

At home during the Christmas and New Year's holiday break, Celeste refused to go to the church Christmas programs with her mother. She refused to leave the house. She slept and lounged. Her mother's badgering with Bible verses about sloth began irritating her. Celeste couldn't wait to return to school.

After a couple months into her second semester, her freedom got the best of her. She started hanging out with her friends more than she took to her studies. They would find something to do in New Orleans every night. And without parental supervision, Celeste and her friends did whatever they wanted. She could hear her mother's voice in the back of her conscience saying things like, "Watch out for the devils," or, "The devil's always watching." This was one of her mother's favorite religious quips to scare her daughter into good behavior. With all of her new social habits, her grades by the end of the semester were below average. She started drinking and even started having sex. She felt out of control but continued her rebellious behavior into the summer semester. She stopped going home on weekends and began lying to her mother about her lifestyle. By the end of the next fall semester, Celeste had forfeited her scholastic scholarships and moved off campus. She began bartending at a local club. She wondered how her life had changed so fast and she felt ashamed. She told herself that she would work and save, and when she had enough money she would continue her education again.

Then she met Kevin Wake. She was bartending at the club one night when Kevin walked in with a few of his friends. Kevin was two years older than Celeste. He had seductive green eyes that seemed familiar, and a smile that, at first glance, won

Celeste's vulnerable heart. Beware of the devils. She pushed her mother's voice from her mind.

"Hello sweetheart," he said.

They hit it off instantly. They started hanging out and he convinced her that he was in love with her. She moved in with him and forgot all about school. She wanted to introduce him to her mother; instead he introduced her to cocaine. The two of them would lock themselves in his studio apartment for days snorting, drinking, and losing track of time. Celeste thought she was happy. The drugs told her she was happy. People would come by at all hours of the day and night to score from Kevin. He somehow always had any and everything he or his customers needed.

After six months, Celeste got pregnant. Kevin took her to a clinic that looked neither safe nor clean. She didn't really want the baby, she wasn't even in a state to take care of herself, let alone a child. She wanted Kevin and would do whatever it took to keep him. In pain, she returned with him to his apartment. He shot a syringe filled with liquid morphine into her arm. Her body relaxed. He laid her in the bed and she slept for days. When she woke, Kevin was there to greet her with a line of cocaine. They both remained in a drug-induced bliss for another six months.

Mrs. Monroe hadn't spoken to her daughter in over three months. The last time she did, Celeste

　　　　Ashley Lauren Mitchell

sounded groggy and discursive. After the first week without hearing from her daughter she was worried, but by now she was distraught. She begged Anthony to find her daughter and bring her home. He promised he'd do everything he could to find Celeste. Mrs. Monroe would walk around her house sending little prayers for her daughter up, hoping they were reaching heaven and the God she wanted to hear them.

Anthony asked numerous people that worked at the club Celeste bartended at about her whereabouts. They said she'd not been there in quite some time. They told Anthony about Kevin and that Celeste had run off with him. He used his police skills to look up Kevin and find where he lived. He arrested Kevin for possession and distribution of narcotics and had Celeste admitted to a hospital. She begged Anthony not to tell her mother. He told her that in return for his promise, she had to promise to make the trip to Donaldsonville to see her mother. They agreed and Anthony stayed by her side through her recovery.

Mrs. Monroe was elated to see her daughter again. "Oh, praise God!" She exclaimed." Celeste didn't tell her mother about the dark life she'd fell victim to or that she was no longer in school. Celeste lived with her mother in Donaldsonville for a summer but longed to return to New Orleans. She was sick of

　　　　Ashley Lauren Mitchell

hearing about God and the precocious, little Lily; the girl that her mother bragged about constantly. Mrs. Monroe told her she should meet the young child but Celeste refused every opportunity. She thought about the abortion more now, and she felt sickened by it. She gave away her child, and her mother's grandchild. Celeste didn't even get her cycle anymore. She knew the trip to the clinic had done something to her. Now she didn't think she'd ever be able to have a baby. That next week she returned to New Orleans without meeting Lily, the child her mother had grown to love.

Celeste found another bartending job at a strip club on Bourbon Street. It had bright, neon pink lights above the doorway. The inside of the club was extravagant, with strobe lights and fog machines creating a mystical wonderland for half naked nymphs and caitiffs. She liked this club. She was there nearly every night and she loved that the city never slept. Anthony would go by the club every week to check on her and report back to Mrs. Monroe that her daughter was okay, but kept his promise to Celeste that he wouldn't tell her about the life she was living in New Orleans.

Tulane University was a distant dream to Celeste by this time. She'd given up on the idea of returning to school and realized her life was in the club. She began stripping to make extra money but her affinity was bartending. She and her mother talked on the phone once a week which was more than enough for Celeste. She hated lying to her mother but she was making such good money at the club. Her mother invited her home for Lily's tenth birthday but Celeste again refused saying she had to complete an internship at a hospital. Her mother was so proud of her. Celeste was so ashamed of herself.

Over the next five years Celeste had moved up to managing the club. It had become her life. She asked Anthony to be the designated policeman to help protect the girls and control the boys. They kept silent about their enterprise to her mother the entire time. They also became close friends and Celeste depended on Anthony more than anyone in her life. Many times Anthony would invite Celeste to ride to Donaldsonville to see her mother and finally meet Lily and Nahdia. Every time, Celeste turned him down. She would use the club as her excuse, painting the picture that it would fall to ruin if she'd left, even for a night. He knew the real reason behind her refusal was because of her shame, but he never pushed her to change her mind.

As the years swiftly passed by, Mrs. Monroe got older and she became ill. At first the cancer was slow and caused her no great pain. Without warning it grew, taking over her withered body. Nahdia and Lily worked together to make her as comfortable as possible but Nahdia knew Lily's teacher and friend didn't have long to live. She told Anthony that Mrs. Monroe should have her daughter by her side when she closed her eyes for a final rest. Anthony concurred and admonished Celeste to go to her mother. Celeste believed he was lying or at least exaggerating about her mother's illness. She thought it was a ploy to get her to Donaldsonville. She said that she would go as soon as she found time in her hectic schedule. She never did and the next week, her mother died. Celeste rode to Donaldsonville with Anthony to prepare for Mrs. Monroe's funeral, crying the whole way.

The funeral was small, but the people Mrs. Monroe loved most in the world were in attendance. At the funeral Celeste finally met Lily, the girl that her mother had mentioned so often.

"Lily," Anthony said, "This is Celeste, Mrs. Monroe's daughter."

"Hi Celeste. I'm Lily."

"Lily? My mother was right. You are the most beautiful little girl in the whole world. And look at those eyes. Wow! How old are you?"

"Thank you. I'm fourteen."

"Fourteen? You don't look fourteen. You look much younger than that."

Lily lowered her head in shame of her inadequate figure.

"Oh baby, no. I didn't mean anything bad by that. Trust me as you get older you'll see that a woman that looks younger than she really is, is fortunate. You should be proud that you look so young."

Lily lifted her head and said, "Yes, ma'am."

"Oh God girl, don't call me ma'am. I'm only twenty-six, far too young for somebody to be callin' ma'am." Celeste joked.

"Girl, you not that young." Anthony said. He and Celeste looked at each other and laughed.

"Well at least I'm not the big three-oh." Celeste said laughing harder.

"That is a pretty bracelet, Celeste," Lily interrupted after listening to Celeste and her Uncle Tony make cracks at each other.

"Why thank you Lily. This was a gift from my dad on my sixteenth birthday. It's my birthstone. Diamond. You know, when the sunlight shines on this bracelet it makes rainbow colors just like your eyes. So, when is your birthday?"

"October...October sixth."

"That makes your birthstone...opal. That's what your eyes look like, a colorful opal stone."

After the funeral Celeste returned to New Orleans. She found solace in her work at the club. She was pleased she had Nahdia taking care of the details of her mother's passing. She told Anthony, on the way back to New Orleans, that she'd never forgive herself for not being there for her mother when she needed her most.

"Your mother loved you Celeste. She also knew you loved her too. Don't be too hard on yourself. You're only human."

"I guess you're right," Celeste said wiping tears from her face.

"I'm always right. You know that." They both laughed. Anthony always had a way of making her feel better. He was there for her and her mother since Mr. Monroe died.

"Tony, you have such a good heart."

"Thank you. It keeps me alive." They laughed again. She looked into his familiar green eyes and she knew then that she loved him.

"Your niece is really something." She said to distract her enamored mind.

"Isn't she, though?"

"How did her eyes get like that?"

"I'm not really sure. She was just born that way. But you know, to say her eyes are so colorful, she can't see color."

"What?"

"She's colorblind."

"Oh, my goodness! All the colors in the world? Can you imagine not being able to see them? She can't even appreciate how beautiful her eyes are. But being colorblind can't be the reason she was homeschooled. Right?"

"No. She, um, doesn't really like being around people."

"Aw, hell. I can understand that."

"No. I don't think you do. In the first grade she got into a fight with some kids and broke one of their noses. She got kicked out of school."

"Damn. She's pretty strong then, and pretty violent." She said giggling.

"Nothing like that has happened since though. She never gives her mother any problems. She reads and likes to play outside, in the sugarcane fields. She's

                    Ashley Lauren Mitchell

a happy little girl."

"And she is, little. A tiny little something for her age."

"She just has good genes girl. That runs in our family."

"Must have missed you then," Celeste mocked. They laughed again.

Anthony dropped Celeste off at the club. "See you later, Celeste."

"What did I tell you, Tony? When we're anywhere near the club, call me Diamond."

"Fine, Diamond. See you later."

***

Since Mrs. Monroe's death, Nahdia and Lily were spending all their time together. Nahdia had retired from the grocery store and had Lily helping around the house. She wanted Lily to go to college and make something of herself like Anthony had done. Lily was extremely intelligent, but she was even more anti-social. She still loved running through the tall sugarcane stalks like she did as a young girl. She

                    Ashley Lauren Mitchell

spent most of her days reading and talking with her mother. She loved when Anthony came to the house. They'd all play games and reminisce. Anthony also wanted Lily to enroll in a college or university. Every time one of them brought the issue up, Lily became reticent. She couldn't imagine leaving her home or her best friend, her mother. Nahdia told Anthony that Lily had her mind made up and trying to convince her otherwise would be futile.

"We wanted her happy, Anthony. She's happy. Let's leave it at that."

Anthony knew that deep down, Nahdia loved that Lily didn't want to leave. And in a way, he didn't want Lily to leave either. He was mostly in the city and he wouldn't want either of them to have to be alone. So he stopped pestering Lily about college, and instead bought her textbooks from university bookstores on many different subjects. Lily liked it better that way, not having to be around anyone but Nahdia, Anthony, and occasionally, Celeste.

In June, 2003, Nahdia started having migraines that kept her nearly bed ridden. She wasn't sure of the cause but she refused to see a doctor. After a couple weeks of persistent pain, Lily and Anthony convinced her to go to the hospital. She was admitted and given an IV. Anthony told her she was hard headed and that she should have gone when the problems first started. She tried laughing at his concern, but it only seemed to worsen the pain.

"Anthony you know I hate hospitals. Now look, you take good care of Lily, just like you promised, and Lily, you mind your Uncle Tony." She took a long, tired breath, "Oh, my babies, I want you to know that no matter what happens to me, you are both my blood, and nothing is more sacred than that." Then she closed her eyes to rest.

Anthony and Lily spent the night watching Nahdia sleep in her hospital bed. They listened to her breathing and hoped she would get well soon, as the small balloon that came with the flowers Anthony had gotten her read. The next morning they tried waking her. They immediately called for the doctor. Nahdia had slipped into a coma during the night. Anthony and Lily paced the floor of the hospital room for hours. They thought about praying, but neither knew how to. They weren't ever really the religious ones. They left that up to Mrs. Monroe, whom they wished was there to say a prayer.

Lily thought about how Mrs. Monroe would sit in the living room of her house and read her Bible. She remembered the painting that Mrs. Monroe told Lily was God's hand reaching down to Adam's, the first man. Lily would stare at the hands and wonder why someone would only want to have pictures of hands, hands that aren't even touching.

                    Ashley Lauren Mitchell

"Aww, sweetie," Mrs. Monroe began to explain, "This is only a small portion of a much larger, much more extravagant painting. This is from a painting called, the Creation of Adam. It is painted on the ceiling of the Sistine Chapel in Italy. The whole ceiling is covered with beautiful artwork like this. One day we just might have to go," she told Lily. They started planning the trip not long before Mrs. Monroe began getting ill.

And now it seemed to be happening to Lily's own mother. Lily started wishing she'd taken Mrs. Monroe's admonishments of God more seriously, and learned to pray every time Mrs. Monroe said she'd teach her; the many times she had offered. She knew that right now she needed it.

When the doctors told them that there was no telling how long Nahdia would be in the coma, Anthony took Lily home to grab some clothes and books, so that she could stay at the hospital with her mother. While packing, Lily looked at the painting on her wall that Mrs. Monroe had given her; the picture of the hands. She touched the one that Mrs. Monroe told her belonged to God, the one on the right, and said, "Please God, if you hear me, please let my mother get better." She bowed her head and fought the tears that were forming in her eyes. Then the phone rang. She answered it. She and Anthony stared at each other for what felt like an eternity. Lily dropped the phone, ran into her bedroom, took the framed painting off the wall and threw it to the ground. The glass flew all over the floor. Anthony ran into the room and grabbed Lily in his arms, holding her, trying to restrain her. "God doesn't exist!" she screamed. They both cried.

Nahdia Leduff passed away at the age of fifty-three. The doctors told Lily and Anthony it was a brain aneurism. It happened so fast that the two of them were left startled and grief stricken.

Celeste went to Donaldsonville to be with them, as they were there for her when her mother died. Lily was only twenty-three years old. She thought she would have many more years with her mother, her best friend. But now she was gone. Although Lily still had Anthony, she knew he would be returning to New Orleans. She wasn't ready to be alone. She wasn't ready to say goodbye to her mother, or how her life had been for nearly twenty years.

Anthony stayed in Donaldsonville with Lily for the rest of the summer. Celeste visited on the weekends, every weekend. Lily and Anthony were coping with their bereavement as best they could, but there was hardly a day that passed that they didn't weep for the loss of Nahdia. Anthony was angrier than he'd ever been. His sister was the only mother he'd ever really known. He and Lily were more like brother and sister than uncle and niece. He too

                          Ashley Lauren Mitchell

thought he would have more time with Nahdia, his only sister, and only sibling he'd ever known. Nahdia had told him about Jean, their older brother that had died, but Anthony had never known his mother, father, or brother. All he had was Nahdia. And now she too was gone.

Lily eventually cleaned the broken pieces of the glass from her bedroom floor. She took the picture from the frame and threw it outside, letting the wind take it where ever it pleased. She had given up on the idea of a god when her prayer hadn't been answered.

At the end of August, Anthony went back to work at the police department in New Orleans. He and Celeste wanted Lily to go back to the city with them, but she wouldn't. She said she still felt her mother's presence at the house and wasn't ready to leave. They understood and let her stay in Donaldsonville.

"She hasn't left that house since she was six years old, you know?" Said Anthony.

"Why not?" Asked Celeste.

"I don't know. That's just how she is. Nahdia told me we had an aunt that was the same way. She didn't leave her house."

"That is so strange, Tony. And she's so beautiful.

I can't believe she just locks all that beauty away from the world."

"I don't bother her about it. If Lily wants to be there, then she wants to be there."

"That can't be healthy, Tony."

"She's fine. But maybe for her birthday we can convince her to come out here and have some fun with us. What do you say?"

"Hey, I'm all for the New Orleans party scene. You know that," chuckled Celeste. "Drop me off at the club please."

"Girl, you should own that place by now."

"I know, right. Don't worry. I'm waiting to finish saving up and I'll open my own club one day. I'll call it...Désirs Cachés. That's French Tony."

"I know that girl. But your dad was French, not you."

"Hey, I'm a little French. And I know how to speak it a little too."

"Greetings don't count," he joked, and they laughed. When he pulled up to the club to drop her off he said, "Bye Celeste. I'll see you later."

"Tony, what did I tell you? Diamond. Call me

Diamond around here. I don't want people knowing my name."

"Whatever...Diamond. Now close my door. Bye."

"Bye," she laughed.

Celeste made herself busy behind the bar of the club. As the manager, she was responsible for making sure the girls and the bouncers were doing their duties. She'd just finished wiping the bar countertop when she heard a voice she'd not heard in years. Her mother's. It was in the back of her mind, "Beware of the devils". She shook her head in disbelief. 'Where did that come from?' she thought. Then she heard another voice she hadn't heard in years.

"Well, well, well. I never thought I'd see you again."

Celeste looked up. It took her a while to speak, "K...Kevin?" She stuttered in amazement.

"In the flesh baby. You sure do look good. So this is where you been hiding, huh?"

"I...I..."

"It's okay, baby. Catch your breath. So they're calling you Diamond now, huh? So, Diamond? What do you say we get outta here for a while and catch up? I haven't seen you since, well, you know?"

"Yeah, no, I know. Um, let me just make sure everything's straight and, yeah, we can go catch up."

"Good. I've missed you, you know?"

Celeste hadn't seen those green eyes in ten years. They reminded her of Anthony's, but there was something terribly different about them. She was surprised they still had the same effect on her as they did when she first saw them. She thought about calling Anthony before going with Kevin, but she knew he'd advise her against it. He was the one that pressed charges against Kevin. But now she saw something else in Kevin's green eyes and convinced herself that she had nothing to worry about, so it was no use worrying Anthony. She grabbed her jacket and met Kevin at a restaurant up Bourbon Street. They talked for hours and Celeste found herself falling for Kevin again. They exchanged telephone numbers and Celeste told him that she'd call him when she got off work that night. When she locked the club, she called Kevin and invited him to her apartment, to finish catching up.

Two days later Celeste opened her eyes. Her vision was blurry. It was hard for her to move. She saw someone walking toward her but couldn't make out

Ashley Lauren Mitchell

who it was.

"Celeste, can you hear me? It's Tony, Celeste. Can you hear me? I'll call for the nurse."

"Nurse? What Nurse?" She mumbled.

"Celeste what happened to you? Do you remember how you got here?" Anthony's voice was trembling.

"Where is here? Where am I?"

"Celeste, you've been in the hospital for two days."

"What? How in the world?" She exclaimed trying to sit up, then grabbing her aching head.

"No, don't move. The nurse will be in here soon. They wouldn't tell me much. They don't know much. You were found on your living room floor by one of your neighbors. They said they'd heard a lot of noise. Your apartment is a mess and some things are missing. Do you remember anything that happened that night?"

Before Celeste could answer the nurse had come in the room and was pushing Anthony out. Celeste watched in fear and confusion as he left. She felt the nurse's touch and then watched as the nurse used a syringe to inject a fluid into her arm. Celeste felt the serum entering her veins and she relaxed. She knew this feeling of relaxation and euphoria. She'd felt it many years ago. It was...morphine. Then she remembered.

"Kevin. Kevin did this to me."

***

Lily was all alone. She walked around the house aimlessly. She tried reading, but her books brought her no comfort. Lily crawled in her bed and cried. For three days, she cried, then slept, then slept, then cried. When she found the courage to leave her bed she was so weak. She hadn't eaten. She felt inert and impotent. She missed her mother. She wanted her Uncle Tony to be there with her again. She poured a glass of water. As soon as she put the glass to her lips she began crying. She didn't want to drink. She didn't want to eat. In a way she wanted her body to simply evaporate from existence. She'd never felt this kind of depressed feeling before.

There was a bang at the front door that startled her so much she dropped the glass of water on her foot.

"Dang it!" She screamed and grabbed her

                    Ashley Lauren Mitchell

toe. The pain that shot through her made her laugh. She was not going to just evaporate from existence or from any sort of pain, physical or emotional. "Who the heck could it be at this hour?" She said limping to the door. When she opened it she didn't see anyone. A cold breeze blew through the screen door and caressed her face. It was familiar, comforting. She opened the door to step outside but something was blocking her exit. She looked down and saw a basket. "Hmm?" She hummed and picked it up.

She sat the basket on the dining room table. It had a bouquet of roses and Zephyr lilies in it. She smelled them and put them on the table. Underneath a silk cover, with a fleur-de-lis motif, was a loaf of bread, a block of cheese, and a bottle of wine. 'I don't even drink,' she thought. She had drinks with her family on special occasions, including her twenty-first birthday, but she claimed she didn't understand what made her mother and Mrs. Monroe so giddy. 'Maybe if I drink the whole bottle,' she thought, and sat it to the side as well.

At the very bottom of the basket was a book. Lily's eyes grew wide. She had a new book. She'd not had a new book since her mother died months ago. The others, she'd read already, and some of them twice. She marveled at the book and ran her hands over the cover. She put the book to her nose and smelled it. 'I think I like this smell better than the

                    Ashley Lauren Mitchell

flowers,' she thought. She flipped through the pages. Mid-way through the book, she saw a bookmark. It was an envelope. She opened the envelope and pulled out a piece of folded paper. Before turning it over, she read the back. For Lamia was all it read. "Who is Lamia?" She asked herself aloud. When she turned the paper over, she gasped. It was the picture that she had thrown out. The picture of the hands.

She ran out the door and looked around. She ran around the house but there was no one there. The wind began to blow. The chilly breeze blew through her long, curly black hair. She closed her eyes and inhaled the cool air into her lungs. A peaceful feeling came over her as she exhaled. She opened her eyes. She went back inside. She took the basket, all its contents, and a glass for the wine, into her room and closed the door.

***

"I'm so sorry, Tony. I know I should have called you first." Celeste cried.

"It's okay now Celeste. We're gonna find that son of a bitch, I promise. He's as good as dead."

"I'd kill him myself if I get my hands on him. I

                    Ashley Lauren Mitchell

can't believe I was so stupid. I thought I saw something different about him. His eyes, something seemed so different in his eyes."

"You can tell a lot by looking into someone's eyes. He was locked up for a long time. That difference could have been any number of things. And I'm sure they're not good things."

"How could I be so blind, Tony? I could have died." She put her head in her hands and continued crying. Anthony sat on the hospital bed next to her and put his arms around her fragile body. She grasped his bicep and instantly felt safer. She laid her head on his chest and allowed his breathing to allay her fears. She knew his embrace so many times. He had saved her more times than she could remember. He was there for her years ago when her father and mother died, and he was there with her then. She wanted so badly to tell him that she was in love with him. But Anthony seemed so pure. She was ashamed of her life choices, which stood in a dark contrast to his. He was a saint compared to her. She knew, for that reason, she'd never tell him.

"Hey look," Anthony said, reaching into his jacket pocket. "He didn't take this."

"Oh my God!" Her eyes were as bright as the sun as he clasped the diamond bracelet around her wrist. Tears rolled down her face again. She kissed

                    Ashley Lauren Mitchell

Anthony on the cheek and he winked at her.

"So," he began again, "Lily's birthday is gonna be here before we know it. I need to find a way to get her out here."

"No Tony," said Celeste. "If she wants to be in Donaldsonville then we should go to Donaldsonville."

"You know, that's a good idea." He smiled. "You can stay at my apartment until you get straight. I probably won't be there much because I'll be helping the boys look for Mr. Wake, and trust me, when we find him..."

"You'll find him Tony. You always find 'em."

"Unfortunately, that's not true. But I wish somebody would get these fuckers. They roam the streets of this city, terrorizing people. There's a guy out there that kills mothers and children for fun. Can you believe that? Charles. That's his name. Charles. Elusive fuck. Somehow the bad guy always gets away." Tony sounded defeated. He was a good guy, a good cop. He hated that innocent people were hurt for others' pleasure.

"Don't worry Tony. One day they'll all get what they deserve."

"Yeah, one day."

Anthony hadn't taken Celeste to see Lily for the whole month of September. He told Lily that Celeste was sick, but the truth was they didn't want Lily to see what Kevin had done to Celeste's face. The two ladies had become close friends since Nahdia's passing. The night of Lily's birthday, Celeste and Anthony prepared to ride to Donaldsonville. He took her by the club so that she could finish some last minute business. Half -way to Lily's, Anthony had the eerie feeling they were being followed. He'd remembered seeing the green Dodge Stratus parked behind him when he took Celeste to the club. He didn't see a driver so he thought nothing of it. But now, there was definitely a driver. Anthony couldn't make out the face. It was too dark outside and the headlights were blinding him.

The devil's always watching.

"Celeste, I think we've got company."

"What?" Celeste asked as she turned to look out the rear window. "Who do you think it is?"

"I don't know but I'm gonna try to lose 'em. Hold on." He said as he pressed the gas pedal to the car floor.

***

                           Ashley Lauren Mitchell

Lily was so happy that she was going to spend time with her Uncle Tony and Celeste for her birthday. She'd not seen Celeste in over a month. She was looking forward to their time together. Lily decorated the house for her own party. It seemed more of a party for Anthony and Celeste than for herself. She placed the food dishes around the strawberry cake she baked.

"Now it's time to take a shower and get dressed."

She took a quick shower and washed her hair. Before she got dressed she looked at her reflection in the mirror. Even though she was turning twenty-four years old, her figure looked like that of a teenager. But she was now more feminine and shapely than ever. She was pleased with the way she'd grown. For the longest time, she assumed she would look like a child forever. She turned around, watching herself in the mirror. She lifted her long, wet hair into a bun at the top of her head, released it, and let the luscious black tendrils fall back to her waist. When she was alive, Nahdia kept Lily's long hair in a single braid platted down her back. With no one to braid her hair now, Lily let the locks flow loosely. She gave herself a huge, gratified smile in the mirror.

                    Ashley Lauren Mitchell

She put on the dress that Celeste had bought for her a year ago. Celeste has great taste in clothes, she thought, holding the dress up and looking at it. The dress, from what Celeste had told her, was red. For all she knew if could have been purple or blue, but Celeste had no reason to lie to her. The dress was a bit too sexy and revealing but she was a woman now and she should start dressing like it. She laughed, who do I have to flatter? She put the nearly sheer dress on her body. The inner layer of the dress was satin and it connected to the sheer, open front, outer layer by a ribbon under the bust. After she put the dress on she looked at herself in the mirror again. She couldn't remember ever being this happy with the way she looked.

She heard a knock at the door. They're early, she thought, as she quickly brushed her hair. When she answered the door, expecting to see her Uncle Tony and Celeste with gifts in their hands, no one was there. Bewildered, she stuck her head out the door and looked around. "Hmm. I could have sworn...oh, well." She shrugged, closed the door and went back to her room to finish getting ready.

The book that was left on the doorstep in the basket was on her dressing table. She picked it up and read the poem that the envelope and picture had marked. It was titled, Lamia and was written by a poet named John Keats. When she finished reading

                    Ashley Lauren Mitchell

the poem she opened the envelope and pulled out the picture. For Lamia. Who is Lamia? And why did someone send this painting back to me? She asked herself.

She heard the knock on the door again. This time it was louder and more ominous. Lily slowly walked to the door and opened it. Again, she didn't see anyone. She pushed open the screen door and stepped outside. With each step she took the wind grew stronger. She couldn't understand why the wind was always so cold, even when it was hot outside. When she turned to go back inside she heard a voice. The words were incoherent so she closed her eyes, taking away one of her senses to strengthen the others.

"Lamia," the voice called. It was resonating through the sugarcane fields. Lily turned in the direction the voice was coming from. Far in the midst of the field she saw a dimly glowing light. She squinted her eyes in order to make out what she was seeing. She started walking into the field. She thought for a moment that the voice was calling her name. Then she heard it clearly, "Lamia," the voice called again. Lily continued walking to the light. "Lamia."

The further she walked into the sugarcane field, the more the light backed away from her. In the distance, she heard a car coming up the road. And it was coming fast. The driver had to have been going

   Ashley Lauren Mitchell

over ninety miles per hour, at least. "Uncle Tony," she said merrily and started running to the house. Before she'd made it to the front of the sugarcane field she saw another car speeding behind her Uncle Tony's. The car was green and long. She thought that it might be Celeste's, but she remembered, Celeste didn't drive a car like that. Then she thought, maybe they had gotten her a car for her birthday, and maybe she would ruin the surprise by being outside when they pulled up. It was too late to try to run to the door, so she hid between the sugarcane stalks and waited.

Anthony's car peeled in the front yard of the house. He tried to run inside where he could grab the gun he had hidden underneath Nahdia's bed. Before he and Celeste could make it to the door, the other car had stopped in front of them, hindering their entrance.

"You fucking bitch!" Screamed the man scrambling to get out of the car.

Lily watched from the stalks as the strange, irate man moved toward her Uncle Tony and Celeste. She didn't know who he was but he obviously knew who he was yelling at. She thought it best to stay hidden.

"You're with this asshole? The asshole, that put me behind bars?" He reached for the gun at the small of his back.

                    Ashley Lauren Mitchell

"Kevin wait!" screamed Celeste. She was shaking and crying. Anthony had stepped in front of her protecting her from Kevin's aim.

"Kevin, put the gun down!" Anthony shouted. He wanted to sound calm but his adrenaline was racing and he couldn't control the pitch of his voice.

"Fuck you! You put me away for almost ten years! I'm going to kill you motherfucker! Then I'm going to have fun with that bitch!"

"Uncle Tony!" Lily shouted as she ran frantically from her hiding spot.

"Lily!" screamed Celeste.

"Lily, No! Stay back!" Screamed Anthony.

"What in the...?" Kevin's eyes were fixed on Lily. He had never seen anyone so beautiful in his life. He loved destroying beautiful things and he wanted badly to destroy her. He started walking toward her. "Lily, eh?" He chuckled.

"You stay away from her!" Anthony yelled a warning.

"Or what?" Kevin taunted as he kept walking forward. Anthony tried running toward Lily and Kevin fired a warning shot by his foot. Lily jumped and turned to run back into the field. "Uh, uh, uh. Don't

                    Ashley Lauren Mitchell

you move!" He commanded her. She knew the gun was pointed at her back and she quickly turned back around to face it. She took a deep breath and braced herself for the man's rough touch. "Oh yes," he laughed twirling Lily's hair on his index finger. "Tell you what officer," he began, "you keep that old bitch, and I'll take this one." He used the barrel of the gun to push Lily's hair from her shoulder.

Through her tears, Lily noticed Kevin's eyes were the same color as her Uncle Tony's. She wished at that moment that they weren't. She hated the green eyes that were staring at her, fiendishly. She hated this man, whoever he was. She had no idea what this was all about but she knew that now she was part of it.

"Don't you touch her mother fucker!" Anthony was livid. His face was red and he started sweating.

"Please, Kevin. Stop!" Begged Celeste.

"Oh I haven't even gotten started. Girl, look at you. I'm going to have the time of my life tonight." Kevin spun Lily around. He wrapped his arm around her neck and pointed the gun at Anthony. "Don't you fuckin move," he said as he started walking backwards into the sugarcane field, dragging Lily with him.

"Lily," Anthony said. His eyes were wet with

tears that had yet to fall. Celeste was holding his arm staring in disbelief as Lily disappeared from their view. "Lily!" He screamed, "Lily!"

Lily heard her Uncle Tony's screams. She knew she was just as strong as Kevin but because of the Rossi .357 pointed at her head, she decided against trying to fight him. Tepid tears streamed down her face. She was more frightened than she'd ever been her entire life. Kevin was dragging her deep into the sugarcane field. He warned Anthony and Celeste not to follow him or he'd kill Lily.

Once they were out of view, Anthony ran in the house to get his pistol. Celeste was pacing, crying, and cursing herself; blaming herself for what was happening. When Anthony ran out of the house he called for Lily, but she gave no answer. He wanted to run into the sugarcane field but he couldn't see where the crazed maniac had taken his niece. He knew Kevin had taken her deep into the field, but he didn't want to think about why. He fired a round into the air and screamed for Lily again. Celeste jumped in surprise. She had never seen Anthony this upset and terrified. Listening, he still heard no reply. He pulled out his cellular phone to call for backup. Before he could press a button, he heard motion in the field. He pointed with the gun and began running immediately in the direction he heard the movement coming from. Minutes passed by before he heard a man's

     Ashley Lauren Mitchell

scream followed only seconds later by three gun shots.

He paused. "Lily?" he whispered to himself, and then he screamed, "LILY!" He ran as fast as he could through the field. When he found Lily, she was lying face down in the dirt. Blood was spilling from her mouth and she had three gunshot wounds in her back, in close proximity to each other. "Oh, my God! Lily! Oh, God, my Baby Girl!" He whimpered. Tears were pouring from his eyes. He knelt down to touch her and saw a finger on the ground by her face. He heard rustling in the field next to him. In a fit of rage he got up to give chase.

***

Lily could feel the perspiration from Kevin's arm on her neck. She wanted to get away from him but didn't know how without being shot. Once he'd gotten far enough into the field, Kevin pushed Lily to the ground. "Take off your clothes, bitch," he demanded, pointing the gun at her face. She lay there covering herself with her arms, staring fearfully down the barrel of the gun. She closed her eyes hoping that he and the gun would disappear.

When she didn't obey him, Kevin pulled her off the ground and started ripping at her dress. She tried

                                  Ashley Lauren Mitchell

fighting him off and he hit her across the face with the pistol. She stumbled backwards bracing herself against the stalks. He came at her again. She felt a stream of blood gliding down the side of her face. He grabbed her by the throat with one hand and forced her back to the ground. He knelt down on top of her and placed the gun to the side. He ripped at the dress again.

Suddenly, they heard a rustling in the field only feet away. Kevin covered Lily's mouth with his hand and listened for the sound. Lily looked at the gun that was on the ground next to them. She knew it was out of her reach, but she had to take advantage of the opportunity while he was distracted. It was too late. When Kevin didn't hear the sound again he resumed trying to desecrate her. Then they heard the sound again. This time it came from behind them. It started moving in a circle around them. Lily listened for the sound, which she hoped was her Uncle Tony. Kevin's head was following the sound as it moved around them. When he'd turned to look back again, Lily made her move.

She grabbed his hand that was covering her mouth. She pushed one of his fingers between her teeth and bit it, hard. He screamed in pain. She spit the bloody finger out of her mouth. She turned on her stomach and struggled to push herself up and run away. She heard the blasts before she felt them. One,

Ashley Lauren Mitchell

two, three shots fired in tandem into her back. The bullets ripped through her flesh. She wanted to scream but her body wouldn't allow it. She hit the ground. She heard Kevin run away. Soon after she heard her Uncle Tony's voice. "Oh, my God! Lily! Oh, God, my Baby Girl!" He cried. He dropped to his knees beside her. She heard the movement in the stalks before her uncle quickly ran after it. She closed her eyes and listened for the last beat of her heart. Lily Antoinette Leduff died October 6, 2003, the night of her twenty-fourth birthday.

***

After several seconds, the blood from Kevin's finger dissolved into the corpse's tongue. It effervesced, like a carbonated beverage, before evaporating completely. It was now in the bloodstream. Although there was no pulse, though no breath escaped from the form that lie absent of life on the night's dark ground, and despite all logic and reasoning that would deem it otherwise appropriate the body began trembling.

Ashley Lauren Mitchell

<u>Chapter 7</u>

October 6, 2003

He called me Lamia.

How did I get here?

When I opened my eyes I saw that I was lying in a puddle of blood. Is this my blood? My body was cold and trembling. In moments, I felt a searing pain in my back that travelled through my body to my chest. I curled into the fetal position in agony. What the fuck? What is this pain? There is something lodged in my back. It begins vibrating. My body starts writhing, twisting on its own. It felt like I was being spun in a powerful, violent whirlpool. The pain was so great! I screamed so loudly I heard my echo. The 'something' lodged in my back was forcing its way out. My fingers grabbed the earth as I screamed again. After a few seconds I put my arms behind me, straining to reach for the source of the pain. Whatever was trying to come out, I wanted to pull it out myself and speed up this painful process. I touched something small and hard, like metal. I was able to grab it and yank it out. A bullet? I felt the prickling sensation as the aperture closed and my

                    Ashley Lauren Mitchell

tendons reticulated back together. I felt another bullet; then another, pushing through my skin. I pulled one of them. The last one pushed itself the rest of the way out. That really hurt! I continued lying on the ground as my body healed. I stared at the three bullets on the ground next to me and wondered who would have done that to me. I couldn't possibly have shot myself in the back. So who did? After a minute or so, I turned over and saw the stars. There were millions of them, shining so brightly. The moon was perfectly round and looked close enough to touch.

Moments later I was able to stand. The pain, a not so distant memory. I looked down and saw that I was wearing a red dress, covered in blood, with holes in it, and not just bullet holes. I wouldn't have put on something with holes in it, would I? I wanted to rip it off but another more pressing feeling took over me. Damn, I am hungry! I tore the top layer from the dress. Underneath was a shorter, red, formfitting dress with thin straps. Better. I felt the wind blow through my hair. It sounded almost as if it were saying something. I listened closer.

"Lamia," it whispered.

I closed my eyes and started walking, barefoot, in the direction the wind was blowing. Then I stepped on something. I looked down and saw a white, bloody finger. It looks like a man's finger. I put it to my nose and sniffed it. It smelled...incredible. The blood was fresh, not even ten minutes ago had it been severed. I heard a noise rushing toward me and a voice crying, "Lily! Lily!"

Who is Lily?

Then I smelled a match for the blood of the finger I was holding. I started running in the opposite direction of the voice calling for Lily. There was a light up ahead. The decadent smell was getting stronger. I ran faster.

By the time I reached an opening in the tall grass, I saw a man and a woman. The man had a gun pointed at the woman. I saw blood dripping from his hand. It must be his finger that I was holding. Another man, of a light brown complexion, ran out of the tall grass behind the woman. The man pointing the gun instantly ran and grabbed the woman. He started shouting,

"I didn't want to shoot her. She bit my finger off!" He yelled, holding up his bloody nub.

The other man with the brown skin said, "Where is she? Where is Lily?"

"I don't know," yelled the other.

The woman was shaking and crying. "Please, stop this," she begged.

I'm so hungry! And I'm getting tired of this scene. I step out of the tall grass and walk toward the three humans. The man with the brown skin notices me first. His eyes grow wide, astonished. "Lily?" He says. He has me confused. I don't know if I know this man. I almost feel a strange connection to him, but I ignore it because I feel hunger more.

The other man, the one with the gun, spins around holding the woman tightly to his body. He has the gun pointed at her temple. Both of their eyes grow just as wide as the other's. The man holding the gun becomes as stiff as a statue. He releases the woman and the weapon. She runs backwards to the darker-skinned man as they all continue staring at me.

The man with the missing finger is not moving a muscle. My eyes are locked on his. I see something in his eyes that I can't quite make out. I tell him to come to me. He obeys.

The darker-skinned man says, "No, Lily."

I don't know who Lily is.

The man continues walking slowly toward me. When he's standing directly in front of me I have a better view of his eyes. They're green, but that's not what I'm focusing on. In his eyes I see a girl lying on the ground. She has on, what appears to be, a red dress; one exactly like the one I am wearing. Then, I realize what

Ashley Lauren Mitchell

I'm seeing. The girl is dead. The girl was me. And this asshole killed me, or...her. I grab him by his scrawny neck and step backwards into the tall grass.

"Lily?" Says the brown skinned man and the woman simultaneously. It would be best for them if they stand where they are. I'm going to feed and I'd rather not be disturbed. Holding the man firmly by the throat I look deep into his eyes. The past hour replays like a rewinding film. I see him ripping at the red dress and hitting the girl in the head with the gun. The images go back further and I see the woman that was standing by the house in his grasp. She is unconscious and he is kicking her. He proceeds to destroy what appears to be a home, probably her home. In minutes I see all of the wretched things he's done throughout his life, just by looking into his eyes. Without realizing it, my grip on his neck gets tighter, and tighter, and tighter. His face turns a shade of blue. An eyeball pops from his head, dangling from its socket. I don't intend for him to die from suffocation before I get my fill.

I bring the man's neck to my mouth. I puncture his skin with my needle sharp teeth. The blood is so warm and refreshing, and delicious. I shut my eyes. Only seconds later, I hear a whisper. It is close to my ear. The breath on my ear and neck is cold but comforting. It says, "Lamia. Stop." I pull my teeth from my victim's neck. I can hear his slow heartbeat. It's a beautiful melody. I lift his body to my other ear and listen until I hear the last beat of his heart. Then I drop the body to the ground. I look around to see where the whisper had come from, but I don't see anyone.

"Lily? Are you alright?" I hear the brown-skinned man yell in the distance. He sounds like he's getting closer. I wipe the blood from my chin and walk to meet him. He halts in his tracks.

I continue walking closer to my next meal. When I'm close enough to reach out and grab him, I notice something in his eyes, something that makes him immune to my hypnotic gaze. However, I'm not certain what it is. I need a better look. I take another step toward him. I can hear his heart racing. His breathing is fast-paced. I see small drops of sweat on his forehead. His cheeks are tear-stained. To my surprise, this frail human, whom I could easily destroy with minimal effort, is in no way off-set by my entity. He looks confused, not shocked.

He reaches his hand to my face, as if he knows me. I withdrew only once. I let him touch me. His hand is soft, gentle. I look into his eyes, searching for an answer as to why I haven't already killed him. When I see it, I nearly jump backwards. This human has no mortal sins? Venial ones, yes, but otherwise this man is, is, innocent? No. No. Why? Why is he innocent? And why does that matter? Why can't I kill him anyway?

                              Ashley Lauren Mitchell

My chagrin forces me back, and I begin walking away from him, back into the depths of the tall grasses.

"L...Lily? Stop. Are you okay, Baby Girl?" He asks hesitantly. "I know I saw you lying on the ground with gunshot wounds in your back. You were...there was blood everywhere."

Lily? Who is Lily? Is that my name? It doesn't feel familiar to me. I stop moving. I don't believe I know him. I don't know where I am. I don't know how I got here. I only know a name. But that name is not Lily. "My name is not Lily" I say.

"What? What are you talking about?" His eyebrows are high above his eyes. He's shaking his head in disbelief. He looks desperate and confused.

A cold breeze blows across my face and I hear it whisper the name again. I close my eyes and listen to it. This name sounds more familiar than Lily. Even if this is not my name, this is what I will tell him to call me. Then I open my eyes and look at the man. "My name is Lamia." I say to him, "Call me Lamia."

 Ashley Lauren Mitchell

<u>Chapter 8</u>

October 6, 2003

Anthony could not believe what he was hearing. He could barely grasp what he was seeing. Somehow, Lily's skin had become darker. It looked as if she'd been playing in the sun for hours, like she does during the summer months. It usually takes a month or so for her skin to return to its pale, white color, when the fall and winter months arrive. But at this moment, it was tanned and glowing. Two of her teeth appeared different as well. They were, long and sharp. This all confused him, but he was so happy that his niece was alive that he didn't care that she looked somewhat different.

"Lamia?" He repeated in disbelief, as he smiled and shook his head.

Just then he heard Celeste calling for them. "Tony? Lily?" She screamed.

Anthony turned his head in the direction of Celeste's voice. When he turned back, his niece was gone. "What the...?" He heard the rustling through the sugarcane stalks. It was moving toward Celeste.

 Ashley Lauren Mitchell

He ran after it. "Lily?" He called out. He kept calling her until he reached the opening and saw Lily standing directly behind Celeste.

"Lily?" He said, breaking the trance. "Lily, please, stop."

She pulled her eyes from Celeste and put them on Anthony.

She stopped. Anthony watched her. With each second that passed, his fear grew. His fear was not of her; his fear was that something had happened to her. Something that could not be undone. His fear was that this creature standing before him was in fact not his Lily at all. The way she walked, talked, moved; they were the actions of someone else, not Lily's. After a moment of revelation he realized what had happened. He knew what she was. He knew how she'd become that way. And he knew he had to stop her.

"I know what you are. Please. Don't kill her."

***

Call me Lamia. I told him to call me Lamia.

"Lamia?" Asked the brown-skinned, green

                    Ashley Lauren Mitchell

eyed man. He smiled and shook his head. What could he possibly be smiling at?

Then I heard the woman's voice calling out. "Tony? Lily?"

Once the man's head was turned, I bolted towards the woman. Perhaps she would be my second meal. When I was standing in front of her, I saw that she was not nearly as innocent as the man. She will be my next victim. I walked to her and she walked to me. I can see that she has some mortal sins that land her right on my menu. I must kill this human. I tell her to turn around and I step behind her. I lean her head to the side and smell her. I open my mouth…

"Lily?" I hear the man yell.

My teeth are almost in her when he says, "Lily, please, stop!"

Stop? He wants me to stop?

"I know what you are. Please. Don't kill her."

"If you know what I am then why are you asking me to stop? Why should I spare this human?"

"Take me instead." He begs.

"Take you?" This piqued my interest so much that I turned to look at him. I gazed at him for a while. Is this man serious? How can any human be this stupid, this selfless? Would he really condemn himself to death for her? How interesting. He bravely walks up to me. In his eyes I see such goodness that it halts me. He is so pure and pristine. He is so intriguing to me. Why? "You would let me take your life to save hers?"

"Yes." He says without hesitation.

"Why?"

"She's my friend. I love her."

"Love her? You love her enough to die for her?"

"Yes."

I was taken aback by his response. No one could really give their life for someone else like that. Could they? "Fine. Then. I'll take you instead." Even as I am about to take him, he shows no sign of fear or anger. He doesn't try to resist me at all. He is not under my spell but I simply won't refuse his offer. I want to taste this unsullied mortal's blood. I want this. He wants this. I walk slowly behind him, admiring the essence of his chastity before I end his meaningless life. He's a bit taller than I am so I have to put him on his knees. I hear his heartbeat pounding in his chest, but he is so calm. I stoop down behind him and bite into his tender, warm flesh. I feel him tense and squirm from the pain; but he allows me to proceed. When his blood hits my tongue I immediately release him. His

                    Ashley Lauren Mitchell

blood! It's so strong! Almost...repellent. It couldn't be because he is innocent. No. This blood, it isn't human. It tastes like...? "Who are you?" I ask as I back away from him.

He stands and covers his neck with his hand. His motions are unsteady at first, but after only a moment of recovery he says, "It's me. Your uncle. You're Uncle Tony."

"My uncle?"

"Yes."

"But you're not..."

"I know. I know what happened to you. You tasted the blood of a human. You are different, transformed somehow."

I didn't speak. I have only flashes of memories surging through my brain. But they are not my memories. They don't feel like my memories. And they are not enough to piece together a better explanation.

"So this is what happens if we taste blood?" He says as if speaking to himself.

"We?"

"Yes. We. You and me. We're related. You won't kill me. Apparently, you can't. I'm your family.

Your blood."

I don't doubt what he's saying; even though it doesn't make sense to me. I don't want to believe him. But what if what he's saying is true? I mean, I couldn't drink his blood.

"Please don't kill her," he begs.

"Her?" I ask. "Oh, yes. Her." I say as we both turn our attention to the female human standing only feet away from us. "Why should I spare her life?"

"We made a deal. I traded my life for hers."

"And yet you live."

He huffed. "Please. She's my friend."

His eyes are gentle. Caring. He's so... fucking, I don't know the word for it. Innocent is not enough. "Fine." I say disappointedly, and then add, "Until, she sins again."

He looks at me and sighs. It could be a sigh of relief. Or, it could be a sigh of angst, for he knows like most humans, she just may sin again and land herself back onto my menu. A moment of thought goes by as he turns to look at her. I can tell he is very concerned for her. But there are only so many times you can save someone from themselves.

"Will she snap out of that trance?" He finally

                    Ashley Lauren Mitchell

asks.

This time I sigh. I walk back to the woman who is still standing motionless with her head leaning to the side. She would have made a great meal. I walk in front of her and look at her for a minute. What is so special about her? Why does she deserve his devotion? Once, I realize I won't find my answers, I look past her, to him. He is watching intensely. Dammit! I hate that I'm going to do this. This will be the only time. Next time, she will die. "What is her name?" I ask him.

"Celeste."

What a nirvana-inspiring name. Celeste. "Celeste," I call to her. Her eyes begin to show signs of life. A pity. Her pupils are growing. I can see recollection coming back to her. Memories being inserted back into her brain. I'd taken them from her. They were to be my memories. Memories of the time she was to be mine. It takes only a moment to return them, leaving any she may have of the conversation I'd had with the man. When I've completed, I call to her again. "Celeste, wake up." I push the words through my gritting teeth.

She obeys. She blinks her eyes and shakes her head rapidly. "Lily!" She exclaims and hugs me. Her sweet smell lets me know I am not related to her. I want so badly to ease my fangs into her neck, which

Ashley Lauren Mitchell

is conveniently close to my mouth.

I wriggle her off me as she continues to ramble and touch my arms, head, and face in quick, uncontrolled motions. "I'm so glad you're okay. I heard those gunshots. Oh God! I thought you were a goner Baby. That asshole was after me, and I brought this all on ya'll. Oh, I'll never forgive myself!"

"Celeste?" Says the man, attempting to gain her attention. But she continues.

"What happened? Where's Kevin? Did you get him Tony? Why are you holding your neck? Are you hurt? Did he hurt you? Oh God. We should leave. We should go back to New Orleans right now. We should take Lily with us. Lily, go get your things packed. You're coming with us."

"Celeste!" The man called again.

"What Tony?"

"I think we should all go inside."

"Go inside? With that maniac out there? I don't think so. We should..."

"Celeste!" He screamed. It startled her, and it was so forceful that I nearly jumped. "Let's just go inside, please," he said with a hand pointed at the house.

                    Ashley Lauren Mitchell

The woman scowled her face and sucked her teeth, making an annoyed, grating noise. She walks to me and placed her arm around my waste pulling me with her into the small abode. "Don't worry about your uncle, Baby. He didn't mean to yell. He's a little shaken up. I think we all are."

Shaken up? What does that even mean? She really has no idea that I'm not this Lily person. The human she is referring to. I'm not cold to the touch so she can't discern from that, but surely she must know I am...different. She doesn't seem like an evil or sinful human. Perhaps she is just a fool, like most mortals. Blind fools who blissfully, naively, fall into a life of sin; only to end up with the same fate as their evil tempters. She has no inkling of what was about to happen to her. I doubt the man wants her to know of it either. However, he had better warn her of her foolish ways, or she could end up someplace she may not deserve to be.

When I stepped through the door I saw colorful balloons, loose and bouncing along the ceiling. The dining table was covered in food platters surrounding a one layer cake with white cream icing and bright red berries on it. It had the number twenty-four sticking out the top of it. From the looks of it, someone seemed to have been celebrating something. A human ritual perhaps.

                    Ashley Lauren Mitchell

The man and woman walked in behind me. Celeste, I suppose I can refer to her by her name, sat at the table and covered her face with her hands before mumbling something through her fingers. "I'm so sorry. This is all my fault."

"It's not your fault," the man, Anthony, said walking to her and putting his hands on her shoulders. I watched, still wondering who these people were, and why I had come to be here, with them. "Lily," he began looking at me. When he saw the look on my face, he corrected himself, "Lamia," with hesitation, "I need to explain this all to her."

The woman looked back and forth at Anthony and me and began asking, "Explain what? Who is Lamia? Lily what's he talking about?"

"Celeste, this isn't Lily."

"What?"

"I mean it is Lily. It just isn't our Lily anymore."

"Ok. Yeah. That makes perfect sense Tony. That isn't confusing at all." She says in a mocking, sarcastic tone.

"Here, I have a better idea. Come with me." He said. He took the woman by her hand and with asking eyes begged me to follow them. He led us to a room with a tub and latrine. On the wall above the sink was a large mirror. He stood her in front of the

                    Ashley Lauren Mitchell

mirror, stepped back and allowed me to step beside them. I must admit, it was a rather clever way to get his point across.

"Holy shit!" She shouted, aghast. Tears began welling in her blue eyes. Half a minute passed before she spoke again, "Oh my God! Lily?" She said. "This is impossible. Where are you? I mean, in the mirror. Your reflection? Where is your reflection in the mirror?" She looked to Anthony, then to me. She examined my face, my skin, and my...teeth. "Lily, you're a...a...a vampire? You're a fucking vampire!" She slowly began stepping away from me. Her hands up in defense. Before she knew it she'd stumbled backwards into the tub, hitting her head against it. Anthony, rushed to help her. He rubbed her head as he pulled her up. She stared at me, ignoring the pain she had to have been feeling. She breathed.

"How..."How? How did this happen?"

"C'mon," said the man, "let's go to the table and talk."

"No! How did this happen? This is...it's...How did this happen to her? Tell me! She's a..."

"I know. Please Celeste? Can we just go back to the table?"

Her stunned look amused me. I gave her a devilish smile before backing out of the lavatory and walking into the dining room.

                              Ashley Lauren Mitchell

She eyed me curiously and cautiously as they walked in after me. She couldn't take her eyes off me. When we were all seated, Anthony started telling a story about when he was a young boy. He mentioned something about him falling ill and a strange man helping him, as well as his aunt, who'd had the same condition. Then he tells us that when the girl, Lily, was born, something was wrong with her and that she'd had a blood transfusion using his blood. He kept on with the story up until he got to the part when Lily...

"So what are you saying?" asked Celeste, with the most perplexed look on her face.

"I'm saying that Lily tasted a human's blood. Now she's...this."

I watched Celeste's facial expressions change multiple times; from confusion, to fear, to disbelief. Then she asked, "So where is Kevin?"

It was not at all the question I was expecting her to ask. And who is Kevin? Anthony gave her a look I didn't quite understand. He said, "Where do you think he is?" Then he glanced at me before looking back to her. She also looked at me before looking back at him. I felt some sort of unspoken message passing between them. Then she asked,

"So, he's dead?"

Anthony smirked and shrugged his shoulders.

                                    Ashley Lauren Mitchell

"I, I believe so."

They both looked at me, then back to each other. Celeste's facial expression changed again. And again, it wasn't what I was expecting. She...smiled. She looked...relieved. "Are you sure?" She asked, hesitantly. They both looked at me, cautiously, I suppose waiting for a definitive answer.

When I finally gave them an answer, I said it slowly, with great care. "If Kevin was the man, out there. The other human I encountered tonight. Then, yes, he is dead."

After a quiet moment I heard a sigh. Then,

"Thank God." Whispered Celeste.

"I know," added Anthony.

Now, I am the one with the confused look on my face. How are these humans not disturbed by this? "And this doesn't bother either of you?" I had to ask.

"First of all Baby girl, that son of a bitch had it coming. If you wouldn't have finished him off, trust me my .40 would have," he said making the shape of an upside down gun with his index finger and thumb. He reared back on the hind legs of the chair he was sitting in.

                    Ashley Lauren Mitchell

Celeste chuckled as he continued, "You kind of took that opportunity away from me. But either way, he was destined to die tonight."

"Yeah," said Celeste, "he basically asked for it. We both wanted to kill him, sweetheart. You just, got to him first. I think you made your Uncle Tony here proud."

Proud? How could any human be proud that I'd taken the life of another human? Why don't they fear me? Why aren't they trying to get away from me? This is all so unusual.

"Well, if it would've been me that tasted Kevin's blood, I would be the one that's a...," he hesitated, "You know what? I am proud, Celeste. But also a little jealous," he said looking back at me. "I should've gotten that bastard first. And I should've gotten him years ago. Instead, my niece got him. My niece. Oh, and I bet that felt good too. Didn't it?" He gazed at me waiting for a reply.

But what does he want me to say? The man was my food. Of course it felt good; and tasted even better. "Yes," I reluctantly answered. But how could he have any idea how good it really felt? He nodded his head as if he understood.

"So why haven't you killed us?" Celeste had the gall to ask.

"Celeste?" Anthony said, reprehensively.

                                    Ashley Lauren Mitchell

"I will, if that's what you'd like," I replied smiling at her.

"She is not going to kill us. Right?" He said to me, with authority.

Who does he think he is? Just because he claims to be related to me in some way, does not mean he can order me around. And just because I cannot kill him does not mean I can't just leave. This pesky human. I don't even want to respond to such a query. I look at him with a devious smile so slight, and slowly shake my head left to right, left to right. That is the only answer he will get to that question. I looked at Celeste with more than a hint of disappointment. She was supposed to be my meal earlier. I turn back to Anthony, the only reason she lives, and I realize he really is not afraid of me. He is not intimidated by me. He wasn't even angry with me. He leans closer to me and says, "And we'll find a way to keep you safe."

"Keep me safe?" I sneer, "Really? Don't you think you humans should worry about keeping yourselves and everyone else safe from me?"

"Look," He started, "You may be different, but I still consider myself your uncle. We share the same blood. Maybe it's just instinct for me to want to help you and protect you. And, maybe, you can protect yourself from a few humans at a time. But, the world is not ready to accept something like...you. Humans fear what they don't understand. And that fear can turn to panic.

                    Ashley Lauren Mitchell

There's no telling what could happen if enough of them panic and come after you."

"I do not need to be accepted by humans. I do not need to be protected by a human from other humans. I do not fear you or them."

"But you don't need to have a shit load of humans after you either." He says with so much care in his expression that it disarms me and I downcast my eyes.

"So what do you suggest?" I calmly ask, avoiding his gaze. But at that moment, I felt my body slump. I became virtually weak and disoriented.

"What's wrong? What is it?" Asked Anthony.

"What time is it? I'm, I need..."

"You need rest. The sun will be rising soon." He said cutting me off. His knowledge impressed me.

"Yes," I replied.

He rose from the chair and said, "Follow me." He led me to one of the two bedrooms. "This was Lily's room. You can rest in here."

In a most peculiar way I felt grateful to him. I nodded and went into the room. One of the walls, the entire wall, was covered with a giant bookshelf with possibly thousands of books. Curiously, I was drawn to it. "These books?"

"They were Lily's. I bought most of these for her.

 Ashley Lauren Mitchell

It's all she ever really asked for. Do you like books?"

I didn't answer him, but apparently, yes, I must have a strange affinity for them.

"Well there's plenty here for you." He says.

As my eyes wandered over the bookshelf with silent delight, I felt him watching me. It was an eerie feeling. I could hear his steady heartbeat. He inhaled a breath as though he wanted to say something, and then retreated. For a second I thought he would leave, but his heartbeat quickened, and he took another breath. He parted his lips, but before he could speak I turned to him and said, "I would like to be alone now."

He smiled attempting to hide his sadness, "Yes. Yes, of course." He turned and began walking out, then stopped to say, "I gotta leave the house, but I'll only be gone for a little while. There's a few things I need to take care of; Kevin's body being one of them." He smiled. "But I'll be here when you wake up. I promise. And Celeste will be here. So we'll watch out for you while you sleep. So don't worry about a thing. Okay, well I'll leave you to it." He paused, "Goodnight."

"Yes." I respond. We stood there looking at one another for a brief time. Perhaps he wanted me to say something else. Or do something else. What do humans do in this type of situation? He was offering

                    Ashley Lauren Mitchell

me a place to slumber. And I suppose it is reassuring to know that I'll have sentries guarding me in this new environment while I do. These humans may come in handy after all. Before he closed the door I swiftly said, "Thank you."

He rushed to me and hugged me softly. He said, "No. Thank you, Baby Girl." Then he snickered. "That man that you...Kevin, he was trying to kill us. Going to kill us. And you saved us."

Saved them? Yes. Perhaps. Unintentionally. He must know that. And definitely not the woman. As a matter of fact, she wasn't saved by me; she was saved by him, from me. He should thank me for not killing her. I'm too tired to contest. He gives another apprehensive smile before finally closing the door behind him. I intend to figure him out. This man. Anthony. My uncle?

Once I was alone, I walked up to the enormous bookshelf and ran my hand along the spines of the books. All of these books. Something about it delighted me. I turned to the night stand. On it sat a lonely book. This must be the book the girl Lily was reading before she...

I picked it up and read the cover, The Complete Poetry of John Keats. John Keats? Hmm. Almost sounds familiar. I flipped through the pages. An envelope was used to mark a page. I pulled it out

                                    Ashley Lauren Mitchell

and opened it. Inside was a folded piece of paper. On the outside, was written, For Lamia. What the hell? I opened it, turned it over and saw two hands reaching for each other, but not quite touching. It feels like I've seen this before. Somewhere. It caused a semblance of a memory to form in the depths of my mind. Red eyes. Red hair. Black smoke. Then, as quickly as it had come, the vision faded away.

I dropped the paper on the bed and looked at the book-marked page. It read, Lamia by John Keats. This is so odd. It is a long poem I realized, as I slowly turned the pages. I wanted to read it right then, but I doubted my exhaustion would allow it. I started reading the first line, UPON a time, before the faery broods... To my surprise I kept reading. I was reading so unnaturally fast that it felt like my eyes had been possessed. The words were the lyrics of a beautiful melody being sung to me. My eyes deftly scanned line after line of the enchanting composition. When I finished, it felt as if I were floating. My defunct heart raced. I felt so light, and peaceful, drifting along in a sea of words; of rhythm and rhyme. I looked at the front cover, at a picture of the poet. He. Looks. So. Familiar.

I soon become aware that I was draining the last of my energy thinking about this poet and his work, when I needed to hurry and get to sleep. I closed the curtains. I took off the red, ripped dress.

                    Ashley Lauren Mitchell

There was a large shirt, with a huge insect on the front of it strewn at the foot of Lily's bed. I put it on. I looked in the mirror of her dressing table, but of course I saw no reflection. There was a picture. I moved closer for a better look. There were three people in the picture. There was a woman with short black hair; the man, Anthony; and in the middle of them was, Lily...me. I took the photograph from the mirror and brought it closer to my face. So, this is what I look like?

Her skin is a pale complexion. But she is beautiful. She was beautiful. The other woman in the picture had skin that was a shade darker than Anthony's, but not by much. Both of them were darker than Lily. All three of them have shiny black hair, so black, that the light made it appear almost blue. In the picture Lily's hair was braided in a long, single braid. The end of it draped over her shoulder and reached down to her waist. It looks like it's never been cut. Then something else in the picture catches my attention. Her eyes! They are so...colorful! The other's eyes don't look like that. I wondered if those eyes were still that way. I glanced at the mirror, forgetting for the moment that I don't have a reflection. I put the picture down.

I crawled on top of the bed and situated myself in the middle of it. Within seconds I felt the bed began to sink, sucking me deep down with it. I pulled myself up and jumped out of the bed. An indentation

Ashley Lauren Mitchell

was left where I'd been lying. I took the covers from the bed, got on my knees and crawled underneath. Lying on the covers, underneath the bed. Yes, this felt better. I wrapped the extra covers over my head and body, turned on my side and closed my eyes. Everything went black. But just before I drifted to sleep, I heard it. I heard it call that name. My name. It's calling me.

"Lamia..."

It calls me Lamia.

Ashley Lauren Mitchell

<u>Chapter 9</u>

The next morning, Anthony and Celeste were at the dining table eating breakfast.

"So, she's under the bed?" Asked Celeste, taking a sip of her coffee.

"Yeah. There was an outline of her body in the middle of the bed. Maybe it's just too soft for her."

"Oh, poor Lily. If all of this is confusing to us, imagine what it must be like for her."

"Yeah, I know."

"How long you think she's gonna sleep for?"

"I'm not sure. Probably until tonight sometime. You know, like in the movies? Oh, I don't know. All of this is so new and alien to me."

"Not alien, Tony. Vampire." Celeste said attempting to liven the mood.

"Wow! You're so cheesy," he laughed.

"I mean, that's what she is though. I think it's so cool."

                    Ashley Lauren Mitchell

"Oh, really?"

"Yeah." Celeste began, "Just imagine, if vampires are real, maybe aliens are real. Maybe God is real. Maybe the devil is real."

"Whoa, whoa. Okay now. We won't go into all that. Besides, there's a difference. We can see her. We can see the sharp teeth. We can see the, we can't see the reflection in the mirror. These are things we can see. Empirical evidence. Those are the only things I believe in, so we won't go into the religious stuff. Okay?" He said. After a moment he realized he was probably a bit brusque with her. Maybe even offensive. He watched her push her eggs around on her plate. "I'm sorry Celeste. I didn't mean to snap at you like that." She looked at him as he continued, "But I think if God were real, he wouldn't have let any of this happen in the first place."

Celeste knew her relationship with any god had been severed when her father died. She would not be the one to judge Anthony for his feelings when she, deep down, thought the same way. "But we still have our Lily. In one way, shape, or form." She said fighting tears.

Anthony reared back on the legs of the chair. He leaned his head back, closed his eyes, and took a deep breath. As he exhaled, he opened his eyes and scanned the ceiling, as if searching for some calming

                    Ashley Lauren Mitchell

thought or answer.

Celeste knew this had to be killing Anthony inside. His niece, whom he loved more than anything, was now something neither he nor Celeste could hardly fathom. She pulled him back, "Tony?" He lifted his head from the back of the chair and looked at her. "It's going to be okay." She said sincerely, hoping it would give him a semblance of hope.

He gave her a forced, half-smile. But as he continued looking at her optimistic expression, his smile began stretching across his face. He realized being disheartened wouldn't solve anything. He also, realized he was glad he had Celeste to go through this with him. He took a sip of his coffee.

"So you think it's cool, huh?" He asked her, still smiling. "So, you're saying you're not afraid of her?" He asked, sounding much more cheerful.

"What, me? No way, Tony. Okay, I do admit, last night I was. It's more than a little weird, but, it isn't like she chose to be that way. To me she's the same little girl she was when I met her ten years ago. It's just, now she has those teeth." She paused to think about those sharp teeth and shuddered. "But, it's not like she'd hurt us or anything. Right?"

Anthony remembered what their, 'Lily,' had told him about Celeste last night. He believed her

                                        Ashley Lauren Mitchell

when she'd said she would kill Celeste if she sinned again. There was no way he could sacrifice himself a second time to save her...from herself. "But she could if she wanted to." He said. "We need to be cautious of her power and abilities and not take them for granted. We also need to make sure we don't do anything stupid that would make her want to hurt us."

"Make her want to hurt us? Like what?" Celeste asked.

"I don't know. But let's not find out." They both took a deep breath. They couldn't believe they were having such a conversation. Anthony was the first to break the uncomfortable silence. "So what do you think? We have to come up with a way to keep her protected and definitely, hidden. We have to watch out for her. We can't leave her out here all alone. But we can't have her around a whole bunch of people either."

"I understand all that Tony, but we both live in the city. Are you willing to move to Donaldsonville and give up your life in New Orleans? I mean, I love New Orleans. It's my home. And I still have my work at the club. And you? You're a New Orleans police officer. Hello? We're not exactly in positions where we can just get up and leave."

"I know that stuff already Celeste." Anthony let out a deep breath and rubbed his hands over his

                    Ashley Lauren Mitchell

head.

Celeste could tell how frustrated he was. She wished she had the answer to this very unusual dilemma they were in. Before she realized it she began voicing her thoughts. "This is crazy. If only I could take off from the club and stay out here with her for a while. But my boss would throw a hissy fit. He hates that. Hell, I'm the one that practically runs the joint. I should be the boss. Man, if I had my own club. I'd show him. And maybe if I owned my own club by now I would..."

"Celeste! That's it!" Anthony exclaimed, breaking her thought process.

"What? What's it?" Celeste asked, surprised. She hadn't realized he'd been listening to her rambling.

"Your own club!"

"Yeah that would be great. Then I'd be my own boss. But Tony, My own club is still a dream in progress."

"But what if you opened it sooner?"

"And how would I do that?"

"Well, what if I helped you get it started?"

"And why would you do that?

                    Ashley Lauren Mitchell

"Think about it." Anthony looked at her for what seemed like an eternity making eye movements, hand movements, and neck movements; using his silent gesticulations to somehow telepathically convey his message to Celeste. She watched him and tried to follow, as he willed her to guess his meaning. Her eyebrows were dancing above her eyes as she watched. The two of them were not speaking but using their facial expressions to do the communicating. After minutes of their silent game of charades, Celeste solved his riddle.

"Oh my god! I get it! Tony, that's a brilliant idea!" Celeste yelled.

"Shhh." He laughed, remembering their sleeping guest. "Those are the only kinds I have." He excitedly, but softly, clapped his hands together and rubbed them in proud delight.

"Hardy har har. Don't flatter yourself. The club is my idea." Celeste said.

"Yeah, yeah, yeah. But housing her there. That's mine."

"Whatever. I'm still so excited! I finally get to have my own club. You know you'll have to be there every night, right?"

"Of course. I can't trust you with something like this."

"Boy, shut up."

The two of them spent the day planning the enterprise. At nine o'clock, that evening, the sun had just gone down when the aberration woke. She stepped into the hall and headed toward the dining room, where she heard the beating hearts of the two humans. Before Anthony and Celeste saw her, they felt the room get colder and looked at each other.

"Did it just get cold in here?" Celeste asked Anthony.

"It sure does feel like it. Hmm, I'll go check it out." When he stood to leave the room he saw the creature standing at the doorway. He saw that she had lost all of the color in her skin and it appeared white as snow. He was standing close enough to her to know that it was her that had made the temperature in the room drop. Chills traveled up his spine. "Oh, hey you." He said, trying to hide his startled reaction. "Didn't hear you coming. How'd you sleep?" He said, giving her a pitiful smile.

"I'm hungry."

Anthony and Celeste looked at each other nervously. They were both surprised by what they were seeing and hearing, but they tried to remain calm. "Yes. Well, I um, figured you would be. I'm sorry Baby Girl, I'm all out of fresh blood right now, but, I went to a blood donation clinic and picked these up for you." Anthony handed her one of the bags of blood. She turned it around in her hands, observing it. She looked at him, chuckled, and tossed the bag on the table. She began heading to the front door when Anthony jumped in front of her.

"Wait. I can warm it up for you." She kept walking. "Wait. Please," he begged, jumping in front of her again.

She gently and easily moved him from her path with one arm. He felt her strength for the first time. He hadn't been handled like that since he, well, ever. Anthony was always the strongest compared to anyone he met. He knew he couldn't physically stop her. "Lamia. Please. Stop." She stopped and turned to face him, but didn't speak. Anthony looked at her, wishing he could undo everything and make her his Lily again. 'Feeding Lily was a lot easier,' he thought. He walked up to the being that once was his Lily and said, "I know you want to go out there and find your own food, but I just can't have you doing that. I don't want anyone to see you. I don't want anyone else besides us," he said pointing to himself and Celeste, "to know about you at all. You may think you can take care of yourself, and you probably can. But there's a whole world of humans, and from what I know, from what probably anyone knows, there's only one of you."

Lamia snorted and said, "I'll take my chances." Again she turned to leave.

"But you're still my niece. No matter what you think or feel. I don't care if you're a vampire. But the world will care. Please just stay with me, with us, for a little while. The world isn't ready for you. Please." She opened the front door. "Lamia?" She took a step outside. "Lamia? Lamia. I can't just let you walk out of here. Please Baby Girl don't go? Lamia? I love you. Please. Don't go!"

***

Call me Lamia.

Love? Me? How can he even say that? Doesn't he realize what I am? He must know it's impossible for something like me to ever love a human? This man is pushing his luck with me. I have one foot outside the door but when he says that, I bring it back in. I turn to face him. Look at him. Look at those begging eyes. Look at that fragile human telling me he loves me. As if that's supposed to change anything. I'm sick of this game with him. It's time I show him who's boss.

As I make my way toward him, I know he can see the fury in my eyes. Celeste stands up from the

Ashley Lauren Mitchell

table with alarm painted on her face. However, she's wise enough not to make another move. This is between him and me. Once I'm close to him I reach for his neck. I grab it and lift him off the ground. Celeste screams, "Stop it! Stop it!" I toss him on the floor near a wall, knocking down a picture frame which falls and lands on him. As I go to reach for him again I catch a glimpse of the photo. It is of him and the girl whose body I now possess. He has his arm around her shoulder and his lips on her forehead. She has her eyes closed and has a smile so wide, all of her teeth seem to be showing.

In that moment I realize that this man will always see me as the girl in the picture. The love he has for her didn't just go away when I took over her body. And I'm hurting him for expressing his human emotions? I am a monster. I shouldn't be here with him. This is some kind of joke from the devil himself. Putting me here with a human I cannot destroy. A man as innocent as a child. It is in me to kill and cause fear and pain. I feel it. Like anger and rage bottled in a small glass waiting to escape. But this human is trying to make it hard for me. I can't be here. I have to go. I look at both of them. They're shocked expressions were enough to let me know I'd done enough damage. "Don't you see human? I cannot be here. I am not this girl you love. I am not your Lily. I...I must go."

                    Ashley Lauren Mitchell

Once again I turn to leave, and the stubborn human grabs my legs. He trips me and I fall to the floor. I make a loud thud and even leave a few cracks in the wooden panels of the floorboards. The nerve of this man! As I scramble to get up he crawls up my legs and tries to wrestle me to stay on the floor. I stifle a laugh. He's light, not as light as the other human, but I could still toss him and send him flying across the room. But I'm so amused and impressed by the fight in him, I allow him to believe he's even close to a match for me. Then I push him away, sending him sliding back to the wall.

He starts speaking, "If you would just listen to me! I've got a plan to keep you safe. We want to help you. We want to take care of you. It'll take cooperation and patience from all of us, but...we need you. The world needs you. I need you. And you may discover that you need us just as much. You have no clue how many mother fuckers there are in this world that I wish you would just go kill. But if you just give me a little time and a little trust, I promise you I can make it so that the world won't fear you, but welcome you."

"Welcome me?" I ask through my amusement. For some reason what this man was saying actually sent a warmth over my cold skin. I looked at him staring up at me from the floor and said, "I'm not some animal you found, and must now take care of.

                    Ashley Lauren Mitchell

I'm not your responsibility."

"No. Not at all. I don't think that. We don't think that."

"And I can leave whenever I want to."

"Yes. We're well aware of that too."

"And I am not Lily."

"Yes," he said, lowering his head, "I know."

"I want to drink from human bodies. Not those bags."

"It won't be for long. I promise. And besides, since you're a vampire, you'll live forever. So what's some years with us? Letting us work with you. For you." He said getting to his feet and brushing himself off.

I was slightly appalled by his frankness. "So just what would you two be getting out of all this?" I asked curiously. There's no way they could be doing this just for me and not getting anything in return. That would be foolish. They looked at each other. Then to me. Anthony spoke.

"We would get, justice and peace of mind, just like you gave us last night, when you killed Kevin." He walked to me. "You see, I'm a cop. I have to follow the law. But some people are just out of the laws reach. These people, I'll bring to you, will be nothing

                              Ashley Lauren Mitchell

short of deserving of whatever you're gonna do to 'em. Don't you see? I feel like you were supposed to be here. You're supposed to be right here with us. And if you are going to make people disappear, I want to make sure it's the right people. I want to protect you. That is what I want."

I'll admit, he intrigued me. And he's right, I had nothing but time. An infinite amount of time. "Fine," I acquiesced, "I'm listening."

"Alright...Lamia," he began, controlling his excitement. "So, our idea is..."

***

On the night of Friday, October 10th, 2003, Anthony, Celeste, and Lamia finished packing and headed to New Orleans. When they entered the city, Lamia found herself looking out the window apprehensively. She watched the people walking along the streets and resisted the urge to jump out of the car and snatch one.

As Anthony drove, he had a thought to himself and smiled. He hadn't had his niece in a car with him this long in nearly twenty years. Her opal eyes sparkled in the city lights. She looked this way and that. He wondered what she could be thinking. He was glad that she agreed to stay with them for a while. He wasn't ready to lose her. It also took some time and persuasion, but she eventually drank the blood from the bags. He had warmed them on the stove in a pot of water. He did it with such care that it felt to him like warming a baby's bottle. Only, that bottle is full of human blood, and that baby is a vampire, that does not want to drink that blood. Still, he loved being able to do for her. "So this is New Orleans, Baby girl," he said.

"And you're sure this is a good idea?" Lamia asked.

Celeste turned around in the passenger seat, "Why wouldn't it be? Can't you feel the energy in this city?"

Lamia could definitely feel the energy pulsating throughout the city. There were so many heartbeats. They'd already passed about twenty people she could tell needed her judgment. She remembered watching the man in the red 1990 Toyota Corolla while they were on the Bonnet Carre Spillway. His balding head. His thick glasses. His splotched skin. She felt the evil in him. He looked over suspiciously at Anthony's police car just long enough to catch her eye. She saw that he had killed a young woman not even an hour ago and was on his way to New Orleans to get lost amongst the crowds. But his

Ashley Lauren Mitchell

night was over when he locked eyes with Lamia. He froze. Fortunately for him, his car eased itself over to the emergency lane. He won't come out of that trance unless by fate Lamia finds him again, destroys him, or reverses the trance. But she will not. And he will spend the rest of his life with a stunned expression on his mute face. That will have to be his punishment.

"As long as we all stick to the plan, everything's gonna be fine." Anthony said reassuringly. "How you doin' back there?" he asked, searching for Lamia in the rear view mirror. It took him a moment to remember why he didn't see her reflection.

Lamia leaned her head against the window. When she breathed her cold breath on it, it left a chilly frost. The bags of blood just didn't warm her the way fresh human blood could. Looking out the window, she no longer saw the bright moon. She remembered looking at it before getting in the car. In Donaldsonville the sky was clear and beautiful. All the stars were visible and the moon was nearly the only source of light needed. Here the sky was veiled by street lights, cars, and buildings. Smoke and miasma clouded the atmosphere. "This place feels very different than where we came from."

Anthony chuckled. "Sounds like something Lily would say. She was only six years old when she left this city? She didn't like all the hustle and bustle out here. But she loved the country. Maybe you two are alike in that way," he said, trying not to think about the fact that the girl sitting behind him wasn't his Lily.

Lamia ignored his statement. "Why are there colorful beads on everything? Is that another human ritual?"

"Colorful?" Asked Celeste. "What do you mean colorful?"

"What do you mean, what do I mean?" Lamia asked, puzzled. "Look. There are blue, purple, green, gold, silver, all different colors of beads on almost everything."

Anthony and Celeste looked at each other, "Lamia, you can see colors?" He asked.

"Yes. Am I not supposed to see colors? Can you see color?"

Anthony felt he'd offended her and quickly explained his meaning. "What I meant is that Lily was colorblind. She'd never been able to see colors."

"Oh." Lamia thought about the picture on Lily's dressing table. Lily's eyes were full of multifarious colors. "So, she'd never seen what her eyes look like?"

"No. She had," Celeste corrected herself, "You have, the most colorful and beautiful eyes on earth. They look like rainbows. And Lily was never able to see that."

And neither will I, Lamia thought. She had seen a picture of a rainbow in one of the magazines on Lily's bookshelf. It's one of those daytime phenomena, like the sun, that she can never see with the magnificent eyes she had. All three of them were silent for the next few minutes. Lamia thought about the girl Lily. The colorblind introvert who liked to read and play in the sugarcane fields. She didn't seem all that spectacular. Why was she chosen to be my host? Or was it all by chance? Lamia thought.

"You're gonna stay at my apartment until we get the club set up. But," Anthony said hesitantly, "it may take a few days."

A few days turned into a few weeks. Fortunately, Anthony had moved into a condominium. The complex wasn't as congested as most living areas in New Orleans. He had few neighbors and fewer, if any, disturbances. There were mysterious vanishings of his neighbors' pets during Lamia's sojourn. He knew it was her, and although he was disappointed in her a little, he was relieved it wasn't any of his neighbors that she'd taken; or any human, for that matter. He was upset it was taking so long to get things set up with the club, so he could only imagine what she was going through. He was surprised and impressed by her patience. He believed she was as well.

                    Ashley Lauren Mitchell

There were some nights when it would be just the two of them. When she wasn't reading, they would talk. Sometimes it would be for hours. Lamia liked when he told her stories about the bad guys he'd caught, and especially about those he didn't. She knew those would be the ones that would be for her. He had a collection of manila folders, his own rogues' gallery; he'd accumulated throughout his twenty-year career. The ones that got away, he called them. But now he would make sure they wouldn't get away with anything, ever again. Lamia watched him when he talked. She saw the passion and desire for the destruction of these villains in his eyes. She gained a deeper understanding and respect for this human and started believing his and Celeste's plan would work. She would help make sure of it. They also decided, in order to keep up with appearances, Lamia was to call him, Uncle Tony. Celeste would be called Diamond, the name she'd always used at the club. And the girl that was once Lily would be called, Lamia. They would all call her Lamia.

It wasn't until October 31st, that the doors to Désirs Cachés were opened, right up the street and around the corner from the club Celeste had worked at for roughly ten years. She wanted to have a huge party. She wanted to be competition for the other clubs. She wanted money and recognition. But Anthony warned her about being too flashy. They didn't need too much attention drawn to the club. It

                    Ashley Lauren Mitchell

was supposed to be more of a covert operation, as opposed to being a pretentious business. They had a grand opening party, which was not grand at all. Customers were not impressed, so the next night brought fewer patrons than the last. Which in their case, was a good thing.

Celeste was able to convince some of the girls from the other club she'd been managing to work at Désirs Cachés. The girls didn't need much convincing. They'd always liked the way Celeste treated them, with respect and kindness; something unusual in the business they were in. In a way, Celeste felt she was just an older version of most of them. She saw herself in their eyes. The girl she was years ago.

The girls also liked that Anthony promised to be there every night. They trusted him, felt secure with him, and knew they'd be safe under his protection.

They were told about his niece, the one that would be upstairs, but was not to be disturbed. "It's for security purposes. She handles the money and the top dollar clients." Diamond told them.

Lamia was allowed to step to the railing of the stairs so that the girls could see her. Proof that she actually existed. She heard the whispers from the girls saying things like, "She's pretty," or "Yeah, yeah, she cute." And, "Lamia? I like that name. It's pretty. Kinda exotic." They didn't ask questions. Like Celeste, they

   Ashley Lauren Mitchell

really only cared for one thing, and one thing only. The money. And as long as they had that, they didn't want to know about Tony's niece that lived upstairs. Except for one. There was one girl in particular that caught Lamia's...attention. Lamia wasn't quite sure why.

Anthony and Celeste decided it would be best not to bring anyone to her the first night. Lamia abhorred the taste of the pouched blood and was anxious for a kill. She'd been patient long enough and was finally going to get her reward. Anthony lured the game to the club using the girls. Each perpetrator had a type, especially when it came to their victims. Each was attracted to something different, but each had the same motive. Murder. Of the fifteen girls that worked at the club, at least one of them was bound to be what each man was hunting for. Anthony could have just as easily had the men arrested when he found them, but after all the years he'd spent as a police officer, he knew they would be out of jail in days, maybe even hours. He wanted justice and now he had Lamia to help serve it.

Lamia's first kill at Désirs Cachés was a man named Milton Cook. Anthony had been wanting to get this bastard for years. When the time finally came, he, Celeste, and Lamia were all eager. They'd planned and prepared as much as they thought possible. Now, it was time to put their preparation to the test. They set up Lamia's room. Celeste had found a beautiful dark red velvet curtain to hang from the ceiling. It spanned the room, wall to wall, and was a perfect addition to the area. They made sure everything was ready. It was time.

***

Call me Lamia.

It's been weeks since I've tasted fresh human blood. I'm in dire need of a kill. Those detestable bags, it seems, no matter how fast Uncle Tony gets them to me, they never taste as delicious as Kevin's blood did that first night. And those pesky animals running around Uncle Tony's neighborhood? It would take too many of them to fill me.

Oh, so I call him 'Uncle' Tony now. It was his idea. 'To keep up with appearances,' he said. I just think of it as a part of his name, even if he is related to me.

While I was living at his home, I learned a great deal about him. He is a pleasant and virtuous human. I found the stories of his police adventures riveting. He showed me how to work a gun, and even showed me the wound he got from being shot before. I, of

Ashley Lauren Mitchell

course, didn't keep my gunshot wounds which healed within minutes of occurring. I'm learning from him, although I am not able to teach him much in return. I feel as if I'd be lost without this human. Where would I have slept? Who would have made sure my slumber wasn't disturbed at the wrong hour? I am surprised by my reverence, and I'm starting to feel it necessary to repay this human for his kindness and hospitality.

Désirs Cachés was Diamond's idea. Celeste told me to call her Diamond now. The club is finally open and I must confess, they did one hell of a job on the place. I was able to view it before they let any humans come in; especially since it will be one of the only times I get to see it like this. Empty.

The girls that will be working here are never allowed to come up to my living quarters. Mostly for their safety. I overheard Diamond and Uncle Tony talking to them the night they told them about me. I had on a mask, to cover my eyes. But they saw enough of me apparently. I heard their whispers, praising my beauty, and admiring my name. If that was praise and admiration. One of them called my name, 'pretty.' And then there was this one girl that stood out from the rest. I wasn't sure why, and I knew Diamond and Uncle Tony wouldn't let me find out. I was forced to ignore the queer feeling and return to my room, where I must remain.

                          Ashley Lauren Mitchell

Diamond has an office across from my room, with a balcony facing Bourbon Street. They wouldn't let me have it because they think I will be tempted to step out on the balcony and get myself noticed. And they're absolutely right.

My room is spacious enough, however. It's divided into two halves by a large, long, dark red, velvet curtain. One part of the room is for when I am to entertain my guests. The other is my private bed chamber with a small shower and sink. I have no need for a latrine, but it sits idly there.

My room has a back door that leads to St. Ana Street, which I plan on using for disposal purposes. In my opinion, the most important area of my room, is my bookshelf, equipped with a copious amount of books from the house in Donaldsonville. On nights that I don't have a guest, I can read until my dark heart is content.

Uncle Tony was able to procure a shiny mahogany casket for me. The inside of it has plush, satin lining. It locks from the inside. It was very considerate of him to have gotten this for me. He also brought the rug that had been in his sister, Nahdia's room. It's unique. He said it was a gift to her from someone. I like that it cushions the hard, wooden floors in my room.

The club has been open for three nights now.

          Ashley Lauren Mitchell

Tonight, the man that I'll be ridding the earth of is called Milton Cook. Uncle Tony told me that he's been one of the most sinister serial killers he's ever searched for. He gave me a folder that had a picture of the brute. Inside was a stack of papers with information on all the crimes he's committed. I listlessly browsed through the folder. I doubt it matters if I peruse his infractions on these mere sheets of paper. I'll see all his foibles, every single one of them throughout his whole life, in his eyes. When I see him myself tonight, he will show me everything I need to know.

I let Diamond adorn me. It pleases her dressing me, like a doll, or a child. One thing I've learned about this woman Celeste, or Diamond, after spending so much time with her, is that she isn't an evil or threatening human; she is simply naive, vulnerable, and because of it she's lived an unwholesome life. She shared with me the devastation she felt when her father died, and even more when her mother died. She told me the complete story of her first encounter with Kevin Wake, my first meal, and all the demoralizing things she'd done with him. She confided that she'd felt, and still sometimes feels, like the most foolish and selfish person on earth. I listen to her. I hear her talking. But, if she continues making the same mistakes because of her weakness, whatever it may be, she will be responsible for her own demise. Not me.

                                    Ashley Lauren Mitchell

The dress she's chosen for my meet and eat tonight with Milton, is made of white lace. It could be one of those bridal gowns, but it isn't quite as elaborate. It's held on my body by lace straps over my shoulders. It's rather form fitting, and a bit too long, falling nearly to the floor. The shoes that she's picked out for me are open toe high heels with clasps around the ankle. I didn't like them and told her I wasn't going to wear them. I'd much rather go without shoes. I'm already tall enough, standing five foot eight; at least two inches, to one foot, taller than all the girls including Diamond. Uncle Tony is taller than me by about four or five inches. But I'm much stronger than he is.

Diamond is styling my hair. I feel it lift from my shoulders. She cut my hair one night by accident. It wasn't much, just a few strands, but she kept going on and on about how sorry she was. I didn't care. It's just hair. Humans must care about superficial things like that. Anyway, when I woke the next night, the cut strands had returned to the length they were before. Now she styles my hair as she pleases. She cuts it as short as she likes. Sometimes she even straightens it. It always returns to a long, black, curly mess when I rise at night. Sometimes she forgets and hands me a mirror to see what she's done. I wait a moment before she remembers why I refuse to accept it.

                                    Ashley Lauren Mitchell

To finish the ensemble, she situates a mask over my eyes. Tonight the mask is white to match the dress. It has crystal and pearl embellishments, with large white feathers on the top. It is covered on the inside by a strip of soft black tulle. It was sheer enough to see through but dark enough to hide my colorful eyes. Diamond takes a step back to appreciate her work. When she's satisfied, she opens the door for Uncle Tony. He looks at me like a doting father would his beloved daughter.

"You look so beautiful, Baby Girl," he says as if he were fighting back tears. "I almost don't want you to do this tonight."

"Oh no," I say, "I'm going to do this tonight."

"I know, I know," he sighs. "Now listen, I'll be waiting out back by the car. When you're done come down and let me know. I'll come help you bring the body out."

"How many more times do we have to go over this, Uncle Tony?"

"As many times as I feel necessary. This is serious business. Nothing can go wrong. We may have gone over it a lot, but what we're doing is still dangerous. We're all at risk."

"The only one at risk here is Milton," I said facetiously.

"Your uncle is right Lamia," interjects Diamond. "We don't want you getting hurt."

I'm sure she'd agree with him if he'd said the world was ending tomorrow. I have a feeling she loves him. Her heart races when he's near her, or when she hears his name, or when she speaks of him. But she hides her feelings, assuming no one knows. But I know. I wouldn't doubt Uncle Tony knows either.

"I won't get hurt. You need to trust me on this. I'm a lot stronger than either of you want to admit," I tell them.

We all look at each other. This is the moment we've been planning for, or scheming for, rather. I can sense their nervousness. I know they have honorable intentions, but I also know that Uncle Tony is concerned about losing his job. I doubt his colleagues would overlook an avocation such as this. But he is taking a risk. And he's doing it for me. I can't let him down. I won't let him down.

"Très bien!" Says Diamond and claps her hands together. She finishes in her lazy French, "Il est temps!"

She and Uncle Tony head downstairs. I pace back and forth in my room. I'm hungry but excited. I don't like that they're worried about me. Even after what happened to Kevin. It must be a human emotion. Worry. I try to remember what it was like to

                    Ashley Lauren Mitchell

have been human. I can't. I push those thoughts from my mind. I need to remain focused on my task. I'm fidgety. I'm anxious. I need to relax.

I go to the bookshelf and find the book with the poem in it, the poem entitled, Lamia. Reading it pacifies me somehow. It's a tragic love story, but it's still very captivating. It is a tale of a serpent-woman who helps the god Hermes find love. In return he gives her a human form. She takes her new gift and finds the man she falls immediately in love with, Lycius. He falls in love with her as well, and eventually wants to marry her. She's afraid he will discover the secret of her true form and leave her, but she lets him have his ceremony anyway, to make him happy. At the wedding reception, Lycius's instructor reveals what Lamia really is and with a final scream, she vanishes. Lycius, bereaved of his Lamia, instantly dies. A love story worth dying for. I read as much of the poem as I could, before I heard the music downstairs become louder. I closed my eyes and sighed, "It's time."

I ran behind the velvet curtain and waited. I listened to the footsteps getting closer. Then I heard the door open, then close, and then, lock. I heard Milton trying to twist the handle of the door to escape. My first dinner guest has arrived. I will not disappoint.

After asking the man to sit, I pull back the curtain. "Bonjour Monsieur."

                    Ashley Lauren Mitchell

French. Diamond's father, Mr. Monroe, was from France. He came to America in the nineteen-thirties. Diamond only speaks a small amount of mostly broken French. But it's the main reason she chose Désirs Cachés as the name of the club. That, and because Louisiana is known for its strong French heritage and culture. Not only does Diamond like the girls to wear Mardi Gras masks, she also likes for them to greet patrons in French. I think it's a rather amusing concept and I don't mind playing along.

"You may call me Lamia," I tell him.

This corpulent man is at least 6' 2" and roughly 300 lbs. His hair is a tawny red, almost orange, color. He has freckles to match on his face and arms, and I can only assume everywhere else on his paunchy, sweaty physique. His body reeks of liquor. His light blue eyes look me from head to toe. He rises from his seat and walks toward me. When he's in reaching distance of me I can see that he's going to let his baser instincts take control. I'd rehearsed all that I wanted to say to him before I allowed my baser instincts to control me; but he ruined it. He wanted me and wasn't going to waste a moment attempting to conquer me.

He came at me with fierce rage in his eyes. I tried moving out his grasp but he had me. He moved surprisingly fast for a large man. His hands were trying to grab my neck, but I held his wrists, and watched

     Ashley Lauren Mitchell

him struggle. I pushed him backwards and his fingers grabbed the string of my dress on his way down. It tore, and one side of my dress fell, exposing a breast. I didn't try to cover myself. Instead, while he was still on the floor I fell on top of him and put each of his arms underneath my knees. He was staring at my visible breast and still trying to fight me as I hurriedly took off my mask. His body went limp. His eyes are now transfixed on mine.

"This didn't go the way I wanted it to Milton, you piece of shit! I had a whole scenario to play out, and you spoiled it. This is going to end a lot sooner than I'd hoped. I won't be too hard on myself. This is the first time. I'll get better at it." I know he can't answer me. I might as well be speaking to a corpse. I put my hands on the floor by his head and lean closer to his face. I inhale, smelling his skin, and exhale my cold breath in his face. "So you are the one that keeps getting away from Uncle Tony, huh? How can an evil human like you be so hard to find? Or catch? You've killed a good bit of people haven't you? I can't wait to catch up with to you. And since you'll be dying tonight, there's no rush. Your methods are interesting. The way you tie up your victims and burn them alive. You know you deserve this. And I am going to savor every moment of it. You should feel privileged to be my first. You've had your fun. Now, it's time I say, Au revoir. It's time to die!"

With great force I bury my nails in the thick skin of his chest and pull his body up by his sternum. Blood sprays all over me. I can feel his heart beating next to my fingers. Holding his chin, I tilt his head to the side and dig my teeth deep into his fleshy neck. Before I drink the last drop, I pull my teeth out and let the warm blood flow down the inside of me. I feel, incredible! I haven't had this feeling in so long.

I hear the slow final beats of his heart. I listen for the last throb and push his defunct body to the floor. I stand over his corpse and look at my stained dress. I probably could've handled that in a neater way. I break the other strap and let the dress fall on top of Milton; or what was Milton. I feel much better this way. Naked, free, uninhibited. Not to mention full, satisfied, and warm. My skin is glowing brilliantly.

I put on my robe and lift the cadaver over my shoulder. I knew I wouldn't need Uncle Tony's help. And now that the body is drained of all the blood, it is surprisingly lighter than I thought it would be. I make my way down the stairs and out the backdoor. Uncle Tony is standing by the trunk of his car. He looks around nervously; making sure no one is looking. I rush to put Milton in the trunk and Uncle Tony immediately closes it.

"All good?" He asks.

I nod. I know it didn't go the way I wanted, but

                    Ashley Lauren Mitchell

next time it will. There will be a next time, just not with Milton. "Thank you for this," I blurt out before realizing it.

"Aww, Baby Girl. I've been hoping for the death of this worthless asshole for years now. And you've just made it happen for me. So, I guess I should thank you." He walked to me and touched my cheek with his hand. "Thank you Baby Girl." He said sincerely. And then he said, "You're warm. Hmm. You haven't been this warm since that first night. Maybe that only happens after you...Ah, well. Let me move this car and I'll see you inside."

I watch him drive away. I look up at the night sky. The stars are so lucid and bright. I close my eyes. After a moment I feel a cold breeze whip across my face. I open my eyes. Nothing. I look around. Nothing. I go back to my room, clean the mess Milton and I made, and wait for Uncle Tony and Diamond to come to me. I can't wait for many more nights like this.

While I'm waiting and after I'm finished cleaning, I continue reading the poem that I'd stopped reading to have dinner. Then, I smell something. It smells like blood. But I'm sure I cleaned my room of all of Milton's blood. I've even taken a shower. I get on my knees where his body was and sniff around. It's not in my room. It has to be the room below mine. I believe Diamond said it belonged to a

                    Ashley Lauren Mitchell

girl they call, Sable. It's her dressing room and private entertainment room. The scent is so strong. I close my eyes.

When I opened them, I was miraculously in the room below mine. And there she was, Sable. She was putting on her make-up in the mirror when I appeared like a shadow behind her. She couldn't see me standing there, watching her in the mirror, wondering what it was about this girl that made me want to devour her. I bent over to smell her and I breathed on her neck. I saw the chill bumps rise on her skin and her nipples instantly became hard. I watched her eyes shift in the mirror to the vent on the ceiling, probably thinking it was the air conditioner that was making her shiver, and not knowing she was only inches away from drawing her last breath. I closed my eyes and opened my mouth.

"Lamia?" Diamond shrieked as she burst through the door. "What are you doing in here?"

Sable immediately turned around in her chair. When she caught sight of me, she froze, like a statue. Her brown eyes wide and curious. I smiled at her shocked appearance.

"I smelled something in this room, and, I, wanted to see what it was." I replied trying not to sound irritated for having been interrupted.

                    Ashley Lauren Mitchell

Later that night, Diamond, Uncle Tony, and I, set a few house rules. And I set the rule that menstruating females can't be anywhere near me! Their scent is too strong. That Sable girl could've been killed tonight if Diamond wouldn't have stopped me. Lucky little minx. I was so close to her. Damn it Diamond! A fucking period? Really? I should've killed Sable just for being here while she's having a period, as a warning to the other girls who think about doing that. Sable, Sable, Sable. She could've been my dessert tonight. She has no idea how bad I wanted her. If she did, I'm sure she'd never come around here again.

Once I've calmed down I ask myself, "How did I appear behind her like that?"

<u>Chapter 10</u>

July, 2005

Call me Lamia.

I still can hardly believe what happened last night. I can't tell Diamond or Uncle Tony that Sable was able to sneak into my room and discover my secret. They may want to take the matter into their own hands. I feel I handled it well. I shouldn't have any more chance incidents with Sable.

Diamond's sitting at my dressing table talking to me, but I'm not listening. My mind is in another place. I'm thinking, maybe, I like Sable. Or, it may be quite the opposite. I more than likely hate her. I hate that she was bold enough to come into my room. I hate that she wasn't afraid of me. I hate that she...loves me. Why do these humans love me? When will they realize I'm a force to be reckoned with? "Damn it." I say aloud unwittingly.

"What's wrong?" Asks Diamond.

"Nothing. I, just, nothing."

 Ashley Lauren Mitchell

"Are you sure?"

"Yeah."

"You've been acting different lately."

"Yeah? Well, I'm starting to feel too confined here. Every night I'm in this room. I need more, space."

"Now sweetie, you know you can't just roam around the streets. It's too dangerous."

"For me or for everyone else?"

"Both." She pulls a chair across from me and sits. "What if Uncle Tony and I take you to Donaldsonville for the weekend? That way you can roam as much as you please."

"I don't want to go to Donaldsonville. I like New Orleans. I want to enjoy it like you and everyone else."

"Lamia, you're not like everyone else. You know that."

"Of course I know that. Hell, I sleep in a fuckin coffin and drink blood. You think I don't know I'm different?" I say caustically.

"I'm sorry," she says sitting back in her chair. "It has almost been two years. I guess I didn't think you would get like this. You were always so content in Donaldsonville."

                    Ashley Lauren Mitchell

"What? No. Lily was content in Donaldsonville. I'm not Lily. I'm Lamia. Remember?" She still thinks of me as Lily? I take a deep breath. "I'm not Lily. How can you not see that? Did Lily kill people?" My words seem to cut right through her. She stood and walked to the door.

"I'll be right back," she said. She looked sad but she still managed a smile.

I'm not sure what to expect when she returns. Perhaps I overstepped. It doesn't matter now. I've already said it. After a few more moments I almost regret telling her the truth.

As I wait, my curiosity overwhelms me. I arbitrarily grab a mask to cover my face. I open the door and walk out. I step to the top of the stairs. I can almost see the entire club from where I'm standing. The strobe lights emit colorful rays all over the room. The floor is covered in a haze of smoke, as if it's rising from the ground.

I see Diamond talking suspiciously to Uncle Tony by the entrance. No one notices me in my long black silk robe and mask. I see Kitty leaning coquettishly over the bar, talking to a man, who's looking at her cleavage. I see Slate at the DJ's booth scrolling through his laptop for the next musical selection. A group of men are laughing with Angel as she sits talking with them at their table. Then I see, her, as she steps on the stage, and steals the spotlight. My gamine. Sable.

She's wearing a cerulean blue fishnet tunic over her matching lacy lingerie. Her eyes are covered by an azure feathered mask and she has on matching stilettos that wrap around her ankles and up her calves. Slate turns the music up. He's chosen Digital Bath by the Deftones. He plays songs like these often. He must enjoy this genre. Either way, it is the perfect song. Sable's hands caress her sinuous body as the first verse begins. Then she grabs the pole, spinning round and round. I watch her slender, flexible body climb and perform lewd acrobatic stunts, and then slide back down. She doffs the tunic and is now in just her bra and lace bottoms. She moves closer to one of the drooling men. I step to the edge of the staircase. She sees me. She smiles and her dance becomes more intemperate with every word of the song, as if she's only dancing for me. I smile back. Tonight, I...feel...like, I feel like more... She begins groping her body and I can tell she wishes it were my hands fondling her. She puts her arms behind her back and pulls the string, loosening her brassiere. Her round, full breasts bounce loosely. She pulls the piece of cloth over her head, revealing two erect nipples. She squeezes her breasts together and jiggles them in her cupped hands. She slowly turns around, bends over and slides the lacy underwear from her buttocks down her shiny, toned legs. She

                          Ashley Lauren Mitchell

steps out of it with one foot and kicks it to that annoying, drooling man sitting in the front, nearly on the stage, staring as attentively as I am. She continues dancing and then puts her finger into her mouth and sucks it. When she removes the moistened finger she slowly puts it to her vagina and moves it in a circular motion. She moans.

Everyone in the club is watching her, entranced by her obscene performance of self-gratification. Everyone, but Diamond and Uncle Tony. They turn to look at the crowd gathering around the stage. Both of their eyes dart to Sable, whose eyes are fixed on me. They look up and see me moving in the direction my eyes are staring. I can feel the humans' body heat rising. I can feel her body heat rising. As I take the third step down the stairs, Diamond and Uncle Tony race to meet me. They each grab an arm and pull me back to my room. Sable smiles seductively and licks her lips, as I fade from her view. I smile back.

"Have you lost your mind?" Asks Diamond shaking with anger.

"Someone coulda seen you, Girl!" Says Uncle Tony. He is just as angry as Diamond; if not, more.

"No one saw me," I say, smiling mischievously.

"Look, I don't know what's gotten into you, but

we've worked too hard for you to blow everything away now," says Diamond. I don't recall having seen her this upset before.

"Sorry," I say, indifferently.

"Lamia," begins Uncle Tony, "Diamond was telling me that you said you wanted more room."

"Oh, really? Actually, I said more space," I said looking at Diamond with a smirk. That little tattletale.

"Now look," he said, "I believe we have been more than understanding of your... situation."

"Right, especially since it was you two who got me into this situation." The words came out faster than I realized and they halted all three of us. I'm not even sure where they came from.

"What?" They asked simultaneously.

"I...I didn't mean to say that."

"Yes, you did," said Uncle Tony. He sighed and said, "And you're right. We did."

"What?" I asked, dumbfounded.

"We can't expect you to be exactly like Lily. As you've said over and over, you're not Lily. And we can't expect you to stay locked in here forever," said Uncle Tony.

I'm not sure where he's going with this, but he has my undivided attention.

"I think that we should all go out one night. Diamond and I can chaperon you to anywhere in the city you want to go. And I just know you're gonna be on your best behavior. Right?" He said staring hard at me, with probing eyes.

"Yes. Right. My best behavior." I say agreeably.

"New Orleans is one of the greatest cities in the world, and you don't even get to enjoy it. That just isn't fair to you." Added Diamond.

I couldn't believe what I was hearing, but I was hearing it. I can't see it but I know the smile on my face is ear to ear. Genuinely happy, I wanted to run to both of them and kiss them. Instead, I just said, "Wow. Thank you both. I don't know where I want to go first." They're smiles were just as big as mine.

"We'll talk about this later. Right now, I need to go downstairs and make sure the guys aren't passing out from that little show Sable's putting on."

"Yeah, I've never seen her be so...free before," said Diamond rubbing her chin, bewildered. "That didn't have anything to do with you, did it?" She inquires, looking at me with askance.

"I don't think so," I say, knowing it's probably a

                    Ashley Lauren Mitchell

lie.

Once Uncle Tony has gone back downstairs, leaving Diamond and I alone together, I thank her for talking to Uncle Tony for me.

"No problem Sugar. I can't even imagine what it's like for you. I want you to know, you aren't alone in this. And you're right, this probably never would've happened to you if it weren't for me and Kevin. I'm truly sorry for that."

"No, Diamond. I'm sorry for saying what I said. I don't even know where that came from. It just, slipped out. You and Uncle Tony have been more than understanding, and have gone out of your way to accommodate me."

She wraps her arms around my frosty body and squeezes me affectionately. "Come here, I want to show you something. But you have to promise me you won't tell your Uncle Tony. He'd have a fit."

"I promise."

She takes me by the hand and leads me to her office across the hall from my room. I hadn't been in there in some time. She had it decorated. It had black and white Marilyn Monroe photographs on the walls. She told me once that the blonde woman was an idol of hers. She saw me looking at the posters on her wall.

                                    Ashley Lauren Mitchell

"The only other Monroe that is as bodacious as I am," she jests. We both laugh. She brings me to the doors of her balcony. "You ready?" She asks. I smile at her excitement. She swings the doors open.

The humid Louisiana heat hits me like a wave. I'm so cold that steam instantly rises from my skin. I'm covered in a hazy halo of smoke, which could easily be mistaken for a smoke machine blast. Beads of sweat form on Diamond's nose. These uncontrollable bodily functions don't bother us a bit as we look below at the assembly of people. It's the fourth of July, and Bourbon Street is packed with party goers celebrating their day of national independence. Nearly all of them have a beverage in their hands, and some even have caps on their heads with straws flowing out of beer containers. Everyone is risible and carefree. Music of all genres is coming from every direction.

Some people look up at Diamond and me, and howl in their drunken stupors. Diamond is wearing a patriotic, red, white, and blue negligee. She has silver, faux star tattoos on her face and arms. She has the same evenly cut, white wig over her brunette hair as she did nights ago. Her deep blue eyes light up as she sees the revelry below her. She starts dancing to the rhythmic zydeco music. She loves this city. I love the energy. Hundreds, thousands of humans, and a few horses, all those heartbeats. It was a delightful

 Ashley Lauren Mitchell

spectacle. I've not fed yet, but I don't feel hunger pangs. I only feel, whatever is resonating from Diamond, and all these humans. Joy. Elation. Happy.

Before Diamond and I turn to go back inside, a figure catches my eye. It's the same mysterious figure I'd seen nights ago. It was glowing dimly, surrounded by a white aureole, like the one emanating from me.

"Diamond," I stopped her as she was walking in. "Do you see that?" I asked her.

"See what?"

"That. There. There's a man looking at me."

"Girl, I'm sure all the men are looking at you, and me too! Whoo-hoo!" She yells and starts dancing again.

I stop her. "No. Look. Right there." As soon as I pulled her closer to me and pointed, he disappeared.

"I don't see anything," she said looking at me. "So? What? You're seeing ghosts now?" she asked mockingly.

I think I'm rubbing off on her. "It wasn't a ghost. At least, I don't believe it was."

"Ghosts, Lamia?" she laughed. "Or maybe it was the devil. You know he's always watching," said Diamond. She shook her head, "Whoa! I sounded just like my mother right there. I think I had too much to drink tonight." She looked around at the scenery. After a moment, she looked almost sad, remorseful. She looked at me and said, "You need to eat something and go to bed. This may be too much excitement for you tonight."

I believe it was too much excitement for her. "Yeah," I huffed, "you're probably right."

We went inside.

A bag of blood was waiting for me in my room when I entered. I dreaded having to drink it, but I dreaded hunger more. I picked it up, grabbed a book from my bookshelf, and sat in a chair to relax.

There was a knock on my door. Presuming it to be Diamond or Uncle Tony, I didn't get up to answer it. They both have a key and would open the door momentarily. When they knock it's usually to let me know they're about to enter. But the knocking continued. I put the bag down and stared at the door. The knocking continued. Hesitantly, I went to open it. Perhaps they forgot their key. Although that rarely ever happens with them. Well, they are only humans. I opened the door. Standing in the doorway with wide, brown eyes was my...was Sable. She had on an opened robe, showing her nude, curvaceous body.

"Hey," she said leisurely, and leaned against the doorway.

I gazed at her skeptically. "Sable, I thought we had an agreement? You know you can't be up here."

"I know. It's just that, when I saw you tonight it made me want you that much more."

"What do you want from me Sable? You know my...condition."

"Yes, I do. And I don't care," she said.

I felt my face wince with surprise and disbelief.

"Well, aren't you going to invite me in?" She asked.

"Sable, I..." she didn't wait for a refusal. She slithered her way past me. I let her. She walked in my room shamelessly. She took her robe off and let it fall to the floor. She turned and faced me.

"I'm here now. Take me," she said.

I looked at her naked body. At that moment I understood why breasts were the first part of a woman's body to gain attention. Her pert nipples were pointed at me like two dark brown irises.

"What? Take you?" I asked.

　　　　　　　　　　　Ashley Lauren Mitchell

"Yes. Take me. I know what you want." She turned her head to the side and rubbed her fingers along her smooth, slender neck, and down the center of her naked body.

I watched, then said, "You don't know what I want."

"Oh, but I do. I'm not stupid. I know what you are. And I've thought about it. I donate blood for money, sometimes. I get like ninety bucks for doing that. This'll be just like donating blood, only now, I'm donating it to you."

I chuckled. It sounded reasonable, logical. Why did it have to sound reasonable and logical? I wanted to resist...I think. I looked at the bag of blood on the chair. I grimaced and turned back to her. "Please, don't do this," I begged. It sounded awkward coming from me.

She approached me and put her hand behind my head, forcing my face to her neck. Goosebumps rose on her skin. Her redolent fragrance filled my senses. She began placing soft kisses on my face. She was so warm against me. She blew her warm breath past my ear. I closed my eyes and kissed her neck once. Then I opened my mouth and bit into her. We both moaned in ecstasy.

It was only after a few minutes that I even

                    Ashley Lauren Mitchell

wondered what was wrong with her. Why did she want this from me? I rubbed my hands along her arms all the way down to her wrists, and I felt them; numerous peeling scars. Why didn't I see this before? She was a cutter, a glutton for pain, punishment, and self-mutilation. I'm sure she'd done this with a needle or a razor. Something as thin and sharp as my teeth. I wanted to keep my eyes closed and keep enjoying the sensations we were both experiencing, but instead I pushed her away.

"You like pain, don't you?"

"What?" She asked, gripping her neck.

"Those cuts on your wrists, they're self-inflicted."

"Yeah. So?" She said abruptly.

"So, I can't do this. I won't do this. I don't want to hurt you Sable."

"But it doesn't hurt," she contested.

"If I do it this time, you're going to want me to keep doing it. I can't. I'm...sorry."

"Oh, you will," she said authoritatively.

"Excuse me?"

She stepped closer. "I said, you will keep doing this. Or I'll tell your little secret to the world."

                    Ashley Lauren Mitchell

Is she....did she just threatened me? Is this really happening? Her foolish words were like a blow to the face. "No one will believe you," I said.

"I guess we'll have to see about that, won't we?" She said, and grabbed her robe from the ground. She started walking to the door.

I wanted to let her walk out. She wasn't a bad, or an evil person, just an incredibly stupid person. A person not deserving of death, but definitely of punishment. Fuck! I can't believe I got myself into this. And this human has no idea the trouble she's getting herself into. I blocked the door. "I need to get my Uncle Tony. He'll know what to do."

"Or," she said, leaning against the door, "you can keep drinking and we'll just keep this between us."

"Sable, if I start drinking you again, I won't stop. I'll drain you of every drop of blood until you die. Is that what you want?" I intended to scare her, but instead, she was thinking about it. What kind of person needs time to think about whether they want to live or die?

She drops the robe and leans her head to the side. The stupid bitch wants to die.

"I want you to understand that you asked for this. You do understand that?" I ask her.

                    Ashley Lauren Mitchell

She nodded her head. "Yes, I understand."

I bite into her again. I drink until I feel her body weaken and she can barely stand. I stop myself, remove my teeth, and step away from her. She tries to catch her breath. Her back was against the door. She used it to keep herself from sliding down. One of her hands was on her neck, the other on her chest. I picked up her robe and threw it to her. I opened the door and pushed her out before she put it on.

"See you tomorrow," she said, dizzily, and arrogantly.   ·

After I closed the door without responding, I sat back down in my chair. I picked up the bag of blood. At that moment I knew I was right about what I was thinking earlier. I do hate Sable.

The next night I told Diamond and Uncle Tony what happened.

"Oh, that little bitch!" Exclaimed Diamond.

"You didn't do it though, did you?" Asked Uncle Tony.

I didn't answer. He knew the answer when I bowed my head in shame. Me? Shame?

"Oh, Lamia," said Uncle Tony, chagrined.

"What was I supposed to do? It's not like this has happened before."

"You're right. You're right. But why didn't you just come to us?" He asked.

"She said she'd tell my secret."

"Oh, that little bitch!" Yelled Diamond. "She won't get away with this."

"Yeah, like she got away with murder," I said unwittingly.

"What do you mean?" Asked Uncle Tony.

"Well, she kind of, well she, killed someone," I said scratching my head. Not that it itched. I don't know what an itch feels like. But the action just seemed like something to do while saying that. An action of confusion.

"Killed someone?" He asked, aghast.

"Yeah, but she said it was in self-defense. She's innocent." I hoped this is what they wanted to hear, but I hated saying it.

"That girl is about as innocent as she is holy," said Diamond.

"Lamia, you did good Baby girl. You did the right thing by not ending her life," said Uncle Tony,

                    Ashley Lauren Mitchell

"But, she's not innocent. I'll make sure she knows that. She'll get jail time for that murder."

"But what if she tells people about me?"

"Who's gonna believe her?" he said. "Wait, I got it! We'll have her committed. She cuts herself, she's killed someone, and she talks of vampires. She'll fit right in."

"Can you do that?" I asked him.

"Oh, yeah. Your uncle can work wonders." said Diamond, heart racing.

"Good. I don't want to have to see her again." I said, positively.

"You won't. But I'm afraid until all this blows over you'll have to be content staying in your room for a while longer," said Uncle Tony.

"Understood," I replied, indifferently.

That next night, the third night, my night, Uncle Tony told me that Sable was successfully admitted to a mental institution. And although she was screaming about a vampire, no one believed her. Instead, they gave her something that would put her to sleep. They found the body of her boyfriend. She buried him in her back yard. How stupid. Uncle Tony showed the cuts on her wrists to the authorities and she made it

     Ashley Lauren Mitchell

easy to put her away. He told me there was nothing to worry about. I believe him.

Since I'd just had fresh Sable blood the night before, I thought Uncle Tony would cancel our arrangement for tonight's guest, Phan Wu, the Chinese acupuncturist, who likes to go a little crazy with his needles. But thankfully, Uncle Tony told me we wouldn't deviate from the plan. This pleased me. I still get to have fresh Asian blood tonight.

When I'd finished, I tossed Mr. Wu's dead body in the trunk of Uncle Tony's car. I watched Uncle Tony drive away. I looked up at the stars illuminating the night sky. I looked across Bourbon Street.

And there he was, glowing luminously and gazing at me.

Maybe it was all the human blood that was making me act so spontaneously. Or maybe it was because I was tired of not knowing who he was. Either way, I wanted to know. I found a path through the crowd and made a run for it. He started backing away but I was able to catch him.

My skin was warm from Mr. Wu's blood, so when this mysterious being touched me, I felt the chills all over my body. He gently rubbed his freezing hand on my cheek.

"Lamia," he whispered.

I closed my eyes for mere seconds to savor the feeling he was giving my skin. The cool, tingling sensation Diamond must feel when she touches me. When I opened my eyes, he was gone, vanished into thin air. I looked around, but I knew I wouldn't see him. I put my hand to my cheek and felt the icy area he'd touched. I went to my room and locked the doors. The poetry book was sitting on the dressing table. I grabbed it and settled into my coffin for the night. I'm not oneiric. What would the dead dream of anyway? But tonight, while I slept, I dreamt.

He was there with me in my dream. We were naked in a lush, green garden. The sun was shining on our skin. I could feel its warmth. I was no longer cold, but my blood pulsated through my body warm and red, like a human's, and the heat of the morning star was delightful. We were surrounded by animals of all kinds. I remember seeing these same creatures in the National Geographic's magazines from the bookshelf in Lily's room. We roamed the land with the animals at our heels. The mystery being and I talked for hours in the arboreal garden. When we laid down to rest, I couldn't fall asleep. I looked at my mystery being, kissed him, and watched him as he slept. All of the animals had fallen asleep as well. I was the only one awake. It was as if my mystery being had some type of connection with the animals. They walked with him. They listened to him. He had even told me he named them, all of them. As I watched him sleep, I admired his perfect figure. He was beautiful. The whole dream was simple and beautiful.

When I woke the next night, I hadn't the slightest clue what the dream meant. I never remember having a dream before. How was I to interpret it? It made no sense at all. Who was he? Why couldn't I sleep when he and all the other creatures could? I can't talk about this to Diamond or Uncle Tony. How could they decipher a dream like this? A dream of mine? A dream of a non-human, who dreams of other non-humans? And what would they say if I told them I'd let another person see me, touch me? They'd really hate that. But this time, I know it's different. He knew me. He was like me. He spoke to me. "Lamia," he said. Lamia.

He called me Lamia.

<u>Chapter 11</u>

August, 2005

After the incident with Sable, the monotonous routine had returned to Désirs Cachés. Again, every third night I killed a killer. I did miss the excitement of the past month, but I like it much better when things aren't so dramatic. I sometimes wonder how Sable is doing at the mental institution, but I won't ask Uncle Tony to check on her. I also thought of how easy it was for him and Diamond to get rid of Sable because she posed a threat to me. I guess I sometimes underestimate how much they want to protect me. The lengths they'd go to please me. Who would become easily expendable? I also sometimes wonder, do they still think of me as Lily?

But I'm not Lily. I am Lamia. That's what he called me. The man from my dream. The mystery being from across Bourbon Street. For the briefest moment I was near him. He touched me and spoke my name. How did he know my name? Better yet, who was he? The mystery being? Would I ever see him again? Where did he go? His hand was so cold when he'd touched me. Then, I had a revelation. It hit me suddenly, like a rush of...wind. He must be the one

          Ashley Lauren Mitchell

that blows past me, creating the cold breeze I feel so often. And his fingers were icy. The way mine are now, before I feed. Could he be a...a...vampire, like me? Why should I assume I'm the only one? In my dream we were both humans, but it was only a dream. Is he really a vampire? Of course he's a vampire. He has to be. What human could be that cold? Or have eyes so dark and large? For a second I felt I wasn't really alone. Although I had Diamond and Uncle Tony, they can't fully comprehend all that I feel; all that I thirst for, being as I am. But he might. My mystery being.

It's mid-August. The year is 2005. Désirs Cachés has been operational for twenty-one months. I've been what I am for nearly two years. I still don't remember anything from before the night I came into existence. Nothing. I don't even know if my soul was in another body before this. I don't know how I even came to be. Was I born? Was I conjured? Why did I know my name is Lamia? Is that really my name? Why am I here?

Even though Uncle Tony and Diamond gave me a recap of Lily's life a long time ago, none of the things they talked about seemed familiar. None of them felt like my memories. Not Nahdia or Mrs. Monroe. None of them. But this Lily person was well loved. I hope she knew that and appreciated it. Perhaps, I was living somewhere deep inside of her.

                    Ashley Lauren Mitchell

Somewhere dark and cryptic, no doubt. She'd just turned twenty-four. Still so young. Seeing from how my body is now, she'd never gotten any tattoos or piercings. She'd never cut her hair. She was probably some type of goody two-shoes. But I can't criticize her. She did a marvelous job of preserving her body. She was, I am, a beautiful creature. I gaze at the pictures of her sometimes, especially since I can't see that image in a mirror. Humans have no clue how fortunate they are to be able to see themselves in a mirror. Something I'm certain many of them take for granted. The only thing that seems even remotely familiar about Lily's appearance, are her, my eyes. These two colorful orbs, like I've seen them before. As if from another life.

I, at times, think about how Uncle Tony and Diamond weren't able to bury or grieve for Lily. Maybe they still do see me as her, just in a different way; a more savage variation of course. Hell, I look just like her. I am in her body. How could they not still see me as her? I wonder if our mannerisms are similar. Doubtful. I'm sure she was nothing like the coldhearted monster I am. I should be thankful to her for giving Diamond and Uncle Tony to me. I'm sure they protected and cared for her just as much, if not more, than they do for me.

The three of us are sitting in my room discussing the next one of my victims. To say I've feasted on over two hundred of these villainous miscreants, I have yet to put a dent in Uncle Tony's collection of files. But, then again, Uncle Tony has been collecting those files for over twenty years. Almost as if he were waiting for something or someone, like myself, to spring to life and slay them all.

Once we've completed devising our plan for Operation Kill Samuel Hicks, Diamond tells Uncle Tony and I about what she'd heard on the news earlier that day.

"A hurricane?" I ask.

"Yeah. They say it's supposed to come right for New Orleans," said Diamond.

"I heard about that too. It's supposed to be a category three," said Uncle Tony.

"That's bad right?" I ask, confused. I remember last year they were talking about a hurricane season. I even did some reading on what a hurricane is and how much damage they could do, but nothing happened.

"Oh yeah," he said, "that's pretty bad. They're gonna evacuate the city."

"God must me angry," Diamond said with her head bowed. She slowly raised her head and looked at Uncle Tony who was looking back at her strangely

                                        Ashley Lauren Mitchell

after she'd said that. She laughed and said, "Sounds like something my mother would've said." Uncle Tony nodded his head but didn't speak. He looked surprised at her. She tried to hurriedly change the subject back to the hurricane issue. "Don't you think we should leave too?" She asked hoping to take the attention away from what she'd blurted out.

"Probably so. I won't. I'm gonna stay and help. I'm sure there's gonna be some hard headed people that won't leave. And a good bit of us officers have decided to stay anyways," said Uncle Tony.

Uncle Tony is so generous. He puts his life in danger everyday being a man of the law. He's brave and noble, and... wait, "So where are Diamond and I going?" I ask, only just realizing what is being discussed. Evacuation.

"To Donaldsonville. You'll be safer there until this thing blows over. Get it?" He nudges Diamond, "Blows over?" He laughs.

Diamond laughs with him. "Oh, Tony, you're so cheesy."

I think I missed the joke. "But why can't we stay here. Won't it be safer here, with you?" I ask.

"I don't think so Baby Girl. It's too risky. Besides, New Orleans is already dangerous enough. Imagine what it would be like if this hurricane is as bad as

                    Ashley Lauren Mitchell

predicted. Pure chaos," he said.

"Anarchy galore," said Diamond.

"Well then, I should definitely stay. I can help maintain order, so to speak. Don't you think?" I say, smiling devilishly.

Uncle Tony laughs. "You're probably right. But I won't be able to watch over you during the day when you're sleeping. Who's gonna make sure no one breaks in here and discovers you? I'll be working."

I looked at Diamond.

She sighed and shook her head, "He's right Lamia. I mean, I don't want to get stuck in this place. No food. No water. Impending danger and riots. We're right on Bourbon Street. I don't want to be trapped here watching your coffin until you wake up. No. No, I think we should go to Donaldsonville until Tony says it's safe to come back."

Always agreeable with Uncle Tony.

"I don't think Katrina will be playing any games," he said.

"Who's Katrina?" I ask.

"That's what they're calling the hurricane. Hurricane Katrina."

"Why do they give them names?"

"Each hurricane is different, so each one gets a different name."

"Oh, like me and Lily?" I said, unwittingly. Shit. Why did I say that? I regret having said it immediately. I notice a slight change in Uncle Tony's and Diamond's posture, but they smile at me and say, "Right."

I know how much they loved Lily. They show me every day by being to me, what they were to her. I have to remember not to mention her as if she's not here anymore. Perhaps she still is here, living inside me, somewhere dark and cryptic, as I once lived in her.

By late August, activity at the club had slowed significantly. At least half of the girls that worked here had already gone. Bourbon Street seemed quiet. But on the television, all of the people in the city seemed to be in a frenzy. I usually don't watch television. I don't have one in my room. I don't remember there being one in Lily's room in Donaldsonville either. Maybe she and I are alike in some ways. No. That can't be. I am Lamia, the Mr. Hyde to Lily's, Dr. Jekyll. Only in this rendition, Mr. Hyde will live on and Dr. Jekyll will die from three bullet wounds in the back.

Diamond has a television in her office. She and

Ashley Lauren Mitchell

Uncle Tony are watching, intently. I step from my room and they don't even notice. Before I join them, I attempt a look at the club below from where I'm standing upstairs. At first, I try stretching my neck, but when I see that Uncle Tony and Diamond aren't paying me any mind, I walk boldly to the edge of the staircase.

The music is softly playing. I hear a television downstairs as well. Kitty, Slate and Angel are still here. There are only three patrons, all sitting around Angel, who is winding around a pole listlessly. Kitty and Slate are watching the flat screen television above the bar. One of the men throws a few dollar bills at Angel's feet and gets up to leave. Now there are only five humans downstairs. I haven't seen the club this empty since it opened. Even by the time I wake in the evenings, the club is vibrating with music and numerous thumping heartbeats. The deserted look of the club bothers me in an odd way. I go to Diamond's office. She and Uncle Tony are quietly talking to each other.

"Hey Baby Girl. Come see this," Uncle Tony says, reaching for me with one hand and pointing at the television with the other.

"What's happening?" I ask. When I look at the television I see images of dozens of people at a grocery store, with carts filled with supplies. One person had a whole basket filled with only cases of

                    Ashley Lauren Mitchell

bottled water. Then the screen changed, showing hundreds of cars on the interstate.

"People are in a panic. They're leaving the city," said Diamond.

"Will they come back?" I asked.

"I'm sure they will, after this storm blows over," said Uncle Tony.

I was expecting him and Diamond to laugh at what he'd said again. I remember the last blows over, line, and they both found it amusing. But this time, they didn't laugh. They didn't so much as crack a smile. In fact, both of them looked eerily, serious and gloomy.

"I think we should go ahead and close the club and send Kitty, Slate, and Angel home. What'chu think?" Asked Diamond to Uncle Tony.

"Yeah. Might be a good idea to get you two to Donaldsonville tonight," he said.

This conversation is moving too fast. "Wait, but what about Samuel Hicks?" I asked, trying hard not to sound too anxious. "We were, I was supposed to...entertain him tonight."

"Oh right, I'm sorry Baby Girl, I forgot to tell you. I can't even find him anymore," he said, rubbing his hands down his face in aggravation. "Hell, he must have left the city too."

I can tell by the way he's speaking that he's upset at the situation. But he must know it is twice as upsetting for me. So then, attempting to sound concerned, I say, "But he'll just keep killing people everywhere he goes."

"I know Lamia, but it's not like I can track him down now. No telling where he's gone. Everything's different right now. It's survival of the fittest times. We need to make sure we survive this hurricane before we start talking about our enterprise again."

I couldn't help it. Now, I was angry. I'd been looking forward to having Sam Hicks for dinner tonight. This isn't fair. Diamond even had a sparkled, all red mask picked out for me. I wanted to put it on and wait for my meal to be brought to me, just as we'd planned, just like it is supposed to be on night three. "It's just some stupid storm! What the hell are you humans so worried about?" I said as I stomped my feet and walked away. I am behaving like a spoiled child, but I don't care. I knew that if I went to Donaldsonville tonight, my dinner would be one of those disgusting bags of blood. I hate them! I hate having to drink from them. I waited for Uncle Tony or Diamond to follow me. I thought one of them, if not, both of them would come to mollify my agitation, like they usually do. Neither did.

Our things were packed, and we were on our way to Donaldsonville. We rode in Uncle Tony's police car. He had his sirens on for most of the trip. Motorists magically cleared a path for us to drive through. Even so, a ride that takes no more than forty-five minutes, took nearly two hours. And I'm certain hours longer for the unlucky others that weren't cheating their way through the congested highways. The streets were filled with bumper to bumper traffic. All the pumps at gas stations were occupied, and they each had lines of impatiently waiting drivers.

Donaldsonville, from what I remembered, is normally a tranquil town. But now it seemed overrun with foreigners. Uncle Tony dropped Diamond off at her mother's house. She'd told me over a year ago that she decided not to sell the house after her mother died because she felt so guilty for not being there for her on her deathbed. For that same reason, she kept everything in the house the way her mother had left it.

"Are you sure you don't want to stay at the house with me?" I asked her.

"Yeah, I'm sure. Thank you sweetheart."

"Why, are you afraid I might eat you up?" I asked her smiling.

They laughed.

                    Ashley Lauren Mitchell

"Good one," she said, "But if I run out of food, I might end up eating you instead." We all shared a laugh before she kissed Uncle Tony and me on our cheeks and gave us each a hug. It still amazes me sometimes how my coldness doesn't faze her. "I'll be over tomorrow night to check on you," she said to me before turning to Uncle Tony. Her heartbeat raced as she spoke to him, "Please be careful out there Anthony." I can't recall the last time, if ever, that I heard her call him Anthony. It's usually just Tony. "I don't want to hear anything about you getting hurt, okay?" she said, looking at him with tears welling in her sad, blue eyes.

"Okay, Celeste," he said. He put his hand on her face and rubbed his thumb across her cheek, like he did to me every time I tossed a corpse into the trunk of his car.

I cannot deny that hearing them call each other by their authentic names, disturbed something inside me. I don't believe it's fear. I've never been afraid of anything or anyone. I don't know what it would have even felt like if I had been. No, this was something else that I was feeling. Perhaps I do care more for Uncle Tony and Diamond than I realized. They were there for me since the day I was, I guess, born, into this world. And from what I was told, Uncle Tony was there since the day Lily was born. He even gave her some of his blood so that she could live. I

Ashley Lauren Mitchell

suppose he gave me blood to live as well, even though I may have just been an invisible parasite living inside of his niece. Even if he doesn't love me as much as he did Lily, he loves me. I know it. Maybe there is still a little of his blood that flows through my veins.

The house that belonged to Lily and her mother, Nahdia, was roughly eight minutes from Celeste's and her mother's, judging from the clock on Uncle Tony's dashboard. I'd only spent a few nights here since the night of my incarnation. We left for New Orleans so swiftly, I didn't have much time to explore out here. I haven't seen this much land and nature in nearly two years, that wasn't in a National Geographic's. I remembered the tall grass. "Uncle Tony, why is that grass so tall?" I asked.

He chuckled. "Lily asked me a similar question twenty years ago. That isn't grass Baby Girl, that's sugarcane."

"That's sugarcane? Where's the sugar?"

He started laughing. I wonder if I made a joke.

When we parked he went up to a sugarcane stalk and broke it. He peeled the chaff and bit into the light colored center. "This part is so sweet," he said slurping down the juices. "This is what sugar is made from." He offered it to me and then quickly took it

 Ashley Lauren Mitchell

back, remembering.

I looked at the stalk in his hand and then back to him, "What if I did try it?" I said, shrugging and reaching for the sugarcane.

He drew it back, further from my grasp. The smile on his face instantly disappeared. He looked at the stalk in his hand and said, "Remember when I told you, you are, what you are, because you tasted blood?"

"Yes, I remember."

"Have you ever tasted human food?"

I thought about it. "No. I've never really wanted to, to be honest."

"Well, I don't think you should. I mean, if you've never tried it and never wanted to try it, then maybe you shouldn't."

"Why not?"

"Well, humans don't drink blood? Do they? What if you aren't supposed to eat human food? I mean, ya know, being that you are...different. You don't know if eating human food could hurt you, or change you, or something worse."

"Like kill me?"

                    Ashley Lauren Mitchell

"Yes, like kill you."

I laughed. "Uncle Tony, I don't think tasting or eating human food will kill me."

He grabbed me by my chilled arms tightly, jerking me. "But you don't know that!" he exclaimed. His eyes were glazed, glossy. He looked like he was going to cry. "You don't know that." He repeated, softly. He pulled me to his chest and wrapped his strong arms around me, crushing me in his embrace. He started crying.

"What's wrong Uncle Tony?" I asked.

After he cried loudly for a few moments, he said, "Oh Lily, I never questioned why you came back to me this way. I was just happy you were alive. I just, guessed, you came back this way because I failed you, and God was teaching me a lesson. I should've protected you. I should've kept you safe from that, that, asshole, but I didn't, I couldn't. I'm so sorry Baby Girl. I'm so sorry! I was supposed to look out for you, be there for you, keep you from harm, and I didn't. Oh, God, I didn't! I can't lose you again. Don't you understand, you're the only family I have left and I can't lose you? I promised Nahdia I'd protect you and I failed. I failed you both. I can't let that happen again. I won't! I promise you Lily. I promise." He wept.

Uncle Tony was finally grieving for Lily, after

　　　　　　　Ashley Lauren Mitchell

nearly two years; and in the same sugarcane field he'd lost her in. He even called me her name, which he respectfully hadn't done in a long time. He denounced himself for his defection, which I can't believe he could be guilty of. He's a good man, a great human, now blaming himself for Lily's death and damned resurrection. I wasn't sure what to say or do, but I knew he needed to say these things. He'd never said them before, and I haven't seen him cry since he lost Lily. I wrapped my arms around his waist, careful not to squeeze him, hurt him. I closed my eyes and listened to his heartbeat as his tears fell to the ground.

We unpacked my things and took them in the house. I made sure that I'd brought all the books back here, to the bookshelf I borrowed them from. I also brought some clothes. Uncle Tony made sure I had enough of the bags of blood to last for two weeks, considering I only drink one a night. I had to leave the beautiful mahogany casket at the club, but Uncle Tony had another one delivered to the house. This one was just as luxurious.

Once we'd finished the chores, Uncle Tony told me he had to leave. There hasn't been a single night that I didn't see him. There hasn't been a single night without his kindness and gentleness. I realized again how lucky a beast I was to have him. Now I know what the feeling was that I couldn't place when we were saying our farewells

                    Ashley Lauren Mitchell

to Diamond. It was worry. I was worried about my Uncle Tony. I was worried about myself. I was worried about being without him. I was worried I'd never see him again. This is worry, the emotion I believed only humans suffered from.

My cold heart ached as we hugged a final time. Before he walked out the door, he brushed a curly tendril from my forehead and kissed it.

"I'll miss you," he paused, "Baby Girl," he said.

I knew he wanted to call me Lily. "I'll miss you too Uncle Tony."

"I'll be back as soon as I can. But if anything should happen..."

"Nothing is going to happen," I said assuredly, cutting him off.

"But, if anything does," he continued, "just know that I love you. No matter what you are now, I know you are still my blood, and nothing is more sacred than that."

We waved goodbye as he drove away. I watched the car get smaller, and smaller, and eventually disappear from view. I watched him drive away. I looked up at the night sky. The stars weren't out tonight. They were hidden by clouds that seemed to be moving as fast as the wind, which was blowing at an extreme pace. It was the advent of imminent danger displayed in the heavens. Strong winds rustled my hair. It wasn't the comforting ones I'd felt many times before. This wind blew with power. I stood outside for what felt like an eternity, gazing at my surroundings. I wanted Uncle Tony to come back. I think I wanted to cry too. But neither of those things happened. I went inside, climbed in my coffin and laid there for hours until I finally drifted to sleep. Tonight, I didn't dream.

***

On August 29, 2005, Hurricane Katrina landed in New Orleans, Louisiana. It is recorded as one of the most powerful and destructive storms to impact the coast of the United States in the previous one hundred years. It blew with winds that reached over one hundred twenty-five miles per hour. Hurricane Katrina left hundreds dead or missing. It caused widespread panic and left much of the city in ruins.

***

He called me Lamia.

The next night I rose from my coffin and heard pounding on the window. I looked outside and saw the sugarcane stalks blowing wildly in the wind. It was raining. Debris was being blown against the glass. I tried turning on a lamp but it wouldn't click on. The power must be out. The phone rang. At least that works. It was Diamond calling to check on me. She remembered what time I wake. She said she was going to come over and see me, but the weather was preventing her. I told her I was fine and that I'd see her tomorrow night.

When I hung up the telephone, I boiled a pot of water and grabbed a bag of blood from the refrigerator. I put it in the water to warm. I sat at the dining table and drank it in silence. I don't remember the last time I heard this type of silence. There was always music playing at the club. Or Diamond or Uncle Tony would be with me. I would at least hear footsteps daily. This was a peculiar silence. I tossed the empty bag on the table. I sat in the chair with my eyes closed and listened. I don't know what I was listening for, but I still listened.

The wind was so loud. It whistled and howled outside, calling me to it. I went to the front door, opened it, and watched Hurricane Katrina through the mesh of the screen door. The wind looked like it would be strong enough to lift me from the ground, so

                    Ashley Lauren Mitchell

I stepped outside to test it. The clouds covered the sky. They were light gray against the dark of night. Plump raindrops drizzled on my skin. Lightening bolted across the sky and the earth thundered beneath my feet. I stood in the clearing, where Uncle Tony parks his car, and spread my arms out to the sides, palms down. I closed my eyes and imagined I was flying. Although the wind was forceful, it didn't move my preternaturally heavy body an inch. The sugarcane tips were whipping vigorously. When the stalks broke off, they flew through the air. I turned to look at them and my hair blew in my face, blocking my view.

When I brushed the locks away with my fingers, I saw my mystery being standing in the road not far from me. He looked as melancholy as I felt, but he was just as beautiful as I remembered. We stared at each other for a long period of time. Both our hair blowing wildly and freely in the savage wind. After so much time had passed, I thought he would come to me. But he didn't. Like always, when I tried to make a move to go to him, he vanished. He left me standing there alone and wondering about him.

I wondered how long he'd been watching me. I wondered where he went when he wasn't watching me. How did he know where to find me? Who was he? What was his name? Why won't he come to me? I hadn't seen him since the night of my dream. I can barely remember it anymore.

Just like the previous night, I stood, in the same spot that I stood watching Uncle Tony drive away. The wind became more furious. I walked back inside the empty house. My eyes adjusted to the darkness. I took a shower, letting the lukewarm water stream down my face. Maybe this is what having tears feels like. Why can't I cry? I wanted to. I wanted to, badly. I believe I was sad enough to cry, but the tears just wouldn't form. After drying off and dressing, I climbed into my coffin. And like the previous night, I lay there, listening to the howling wind, until it lulled me to sleep.

Diamond and I were watching the newscast in the living room of her mother's house. It had been two long nights since the hurricane. We'd been trying assiduously to reach Uncle Tony. The pictures on the television showed distraught people on roof tops surrounded by high, murky waters; people crowded in the Superdome; people walking on the interstate; people looting; and people being arrested. They were devastating images. Diamond cried, not only for the misfortune of those distressed people, but also for the ravaged city of New Orleans that she called home. If anyone loved New Orleans it was Diamond. And seeing it like that, I could tell, was breaking her mortal heart.

She and I have called every person we could think of to locate Uncle Tony. His cellular phone won't ring or go to his voicemail. Diamond paced the floor

                              Ashley Lauren Mitchell

and cried, for hours. I sat curled on the couch, my chin resting on my knees, watching the news. We....I... felt so helpless. The man we both loved, albeit in different ways, was missing. We both hoped we'd get a glimpse of him on the television, so that we'd at least know he lived. We shouldn't think such things. Uncle Tony is brave and strong. He can take care of himself, we hope. It's difficult to be optimistic when you feel such desperation.

We spent the entire night there in the living room. We have a repeat of this night for a week. No word from or about Uncle Tony. Every morning before sunrise I make the lonely trek back to Lily and Nahdia's house. My defeatist attitude consumes me. Most nights I want to keep walking right to the end of nowhere. Maybe if I keep walking I'll find Uncle Tony, my guardian angel. But I can't keep walking. The closer the morning star gets to making its appearance, the more languid I become. The longing for my dark coffin grows stronger. All I can do is succumb to that feeling.

It's now been two weeks since Uncle Tony brought Diamond and I to Donaldsonville. We have yet to receive information on him. He hasn't called or come to us. We are beyond worried. What's almost just as bad is that I have run out of blood pouches. I know I can at least make it one night without sustenance. I know this because the first night I tasted

                    Ashley Lauren Mitchell

a bag of blood it repulsed me so much I refused to keep drinking it. The following night, on the way to Uncle Tony's condo in New Orleans, I was so hungry that I gave in and reluctantly drank from the nauseating bag. They give me just enough energy to make it through the night, considering I only get about ten hours of being awake. And although I don't like them, I wish I had one tonight.

I told Diamond it wasn't safe for her to be near me. Her scent was becoming irresistible. And before I do something regrettable, like drink her, I'll abstain from her presence completely. This is hard for both of us. Being around each other brings comfort from the absence of Uncle Tony. We talk on the telephone, but it doesn't feel the same.

By the end of the week, I'm too inept to leave my coffin. I lay there wanting to sleep, but sleep won't come. I try reading, but even reading feels like it takes too much energy. Energy I do not have. I continue lying there, motionless. I'm expecting the phone to ring so that I'll have a reason to get up. Instead I hear a knock at the front door.

Peculiar.

I climb out of my coffin and slowly walk to answer it. Before I open it I already know it's a human. Only a human can smell this good, this, inviting. I wanted it to be Uncle Tony, for so many reasons. And for so many reasons, I needed it to be. I felt the hope rise in me as I put my hand on the doorknob and twisted it. For the briefest moment I believed he was here to make all of this anguish go away. But it was Diamond. Her eyes were swollen from all the crying she'd been doing. She looked gaunt from inanition. She looked at me with her red, puffy eyes. Then, suddenly, she grabbed me, hugging me tightly to her. She smelled...amazing. I closed my eyes and opened my mouth...

"Diamond! What the hell?" I yelled, pushing her away from me. "What are you doing here?"

"I'm so lonely over there by myself. I miss Tony so much! I miss you, I miss everything. I'm not used to this silence, this loneliness. I want him to come back! Where is he? Where is he?" she screamed.

I empathize with her, I really do, but I need to do it from a distance. "Diamond you need to go. Please," I beg her.

She looks at me with distraught eyes and says, "Just kill me."

"What are talking about?"

"Just kill me already."

"Do you hear yourself?"

"Yes! Lamia, I know you almost killed me that

                                    Ashley Lauren Mitchell

first night and Tony stopped you. I figured it all out over time. But I don't care. I deserved it. I still deserve it. Kill me! I'd rather die than live in a world without him. I love him so much! I'm so stupid for not telling him how I feel about him. He's, my everything! He's the reason I breathe! Just kill me and get it over with!"

I can't believe what I'm hearing from her. I always knew she loved Uncle Tony, but she was implying that I should take her life. "No," I said, "I won't do it. I know how you feel, I really do, but I won't kill you."

"Yes you will. If I stay here long enough, you will."

"Diamond, please go. You're being psychotic. Killing you won't be the answer. And when he comes back? What will he think of me if I did something like that?"

My questions moved an emotion in her she'd not felt for some time. Hope. She took a breath and said, "I'm sorry for acting this way. I'm, I'm losing it. I can't be as strong as you. I'm only human." She took a long breath. "I'll just go. I'm gonna call you when I get home. Okay?"

I smiled at her. "Okay." I respond.

She turned and walked out the door. The whole scenario seemed surreal. But then again, so did

Ashley Lauren Mitchell

everything else that was happening. Diamond hadn't done anything deserving of me taking her life. She is a good human. I didn't want to kill her. It made me think of the first night, and how badly I did want to kill her; but Uncle Tony sacrificed himself to save her. That's the kinds of things he does. He did it for her, and I know he would do it for me. I miss him so much! However, I cannot say that I've thought of killing myself because he is gone.

I went back to my coffin. I stood and looked at it for a while. Was I going to lie in it until Uncle Tony returned? What if he never came back? How would I survive? I recall him saying something about 'survival of the fittest'. Was I one of the 'fittest'? If I were to just lie here and wait for him to come, and he never did, would I just, die? Would that be the same thing as what Diamond wanted to do? To give up? To surrender to death? Was I subconsciously trying to kill myself?

It does seem like an easy way out.

"Wait. What am I thinking?"

I went to the dining room and waited for Diamond to call me. Hours passed and I still hadn't heard from her. Another hour passed. In the state she was in, she was liable to have done anything. Maybe she decided to keep walking until she walked right into Uncle Tony, like I'd imagined doing days ago

                    Ashley Lauren Mitchell

walking back here. I thought about going to her house. The sun will rise soon. I wouldn't be able to make it there and back in time. I feel too fatigued anyway. I'm sure I'll hear from her tonight. I went to my coffin to rest.

That next night I woke, I called Diamond. There was no answer. I let it ring, and ring, and ring. I tried every hour. She didn't answer. Maybe I should go to her house. But I'm so weak. And what if I run into a human? I don't trust myself enough at this point. My hunger is too great. It took so much self-control not to give Diamond what she asked for last night. We both would have had instant satisfaction, but I would be the only one who'd live to regret it. I could've fed from her like I'd done Sable, but Diamond looked just as depleted as I am. I'm sure she'd not been nourishing herself. She wouldn't have survived my consumption.

I'd run out of options. I had to find the strength to go to her. Slowly I stood and began walking. I felt dizzy immediately. I used the wall to steady myself as I made it to the door. My head was spinning. My vision became blurred and I felt like I needed to sit down. I rested my forehead against the door. I started breathing deep breaths, in and out of my cold lungs. In and out. In and out. In and...I smell blood. I smell fresh blood. And it smells so close, as if there's a human standing on the other side of the door. It could be Diamond. I hope it's Diamond. I hope she's

Ashley Lauren Mitchell

alright.

I opened the door and didn't see anyone. I tried opening the screen door to step out, but there was something hindering it. I looked down and there, on the step was a tall glass. A handkerchief with the initials N.V., was placed on the rim, covering it. I picked it up and removed the cloth. I smelled the contents. It was blood, or at least I hoped it was. I was apprehensive to drink it. What if what Uncle Tony said was true, and if this wasn't blood, it kills me? What would I become then? Do I have a choice? I would perish eventually anyway at the rate I was going. I dipped a finger in the glass to check its consistency. It looked like blood. It smelled like blood. It felt like blood. But now the final test, I put the finger to my mouth and closed my eyes. Here goes. I put my finger into my mouth and waited to see what would happen.

Nothing happened. The blood was so delicious I had licked it all off my finger in one taste. I put the glass to my lips and drank it. It was still warm. It was fresh. It wasn't until I'd drunk every drop that I thought about where the blood could have come from. And more importantly, who the blood could have come from? Could this be from Diamond or Uncle Tony? Why didn't they come to see me?

Once the blood had settled in my body, and I felt revitalized, I walked to Diamond's house. Luckily, I

Ashley Lauren Mitchell

didn't encounter any humans along the way. When I arrived at her house I knocked on every door and window. She didn't answer. After trying a few times I gently broke open the backdoor. I searched the house but she wasn't anywhere to be found. I waited. I sat in her living room and waited for her to come home. I looked at the handkerchief with the initials N.V. embossed on it. The one that was placed over the delicious glass of blood.

Who could this belong to?

It's four o'clock in the morning. Today is October 6, 2005. And I just realize, that two years ago on this day I became, this. I guess that makes today my birthday. Two years ago I'd just met Uncle Tony and Diamond. Two years ago everything was different. I needed to get to my coffin before the sun came up. I wrote a note for Diamond, telling her to call me and that I was concerned about her. I started walking home. With each step I felt lonelier. I'd lost contact with the only people in the world that I knew. It's been three weeks since I'd seen or heard from Uncle Tony and this is the second night I haven't seen or heard from Diamond. Something is terribly wrong, and I can't do anything about it. This impotence and emptiness is absorbing me. I have no clue what to do. There's no one else I can talk to. No one else that knows of me. All the other humans that knew I existed are dead, because of me. I thought of Sable. She

Ashley Lauren Mitchell

wouldn't be in New Orleans, and if she were, she wouldn't want anything to do with me after what we'd done to her. Sending someone to a mental institution I'm sure isn't the best way to guarantee a lasting friendship. I am alone, completely and utterly, alone.

When I rounded the corner to Lily's house, there he was, standing on the front step of the house. The mystery being. My mystery being. He had a glass in one hand and a bouquet of flowers in the other. They were roses and some other type of flowers with white petals. But the glass. It looked familiar. It looked like the same glass from earlier. I looked at him as he looked at me. Neither of us spoke. I walked up to him and he handed me the glass. I took it and drank the contents. It was the same delicious blood from earlier too. And it's still warm.

He took the glass from me when I'd finished. My body became only slightly warmer, but I felt much better. He handed me the flowers. "These are for you," he said. I took them. Then he said, "Happy Birthday, Lamia." His voice was deep and resonating. He had an accent unlike any I'd ever heard before. I smiled at his statement but for some reason I couldn't speak. Assuming the handkerchief belonged to him, I reached in my pocket, pulled it out and handed it to him. He accepted it. I moved past him and opened the door. I stood in the doorway with the door open,

Ashley Lauren Mitchell

inviting him in. He stared at me with his large, black eyes until I walked inside. When I turned to look at him again he was gone.

Ah, Lycius bright, and will you leave me on the hills alone?

Lamia. The poem that I'd read so many times. I got the book from the bookshelf, and took it and the flowers in my coffin with me, and closed the cover.

That night I had another dream. Well, I shouldn't say another dream, because it wasn't another dream. It was the same dream I'd had weeks ago. It started the same way. My mystery being and I, naked in the lush garden. The animals all around us. He falls asleep, the animals fall asleep. I kiss him and watch him sleep. It is my only comfort. It was the only time I'd smiled in a long time

 Ashley Lauren Mitchell

<u>Chapter 12</u>

October, 2005

That night when I rose from my coffin, I knew my life had been radically changed. The wilted flowers fell to the floor, along with the poetry book. I left them scattered there. I tried to call Diamond on the phone. There was no answer. Surprisingly, I still felt I had enough energy from the glass of blood last night to walk to her house. Hastily, I made the journey. I went straight into the house through the backdoor I'd broken open the previous night. The note that I left her hadn't been touched, and more than likely, hadn't been read. I searched the house. Nothing. Not one sign she'd even made it back the other night from her visit with me.

I sat at her dining room table. I thought I'd wait there again, the entire night. Perhaps she found a way to go back to New Orleans and was searching for Uncle Tony. I'm certain if my circumstances were different, I'd do that. A morose feeling swept over me; that I wouldn't see Uncle Tony or Diamond ever again. I crossed my arms on the table and put my head down on my forearms. I wanted to cry so badly that I shut my eyes and opened them repeatedly,

          Ashley Lauren Mitchell

attempting to strain a tear out. Nothing.

I trudged, vanquished, back to Lily and Nahdia's house. When I rounded the corner of the house I thought I'd see the mystery being. Nothing. I didn't want to go into that lonely house at the moment so I walked into the sugarcane field. I walked until I believed I'd reached the exact location that I'd come to existence in. I laid on the ground. I looked up at the night sky. The stars were back. I watched the sparkling gems for an hour or so and remembered what it was like the first night I saw them, looking at them from this precise angle. I'd changed dramatically since that time nearly two years ago. I'd come to care so much for the two humans that I'd met that night. I wouldn't doubt that I'd sacrifice myself for them. I'd do anything to have them back. Diamond and Uncle Tony seemed perpetually distant. The two that started out as strangers, were the only family I knew. Now they're gone and I really do understand Diamond. I want to die.

I went back to the house. I got in my coffin and this time I concluded to let death come for me. Or maybe Uncle Tony or Diamond would come for me. Or if I cannot have death, then I will sleep forever. Right before I closed the lid of my coffin, for what I was sure would be the final time, I heard movement in the house. The wooden floors creaked as someone

                    Ashley Lauren Mitchell

stepped on them. Someone was in the kitchen. And I smelled blood. It wasn't just my hunger beguiling my senses, I actually smelled blood. It was a strikingly powerful scent. I sauntered into the kitchen. On the counter was another glass of fresh blood. I drank it wholly, swiftly, as if I didn't drink it that way, it would disappear. When I'd drunk it all, I stood holding the glass. In the living room I heard footsteps. I set the glass back on the countertop. Wiping my mouth with the back of my hand, I went to the living room.

Standing across the room was the ever transient creature, my mystery being. He looked like a painting standing there with his hands in his pockets, looking out the window. He turned his eyes from gazing out the opening, to gazing at me. We stood in silence for a time. I walked steadily to him. His skin wasn't as luminous as it was other times I'd seen him. It was tan, like mine after I feed. His wavy brown hair was pulled into a sleek ponytail. He was just as tall as Uncle Tony. He was wearing a gray V-neck t-shirt that clung to his lean, muscular chest and abdomen. He had on black jeans that fit as if they were tailor made for him only. His boots were just as black. There was also a black leather jacket thrown indifferently on the couch.

When he touched my face, his fingers were warm. His soft, pink lips were full and ripe. The dagger tips of his teeth were resting on his bottom lip. His eyes were completely black, like the pupil had expanded to cover his entire eye. When I looked into them I didn't see his past actions or future intentions like I did with every human I'd ever seen. But he wasn't human, was he? When I looked into his eyes, I saw...myself. My reflection was shown in those black, gleaming eyes. They were like mirrors. Black, shiny mirrors. Everything about him made me want to keep staring. He is like me. Yes, he is.

He brushed a tendril from my face, and he spoke, "...And for her eyes; what could such eyes do there but weep and weep, that they were born so fair?"

His voice was low and soft; and that accent that I still cannot place, made me quiver. The words he spoke, I knew those words. I remember reading them in the poem just last night. I gazed at him in disbelief. "Who are you?" I finally asked him. "Tell me. I can't go another night without knowing."

"My beautiful Lamia. I've wanted this moment for so long. To have you all to myself." He took my chin in his hand and rubbed his thumb across my bottom lip. "My name is Nathaniel. Please," he smiled, "call me Nathaniel."

I gulped. "Nathaniel," I repeated.

He wrapped his arms around my body and

pulled me to him. He smelled like nothing I'd ever smelled before. The sweet fragrance penetrated my nostrils. I closed my eyes and inhaled. I felt safe and cared for again, enclosed in his warm embrace. I exhaled.

There were so many questions I wanted to ask him, but I feared if I said too much he would spontaneously disappear. I wanted him near me. I didn't want to be lonely anymore.

"I think you need to feed," he said.

His presence made me forget my hunger. The glasses of blood weren't nearly enough, but I was grateful for them. "My Uncle Tony usually takes care of feeding me. I don't get my own food."

He chuckled. "Don't get your own food? And who is this, Uncle Tony? And why is he not feeding you then?"

"He's gone. I don't know where he is."

"He's gone?"

"Yes."

"So what are you going to do now?"

"I...I don't know," I said, shaking my head and shrugging my shoulders.

  Ashley Lauren Mitchell

He laughed. I wasn't quite sure what he was laughing at, so naively I laughed along with him. He said, "You don't know?" He asked sarcastically. I stopped laughing. "You do know," he said, "you're surrounded by food?" I didn't speak. I felt he were mocking me. "Come," he said, "I'll show you." He grabbed my hand, slipping his fingers between mine. "Close your eyes."

He had an infectious, contagious smile. I wanted to turn away from him but he was irresistible. I smiled and shook my head. He slowly walked behind me. He put one arm around me, shoulder to shoulder, and used the other hand to cover my eyes. He leaned close to my ear and repeated, "Close your eyes." I closed my eyes. A few seconds later he removed his hand and said, "Now, open."

When I opened my eyes we were in the yard of a small wooden house, not very unlike Lily and Nahdia's. But there were apple trees and orange trees around it.

"How did you do that? How did we get here? Where are we? Who lives here?" I fired questions at him one after another.

He put his index finger to his lips and said, "Shhh." He strode boldly to the front door of the house. I scurried behind him. He knocked on the door.

An old man, nearly seventy years old, answered. He looked at us curiously, squinting his eyes, and leaning closer. "May I help you? He asked.

Nathaniel smiled and nodded. He brushed past the man and walked into the house. The old man and I watched him, stunned. The old man looked at me. I gave him a shrug. We both walked in after Nathaniel. A woman, just as old as the man, was sitting in a rocking chair, rocking and watching television. She looked up at us and smiled when we entered the room. "Oh? Hello." she kindly said.

I was waiting for Nathaniel to say something. I thought he knew these people until he looked at me and said, "See? Food."

I wasn't quite sure what he meant but I know it wasn't anything good. "What? What do you mean food?"

"These humans. They are food."

"We, we can't just feed from them."

"Why not?" he asked. The man and woman looked at each other. I could see traces of worry forming on their faces.

"Because, they, they're good people."

"Good people? And how do you know they're

                    Ashley Lauren Mitchell

good people?"

"I can see it in their eyes. Can't you?"

"No. I can't. And I don't discriminate when it comes to my food. But that's right," he said walking to me. "You're the vigilante vampire, aren't you?" He laughed. "How admirable." His words were sarcastic and incisive. He put his hand on my chin, "And adorable." He said and continued laughing. I jerked my face from his hand. I couldn't believe his crass. The old man quickly moved over to his wife. Suddenly Nathaniel's face became serious, "If you do not feed you will die. I won't allow that. You should know that by now."

"You?" I asked.

"Yes. Me. Why do you think I gave you the glasses of blood?"

I didn't answer him.

"Lamia, you're a vampire. What else could you be? An angel sent to help rid the earth of scoundrels, like the ones you'd toss in the back of that car? You're not an angel. If anything you're more of a demon."

"I'm not a demon," I said, becoming increasingly annoyed by the way he was speaking to me.

                                    Ashley Lauren Mitchell

"No. But you are a vampire. You feed on mortal blood in order to exist. Your teeth. Your strength. Your sleep patterns. You're a vampire." He sighed and stepped closer to me. "You must accept that."

"I do accept that. How dare you say such things to me?"

He grinned and grabbed my hand, ignoring my inquiry altogether. He said, "Here, let me show you something else. Close your eyes."

"If it's another..."

"Just close your eyes."

I looked at the old man and woman. They were holding each other's hands, staring at us, fearfully. I wanted to leave them as soon as possible, so I did as Nathaniel told me and closed my eyes.

When I opened them, we were in a land vast and verdant. The air was stale and mild. The sun had just descended into the earth, leaving the sky in a colorful array of purple, pink, and orange. I heard animal noises of all sorts all around me. A herd of zebras were stampeding away from where we were standing. It reminded me of...of my dream. In my dream, he and I were standing in a land much like this. With animals all around us. Only, in the dream we were humans land were standing in the sun. But we aren't humans. And the sun is not high in the sky, but disappearing all together.

"Where are we?" I asked as the dusty, dry breeze blew softly past us.

"This is Africa. The Serengeti, to be more precise. The endless plains."

"Africa?"

"Yes. Haven't you ever been to Africa?"

"I've never left the State of Louisiana." For some reason I felt asinine for saying that. "So, what are we doing here?" I asked.

"Look, I want you to see this." He put his hands on my shoulders and turned my body around.

A short distance away from us were three lions. One had a mane and the other two didn't. From the National Geographic's magazines I'd read, I knew that the one with the mane was male and the other two were his female consorts. The three of them were circling an injured zebra that was yelping in pain. Its front right leg was broken and dangling. It reminded me of the time Derek and Michael were circling me. Only this time, the one in the center wasn't the predator. Nathaniel wrapped his arm around me, leaned close to my ear and whispered, "Watch."

                    Ashley Lauren Mitchell

Within seconds, the three lions all pounced viciously on the frightened zebra. They started ripping the animal apart. Blood and entrails splattered on the dirt as the zebra continued screeching. My eyes grew wide at the horrendous sight. I think I wanted to look away, but I couldn't. I was mesmerized by the bloody spectacle. The zebra finally surrendered to death. We watched as the three savage beasts devoured their prey, and lick the bones clean.

When they'd had their fill, the male lion looked up and stared at us. It stood on its massive paws and began walking toward us. Nathaniel held me steady as it came closer. When it was only a few feet away from us, it sat, like a dog following a command. "Touch it." Nathaniel whispered and gently pushed me forward.

I waited and stared at the animal. After a moment, I reluctantly stepped forward and reached my hand out toward the beast. It didn't move. I cautiously touched the bridge of its nose and rubbed up to its dirt and blood covered mane. It licked its lips and then licked my arm. Its tongue was rough and smooth simultaneously. Touching this animal reminded me of the time I pet the horses in New Orleans. I knelt on the ground and put my face close to the lion's. His breath was hot and steamed on my flesh. It smelled like, blood. His eyes looked kindly into mine and all the anxiety I felt went away. I touched

                    Ashley Lauren Mitchell

one of its long, cone-shaped, canine teeth, and then I boldly wrapped my hand around it.

"This is the most beautiful thing I've ever seen. He's beautiful," I said.

"I knew you would enjoy this," Nathaniel said smiling. "I wanted you to see this because I need you to understand that some creatures must be sacrificed so that other creatures may live."

I looked up at him before I rose to meet his eyes. "But we aren't beasts like this."

"Oh, but we are. Don't you see? Humans see us the same way that helpless zebra saw these lions. We're a threat, no matter how you look at it. We are the hunters and they are the prey. You must feed Lamia. It is, I guess," he paused, "the survival of the fittest, even with these lesser creatures."

I remembered Uncle Tony had said those words, survival of the fittest. "But why can't we just pick out the humans that are bad?"

He laughed, "That are bad? Like what, rotten fruit? Oh my love, all humans are the same; capable of the same things when tempted. You can't just wait for the bad ones to present themselves to you now, as they did in the past. Your food won't be brought to you anymore. You are a killer. You must kill."

I turned away from him and watched the lions walk to a tree. They stretched and yawned, and made themselves comfortable. Their eyes grew heavy as they fought sleep. I, too, felt a languid feeling taking over me.

"I want to go home," I said.

"Alright." He grabbed my hand. I closed my eyes, opened them, and we were back in the living room of Lily and Nahdia's house. He said, "I'll let you make the decision on your own. When you're ready I'll come back."

"No, wait. Don't..." He was gone.

He left me standing there wanting and hungry. I regretted not taking the opportunity to feed when I could. Now he was gone again and I didn't know when he'd return. His leather jacket was still on the couch. I left it there. I put my hands on my head and wiped them down, over my face, neck, and shoulders. I let out a sigh of aggravation. I'm not like him. I won't feast on innocent people. There was that word I hated again. Innocent. Who was really innocent? What was innocence? Why did I hate that word? I didn't want to think anymore. The night seemed like a dream. It all happened so quickly. I wanted the moment back. I wanted Nathaniel back. He was only trying to teach me that I needed to get my own food. Right? I can't really expect Uncle Tony

     Ashley Lauren Mitchell

to come back just to feed me. He was gone. Everyone was gone. I was either going to die or survive. Right now I just wanted to rest. I got in my coffin and closed the lid.

My dream. I should have known I would have it tonight. But tonight it kept going, like a movie. There is more to my dream. It started off the same as the last time. My mystery being, whom I know now to be Nathaniel, is with me. We are in a land much like the beautiful land of Africa. I am watching him sleep but this time...I hear something. I hear a voice. It's a woman's voice. She was calling me, calling my name. "Lamia," she called, "Lamia." Her voice is soft, alluring, enchanting, and...familiar. I rise, careful not to wake Nathaniel and the animals and I begin moving in the direction of the voice. In the distance I see an enormous tree, one like I'd never seen before. It was gigantic. Its branches hovered over my head, blocking the sunlight. It was covered in a bold colorful fruit, a fruit unlike any I'd ever seen. A piece of the fruit fell to the ground. I picked it up, turned it round and round, and eyed it suspiciously. I heard the woman's voice again. She said, "It's alright my Lamia. Take a bite." I looked for her, to see where the voice was coming from. When I couldn't find her, I looked at the beautiful piece of fruit in my hand. I smelled it. It smelled delightful. I brought it to my lips and opened my mouth.

                    Ashley Lauren Mitchell

The dream ends. I don't know whether I took a bite or not. It just ends. It is such a strange dream. It almost feels like a memory. It serves no purpose, lends no help, and gives no answers. It only creates more questions. Questions that I may never have the answers to.

***

The moment I opened my eyes the next evening I knew he was there. He was leaning with his back against the front door holding a glass of blood. I smiled at him, happy that he'd come back, I said, "I didn't want you to go."

He didn't smile back. "Here, drink this," he said handing me the glass. I took it. We looked at each other while I drank. When I'd finished and set the glass on the table next to the door, he said, "Did you like that?"

"Yes," I moved close to him, "Thank you." I said. "Is that what you were waiting for?"

"What? A Thank you?" He stood upright from leaning against the door. His tall frame towered over me. His black eyes gazed into mine. His face was solemn as he said, "No. It wasn't. And don't thank me just yet." He stared at me a moment then asked, "Do you know where that blood came from?"

I smiled devilishly and said, "A human?" in the same sarcastic manner he'd used with me last night. He'd called me a vigilante vampire. I didn't care about avenging those people my victims killed. Did I? Still, the way he said it, was as if he were trying to insult me. It irritated me, like I'm trying to irritate him. He looks at me and winces. He twists the doorknob, and pulls the door open. Then he swings open the screen door with one push, nearly sending it flying off the hinges.

I see a man lying on the ground. It was the old man from last night. His body was curled into a ball. He was obviously in great pain. Nathaniel smiled wickedly at me and said, "That is where the blood came from. If you want more go get it. It's right there."

My mouth dropped open. I couldn't believe he was doing this. I ran out to the man on the ground. I fell to my knees beside him and checked to see if he'd been severely hurt. I gently turned him on his back in my lap. His sad and begging eyes looked into mine. After only seconds of gazing, I saw the affair he'd had on his wife with a red head woman many decades ago; I saw that he was a habitual swearer; and that he and his son had not spoken in years because of an argument he caused, and regrets. Other than that this man hadn't killed anyone. I didn't

                    Ashley Lauren Mitchell

want to take his life. I sat him up and checked his injuries.

"What are you doing?" Asked Nathaniel as he casually walked toward us.

"This man didn't kill anyone. I don't want to kill him."

"What? His blood tastes the same as a killer's blood. You didn't seem to mind drinking it from the glass. Would you like me to drain him and hand the blood to you that way?"

His tone infuriated me. I got up and walked to Nathaniel. "Why are you doing this?"

He laughed. "You need to learn to get your own food and stop depending on humans to bring it to you."

I was shocked at his candor.

"Lamia," he said seductively, "Humans slaughter animals for food all the time." He laughed, "There are even such things as cannibals. You know, humans eating humans."

"Stop this. You're being ridiculous."

"Am I?" He asked. He was no longer being jocular. "Or are you just afraid to admit what you are? You don't even embrace what you are. You don't know the wonderful things you're capable of as a vampire. And you're letting it all go to waste, waiting on humans to come to you. There are too many of them not to be able to find your own. You need to stop being so pathetic and needy, and feed yourself. We aren't meant to be helped by humans and we aren't here to help humans. We kill humans. Now, kill that human!"

No one had ever spoken to me like that before. No one had ever told me these things. Feed myself? I don't remember the last time I had to feed myself. I chose not to as a favor to Uncle Tony, who proved to be worth it. But who was Nathaniel to say this to me? I hated him for telling me this. But what I hated more is that it was true. I was angry and embarrassed. This is the one time I actually wanted him to disappear. But he didn't. He stood there and watched me. It felt like he knew what I was thinking. He walked past me and my eyes fell to the ground. He looked down at the old man and said, "Well at least end this man's suffering. Or if you don't, I will."

What was I supposed to do? If I wait for Uncle Tony or Diamond, I could starve to death. Was I going to search down every corrupt and murderous human I could find and make them my meals? Or was I going to give in and listen to Nathaniel?

I turned and faced him. I walked over to the old man and knelt down beside him. Nathaniel knelt

                    Ashley Lauren Mitchell

with me. He held the man still and lifted his arm to me, offering me the wrist. I took it. The man was looking at me. His eyes were sodden, and begging me not to do what I was about to do. "I'm sorry," I tell him. Nathaniel turned the man's head away from me so that I couldn't see his eyes anymore. I looked at Nathaniel. I saw my reflection in his eyes. I looked gaunt and pale. If I don't feed, I don't live. Survival of the fittest, right? I surrendered and bit into the quivering wrist. The man's body pulsated from the initial piercing. Then he relaxed and slumped in Nathaniel's arms.

I watched myself in Nathaniel's eyes. Then I closed mine as the first drops of blood slaked my dying thirst. It had been one month, twelve days, nineteen hours, seven minutes, and forty-three seconds, forty-four seconds, forty-five seconds, since I've had fresh, human blood, straight from the source. I listened to the man's slow heartbeat, a melody I hadn't heard in, what felt in that moment, to be a thousand years. I dropped to the ground from my knees and sat on my buttocks. The blood was so good. It tastes so good. How could I have gone without this for so long?

Nathaniel was still looking at me, only now he had a grin on his face. When I'd finished drinking the old man and listening to his last heartbeat, Nathaniel released the body and stood up. He extended his hand to help me from the ground. I let him pull me to

Ashley Lauren Mitchell

his body and he said, "See, that wasn't so bad, was it?"

I didn't respond. He knows how the blood makes me feel. I'm full and satisfied and I quickly forget the man at my feet. Nathaniel brushed a lock from my forehead and kissed it. He said, "You did well tonight. You'll get better at this. I'll teach you all you need to know about what you are. You will love it. You will love yourself." He touches his lips on my ear, "And you will love me." My warm body shivered. "I'll take care of this body tonight," he said, looking at the corpse on the ground, and then back to me, "And I'll return tomorrow night...and every night after. Oh, my Lamia, you have so much to learn."

I feel heavy and want to lie in my coffin. It's been so long since I drank this much blood. Only one frail human's blood made me this lethargic. Nathaniel kissed my hand and said, "Sleep well, my Lamia." I gave a wincing smile at him and went in the house. I needed a shower but that would have to wait. I felt inebriated from so much blood. I fell into my coffin and closed the lid. I hadn't fallen asleep so suddenly in far too long.

The dream, it came to me again. It continued. I am standing underneath the giant tree. A piece of its colorful fruit falls near my feet. I pick it up. I hear the woman's voice. She tells me "It's alright my Lamia. Take a bite." I look around to see if I can spot the woman with the alluring voice. Then I hear her say, "Once you taste the fruit, you will see me," as if she's reading my mind. I take a final look at the bright colored fruit. I put it to my mouth and I...take a bite.

Chapter 13

October, 2005

He calls me Lamia.

Nathaniel was in the living room waiting for me when I woke. He had on all black. His hair was in a ponytail. He looked like he was going to do something clandestine. He handed me a bag.

"What's this?" I asked.

"Tonight you're going to learn how to hunt."

"Hunt?"

"Yes."

"What's in the bag?" I asked, eyeing it warily.

"That's what you're going to wear."

"What I'm going to wear?"

"Yes."

"Is this necessary?"

He sighed, then said, "Thank you, are the words

                    Ashley Lauren Mitchell

I'm looking for this time." He stepped closer to me. He gave me one of his tempting, conniving, prepossessing smiles. When he touched me, I could tell he hadn't fed yet. He was just as cold as I was. "Here," he said, "go put it on. I picked it out myself. I think it will suit you."

I went into Lily's room and put the skin tight outfit on my body. Everything was black, even the zippers. It was light weight and comfortable. It was so formfitting, it seemed like it was made to fit only my body. I wasn't sure of the material but it was smooth and elastic. It hugged me like a second layer of skin. I was impressed with his choice. When I went back to him, his eyes searched me and he said, "Now you're ready," with a pleased, proud smile on his face.

The first thing he taught me was how to control when and where I wanted to go when I close my eyes. He said, "It's not time travel. We can't go backward or forward through time. We simply meditate on a place in the present that we want to go and we go there, instantly. I call it teleportation."

I remember I'd subconsciously done that twice with Sable. I'd closed my eyes, and when I opened them, I was in her room below mine at the club. I didn't realize I could conjure that power whenever I wanted to. "Teleportation," I repeated, testing the word out.

Nathaniel took my hand in his. He said, "Come on. We're going to go eat. Close your eyes."

When I opened them we were on a dark, quiet rode. There were tall trees with long branches that curved over the top of us, creating a black tunnel. Two people, a younger couple, were walking ahead of us. They looked like teenagers. They were holding hands and talking. They had no clue we were behind them. The girl shivered and started rubbing her arms, and the boy put his arm around her. I'm certain it was because of our presence that she felt that chill.

"Them?" I asked.

"Why not?" He said casually.

"They look so..."

"So, what? Innocent?"

I didn't respond.

"You must get over this now. You will feed. It doesn't matter how humans behave or who they are. They are food. They all will die inevitably. But we...we will live. That, my dear, is survival of the fittest." He started walking away from me and toward the young couple. I knew he wouldn't wait for me. He was cold and hungry, just like I was. I believe that he would take them both if I didn't take one for myself.

                                    Ashley Lauren Mitchell

I walked swiftly to catch up with him. Then he yelled, "Hey!" The couple turned around and saw us walking to them. At first, they stopped and looked at us curiously. I don't know if they sensed something or if they saw something in our eyes that told them to run, but they turned back and started running. Nathaniel stopped me with his arm on my stomach. "Wait a minute," he said, watching them run. I looked at him, then at his arm, then at the couple, that was now a good distance away from us. "Now...go!" he exclaimed and took off.

Even with the lead they had on us, we were so fast that we cut the distance in half in less than a second. My adrenaline was rushing by the time we caught them. Nathaniel's face showed how good it made him feel, the thrill of the chase. I grabbed the female, and he, the male. We were both facing each other. The couple was staring into each other's eyes with sorrow and trepidation. I looked at them and then to Nathaniel.

"Don't think about it Lamia, just feed," he said, watching me, knowing I was second guessing this situation.

I took a deep breath, "I'm sorry," I whispered in the girl's ear, and closed my eyes.

Her body shook for a few seconds, and then rested in my arms. Nathaniel was right, her blood

                              Ashley Lauren Mitchell

tasted no different than a killer's blood. Nathaniel finished before I did. I never knew what Uncle Tony did with the bodies I deposited in his trunk. I don't believe I even thought about it until that moment. Nathaniel put the bodies on top of each other and pulled out a bottle of what smelled like gasoline. He poured the liquid on the bodies, lit a match and dropped it. The bodies burned instantly before my eyes.

Although I felt satiated by the girl's blood, I also felt something else while watching her and the boy's bodies burning. The flames crackled, danced in the air, and then dissipated. It was hypnotizing. It almost seemed like it was taking me to another lifetime. The bodies were so dried out they turned to dust and ashes within minutes. Nathaniel and I took each other's tepid hands and walked away.

"It will get easier," he said. "But you will have to stop seeing them as good and bad. You are not one of them, with the same feelings and desires."

I pondered what he said, then said, "But it seems that we do have the same feelings and desires. They feed, they kill, and they need pleasure. How do we not have the same feelings and desires?"

"No, you don't understand." His face looked disappointed. "We are not humans. We are not even just vampires. We are demigods. So much more than

     Ashley Lauren Mitchell

humans, and only slightly less than gods. We are immortal, and strong, and powerful. But instead of giving life, we take it. It's just what we do."

"So we can't die, ever, in any way? But you said I'd die if I didn't feed?"

"You won't die from not feeding but you won't be able to move or respond. You won't be able to do anything for yourself. You take a form like death. And you won't be able to wake from it." He looked at me with his brilliant black eyes. "But you don't need to be concerned with that. I won't let that happen to you, my Lamia. Come, let's go," he said taking my hand.

We teleported to Lily and Nadia's house. Nathaniel kissed my forehead. He told me to rest and that I needed time to think. And then, he was gone. I didn't know where to, so I couldn't teleport to follow him. I took a shower. My body was so warm, the cold water steamed on my flesh. It was refreshing to wash the dry blood and ash from my hair and skin. The water relaxed me, cleared my mind for a moment.

I tried thinking about what Nathaniel said, and what he meant. Was I being naive? Was I too feeble to be a vampire? Did Nathaniel want me to be vicious and unrelenting like those lions or like him? I remember being more vicious at the club, but that was with my victims. That seems like a lifetime ago. Nathaniel is implying, no, commanding me to treat

                    Ashley Lauren Mitchell

everyone the same way. Could I even do that? What would Uncle Tony think? Where is Uncle Tony? What if I never see him again? Maybe, maybe, I should just face the truth about what I am. Maybe Nathaniel is right. I don't know. But he's right about one thing, I need more time to think about this.

The dream came to me again, but it ends after I bite into the fruit. It starts over and ends when I bite into the fruit; like a movie on repeat. No alternate ending. No ending at all. It just goes on and on, with no ending, over and over again.

***

The next night we found two men hiking in the woods. Nathaniel did the same thing he'd done to alert the young couple from last night. "Hey!" He yelled. The men ran in opposite directions. I chased one, and Nathaniel, the other. When I caught up to the panicked man, he stopped and faced me. We looked at each other as we walked in a circle. I didn't see any evil in his eyes. He was innocent, but I cannot let that stop me now. I am too hungry. He let the promenade go on for another minute before lunging at me. He aimed a knife for my throat but I threw him to the ground. He jumped to his feet and lunged again.

                              Ashley Lauren Mitchell

This time he sliced me across the face. I put my fingers on the cut. It actually hurt a little. When I saw my blood, I found myself feeling no sympathy for the man anymore. I looked at him and smiled as my body healed itself. When he saw the wound fade, his face showed his utter shock. His eyes grew wide. I watched his nostrils flare with fear and rage at the sight of an alien creature. He came at me again. This time I grabbed his balled fist in mine. I squeezed until I heard his knuckles crack, pop, and then shatter. He screamed in agony and knelt in pain. I pulled him up and spun his body around, putting his back against my chest. I bit into his sweaty skin and drank. I did not say, 'I'm sorry.'

Nathaniel had two streams of blood on his chin, and a cadaver in his hand, when he bolted to me. He watched me feed, with a look of pride on his face. When I drained the body and listened for the last heartbeat, I dropped it and walked to Nathaniel. I licked my thumb and used it to wipe the blood from his face. He did the same to me. Then we held each other before igniting the dead bodies on the ground.

Every night he found two humans in a remote and deserted place. One night we were feeding on two college girls. They were walking to their dormitory from a loud party, blocks away. The girl that I fed from was menstruating. I recalled that night at the club with Sable. The smell was so strong and sweet. I enjoyed finally being able to bite into the flesh of a menstruating female and drain her before nature could. Her blood was so warm, almost hot. I tried not to think of all the girls at the club that I could have fed from, and had this thirst quenched many times over.

On the last night of October, Halloween night, Nathaniel took me to a hospital. We stood outside for a while, staring at it. Some humans were walking in wearing costumes of all sorts. Gremlins, ghouls, demons, and...vampires. It all amused and bewildered me.

"What are we doing here?" I asked. "Are we just going to look at them, or are we going to eat?"

He looked at me and said, "Do you see that human over there?" He was pointing at a bald man wearing a hospital gown. He was alone and leaning against the hospital smoking a cigarette, flicking the ashes after every slow drag. He didn't look at all interested in the holiday festivities.

"Yes, I see him."

"Go drink him," Nathaniel said, smiling facetiously.

I returned a furtive smile and casually walked over to the man. Nathaniel followed. When I'd walked up behind him I snickered quietly at his exposed buttocks and said, "Can I bum a smoke?" The man turned around, grasping at the back of his gown, obviously embarrassed and surprised. "Oh, yeah, sure," he stuttered before looking into my eyes. Once he did, he froze. "Wow! Are those contacts? Pretty fuckin sweet! Best costume I've seen all night." He said, handing me a cigarette. I didn't care about the venial sins I saw in his eyes. It didn't matter anymore. He was just another human. I smiled wider, grabbed his extended arm and turned his back to me. I cocked his head to the side and opened my mouth. An odor like I'd never smelled before, hit my nose like a cudgel and stopped me from sinking my teeth into him. I closed my mouth and smelled him curiously.

"What is that?" I asked the man...or Nathaniel. It was so putrid, I was asking anyone that would answer me.

Nathaniel laughed. "You smell that?"

"Ugh. Yes. What is it?"

"This man has cancer?" he said.

"Cancer?"

"Yes. Cancer. That is why you don't want to drink him. His blood is too noxious, like a poison. It won't kill you, but it will make you feel weak if you drink it. He probably got it from these." Nathaniel bent over and picked up the still lit cigarette the man had dropped and eyed it curiously. "Humans

                                    Ashley Lauren Mitchell

and their vices. Even if it kills them, they do them. Slow, self-mutilation at its finest."

I smelled the man again just to make sure I'd remember the odor if it ever hit my olfactory glands again. I doubt I'd ever forget it. Nathaniel snapped the man's neck quickly and easily. "He saw us. We don't need him running his mouth now, do we?"

"No. I, I guess not." I said looking at the man's defunct body, lying sprawled on the ground. "But it is Halloween. It's not like anyone would've believe him anyway."

"Why Lamia? That isn't sympathy I hear in your voice, is it?"

"What? No. Not at all. He's just a mere mortal, right?"

Nathaniel flashed his captivating smile at me. "Good girl."

We found a quick bite to eat and he took me around the hospital making diagnoses. We walked. He talked.

"This man has pneumonia. This woman, ovarian cancer. This one, malaria. This one, typhus. This one Ischemic heart disease. This one tuberculosis. And this one just has a common cold. We could feed from him and be fine."

                    Ashley Lauren Mitchell

"How do you know so much about this?" I asked him.

"I'm sort of a scientist, a doctor I guess you could say."

"A scientist? A doctor?"

"I've been around a lot longer than you have. I've done enough trial and error on myself over the years to know these things. But, never mind that. That was long ago. My Lamia, pay attention. Now, you need to know these things. I wouldn't want you to become weak."

After a long night of medical education, more of an anatomy and physiology lesson, we went back to Lily's. He kissed my forehead and disappeared. I showered and took to my coffin. Before falling asleep, I replayed the night in my mind. Nathaniel had said he was, some sort of a scientist...a doctor? I wondered what kind of scientist. How does one become a scientist? By simply making observations or must one conduct experiments and research? How old was Nathaniel? What does he do when he's not with me? Scientist stuff?

He started letting me choose where we'd dine after some weeks. I used Lily's collection of National Geographic's magazines. I'd flip through the pages and chose a different location every night. I could feel myself evolving. The new Lamia was becoming empowered. She was becoming the murderess she is supposed to be. The murderess Nathaniel was teaching her to be. I enjoyed it. All of it. Myself; what I am; the hunting and killing; the teleporting; and best of all, Nathaniel.

One night after we'd eaten, he said, "I want to teach you something extraordinary."

"What is it?" I asked, intrigued.

He took a step back. His feet lifted from the ground and he rose into the air. "Did you know you could do this?"

I took a deep breath. "Oh my god! We can fly?" I asked, mesmerized.

He laughed, "No, I am no god, and we cannot fly. Vampires do not fly, we levitate. We cannot touch the clouds and the stars, but we can defy gravity and become weightless. We can only go so high and so far, before our bodies are pulled back to the earth. And the more we feed, the more we weigh, so the faster we'll descend." He let his feet touch the ground. "Do you want to try it?" He asked. I couldn't disguise my enthusiasm. I acquiesced and he stepped close to me. "Look up," he commanded. I did. "Now tell your body to lift, not with your mouth, with your mind." I did. He said, "Now look down." I did, and saw the ground several feet below me.

"This is incredible!" I exclaimed.

Nathaniel smiled and said, "We have so much to appreciate about our existence. Don't you see that now?"

I didn't speak, but I smiled as we rose higher and higher. I could see for miles ahead of us and behind us. We were gliding just above the trees, our feet grazing the leaves. Once we'd descended, I felt the urgent need to feed.

"I know where I want to go," I said and took his hand. "Close your eyes."

When we opened them, we were on top of a cliff, somewhere in Hawaii. I'd seen a picture of it in one of the magazines. Three people were taking turns diving from the cliff into the dark, foaming waters below.

Nathaniel looked at me and then back at the humans. "Good job Lamia. This is a perfect location," he said. I smiled, feeling proud of myself.

We walked quietly to the top of the cliff. Two of the men were cheering as one was just making his daring jump. As soon as he'd hit the waters below, Nathaniel and I grabbed the other two. Before we finished feeding, the one in the water was climbing back up the cliff and yelling, "Dudes? Hey? Brett? Damien? Did you see that? That was fuckin awesome! I'm the man! I'm the man!"

Nathaniel and I threw Brett's and Damien's bodies into the ocean. We jumped over the cliff and floated there while the diver searched and called for his recently deceased friends. Nathaniel went up first. I heard the man gasp. He started backing away. I went to the other side and trapped him between us. Nathaniel and I walked in a circular motion around the human, as he looked back and forth at us. "What the hell? Who are you people? And where are my friends?" he said, nervously. We both went for him at the same time. Nathaniel on one side of the man's neck, and I on the other.

The man was drained in no time. We dropped the body to the ground and looked at each other. We watched each other grow darker as we became warmer. Nathaniel's eyes were as black and as shiny as I'd ever seen them. I saw my reflection in them. My iridescent eyes sparkled like a million stars. Nathaniel put his hand on my face and ran it through my hair. He gripped it at the nape and pulled my head so that our faces were almost touching. He looked all over my face and smelled me. I know I had to smell exactly like him. Bloody. Tantalizing. He tilted his head to the side and kissed me. I closed my eyes and let him lead. His sharp teeth bit into my tongue before mine bit into his. After the initial pain subsided, it was wondrous. We sucked on each other and drank each other's bloody juices. He put his arms around my waist, clenched my body to his, and lifted me off the ground. I put my arms around his neck and we sucked harder and harder. His blood was more pungent than any humans' had ever tasted. It made my taste buds tingle. It stung slightly going down my throat, but it was the most delicious blood I'd ever tasted.

When we finally pulled away from each other, we were both panting like lions. I practically stumbled backwards. My legs felt weak and my vision was blurred. This kiss was nothing like the one I had with Sable. This was so much more intoxicating. When we were both able to stand correctly, he said, "I've wanted to do that for so long."

I caught my breath, "I wish you would have. I never imagined that's what it would be like."

After we stared at each other for a time, I walked to the edge of the cliff and breathed in the night and the salty air. The waves crashed into the rocks below. I watched the foamy white lines move across the span of the ocean. Nathaniel came up behind me and held me. He repeated, verbatim, Lamia, by the poet John Keats. It was so beautiful coming from his lips. It was like a song. It was as if I were hearing it for the first time. But this time the words saddened me. The tragic love tale. To be with someone, to have someone, like Lamia had her Lycius. Nathaniel is my Lycius. This, time... these, moments, spent with him, are blissful. I wondered how he knew that poem so well. When he came to the end, we watched the ocean and the stars in silence.

We went back to Lily's house and he kissed my forehead before leaving me to rest. "I'll see you tonight my Lamia," he said and vanished.

I still don't know where he goes when he leaves me. I still hadn't gotten around to asking him all that I wanted to ask. I was just elated that I wasn't alone anymore. I loved that I had someone like myself. Nathaniel was teaching me so much. I was becoming more and more fascinated with my...condition. And of course, with Nathaniel. I wish he would tell me more about himself. Who is he? Does he remember anything from when he was a human? How is it that he's a scientist? A doctor? How does he know so much? Who is he? My mystery being. My Nathaniel.

Chapter 14

Saturday, December 31, 2005

It's been four months since Hurricane Katrina took Uncle Tony and Diamond away. I thought of them as soon as I opened my eyes. Their images flashed through my mind, along with memories of us at the club. I miss the three of us having our nightly conversations, and watching the two of them bantering playfully. There was hardly a night that went by that I didn't see them. Holidays to them only existed at the club with us, together. The more I think about it, I was their life. Their only desire, their only real obligation, was to help me survive. They never treated me like a burden. They opened Désirs Cachés for me, so that I could be with them. And where are they now?

Months feel like years sometimes, now that I've met Nathaniel. On some nights with him, time goes by so swiftly. On others, it feels like time has stopped. I enjoy his company, but what do I do about missing my humans?

Nathaniel was waiting for me in the living room when I woke. When he saw me, I guess it was written

     Ashley Lauren Mitchell

on my face because he asked, "What's wrong?"

"I was thinking about...," before I went on I looked at him. I wondered if I told him that I missed my humans that had been with me for nearly two years, would he perceive me as being a traitor in some way? I'd come to be quite the executrix with his help. I had evolved during these last few months. I'd lost most of the compassion I once, perhaps foolishly, had for humans, and it pleased him. I did not want to mess that up now. "Never mind. I'm not really sure what's wrong," I said, lying to him.

He walked to me and brushed the hair from my shoulder. "Well, I was thinking about last night."

"What about last night?"

"The way you taste."

"Oh, that."

"Oh, that? Lamia, you're different tonight. Have I upset you?"

"No. No. I didn't mean, 'Oh that'. It's just, well," while I had his attention I figured I'd ask something else that I'd been thinking about, "Do you remember anything about who you were before you became a vampire? How long have you been a vampire? And, where do you go when you leave me?"

Nathaniel took a step back, "I guess you have been thinking haven't you?" he asked, snickering.

"I've only been a vampire for two and a half years. I do know some things about the girl, Lily. She's the human whose body I, I guess, possess. Do you know anything of the human whose body you possess?"

"Possess? I should've seen this coming. You want to know who I am, or, who I was, before my transformation," he said shying from my eyes.

"Yes, I do. Don't you ever think about it? I mean, you were human once, right?"

"Lamia?"

"Right?"

He sighed. "Lamia, that doesn't matter now. None of that matters."

"Please Nathaniel, tell me. It matters to me. You're teaching me about who I am, what I am. But I want to know about the one who's teaching me these things." I hated that I couldn't see into his pitch black eyes and see his life, like I could humans'.

"Why? Why must you ask these things?"

"I know nothing about you."

"Yes you do. You know enough."

"I want to know more.

"Why?"

"Why not?" I said. "Don't you want to know more about me?"

"More about you?" He snorted, "Do you even know who you are? It seems I know much more about you than you know of yourself?"

"What does that mean?"

"When I met you, you were barely a vampire. Letting yourself waste away, being inert. Not feeding. Waiting for..." he stopped and stared at me. His words took us both by surprise. I knew what he wanted to say, but he resisted the urge. He was aggravated but he also looked hurt. "Lamia we are, what we are. Why think of what we were, or what we will never be?"

"Because I do think of it. I can't help it. What am I supposed to do? How am I to not think of questions that randomly come to my mind? You're telling me you never think things like this? I am the only one?

"Yes. That's exactly what I'm saying."

"Then who is N.V.?"

His eyes seemed to grow wider. He was no doubt surprised by the question. "How do you know that?"

"I remember those initials from the handkerchief. It was your handkerchief, right? So are those your initials? Or were they the human's initials?" He didn't answer me. But he looked at me in a way that let me know I'd repaid his candid statements with some of my own. I remembered the initials from the handkerchief he laid over the glass. They had to be his initials. But if he says we are not the same as the humans we once were, then why keep the memento? "What does the 'V.' stand for?" I asked.

After a moment he moved to sit on the couch. I joined him. He looked at me and said, "Those are not things worth thinking about. It won't help you. It won't help me. You should only think about us as we are now."

I wasn't satisfied. I didn't understand why he wouldn't tell me. I thought having someone, something, like myself, would be different. I believed I'd be able to discuss things like this with him, but he wasn't being very open to discussion. How disappointing. I sat back on the couch and leaned my head back. I stared at the ceiling. Is this all we are? Vampires? No past, no real identity? Just blood sucking, haunting, vagrant, vampires? At least, once, I felt I had a purpose. I felt needed, like my existence wasn't just an existence. Uncle Tony and Diamond made me feel as though I was a hero or a savior. Now, I feel like nothing more than a killer. Is that what I want? Is that all there is to this life? Oh, and what a life. What a long, long, extremely long life I will have. A never-ending life? It is too much to bear right now. I sigh with frustration. Kill. Kill. Kill. Because I am a killer. That is all I will ever be.

"I've grown tired of this talk," he says. "Come." He grabs my hand, pulling me with him as he stands. "I have something to show you."

Ashley Lauren Mitchell

Chapter 15

Nathaniel had to distract Lamia's mind, which was racing with questions. He knew she'd been thinking about the two humans that had taken care of her for well over a year. He knew she was curious about him, and who he once was. But he also knew he wasn't ready to tell Lamia the truth. He didn't know what she would think or do if he did tell her. After all the time they'd spent together. After all that he'd taught her. He didn't want her to know who N.V. was. Everything about Nathaniel's existence was a secret. He was not even supposed to be. He, long ago, accepted the fact that who he was, was never to be known, by anyone. He was supposed to be this, a ghost, an empty soul roaming the earth. With no real attachment to anyone. Until he found her.

N.V. stood for Nathaniel Volta. He was born in Florence, Italy in 1819. His mother, Isabella, was an intelligent and beautiful woman with many admirers. She had an intriguing oval-shaped face, a pointed noise, dark brown eyes, and full wavy brown hair. In 1795, when she was sixteen years old, a man named William Jones asked Isabella's mother for her

                    Ashley Lauren Mitchell

daughter's hand in marriage. Her mother overlooked the fact that William was nearly ten years older than Isabella, because of his genteel English background, and his aspirations of becoming a high ranking lieutenant in the British Royal Navy. Isabella was forced into marriage. After their hasty wedding, young Isabella reluctantly moved to England with her new husband, leaving her family behind in Italy.

Many years passed as Isabella adapted to her role as Mrs. Isabella Jones. William had wanted a large family, with lots of sons to carry on his name. But unfortunately, Isabella was unable to conceive children for him. He blamed her for being barren and their marriage began to suffer. For over ten years Isabella tried to get pregnant, and was met with much disappointment. William would spend days away from her, leaving her alone with her books, and a parrot that he'd bought for her when they were on the ship leaving Italy years ago. Isabella was young, alone, and felt trapped being William's wife.

William eventually did become a lieutenant in the Royal Army, as he'd told Isabella's mother he would. In 1805, a battle occurred between the British, the French, and the Spanish navies. William fought with the rest of his naval fleet crew just off the coast of Cape Trafalgar in Spain.

When Isabella received the letter informing her that William was killed during the war, she was forced to hide her relief. She was now the widow of a war hero. She was still young, beautiful, intelligent, and now, free. She began making a name for herself and started, finally, living her own life, her way. Years passed, and Isabella never remarried, although she was associated with prominent men in political parties. She never had a child and assumed she never would.

One evening in May, 1817, at the age of 38, Isabella met a very young man named John. After John's brother died, Isabella comforted him and the two eventually grew intimately closer. For months they met in secret, until Isabella had to tell John she didn't love him. It broke his heart. Isabella's mother had become ill shortly after John and Isabella's separation. Isabella sadly returned to Italy in 1819.

While in Italy, Isabella discovered she was pregnant. She couldn't bring herself to tell John. She was then forty years old, far too old, she felt, to start a family. And especially with someone as young as John. She realized if she returned to London with a bastard child, she would ruin both her and John's reputations, so she spent the remainder of her gestation in Florence, under the care of her brother Rudolph.

In November, 1819, Isabella gave birth to Nathaniel. Once she saw her precious baby boy, she knew she would stay in Italy, away from all those she once knew, to raise her and John's love child.

Nathaniel's uncle, Rudolph Volta, was the man that helped Isabella raise her son. Rudolph was a peculiar man, and an even more peculiar apothecary. He would concoct poisons, tonics, and elixirs and sell them for substantial amounts of money. Money he used to take care of his sister and nephew. He taught Nathaniel everything he could about the enterprise, and the boy eventually became his apprentice.

As years passed, Nathaniel grew to become an extremely attractive and intelligent young man. He had wavy brown hair and deep, dark brown eyes. He was the male version of his beautiful mother. Only, he was virile and masculine. His style was austere but eccentric. He preferred being comfortable rather than looking dapper. His undeniable good looks and charm allowed him to be that way, and still entice any woman.

At the age of thirteen, Isabella told him of his father and gave him a small black book with poems written in it. She told him his father, John, was an apothecary like Rudolph, when he was younger. But as he got older, John found his calling was poetry. With deep regret she also told him that John had died when Nathaniel was only a baby. Nathaniel took the book in sadness, but appreciated having some knowledge of his birth father. He read the poems daily over the

                    Ashley Lauren Mitchell

years, and soon had some of them memorized.

After secondary school, Nathaniel was sent to the university to become a doctor like his uncle. While there he also became a philanderer, seducing different women daily, using his father's poetry as dulcet melodies. He'd profess his love for the naive, young women and leave them in the same week. When he wasn't dallying with one of his many lovers, he worked with his uncle on nefarious powders, viruses, and miasmas. Their work was lucrative. Their clientele was surreptitious.

One night, he was on his way home, when he realized he was being followed. When he turned around he saw a tall figure moving toward him. It wore a long dark, cloak, with a hood. The figure's face was veiled by the shadow cast by the head covering. Nathaniel stood intrepid and readied himself for a fight. But as the figure got closer he saw the cloak wasn't black, like he'd thought, it was a deep, dark purple. As it got closer still, he realized the figure was a woman, a beautiful older woman with colorful eyes, and bright red hair. She wore delicate golden jewelry in her ears, around her neck, and on her wrists. The jewels sparkled with every step she took. She was enticing, yet intimidating.

She spoke to him with an alluring, resonating voice, "Hello, Nathaniel," she said.

　　　　　　　　Ashley Lauren Mitchell

"How do you know my name?"

"I know a lot about you."

"How? Who are you?"

"I knew your father many years ago."

"My...my father? You knew my father?"

"Yes. I believe he was a poet, was he not?"

"Yes. Yes he was."

"And his name was, John? Yes?"

Nathaniel was astonished by the woman's knowledge about his father. She convinced him to go with her to her living quarters, using the promise of more information about John.

She told Nathaniel to call her, Onaya. She had a hypnotizing gaze that captivated Nathaniel. When they were in her home, she told him that she knew exactly who he was, and what he and his uncle did for money. She told him that she would pay him a large sum if he developed a special virus for her. She warned him that he was to tell no one of her; or of their business venture. When he asked her about his father, she told him that when they met again she would tell him all he wished to know. She gave him a small, glass vial; told him that she would find him in days to come; and sent him on his way.

Ashley Lauren Mitchell

Nathaniel rushed home and into to his uncle's laboratory. He studied the contents of the vial. It was blood, he was sure of it. He spent hours locked in his uncle's laboratory working tediously on the virus. Finally, he felt he'd done it; he'd discovered a rare virus with the help of the vial. But, he needed to give it a final test before he could be sure. He injected a mouse with the serum and watched as its body slowly, painfully, shut down and the small animal closed its eyes to die. Nathaniel was pleased.

Minutes later he heard a soft, scratching, chirping sound coming from the dead mouse's cage. He leaned closer for a better look. Instantly, the mouse jumped to its small feet. Nathaniel jumped backwards. The rodent started ramming its body against the cage attempting to reach the mice in a nearby cage. The mouse was rabid and violent. Nathaniel's curiosity overtook him. He wanted to see what the infected creature would do if it were able to get to the other mice. As he was moving the animal to the other cage, it latched on to him. He shook his hand roughly trying to free his finger, but the rodent's sharp teeth were deep in his flesh. He hurriedly found something, a hammer, to smash it with. He beat the small ferocious mammal until it stopped moving. He pulled one of the long, sharp teeth that had gotten stuck, from a hole in his finger. Without thinking, he immediately, and ignorantly put his bloody finger to his mouth and sucked the blood away.

 Ashley Lauren Mitchell

Once he'd taken the wounded finger from his lips, he saw the two needle point bite marks that were beginning to swell. His eyesight became hazy as he tried to focus on cleaning the bloody mess he'd made bludgeoning the animal. While reaching for a cloth to clean with, Nathaniel's legs became paralyzed and he fell to the floor. He lay there, trembling with fever and writhing in pain, for only minutes; but to him it was eternity. His screaming became so loud it woke his uncle, who quickly ran downstairs to the laboratory. When he reached his nephew on the floor, he was cold, and stiff. Rudolph gently touched him and then with trepidation, started shaking him. In an instant, Nathaniel jumped to his feet. He grabbed Rudolph and bit into his neck, sucking the blood from his uncle's body voraciously.

It wasn't until Nathaniel had drained the last drop of his uncle's blood that he realized what he'd done. He ran to his mother's room, intending to explain how he was responsible for Rudolph's death. When he arrived at her door he stopped himself. He rested his hand on the doorknob, then pulled away. He couldn't face his mother. He didn't want to tell her that he had killed her only family. He didn't know what was happening to him, or if he would do the same thing to her. So he turned and left.

He ran to Onaya's house. When he got there, he stood, shocked. The entire house was gone; as if it

     Ashley Lauren Mitchell

had never been there. He thought, maybe he was confused and that he was just lost. Then he looked down. On the ground was a single, long strand of bright red hair. He had only seen one person, his whole life, with hair like that. He bent down to pick it up. When he raised it up to the moonlight for a better look, it ignited, and slowly burned from the tip all the way to Nathaniel's fingers. He didn't even feel it burn his fingers before it died out. He felt worried, confused, and soon he felt something else. His body was becoming weary. It was nearly morning and he didn't know the sun was now his enemy. He felt weak and had to find somewhere to rest. He used the last of his strength to run away.

He found a large ship preparing to make sail. He hid in a cargo crate as it was being lifted onto the ship. He remained in the cramped box for two nights before erupting from the small carriage with hunger. He'd fed on over half the crew by the time the ship arrived at its destination in Ethiopia. Nathaniel was lost in Africa for months. He found a cave beneath a waterfall to hide himself in during the scorching days, and he hunted for food at night. He'd recite his father's poems from memory so that he wouldn't forget them, since he'd left the small book and all of his belongings behind in Italy. He wondered about the mysterious woman, who he began to blame for his present situation. He had no idea what had happened to her, but he wished he'd never met her

Ashley Lauren Mitchell

at all. He fought the memories of killing his uncle and leaving his mother. But he was something else now. Something that couldn't go home to its mother. Something that would be feared and would be branded a pariah the rest of its life. More than an animal. More than a human. More than a monster.

One night he came upon a small pride of lions, or rather, they came upon him. He eyed the three predators cautiously, as they circled around him. The male lion pounced first and Nathaniel threw it to the ground. One of the lionesses came at him; he punched it, knocking it unconscious. The other lioness paced back and forth watching him, planning her attack. She lunged and he grabbed her. He had her by the throat, gripping tightly. He watched as her body became still. Before her eyes went dead, Nathaniel released her and she backed away panting deeply. The male lion stood over the other lioness that was lying unconscious, protecting her from Nathaniel. Nathaniel approached the beasts. He and the male lion looked at each other before the animal backed away from the lioness. Nathaniel knelt down and picked her up. The male lion and the other female lion followed Nathaniel to his hidden lair.

During the day, the three lions guarded the cave while their master slept, and at night they would all go hunting together. Nathaniel was just as quick and ferocious as his new pets. He and the male lion would wrestle and race. He was with them when the cubs were born, and helped protect and raise them. Whenever the unusual pride came upon another pack of hunters, they never attacked Nathaniel. They sensed he was a predator, like they were, but also that he was much more powerful. Nathaniel lived and hunted with the wild animals for over a year. They roamed the plains of Africa, easily taking down any prey, human or animal, they chose. Nathaniel felt more like a lion than a human. But then, he knew he wasn't really human anymore.

On another night while hunting, Nathaniel came upon a small village in South Africa that had been invaded by Portuguese sailors. He watched as at least two hundred Africans were pulled in manacles and chains and marched into the ship. He said a farewell to his lion friends and once again hid himself as a stowaway on a ship readying to take sail. He hid near the cargo. Only this time, the cargo contained swarthy men and women being held captive.

On the sea, Nathaniel would sneak at night and drink an African man or woman. The Portuguese sailors would toss the dead body in the water the next morning, assuming the person had just been too feeble. One night, an African man begged Nathaniel to take his life so that he wouldn't have to live as a slave in a distant land he didn't know. Nathaniel did as the man requested, but afterwards he stopped feeding on the Africans and started picking off the crew members one by one, and soon, two by two, then three, four, five, until there were only a few left. Eventually, he released all the shackled men and women.

Although they were appreciative, most of the Africans feared the blood sucking, white man. Nathaniel chose the few that weren't afraid, and explained to them his condition. One of those people was a beautiful and courageous young woman named Tati. She had been taken from her family and village and was all alone. She was very brave and had no fear of Nathaniel. She helped kill and capture the remaining crew members when Nathaniel set her free. Now it was she, who guarded his box during the day while he slept, and waited for him to rise at night. Nathaniel would watch over her while she slept at night so that none of the other men would bother her. He was surprised he didn't want to take her life. Tati and a few of the others helped Nathaniel plan how they were going to get away with having hijacked the ship when their journey on the sea came to an end.

A month later, they spotted land. They stopped the ship a few yards off the shore of an island and jumped out. They ran for safety under the veil of night. Tati, Nathaniel, and a handful of the others ran deep into the thick forests of the island. Hours later, they came upon an enormous white house with columns as tall as trees. They seized the house, and killed its owner, an old sugarcane plantation master. The slaves he owned were overjoyed to be free of the authoritarian ruler. Many of them left, leaving the house to Nathaniel and the Africans, who he now called his friends. Nathaniel pretended to be the new owner of the plantation when the house was approached by slavers. He would free all the slaves and kill the others. Nathaniel became well loved by his new accomplices, especially Tati.

Nathaniel and Tati would spend many hours of the night together. He told her everything, anything he remembered from before his transformation. She encouraged him to find a cure and encouraged the others to help build a laboratory in the basement of the house. They gathered rodents for testing the new developments Nathaniel produced. Time flew by and none of the concoctions worked. Until one night he believed he'd found his cure.

He tested the new formula on a squirrel that he'd already infected with his diseased blood. It had transformed the rodent. He'd had the squirrel for nearly a month, preparing it for the experiment. He liked to watch it feed on other rodents. After a while, he even considered the little beast with his

Ashley Lauren Mitchell

internecine blood in it, a pet. But this night, to his surprise, one of his mixtures worked. The squirrel curled into a ball and let out a loud shriek, before lying still for nearly a minute. Then the small animal blinked its eyes and lifted its head. It climbed to its feet. Nathaniel put another squirrel in its cage and his pet did not attack. It was just a normal squirrel again.

Nathaniel immediately injected the serum into his arm. After minutes of pain, his sharp teeth retracted, his pupils shrank down to size. His body became lighter, not hard and heavy like that of a vampire. Miraculously, Nathaniel was human again. Or at least looked and felt human again.

That very night the members of the house threw a great celebration party for Nathaniel at the mansion. After a while, Tati and Nathaniel snuck off to a small house, two or three miles away, during the festivities, for some long awaited time alone. They kissed each other madly before ripping off their clothes. Tati received Nathaniel with pleasure as he stroked inside of her aching body. He realized he hadn't lain with a woman in over three years, as he pushed himself inside of her again and again while she moaned in ecstasy.

When he leaned in to kiss her neck, he felt as if he'd blacked out for a second. He became freezing cold and his eyes filled completely in black. He bit into Tati's neck and she cried out before becoming

Ashley Lauren Mitchell

resolutely still. He couldn't bring himself to release her and he dried her body out within minutes. Not knowing what else to do but get her to his laboratory, he picked her up and raced back to the mansion. He tried making it to his laboratory before anyone noticed him holding the dead body. He loved Tati and was going to do whatever it took to bring her to life again.

One of the men in the house, who considered himself an authority figure because he was one of those that remained after the arrival and extended stay of the others, stopped Nathaniel and asked what was wrong with Tati. He saw the panic on Nathaniel's face and the black eyes that he'd pretended not to fear so often. Then he looked at Tati. Before Nathaniel could speak, the man yelled "Satan," and footsteps from all over the house ran to where they stood, by the door of the laboratory. They tried taking Tati's body away from him, and somehow succeeded. The men all surrounded Nathaniel. They attacked him, but Nathaniel was too strong. He didn't want to hurt them so he knocked them back with a single swing of his arm. People began running fearfully away, trampling the injured on the floor. That night, Nathaniel was left all alone on the plantation.

He went to the basement laboratory and saw the squirrel he'd tried his elixir on, chewing through its metal cage savagely. He stomped the squirrel to

                    Ashley Lauren Mitchell

death with the heel of his shoe and lamented for his lost love, Tati.

Over the years, he continued trying his experiments, only now he didn't use rodents for guinea pigs, he used those humans that had been left behind by their cowardly comrades; or any human that stumbled upon the mansion. To his disappointment, the results of his work turned out the same way every time. The victims' eyes all rolled to the backs of their heads so that only the white would show. They couldn't speak, they only groaned. They ate...humans. But they didn't just drink the blood like vampires did. These creatures ate everything, all parts of the human body in its entirety. Nathaniel didn't want that for Tati. He wanted her to be a vampire, like him, so they could be together, forever. But it was too late. By the time he'd put his blood in her, she had already been dead too long. Nothing revived her.

One lonely night, Nathaniel closed his eyes tightly and wished he were in Italy with his mother. He hadn't seen her in years and he felt more alone now than ever. He'd never told her goodbye. He'd never told his uncle goodbye; or Tati, goodbye. He wondered if his mother was still alive. At least he was certain he hadn't taken her life. He imagined he was standing at Isabella's bedroom door, like he was when he'd made the decision to leave. When he opened his eyes, there he was; in Italy staring at a building that was once his mother's home.

Once he recognized where he was standing, he felt a strange sense of panic. The house that was once there, the house that he'd grown up in, the house that he'd taken the life of his uncle in, had been replaced, built over by another. Nathaniel looked around for someone to ask what had happened. Any answer to end his confusion.

Then he heard a voice. It was the voice of the woman he had only met once. It was the voice of the woman that changed his life forever. He quickly turned to face her. Her colorful eyes and aura, distracted his anger and fear. Her red hair glistened in the moonlight. She was draped in her purple cloak and bedecked in her gaudy, gold adornments. Nathaniel asked her if she knew what had happened to the house that had been there. She looked at him remorsefully and told him that what had happened to the house was his fault, an accident he caused. The night he ran away, the night he'd killed his uncle, he left the fire on in the laboratory, and the house burned in flames. In a breath he asked, "And my Mother?" The beautiful creature shook her head and told him that his mother had died in the fire. Isabella Jones had died in 1843, at the age of sixty-four, by tragically burning to death.

Nathaniel dropped to his knees and let out a cry. Onaya went to him and held him. She consoled

Ashley Lauren Mitchell

him by telling him that they were now both in the same, bereaved state. She stroked his head and said, "I, too, am without a loved one. My daughter is gone, and I cannot find her." She lifted Nathaniel's head and held his gaze in hers. She told him that he had no need for an earthly mother anymore. She would be his mother now. Then she told him to close his eyes.

When he opened them he was standing in the middle of a large, elaborate building. The walls and ceiling were covered with ethereal, fresco paintings. She told him to look up. She directed his gaze to a scene on the ceiling. He saw a man, a woman, and a large tree. Onaya told him to rise from the ground and get a better look. She ascended from the floor. He watched in amazement, but he wasn't sure if he could do what she'd said. He willed himself to lift from the ground, and surprisingly rose fifty feet into the air. At that moment he realized he didn't even know his full potential and everything his immortal body was capable of. When he was close enough to the ceiling, Onaya said, "Look. Do you know what this painting is?"

"Who doesn't?" he said with a smirk.

"Who doesn't? You say it like it's nothing." Onaya said with an offended tone.

Nathaniel snickered, "It's one of the most popular artworks in history. I've seen this before with my mother, many years ago."

"Really?"

"Yes. I was raised in Italy. I've seen this building many times."

"Then what is it called? This painting?"

"It's called, Fall of Man."

"And do you know who the artists is?"

"Of course, Michelangelo."

"The great Michelangelo," she said with force. "He was a talented artist. I knew him once, just as I knew your father."

"My father? But they lived centuries apart."

This time Onaya snickered, "I am thousands of years old. Something you couldn't possibly comprehend. I've met and influenced countless artists all over the galaxy, and throughout time. You see, I have a powerful attraction to artists, of all types. In a way, I feed off their creativity, I need it. In return I make them...better. I give my artists the one thing they want most for all of their creative efforts."

"And that is?"

Onaya smiled and said, "Immortality."

                          Ashley Lauren Mitchell

"Immortality?"

"Yes."

"How?"

"You said so yourself not too long ago, that this is one of the most popular artworks of all time. Don't you see? For centuries, for perhaps even millions of years to come, the artists that I've met and influenced will live on through whatever medium they've use. Whether it be painting, sculpting, poetry, dance, music; any way a true artist may express themselves. As long as their work is remembered by those that live, these artists will never truly die. They attain their immortality through their artwork, and their souls live on forever."

"But I am no artist."

"No, you are not." She looked Nathaniel from head to toe, "But, you will serve a far greater purpose than any of the artists I've touched."

Nathaniel's eyebrows furrowed. "How so?" He inquired.

Onaya floated behind him. Her long frame hovered over him as she lifted his eyes back to the painting. "Look again at the painting. Tell me what you see."

Nathaniel huffed with agitation, "I see Adam and Eve, I see the tree, I see the serpent, I see the..."

Before he could continue, Onaya said, "Ah, hah. Now look at me." He did. Then she said, "Tell me what the serpent looks like, without looking at the painting."

"Well, it's red. It's long. It was wrapped around the tree..."

"It was half-human? Was it not?" Nathaniel tried to steal a quick glance at the painting. "Ah, ah, ah."

"Yes. I believe it was."

"You. Believe. It. Was." She said each word with increasing chagrin. "You've never really paid any attention to this magnificent artwork, have you? The time, the detail, the labor put into this work." This time it was she who huffed in agitation. "Can you at least tell me the gender of the serpent?"

"Gender? It's a male." He said assuredly. "Satan is always depicted as a male. Right?"

"Just stop speaking you fool! You are going to anger me. How can you be so blind? How can you not see what you have been looking at all those years? This beautiful creature that you so casually overlook is more than a serpent. More than any depiction of Satan. I want you to look again. And this time I want you to tell me what you really see."

Nathaniel looked at the painting. He saw the vermillion color of the elongated body and hair. And then he saw...breasts. "The serpent is a woman!" he exclaimed.

"Yes," Onaya hissed. "She is!"

"Why would Michelangelo make the serpent a woman?"

"Because this isn't any serpent. I am the one that gave Michelangelo the dream, revealing the truth to him. He painted her this way for me. And, it is the most beautiful thing I've ever seen. And your father, wrote for her, one of the most beautiful poems I've ever read."

"For her? Why? Who is she?"

"She...is...my...daughter."

"Your daughter?"

"Yes. You must do something for me, only then will you earn the right to know the truth."

"The truth about what?"

"The truth about everything, and anything. All the mysteries of the earth."

Nathaniel reflected on her words. Was he sure he wanted to do anything for this being? The last time he did it left him, changed, forever. She was already indebted to him. Or was he indebted in some unbeknownst way to her? He thought about his father, who may have once actually known this, Onaya. He thought of why he would be chosen for such a task.

"Because it is your destiny," Onaya said, answering his unasked question.

Nathaniel looked at her, appalled.

"Yes. I can read your mind. I have unimaginable powers; powers that you wouldn't believe. And I know you will perform the service I request of you. I also know that even if you don't want to do it, you will, inevitably do it. It is your destiny. It will happen whether you want it to or not."

Nathaniel slowly shook his head. What she said made sense in a way, but he'd given up on the idea of a 'destiny' when he became no longer human, and bound by the laws of their world, and of logic. He gave in. "What must I do?"

"She is the only child I have. She, is the most important thing to me. I need you to find her."

"Find her?"

"Or I should say, let her find you."

"And how will she find me?"

"You're an immortal with my blood in you."

"Your blood?"

"What do you think was in the vial?"

Nathaniel thought about the night he met her. He thought about the small bottle of blood she gave to him. He never knew whose or what's blood was inside. But she was inside of him, coursing through his veins. He shivered.

"When she comes back to life this time. She will be drawn to you. She will try to fight it, but she will have no choice. She is not held by space and time. And she is so powerful, but will have no knowledge or understanding of her power. You will help her. You will guide her and teach her all she needs to know."

"Why won't she find you? Or why can't you find her yourself?"

Onaya looked up to the painting and stared for some time before saying, "I believe she is angry with me. Many years ago I tried to tell her the truth about who she really is. She refused to listen to me. She disappeared and I haven't been able to find her since. I know one day she will return to earth. I've grown weary of chasing her around the universe. I've done all I can to make her come back to me. But her anger is too menacing. The closer I am to her, the more...distant she becomes." She looked at Nathaniel with promise in her sparkling eyes. "That is where you come in. Since it is my blood that is in your veins, the reason you are what you are, she will come from you. From your blood. Our blood. She will not know who you are. She will not know who she is. She will take possession of a human body and stay there until she and I are united. When it is time, she will emerge. You must teach her who she is. It cannot be me. It must be you."

"But why?"

"It is the only way she will listen."

"How will I know it's her?"

Onaya laughed. "Your father asked the same questions when I brought him here."

"My father?"

"Yes. Nathaniel. Your father. I am using his bloodline as well. You are his son. Even if the world denies you. Even if they see you as no more than a bastard son, born of a whore."

"My mother was not a whore."

                    Ashley Lauren Mitchell

Onaya laughed. "Yes. Of course not. My apologies if I've offended you."

Nathaniel felt a strange sense of deception in her laugh.

She said, "But I am the one who can tell you everything you want to know about your father. That is more than your mother did for you. She kept the truth from you."

"And how would you know that?"

"Silly boy. You were so eager for even the slightest bit of information about John, and from a complete stranger. That is how I know. You don't know half as much about your father as I do. And there is no one alive who does either. There is something you want from me. And there is something I want from you. We can help each other."

Nathaniel looked down at the floor that was many feet below him. He didn't want to be in Onaya's presence anymore. She sensed it and put her index finger under his chin, tilting his head back until his eyes were forced to meet hers. He stared at the colorful orbs. She said, "This is your destiny, Nathaniel. She must find you. You must teach her the things I will show you. You must prepare her for the truth. Only then will you get your truth."

He knew he didn't have a choice. He knew if

he tried to think of a way to get out of this deal with Onaya, she would know. "How will I know her?"

Onaya smiled at him. "You will know. It may take years, but you will know. You will see it in her eyes. And you will call her, what I told your father to call her, what I told those before your father to call her. You will call her, Lamia. She will know that name, but nothing of who she is."

"Lamia?" Nathaniel repeated as he looked back at the painting. "My father's poem. That is Lamia?"

"Yes." She smiled at his revelation, "You understand now."

Onaya moved behind Nathaniel. She placed her hands on his head and transferred all of the things Lamia should be taught by him, and nothing more. Then she disappeared in a ball of fire, leaving him floating alone in the Sistine Chapel.

Nathaniel returned to the plantation. He thought that if he would just stay there, and never leave, he wouldn't have to find Lamia. If she were really going to find him, she would find him there. He spent the next one hundred years in Haiti, terrorizing the land around the mansion like an evil spirit, and waiting for the creature that would have to find him. When travelers wandered too close to the house, he'd usurp them, taking them captive in the villa. Onaya never returned to him. Lamia never found him. He kept working like a mad scientist in his laboratory. He'd given up on finding a cure for his condition. He realized that he'd spend eternity as a vampire. Over time he discovered miraculous things about his malignant state. He began to like it and after many decades, he began to love it. He learned to speak every language and play every instrument. He learned every one of his father's poems, and read thousands of other books. After so long, he became bored.

In 1967, a woman named Naitana bravely came to his house with a pair of twins; a boy and a girl. The small girl was deathly ill. Nathaniel had wanted to kill the children and the woman, but once he looked into the woman's eyes, he knew he wouldn't. Something about her reminded him of...Tati, his African paramour. Naitana was so pristine, selfless, and courageous. He hadn't seen such bravery and compassion since Tati was alive. Nathaniel took the child to his laboratory and treated her. He gave Naitana and the small children a house, the one that held the memory of what he'd done to Tati. He requested that Naitana live there and use her charm to lure men to Nathaniel as payment for helping her niece.

At night Nathaniel secretly watched the young

                                   Ashley Lauren Mitchell

girl, Antoinette, to see how she was reacting to the treatment he'd given her. He wasn't sure if she would be able to handle his powerful blood in her veins. And he knew if she ever tasted blood, she would either die, or become an immortal like him. However, he soon found that she never became ill and she had incredible strength. Over the years he also noticed she grew at a very slow rate and that she didn't like leaving the house. He continued to watch over her and even more so when her brother, Antoine, left with his new family; and her Aunt Naitana died. He, in a way came to care for his first successful experiment, especially since she had his blood coursing through her veins.

One day, when she was much older, Antoinette heard a knock on her door. Standing there was a young girl holding a baby. Nathaniel wondered who the girl was, and why she looked mysteriously like Antoinette. He wondered if that was her son, even though she looked too young to have a child. The two youngsters lived with Nathaniel's experiment, Antoinette, for a couple of years before the baby boy became deathly ill. The young girl, Nahdia, was sent to find Nathaniel so he could help save her little brother's life.

Nathaniel made the short distance to the house of the woman he'd helped over fifty years ago. He was carrying Nahdia in his arms after she'd passed out from panic and fatigue. As he looked at her limp body, he felt a strange sense of some future connection between them. He then thought about what it was going to be like finally meeting and talking with Antoinette after all these years. He knew she wouldn't remember him. She was so young when he'd treated her. When Antoinette opened the door to let Nathaniel in, she felt a chill all over her body. She gazed at his eyes as he took Nahdia into the house.

Nathaniel followed the same procedure on the small boy, Anthony, as he'd done for Antoinette when she was a child. He placed Nahdia in the bed next to her brother. Then he attached a bag of blood to a tube flowing into Anthony's arm through a needle. Antoinette led Nathaniel to the kitchen and thanked him. They sat down and Nathaniel explained what he'd done for the child, and what he'd done for her when she was just as young as Anthony. He told her about her Aunt Naitana's secret missions that had been arranged as payment for treating her. He intended to request she do the same thing, but he knew Antoinette was not fond of leaving the house. He said that he would return one day for payment and until then she was to watch over Anthony, who now had Nathaniel's blood flowing through his small veins.

Two years passed. The teenage girl, Nahdia that Nathaniel had carried back to the house, had

 Ashley Lauren Mitchell

grown into a young woman and wanted to leave Haiti. She wanted to take Anthony with her. Nathaniel was sure Antoinette would say 'No'. However, one morning, while Nathaniel, was still sleeping in his coffin, helpless and clueless, Antoinette helped the two young people leave for a new land. Nathaniel was angry at her for letting them leave. He told her he needed to be able to watch over both of his experiments and make sure they never tasted blood and became what he was.

Nights passed before he went back to Antoinette's house for his long awaited payment. She'd been crying because she missed Anthony and Nahdia. Nathaniel knew how much she missed them. He made a deal with her. He promised to watch over them for her, but she had to tell him where they were. She did. Nathaniel then took Antoinette from the small house to the plantation.

Nathaniel found Nahdia and Anthony in a city called New Orleans, in a state called Louisiana, in the United States of America. He watched as Anthony grew slowly over the years. When Anthony was a teenager, Nahdia, his sister gave birth to a baby girl with beautiful colorful eyes. When the baby was brought out of the hospital Nathaniel saw her and gasped. He remembered those eyes. He'd seen eyes like that before. But there was something else about this baby that Nathaniel couldn't quite figure out yet.

 Ashley Lauren Mitchell

Many nights he tried getting close to the infant. It had been nearly a hundred years since he spoke with Onaya, but he could never forget her eyes. Eyes just like the baby's.

Nathaniel began watching the child more intently than he did his second living experiment, Anthony, who had grown into a strong human. But the baby grew slowly. Nathaniel wondered how she could have the same symptoms as his first two experiments but he'd never performed a procedure on her. Then he realized, it was Anthony, the child's uncle. Somehow Nathaniel's blood was passed to her from Anthony. Anthony had no idea the powers his blood possessed, or the severity of what he'd done by giving the baby his blood.

Nathaniel watched the baby, Lily, grow; from a distance. He loved looking at her familiar, colorful eyes. He loved her aggressive manner. Lily reminded him more of Antoinette, his first successful experiment, than of Anthony. The girl even shared the woman's name as a second name. She didn't like to be around very many people, save her family, and she rarely left from her home, her safe haven.

Nathaniel became more intrigued, when the girl grew into an even more beautiful young woman. When her mother, Nahdia, died, Nathaniel left Lily a basket of gifts on her front step. Lily had not been eating so he left her a snack of bread and cheese,

                    Ashley Lauren Mitchell

and a bottle of wine. He also placed inside a bouquet of roses and Zephyr lilies, and a copy of the book containing the poems his father wrote; which had been published and had become quite popular to humans. Nathaniel found the picture of the two hands that Lily had thrown out. He remembered the hands from the painting, The Creation of Adam, painted on the ceiling of the Sistine Chapel. He wrote on the back of it, the secret name he'd called her when he first saw her colorful eyes. He remembered a passage from his father's poem:

She was a gordian shape of dazzling hue,

Vermilion-spotted, golden, green, and blue;

Striped like a zebra, freckled like a pard,

Eyed like a peacock, and all crimson barr'd;

And full of silver moons, that, as she breathed,

Dissolv'd, or brighter shone, or interwreathed

Their lustres with the gloomier tapestries -

So rainbow-sided, touch'd with miseries,

She seem'd, at once, some penanced lady elf,

Some demon's mistress, or the demon's self.

 Ashley Lauren Mitchell

He called her, Lamia. He used the picture to mark the pages he wanted her to read, the pages of the poem, Lamia. He loved that Lily started letting her long, black, curly hair flow freely; not tamed in a single braid down her back as she did when Nahdia was alive. He loved how she had blossomed.

Only months later that same year, on Lily's twenty-fourth birthday, something terrible happened to her. It happened so unexpectedly that Nathaniel wasn't able to stop it. He was luring Lily deeper into the sugarcane field, playing with her as he'd done so many times throughout the years, when he heard cars driving up. He teleported back to his laboratory in Haiti so that Lily could be with Anthony and the human woman. Moments later he sensed that something was wrong. He heard the gunshots ringing in his head and knew it was too late. One of the humans with his blood in them had been shot. He wasn't sure if it was Anthony or Lily. He immediately teleported himself to Donaldsonville, Louisiana.

He was shocked when he saw Lily lying on the ground with three gunshot wounds in her back. He knew he couldn't save her life; but perhaps he could save her body. He pulled a vial from his jacket pocket and poured the contents in her wounds. The immortal blood mixed with the blood of the evil human she had bitten a finger off of with her incredible strength. When he heard the screams he was certain she'd

Ashley Lauren Mitchell

changed. He watched her in amazement as she moved, as she watched the stars for a minute, and then as she rose from the ground. She wasn't Lily anymore. No. She was something different, something much more than mortal. Nathaniel whispered her name to her over and over, and tried again to get her to come to him. He was just about to take her, when he heard Anthony running toward them. As Nathaniel reached for Lily's hand she started running, away from him, toward an opening in the sugarcane field; surprisingly faster than Nathaniel could catch up with. When Nathaniel saw her again, she was feasting on the blood of a human, the human that was missing a finger. He kept watching her until she disappeared into the house with Anthony and the female human.

A couple nights later Anthony took, what once was Lily, to New Orleans. She stayed with Anthony for a while, then he took her to an establishment off Bourbon Street called Désirs Cachés. She was there every night afterwards, for nearly two years. Nathaniel loved the nights when she'd walk out the backdoor of the club to toss a cadaver into the back of Anthony's police car. She was so strong. And so beautiful. Nathaniel felt himself feeling more and more enamored with her, but he was unsure how to approach her.

One night she spotted him watching her and

                    Ashley Lauren Mitchell

ran to him. He touched her warm face with his icy fingers. 'Lamia,' he said, as he caressed her cheek. He knew in that instant what he must do. He wished he could have her all to himself. But there were other directions he must follow. Instructions he must obey; beyond his control. Then he disappeared, leaving Lamia standing there, both of them awaiting their next encounter.

Chapter 16

He called me Lamia.

"Come." He commands, grabbing my hand as he stands. "I have something to show you."

I pulled from his grasp. For some reason, I felt he was hiding something from me. I wasn't in the mood for his company anymore. "I think I will dine alone tonight."

"Alone?"

"Yes."

"Why?"

I looked at him but I didn't speak. What was I to do with all of these unanswered questions? I couldn't just stop thinking them. That is easier said than done. I started walking away from him.

"Wait. Lamia. Wait." He called to me.

"What Nathaniel?" I retorted.

"Fine. You win. Ask away." He said giving me a

very slight, beguiling smile as he sat back down on the couch. "Sit. What do you want to know?"

Did I really win? Was he really going to tell me the answers? And if so, was he going to tell me the truth? I only see myself in his eyes, not truth or lies, like I can with humans. How will I know if he's being honest? I slowly and unsurely, sit on the couch next to him. What if, he only knows as much of his host as I know about Lily? I was informed by my humans of the girl, Lily. Did someone tell him about who he possesses? What should I ask him first? I looked at him. All the while he had been staring at me, awaiting my interrogation. I started. "Was the name of the man you changed from also named Nathaniel?" I asked him.

"Yes. His name was Nathaniel Volta," he answered.

So far, so good, I suppose. It makes sense because of the initials on the handkerchief. The 'N.V.' I continued, "Where was he from?"

"I was...he was, born in Italy. He was a doctor, of sorts. He worked with chemicals and medicines. I retained much of his knowledge, as you, also, have kept much of the knowledge from the human you possess. Although, memories? Not so much. I believe it's rare to have too many memories of the humans' lives. You aren't that human girl. As I am not that

                    Ashley Lauren Mitchell

human man."

"But, how did we come to be this way? Why are we vampires?"

He took a minute to consider my query before saying, "I cannot answer that question. I'm still trying to figure that out myself. I believe it's more complex than either of us can understand. I've been this way for two hundred years. I've killed more humans than I can remember. Or that I care to remember. I understand your curiosity. I was once that way. But after so many years of being like this, you realize, you will always be this way. No question or answer will change that. I did the only thing I could do. And that was to keep feeding. Until I found you." He turned to me and took my cold hands in his. His dark, deep eyes gazed longingly at me. His beautiful sharp teeth dazzled in his mouth as he smiled at me. "Lamia, when I found you, it finally felt after two hundred years, that I wasn't alone. I won't have to spend eternity alone. I wish I had all of the answers you seek, but I don't. All I know is that I want to be with you, and that we now have each other."

I suppose I don't have much of a choice. I cannot continue to press him for answers. And he's right, they will be answers that won't change anything about what we are. I didn't speak, but I gave a smile that let him know, I understood. Even though I will continue thinking my badgering thoughts, I must accept that we are, as we are. And nothing will change that. What was I going to do? Question him until I understood that I will never have all of my questions answered? And if I don't like the answers? What will I do then? It may be better if I don't know. If in this ignorance I find bliss, I will cease seeking knowledge.

He smiled and nodded. He seemed content with my acceptance. "Now, let's go eat. I have something to show you. It's something I know you've never done before."

"Oh really?" I said in a lighter tone than the one I had only minutes ago. I must take advantage of the time I spend with Nathaniel. My mystery being, whom I now have. I will enjoy our infinite time together.

"Yes," he laughed. He stood and pulled me up with him. He grabbed me by the waist and wrapped me into him. "Now, my Lamia, close your eyes."

Lamia. He calls me Lamia.

Chapter 17

December 31, 2005

When I opened my eyes, we were standing in the vestibule of a casino, surrounded ...by...humans. Hundreds of them. There were slot machines, card tables, liquor bars, and music; very loud music. Women were prancing around wearing rabbit ears, pink bikini tops and short black skirts or shorts with a fluffy ball on their rears. They were strutting the embroidered floor of the casino carrying, trays with boxes of cigarettes, poker chips, drink glasses, and other items.

None of the humans paid much attention to Nathaniel and me. They were all at some level of intoxication. The temperature of their blood is so much warmer when they've been drinking, or taking some other type of substance. Their scent is stronger as well. This whole room is filled with the scent. A lot of the patrons had headbands or hats with 2006 on their heads. Every now and then a few would shout, "Happy New Year!" across the room. There were people at slot machines that looked like they'd been sitting there for days. They were so entranced that they didn't even look up as Nathaniel and I passed them. Our cold bodies felt even with the temperature of the room. The scenery made me nostalgic for Désirs Cachés. Watching humans be sinful in one way or another. Strip clubs, casinos, nightclubs; drunk humans throwing away money. In a strange way, I felt comfortable being at the casino, except for the fact I wanted to grab a human to quench my dire thirst.

"Where are we?" I shouted over the music.

He smiled and shouted back, "Las Vegas, the Palms Hotel."

"So this is where we're eating tonight?" I asked. He smiled and nodded. "It's taking a lot of restraint not to snatch one of these humans. What are we doing here? Why did you chose this place?"

"You are always full of questions aren't you?" He laughed. He put his arm around me, "I'm going to show you something tonight. Just follow my lead. I promise you'll enjoy this."

He took my icy hand in his and led me into an empty elevator. The whole elevator car was made of lights and mirrors. I was relieved Nathaniel and I were the only ones there or we would have had to kill the witnesses. Then again, I'm not relieved. We'd gladly kill the witnesses.

                                          Ashley Lauren Mitchell

Nathaniel stood leaning over me. His arms were on either side of my head, with his hands on the glassy wall behind me. "Happy New Year," he said looking down at me smiling. "And many more to go."

I flashed a coy grin at him and looked away. He raised my head back to his until our eyes met again. His dark eyes gazed at me. They revealed the only reflection of either one of us in the whole mirrored elevator. It was my reflection. I loved seeing my eyes in his. There is something poetic about it. In all the people I'd ever seen, or killed, I'd never seen eyes anything like his. And definitely not like mine.

"Can you see your reflection in my eyes?" I asked him.

"Somewhat. But it's distorted by all the colors. It's actually quite beautiful. It makes me look like I'm in some colorful, abstract painting."

"I wonder how my eyes got like this. Have you ever seen eyes like these before?" I asked fluttering my eyelashes flirtatiously.

He snickered and looked away. His expression became solemn. It took him a minute to answer me. When he did he was hesitant to speak, "No, my Lamia. No, I haven't."

"The girl, Lily, was colorblind. She never saw her eyes how they truly are. Such a shame."

     Ashley Lauren Mitchell

"And until me, you had never seen how they truly are either," he said pointing to the elevator car's back mirror, with neither of our reflections in it.

He was right. If I'd never met him, I would never have seen the prisms that are my eyes staring back at me. This is me. This is my reflection. Lily's pictures could only show so much. The flashes of the cameras made her eyes glow and the colors weren't as breathtaking as they are in Nathaniel's eyes. That little fact made me appreciate looking at him even more.

He was grinning his devilish grin at me. I felt excited and nervous with this strong, tall figure towering over me. We stood looking at one another for a few seconds longer, then the elevator dinged to a stop.

We were on the top floor of the Palms Hotel. We walked into a club with colorful lights crisscrossing the ceiling, the floor, and the walls. Just like at Désirs Cachés. Humans were dancing all around us. My hunger grew when I smelled their sweaty bodies, and heard their hearts thumping louder than the music. I clenched Nathaniel's hand tightly in order not to clench one of them tightly. There were so many, I doubted Nathaniel and I could take them all. Or maybe we could. It wasn't worth the risk...of discovery, that is.

He led me to the outside patio. Fewer people.

                                    Ashley Lauren Mitchell

The fresh night air calmed me and the view distracted me. Dazzling lights across the city were shining against the darkness of the sky. It made me think of New Orleans, and the first night I went there - the lights, the people, the city. I looked at Nathaniel and said, "I'm going to kill one of these people if I don't feed soon. Why do we have to be around all these humans?"

"I want you to feel that way. Hungry, aching, feigning," he said laughing. "But you must control yourself for just a while longer. You have many years ahead of you. You need to learn to enjoy it. You need to learn to look forward to all the different things you must try in order not to feel ennui, the type of boredom that creeps up on you and consumes you. There are so many things you've never experienced. You can walk amongst humans and not always have to kill them...immediately. You should appreciate watching them, studying them, learning their secrets...and desires. Désirs cachés. Right?" He gave my cold body chills the way he'd said it. It was almost mocking but in a jesting way. How does he do that? He slithered behind me and whispered in my ear, "Now look."

He turned me and pointed my gaze to a couple sitting in a booth. They were a very attractive pair of humans. The woman had long, layered blonde hair, blue eyes, and dazzling jewelry. The man had brown hair, freshly cut and natty. He donned a

                    Ashley Lauren Mitchell

business suit and a platinum diamond encrusted watch. He was nuzzling her neck while she smiled and moved her arm back and forth underneath the table.

"What's so special about them?" I asked.

"Don't they look appetizing?"

"At this point, any human looks appetizing."

He laughed, "Patience Lamia. I promise you'll enjoy this. Just follow my lead. And act natural."

He told me to 'act natural.' But, if I did that, all of these humans would be dead by now. He ordered us two drinks from a badgering bunny. Of course, we didn't drink them. We held them and looked, I guess, 'natural.' Whatever the fuck that means. He also sent two rounds of drinks anonymously to the enamored couple he made me keep watching. He told the bunny to tell them it was 'on the house,' and he gave the girl a large tip. I would have given her a tip too. If you want to live another second, stay the hell away from us.

Humans were dancing and frolicking. A tedious half hour later, we stood, still watching the couple. They'd started kissing so vigorously, I thought they'd start having sex right there, in front of us and everyone. Once they'd guzzled the drinks Nathaniel sent them and were getting up to leave, Nathaniel grabbed my hand and we followed them. They were

                    Ashley Lauren Mitchell

kissing by the elevator when we saw them again. Nathaniel waited for them to enter their elevator car and push a button, before we entered the one next to them and he pushed the same one.

"We could just teleport there." I said.

"Always logical, huh?" He snorted. "We could just teleport everywhere. I could teleport two inches if I wanted to. But why not enjoy the rides, the walks, the levitating? Remember my Lamia, we have forever. We are in no rush. And besides, I wanted to be alone with you again in here." He was smiling suspiciously. His hands were in his pockets and he was standing eerily still. I turned and put my back against his chest and watched the lighted numbers of the elevator car descend.

Nathaniel leaned to my ear and whispered, "Have you ever seen humans having sex?"

The question caught me off guard. "No," I laughed. "Why do you ask?"

"Because," he took a deep breath, "You're about to."

"Oh am I? And why is that?"

He took his hand from his pocket and wrapped it around me. "When humans have sex, their heart rates increase significantly," he put his hand over my heart, "the temperatures of their blood increases significantly," he trailed his finger down my abdomen, and their vulnerabilities increase, significantly." He slid his hand down my pants and held it there. "They taste so much better when they are having an orgasm," he said.

"And how do you know that?" I asked teasingly.

"Experience. Like I said, I've been a vampire for a long, long time. And I was also a human for a long time. Some things, some cravings, just don't go away. Trust me, their blood is hotter than you've ever tasted, at their point of climax." Nathaniel rubbed his lips on my ear and whispered, "I want you to try it with me."

I smiled nervously. I wondered if he knew that I was uncomfortable with the idea of watching humans in the act. He kissed my neck and removed his hand from my pants as the elevator came to a stop. The horny couple on the car next to us stumbled, laughing down the hallway, supporting each other's weight. When they reached their room the man put the woman's back against the door and her arms above her head, pinning her body. He started kissing her on her neck and chest. He put both of her wrists in one of his hands and kept them held high. He used his other hand to grope her body. The woman's eyes were closed as she laughed and moaned with pleasure. The man reached in his pocket and pulled out a card. He slid it in the card reader next to the door. The tiny bulb above the door turned green. He let the woman's right arm fall and she used her hand to find the knob and open the door. They backed into the room as the door closed slowly behind them. Nathaniel looked at me and said, "Run."

We sprinted down the hallway and caught the door before it closed. As we were running, I felt a surge of excitement rushing through me. My feet were barely touching the floor. I knew what we were doing was just as taboo and forbidden as anything we'd ever done, but I also knew something about this time, was different. Only then, did I start understanding Nathaniel's thrill of the hunt.

We squeezed through the tight opening just as the door closed shut. The couple made it to the bedroom. Nathaniel crept close to the bedroom door and signaled me to go to the outside. "There's a balcony. Let's watch from there," he whispered. We closed our eyes and teleported ourselves to the balcony. Nathaniel stood behind me and whispered in my ear, "Watch closely Lamia. And when I say so, you take the female and I'll take the male."

We watched.

***

I'd never witnessed humans having sex before. There's something animalistic about the act. The sinful, carnal pleasure. The couple continued kissing passionately. The man rubbed his hands all over the woman's slender body. Then he put his hands under her buttocks to lift her from the ground. Her legs wrapped around his waist and she arched her back. He kissed her chest and neck as he unzipped her dress.

Still holding her, he moved closer to the bed and dropped her on it. She pulled her dress over her legs and threw it across the room. The man quickly took off his jacket and tie and unbuttoned his shirt. He'd just taken them off when the woman, now in only her black strapless bra, black lace panties, and black stiletto heels, reached for the belt of his pants. Her hands were shaking with anticipation as she unfastened the clasps. She unbuttoned and unzipped the pants with one single, fluid motion. The pants had not yet dropped to the floor before her hands were gripping the man's erection. She opened her mouth wide and shoved his throbbing member into it. His body trembled before going stiff. He inhaled and let his head tilt back as he moaned.

Outside, Nathaniel ran his hands up my back all the way to my head. He grabbed my hair into a ponytail with his hand and leaned my head to the side. He whispered in my ear, "See how his body is

                    Ashley Lauren Mitchell

paralyzed by the sensation? That's what happens when we feed from them. First, their bodies tremble from shock, and then relax with pleasure." Nathaniel's free hand slid across my stomach and went under my shirt. His hand was just as cold as my skin but it still made me shiver. The curve between his thumb and index finger cupped under my right breast and he squeezed it gently. My eyes felt as if they would close and my breathing became slower. He whispered, "Keep your eyes open Lamia. Watch."

The woman's head was bobbing back and forth as she sucked on the man ravenously. She pulled him from her mouth and licked him from the base of his penis, up the long, hard shaft. Her tongue flicked at the tip and the man looked down at her. They smiled at each other before she put him back in her mouth. She used one hand to grip and stroke him, and the other to caress his testicles. The man put his hands on her head and grunted with delight. He held her head still while he pumped his penis into her mouth. She gagged and he stopped. When she'd caught her breath, he inserted again and continued pumping.

After a while, he pulled her body up by her arms and unclasped her bra. He grabbed both of her breasts in his hands and began licking and sucking on her hardened nipples. He nibbled at one of them gently with his teeth as she moaned and ran her fingers through his hair.

Out on the balcony, Nathaniel's hand was still searching my body. Every time I tried closing my eyes to concentrate on the feeling he was giving me, he whispered, "Watch." So, I kept watching.

The man kept sucking each of the woman's soft breasts as he slid her panties over her buttocks and down her thighs. He pushed her to the bed and finished taking them off, sliding them over her knees and feet. His hands felt along the length of her legs and he bent over to kiss the insides of her thighs. He dropped to his knees at the foot of the bed. His lips kissed up to her hairless pubic area, as his hands gripped her breasts. Her body arched as she cried out in ecstasy. The man's head started moving in small circular motions as his tongue licked at her clitoris. Then his lips covered her vagina. His hands moved from her breasts, down her waist, to her thighs. He squeezed the soft meat of her buttocks and then slapped it. When he pulled his head away, a string of clear, slimy fluid went with him. He wiped his mouth with his hand and flipped the woman over on her stomach. He roughly pulled her up by her hips, onto her knees. She was on the bed on all fours, like an animal. He grabbed his firm, pointing penis, rubbed it and patted it on her butt cheek. Then, he slowly pushed himself inside her. She whined loudly and he groaned with her as their bodies tensed from the

Ashley Lauren Mitchell

sensation.

At first the man's motions were slow and tender as his hands caressed her body. He massaged the dimples in her lower back with his thumbs. He rubbed one of his hands up the center of her back and grabbed her breasts. He pinched her hard nipples and she gasped. He gripped her hips and grinded himself into her. After several minutes he pulled his penis out of her and look at it. It jumped up and down for a few seconds and then he watched it as he slowly penetrated her again. Many minutes passed and he started ramming himself into her and grunting fiercely. The woman screamed, "Oh God, Yes!" in delight. "Fuck me, fuck me!" she yelled. The man grabbed a hand full of her long blonde hair and pulled her body up on the bed. Her back was against his chest. The impact of his poundings made her breasts bounce wildly as the man clenched one in his fist. His force became faster and harder. Their bodies were glistening with sweat. Their breathing was loud and heavy. Their moans seemed in sync with each other. Their heartbeats were so loud it sounded like Nathaniel and I were standing right next to them.

Nathaniel whispered, "They're both about to come. Get ready."

My excitement had grown with every push the man made into the woman. I didn't know what Nathaniel meant by come, so I listened for his queue.

                                   Ashley Lauren Mitchell

Both of the humans' cries became louder…louder…louder…louder, and then the man pushed the woman away and quickly stroked his moistened penis.

"Now!" screamed Nathaniel, and in an instant we both had the squirming couple in our grasp.

As I bit into the woman's neck, her blood exploded from the puncture wound. It looked like a volcanic eruption. It sprayed all over my face. Her heartbeat was so loud and fast, I thought her heart would pounce from her chest. Her blood was so hot. When I slowed down and opened my eyes, I saw Nathaniel's face covered in the man's blood. The man's body looked like it was suspended in mid-air as Nathaniel held him by the spine. The man's face was frozen in shock, but it didn't look like a shock of pain or terror. He still looked like he was having an orgasm, like he was still in a moment of pleasure. My eyes travelled down to his penis that was still throbbing and jumping up and down. Semen was shooting from the tip of it. But as Nathaniel dried the man out, the white fluid lessened and dripped slowly to the floor.

When Nathaniel and I had both finished, we slung the empty bodies across the room; like the woman had done with her dress. Our faces were both drenched in blood. Nathaniel ripped my clothes from my body. I stood naked in front of him, like I'd done with my victims at Désirs Cachés before killing them. He pushed me on the bed and we began kissing madly. Our tongues pierced through each other's warm, slippery skin and we sucked the hot blood from each other. He straddled me on top of him. He grabbed my breasts and kissed his lips down my neck and chest. He kissed and licked my breasts. His teeth sank into the soft flesh surrounding my nipple and he began sucking it, pulling the blood from me like a nursing infant. My fingernails pierced the skin of his back. My head fell backwards as he suckled harder. After some time my body began getting weak. He pulled his teeth out. I grabbed his hair and leaned his head to the side. I kissed him and bit into his neck, sucking on him until I felt my strength return to me. We both sucked on and fed from each other for a long time. When we were both satisfied, we laid on the bed, panting...like lions.

Happy New Year, indeed.

***

"That was incredible!" I breathed, when I could finally speak. We were both covered in blood, as if a massacre had occurred in the room.

"Yes, it was," he said, huffing. "That's why I wanted you to experience it with me. You enjoyed it, right?"

"Yes," I laughed. "I'd always assumed that sex for humans was like feeding for us. But I had no idea it was so intense."

"Sex is one of the most pleasing and addictive drugs known to humans. It can cause them to do unthinkable things."

I looked over at him. He was still staring at the ceiling and breathing heavily. "Why can't we have sex?" I asked.

He paused, then looked at me, somewhat surprised. "Lamia, we cannot reproduce. Sex is for creatures to give life. We are vampires. We take life. Besides, our bodies don't have the same functions or reactions as humans, because we are not humans. Watching sex is fun, but we can't actually have sex."

I turned away from him and looked at the ceiling. Even after all the pleasure I'd just seen and experienced, his words pulled me back down to the preternatural state I was...suffering from. "We have the same effectors, why can't we use them the same way?"

"We just can't Lamia. Don't you get it? We're not just nocturnal creatures that feed on human blood. We are specters, ghosts, un-living things, whose only purpose is to kill. We kill to live and live to kill. That is our only true pleasure. Our only true purpose. Killing." His tone was harsh. He sat up on the bed.

I sat up next to him. His head was down and his eyes were closed. He looked more sad than angry. I let my eyes wander the room during our moment of silence. Not for the dead bodies across the room, but for us, the un-living.

He squirmed uncomfortably next to me. His voice was softer when he spoke again, "It's just that, that is how things are for us. We can't do many things reserved only for humans, like they can't do many things reserved only for us. We can't have sex, but we can teleport ourselves to any place on earth. We can't dream, but we can levitate. We have supernatural strength and power. We cannot give life, but we have, everlasting life."

It was that, what he'd just said, that made me remember my dream. "But we can dream."

"You're mistaken. That's impossible. Dreaming is for humans. Immortals do not dream. In all the years I've been an immortal, I've never had one dream."

"But I do. Well, I did. Not every night. It started the first night you touched me," I touched my cheek in the memory. I smiled, "It was about you and me."

"How? But? How?" He asked, dumbfounded.

					

"I don't know. You tell me."

"Well, what was it about?" He asked, turning his body to face me. He looked like an eager child about to be told the secret of magic.

"It's always the same." I looked at his naked body. "It reminds me of this moment, right now. You and I were naked, and we were in a land; a land like Africa, where you took me to see the lions. Animals were all around us. We were walking and talking. Now, I believe it was you that was doing most of the talking. Teaching me things. Showing me things. Just like you've been doing since the moment you finally came to me."

"Keep going," he said. I could see his anticipation, and it made me smile. Although, he wasn't smiling. His expression showed a hint of...worry.

"We were surrounded by trees and animals. We were...," I looked at him before I said it, then averted his gaze when he looked at me curiously, "humans."

"Humans?"

"Yes. And we were standing in the sun and it didn't hurt our skin."

He looked so confused. I'm certain I looked just as confused the first time I woke from the curious dream. He asked, "Then what happens?"

                    Ashley Lauren Mitchell

"Then we grew tired and laid on the green earth amongst the trees and animals. You fell asleep. I, for some reason, couldn't. Then, I heard a voice. It was a woman's voice. She was calling to me. I got up to follow it. But it isn't her that I find. Instead I find a humongous tree with fruit on it. It was the most colorful fruit I'd ever seen. It looked like my eyes. A piece of it falls on the ground. I pick it up and the voice tells me to eat it. She says if I eat it I would see her."

Nathaniel's face froze in shock. I noticed as I was telling the last part, he looked more and more uncomfortable. He no longer looked intrigued. He looked, I don't know, disturbed.

"What's wrong? What is it? Do you know what my dream means?" I asked.

He shook his head but didn't speak, as if what I'd just told him had stunned him in some way. He swallowed hard and I saw his lips part. He quietly asked, "So, did you bite the fruit?"

"Yes. I did. But nothing else happens. I don't see the woman or anything. It just ends."

He looked away from me. His eyes searched the room. Then he looked back to me. He stood and said, "Come on, the sun will rise soon. You need to get home."

"What's wrong? Was it something I said?"

His back was turned to me. He took a while to come up with an answer. "No. I'm kind of, overwhelmed, I suppose. I feel I need to rest." He turned and reached for my hand. But his eyes, the way he looked at me, almost made me uncomfortable. I began to regret ever having told him about my dream. I should have kept it all to myself. It seems that not even an immortal can decode the enigma that is my mind.

When we were back at Lily's I asked him, "Where do you go when you leave me?"

He smiled gently and said, "Home."

"Where is your home? Why haven't you ever taken me there?"

"One day I will," he said. He kissed my forehead with his warm, soft lips and disappeared. I wanted to find him but I had no clue where he went. I showered, got in my coffin and drifted to sleep thinking of where he could be and what he really thought of my dream. I hadn't dreamt it in a while. It didn't matter. It was always the same. So I didn't care if I'd ever have it again. Or perhaps I should care. Perhaps there was something I missed, or something I should have paid more attention to. But I cannot will the dream to come. I can only hope the next time I

                                   Ashley Lauren Mitchell

have it, I will remember to pay closer attention.

***

"Come, I want to show you something," said Nathaniel, that next evening.

Perhaps he was taking me on another sexual escapade. Last night was fun, just like he said. I took his hand and closed my eyes. When I opened them, we were standing in a domestic setting. It was a two-story house with expensive looking decor. I walked around the house quietly, carefully. The kitchen was spacious. It had shiny, silver pots hanging above an island. The cabinets were made of dark Oakwood and the countertops were black marble. The refrigerator was just as shiny as the pots. Everything was perfectly placed and meticulously cleaned. I could feel Nathaniel's eyes watching my every move, studying me in a skeptical way as I walked throughout the room.

The next room over was the dining area. The dining table was long and had ten chairs around it. Maybe this is where Nathaniel and I will dine tonight. It was covered in party supplies. The color scheme was light blue and white. Balloons of white and blue were tied to chairs. I rummaged through the mess and saw

　　　　Ashley Lauren Mitchell

a sign that read, 'It's A Boy!

"So," I said in a low voice and pointed to the ceiling, "Are we going upstairs?"

"No," he said calmly. "You can, but your dinner isn't home yet."

"O...kay...," I replied back curiously. I wondered why he said 'your' dinner and not 'our' dinner. I hardly ever knew what Nathaniel is thinking. But as long as he was with me, I felt ready for anything. "Is it something sexy like last night?" I asked, moving to him, putting my arms around his waist.

He wrapped his arms around me and put his chin on my head. He inhaled and breathed out, "No."

It was a brusque and singular answer. I thought he'd give an explanation, or at least say something else; but he remained silent.

Headlights flashed through the front windows of the house, as a car pulled into the driveway. One door of the vehicle opened, then closed. The headlights flickered as the car alarm beeped once. Footsteps. A jingly set of keys were being put in the outside keyhole. Nathaniel looked at me and put his index finger over his lips. He whispered, "Shhh, come this way." I smiled and tiptoed behind him. We hid behind a wall and watched the human enter.

                    Ashley Lauren Mitchell

A wide woman came through the door carrying small bags. She walked to the dining room and placed the bags on the table. She was bundled in a scarf, hat, coat and gloves. When she took off her coat I saw that she had a huge, round, bulge of a belly. She hung the coat, hat, and scarf on a hook and was walking toward Nathaniel and me. Or so I thought it was where Nathaniel and I were standing. When I looked around me, I didn't see him. The woman was getting closer. With each footstep I grew tenser. Closer. Closer.

She was removing her gloves from her hands as she turned the corner. When she saw me, she dropped the gloves and froze. Our faces both had the same confused looks on them. Nathaniel appeared behind her and grabbed her by the back of her neck. The woman's hands grabbed at his hands as she tried freeing herself. She was gasping and kicking her legs wildly. She was still staring at me. Eventually she tired and her body stopped moving. She was still breathing, but barely, and her eyes were wet and glossy. I looked at Nathaniel, then to the woman, back to Nathaniel, back to the woman, then to her belly, back to her, then to Nathaniel.

"What's this?" I asked him, gulping.

He smiled and said, "Your dinner."

I took a deep breath before looking back at

Ashley Lauren Mitchell

the woman. I couldn't speak. I just, looked at her.

Nathaniel asked, "Aren't you hungry?"

I didn't speak.

"I chose this as your dinner tonight. Come on Lamia, here," he said and pushed the woman to me. I caught her in my arms before she hit the ground. We stood up, together, looking into each other's eyes. I gulped again.

Nathaniel had said my name. This woman knew too much about my existence to live another day. I knew that if I didn't kill her, Nathaniel would, and he would be disappointed in me for not doing it. For a second the question of 'why?' crossed my mind. Why did he choose this woman? I'd never fed from a pregnant woman before. I don't really know why. I just, haven't.

"This is killing two birds with one stone," Nathaniel said to me.

I looked at him and remembered I'd thought that same quip when I killed Derek and Michael at Désirs Cachés many months ago. Nathaniel saying it at that moment, however, unnerved me.

"Or at least, it's killing two humans with one bite," he said walking to me and the woman.

                    Ashley Lauren Mitchell

His merciless tone sent chills through me. But not like the chills he'd given me last night. Who is this man? This thing? This...being?

"Go on," he said. "You know it will be done. So just do it already."

His voice seared through me. I kept looking at the woman. I saw it in her eyes. Her innocence. But I could not let her live. She would tell anyone that listened about Nathaniel and me. But, if I let her live she would say I spared her life and that vampires aren't bad creatures.

What am I thinking? She would also say that Nathaniel wanted to kill her and she was afraid of him. Humans would be more moved by that, than by a nice vampire, that spares humans. I realized I needed to protect Nathaniel's existence more than my own at that point. I looked away from her as I turned her around so that I couldn't see her pleading, teary eyes. I enclosed her gently in my arms and leaned her head to the side. My fingers brushed her hair from her neck. Her heart was pounding against my arm. She was sobbing but she wasn't fighting me; as if she knew it would be a losing battle. When my teeth entered her neck I squeezed her body softly, holding her while she shook. Then we both relaxed and closed our eyes.

At first, all I saw was black, a consuming

     Ashley Lauren Mitchell

darkness I thought I'd never escape. Then, I felt like I was falling, deep, down a suffocating hole. There was a light at the other end. I fell into it. When I reached it, I was submerged in cloudy water. It was bright red and orange. Vermillion. I turned over and looked up. Then I saw it. Like a god hovering over me. The baby. It was curled into a ball with its thumb in its mouth. The other hand was curled around the umbilical cord. Its eyes were shut tight. Its skin looked fuzzy, like a peach. The heartbeat was small and quick and loud. It was beautiful. I was so close to...him. It was a boy. His tiny leg twitched and kicked the tight skin that enclosed it. He was so warm. He kept getting warmer. I kept getting warmer. The fetus started kicking his legs and opening and closing his tiny fingers into fists. His heartbeat was slowing. He pulled his thumb from his mouth and looked like he was gasping. He curled tighter into a ball.

I opened my eyes. I didn't want to see that image any longer. The woman was already dead, slumped in my arms. I was now killing her baby...boy. I stared straight ahead avoiding Nathaniel's gaze. I didn't want to see his proud, satisfied smirk. When I heard the last little heartbeat, I gently removed my teeth from her neck. I rested my forehead on the back of her head. I wasn't sure what I was feeling. Perhaps I should feel how Nathaniel is feeling. Gratified. Satisfied. And since I'm the one that fed, maybe even better than he does. But I don't. I feel,

                    Ashley Lauren Mitchell

nothing...or something. Something I can't discern.

I picked the woman up and put her body on the couch. Photographs of her and a man, whom I presume to be the father of her son, were on the walls.

I looked at Nathaniel and said, "I want to go home."

"Didn't you enjoy your dinner?" he asked smiling sarcastically.

I didn't answer. I didn't know this, being. No. He is not a being. He is something else. A monster. Like me? Is he like me? Am I like him? Am I a monster...like him? I feel like a fucking monster. I closed my eyes tight, and teleported myself home, to Lily's house.

Nathaniel showed up a second after me. He grabbed my shoulders, jerking me. "What's wrong with you?" He barked sternly. "Having dreams? Having sympathy for humans? You are no killer!" I stared indifferently at him. "Lamia?" He yelled. I looked away. He shook his head and stepped back from me. "I wanted you to see what it was like to see life like that," he said.

"Life like what? One that hadn't even begun?" I snapped back.

"Lamia! You need to drop the fucking

                    Ashley Lauren Mitchell

sentimental bullshit! You are not supposed to be sympathetic and remorseful for the lives you take! You aren't supposed to dream! You aren't supposed to be like any human! So, stop dreaming! Wake up! Damn you!" Then he disappeared. His words cut through me like a knife. They'd stabbed somewhere deep inside me. It infuriated me!

I was so angry I started throwing things across the room. I threw a lamp through the wall. Then I screamed. I didn't know who I was more upset with; Nathaniel, for treating me the way he did; or myself, for being the way I...am. Maybe it was the fact that he'd left me without having the opportunity to retort to his tirade. And I still had no inkling of where he went. This only enraged me more. "Fuck!" I screamed. "I shouldn't have told him!"

I ran outside the house and into the sugarcane field. After running for miles I stopped and fell supinely on the ground. I caught my breath. The cool night air filled my lungs. I ran my fingers over the prickly grass. The moon was so big, and round, and white. It had a thick aureole around it that nearly overshadowed the stars. It was breathtaking. I calmed myself and tried thinking. A couplet from the poem came to my mind,

And so he rested, on the lonely ground, pensive, and full of painful jealousies.

                                    Ashley Lauren Mitchell

I wasn't jealous. Was I? Jealous of what? Humans, because they were humans? Or Nathaniel, because he could be so callous and unfeeling toward humans? The perfect killer. The perfect killer? What was happening to me? I've been with Nathaniel for so long now that I've forgotten how I was before I met him. I forgot about the life I had. Is that wrong that I miss it? Nathaniel would think it's wrong. Damn it! Where is he? Why is he being this way with me? I thought he wanted me? What's changed? What did I do?

Once I'd calmed myself and cleared my mind. I rose from the ground and ascended into the air. I glided over the sugarcane fields all the way back home...to Lily's house. My home. The wind blew through my hair. I looked into the full, bright moon. It felt even closer and I wanted to reach up and grab it. This was better. This, I do love; about whatever I am.

When I reached the house and landed on my feet, I was empty. I didn't want to think or feel anything for the rest of the night. I crawled into my coffin, locked it, and shut my eyes. I did think, or hope rather, that I would dream. But the dream didn't come.

<u>Chapter 18</u>

Nathaniel was enraged when he teleported back to his dark, lifeless plantation home in Haiti. He paced the halls and rooms, trying to calm himself. He feared the time had come to do what he was destined to do all along. He wasn't ready to give Lamia up. He didn't want to spend eternity alone, and he knew if he gave her away, he would have to. He also feared that Lamia would dream again and that the dream would reveal something he wasn't ready for her to know. He was confused as to why she could dream, and he couldn't. He hadn't had a dream since he transformed, changed, turned into whatever he was. When he slept, he only rested. His body could not respond during the rest, but he could still hear everything for miles. Every heartbeat and footstep a human made, he heard, but was under inertia's spell, unable to move or react. A living death.

He needed answers. He needed to know why these things were being shown to her. He needed to know why his first touch triggered her dream sequences. He'd done all he could to corrupt her; to turn her from all love for humans. He wasn't human. She wasn't human. What good is it to love a human?

                    Ashley Lauren Mitchell

He knew better than that. He learned that the hard way when he'd killed every human he'd ever loved. His uncle. His mother. Tati.

He hadn't meant to be so harsh with Lamia, but she was making it difficult for him to do what had been instilled in him to do. He'd gotten rid of Lamia's humans, in a sense. Or at least had them held captive. He wasn't sure if he should kill them just yet. But he was starting to feel that if he could not have her, no one, especially not any human, could have her either.

His body was weakening. One of his trained house attendants came to him and assisted him as he prepared to settle in his sleeping chamber. He couldn't stop thinking of Lamia's dream. He wanted answers. He wanted Lamia with him. He wanted...rest. His body was shutting down. No answers would come tonight. But he knew how to get them. At long last he knew it was time. He knew he must find Onaya.

***

The next night, he woke and dressed immediately. He knew Lamia would be waiting for him in the living room of the house in Donaldsonville, but he had to get the answers he needed. Tonight, he had to make her wait.

                    Ashley Lauren Mitchell

Once he was ready, or as ready as he could be for this meeting, he closed his eyes and teleported to the last place he'd seen Onaya, the Sistine Chapel in Rome.

The building was dark and quiet. Unusually dark and quiet, as if it had been deserted for years. It was so quiet, that he heard his hard footsteps on the floor as he walked the length of the chapel. He sensed something strange. A presence. He looked up at the magnificent painting. He rose to the ceiling. When he was inches from the figure, he reached his hand out and touched it.

"Oh, Lamia." He whispered.

"You've fallen in love with her, haven't you?" Asked a voice. A voice which he hadn't heard in nearly two hundred years.

He looked down. There she was. Still cloaked and hooded in her dark purple covering. Sparkling jewels. Bright red hair. Still beautiful, captivating, and graceful. Those familiar, colorful eyes, that he'd come to love.

Onaya lifted slowly toward him as she spoke again, her voice resonating throughout the building. "Yes, you have fallen in love with her. I can see it in the way you gazed upon her countenance on the ceiling. She is beautiful, isn't she?"

                    Ashley Lauren Mitchell

Nathaniel didn't speak. He remembered, in that instant, that Onaya could read his thoughts. He'd forgotten how vulnerable it made him feel, someone reading his mind, like a book.

"Yes, Nathaniel. Like a book." Onaya laughed.

"You know why I've come," he said with aggravation.

"Yes. And I know why you have not brought my daughter with you. You've fallen in love with her. Just as I thought you would. But to think you can keep her from me? Tisk Tisk." Onaya wagged her finger at him, playfully, knowing he was far from being in a playful mood.

Nathaniel, again did not answer. Onaya moved closer to him. "How long Nathaniel? How long do you think you can keep her from me?"

He stared at her with purpose and said, "You told me she's angry with you, that she wants nothing to do with you. So, it isn't me that's keeping her from you. And just what makes you think she will want to be with you now?"

Onaya's smile slowly faded. Her colorful eyes began glowing and the red pigment took over the orbs. She matched the color of fire as her anger kindled. "Now you listen to me! What are you trying to prove? I gave you, I encrypted you, with specific

                    Ashley Lauren Mitchell

instructions, and you have completed them. Now your time with her has come to an end. You should feel fortunate enough to have had as much time with her as you've had, as much time as I've allowed you to have. You've only taught her and showed her, what I've let you teach and show her. Don't get egotistic and forget your place. You will bring her to me."

"Or else?"

The smile reappeared on Onaya's face, "I could destroy you if you don't realize it. But that would be too easy, and not as much fun as this. I still have something you want. Something you've wanted from the beginning."

"And that is?"

"Answers, my dear boy. Answers to your existence. Answers to all your questions about your parents. Answers you've wanted your entire life," she circled around him, forcing him to turn his head to follow her, "And death." She laughed.

"You've promised that before. I don't believe you."

Onaya pulled a small black book from her cloak. "This is your mother's diary. She lived a great deal longer than your father, so she has much more information about him. And about who you... were."

                                    Ashley Lauren Mitchell

Onaya tilted her head to the side and gazed at Nathaniel. Her eyes mocked him as she said, "And she never even told him you existed."

"You're lying!"

"Perhaps. But you'll never know until you bring me my daughter." Onaya tossed the booklet to him. He caught it and quickly thumbed through the pages. He landed on a page with the date 1818, October 6, on it, in his mother's handwriting. He attempted to read as much of the text as he could. He'd read just enough to intrigue him before, in a cloud of smoke, the booklet disappeared from his hands. "You can have it back when you bring me what I want."

Nathaniel took a deep breath. He understood he'd never get that book from Onaya without giving her what she wanted first. It was all happening faster than he could comprehend. He regretted coming to find Onaya. He simply was not ready to be without Lamia. "One more night with her, then I'll bring her to you."

"You're making a deal with me?"

"Yes."

She pondered. "Fine. One more night." Onaya reluctantly agreed. "And that is all. Now go to her. I have a feeling she's taken initiative in completing what you two started last night." With a bright flash of light, Onaya vanished.

Once Nathaniel lowered his arms, shielding his eyes from the bright glare of Onaya's exit, he wondered what she meant when she said, "Completing what they started yesterday." He was left to sift through the maze that was his thoughts. He looked at the painting on the ceiling. He felt anguish rush through his hard, cold body. He felt trapped. Cornered. Without options. He had to give her up. One more night was all he had to show her all she wanted to know about him.

Thoughts of eternal loneliness crossed his mind as he turned his pitch black eyes from the ancient, but still beautiful portrayal of his beloved. He was cursed. In that moment, as in so many other moments in his existence, he realized he was eternally cursed. Cursed with immortality. A lonely, companionless immortality.

<u>Chapter 19</u>

January, 2006

When I stepped from my coffin the next night, Nathaniel wasn't there. This is the first time he hadn't been present when I woke in months. After last night, however, I wasn't sure I wanted to see him. Who was he that he could speak to me like that? Better still, who was he? The only things I knew of Nathaniel were that he was a vampire, his host was born in Italy, and he's cruel and unfeeling, I guess, as I should be.

Was that all there is to it? Is that all there is to being a vampire, like me? Yes, like me. He is like me. A killer. Like me. It's not like I have any of Lily's memories. It's as if she and I are just two different souls that shared the same body. Her body.

What if Nathaniel is the same way? What if he really doesn't have any recollection of Nathaniel's, the human's, past? Maybe, I shouldn't have pressed him so. Right? I'm so confused about everything. Where is he tonight?

I walk into the living room. He's not there. I walk outside. He's not there. I allow another hour to pass.

Ashley Lauren Mitchell

He's still not there. I must have really upset him last night if he's not...here. I replayed last night in my mind. I saw images of the immaculately clean house, the round woman walking through the door, her frightened and sodden eyes, and her...baby. Then Nathaniel's raging rant. How did he become so cruel? Why does he want me to be so cruel? And why can't I be?

Another hour passed as I sat waiting in the living room, flipping through the poetry book. I'm not sure why I was drawn to this book, like it possessed the answers to my questions. Had this book been for me? The card in the envelope read, For Lamia. Did that mean this was my book? Was it here before I'd become a vampire or did it appear somehow when I came into existence? The poem with my name as the title, was it written for me? Does it have something to do with who I am? Who I was? A past life perhaps? What does it all mean?

The only conclusion I came up with, is that even though I'd finally met Nathaniel, and we'd spent so much time together; he is still a mystery to me; still the mystery being he was before I ever knew his name.

Should I be grateful to him for teaching me so much about what I am and leave it at that? What if he gives up on me if I don't continue to be the killer he is teaching me to be? I don't want to lose

                    Ashley Lauren Mitchell

Nathaniel. He's the only, thing, I have. No one other than him must know the loss and loneliness I'm feeling.

Wait, then again, there is.

I close my eyes and teleport myself to a place where loss and loneliness are the only things one person must be feeling.

The house feels empty. The house is empty. I walk around the corner and see the blue and white balloons still tied to the chairs, and the party decorations still spread across the table. I walk into the room where I took the woman's life, along with that of her child's. I stare at the pictures on the wall; the pictures of the couple. They look so happy. And I destroyed that. All because of Nathaniel. Why did he have to tempt me? Why did he have to choose her? Why did he want me to take that innocent baby boy's life?

Then I hear a car pulling in the driveway; or more like screeching into the driveway. The car door slams shut. Keys jingle frantically as one is jammed into the keyhole. The knob turns. The door opens. A man, the man from the pictures, stumbles through the door holding a glass bottle. His face is streaked with tears. I hide behind the wall I hid behind last night as he languidly plops onto the couch. He starts speaking but his speech is erratic, discursive. Then he yells, "Dana? Dana?" As if she were about to come running

Ashley Lauren Mitchell

to his bellow. He sobs.

He pushes himself from the couch, holding himself up by his fingers on the coffee table. Once he can stand, he drags his feet to the dining room. I watch him rub his hands over the blue and white mess on the table. He screams, "Dana? Dana!" and brushes his arms across the table swiftly, knocking the materials to the floor. He keeps screaming. He takes the nearly empty bottle in his hand and shatters in on the table. He takes a piece of the sharp, broken bottle and pops the balloons tied to the chairs. He throws the piece of glass and bangs his hands on the table, cutting them on the small shards. He screams with pain, both emotional and physical.

Instantly, the scent of his blood fills my nostrils. I start breathing slowly attempting to control myself from rushing to him. I keep watching. Just like Nathaniel instructs me to do, "Watch."

The distraught man runs to the kitchen sink and rinses the blood down the drain. He takes a cloth from a drawer and wraps in around his injured hands. He goes back to the living room and plops back down on the couch. He puts his wrapped hands on his head and weeps.

The smell is so strong. He is so close to me. For some strange reason I feel like I'm in my room at Désirs Cachés, watching one of my soon to be victims from behind my curtain, before making my entrance. At that very moment it hits me. This man is my next victim. Killer or not, he smells like my victims do. He is only...human. I shouldn't want to feel sympathy for this man, and I won't. Nathaniel would be proud if I took this innocent man's life, without having to be forced. I need to start being the killer, the vampire, I am supposed to be. Right? Here is my chance. I must prove to Nathaniel, and to myself, that I can kill even the innocent, on my own. It is only survival...of the fittest. I shouldn't feel bad about that. I shouldn't feel anything but satisfaction. This is what I'm supposed to do. So, here goes.

"Bonjour monsieur," I say.

The weeping, startled man quickly takes his hands from his face. He looks around and says, "Who's there?"

I wait only a moment before I step around the corner and say, "Call me Lamia."

"What are you doing here?" he asks, sniffling and wiping his tears and mucus away on the towels he has wrapped around his injured hands. He is so innocent that he isn't entranced by my eyes, like a killer would be. He's as conscious as his intoxication will allow. It's surprising enough that he can see me, talk to me, and understand me, in the state he's in. He stares at me for a moment, taking my countenance in. He focuses in on my protruding teeth as I smile at him. He gasps. "It was you. You killed her. Didn't you?"

"Yes. It was me. I killed her."

The man jumped to his feet and ran at me. I could only expect such a reaction. He tripped over his own feet after a few steps and fell to the floor. He pushed himself up again and tried swinging one of his bloody fists at me. I stepped backwards and he missed. His whole body spins as he stumbled into a wall; which actually helps him catch his balance. He then pushes himself off the wall and attempts another swing. This time when I dodge and he spins, I catch him and hold him tightly, resting my head on his back, since he's much taller than I am. He struggles, but he is not be able to free himself. I hear the frustration in his breathing as his anger turns back into depression. He cries and screams out, "Dana!"

Of course this wouldn't be easy, for either of us. His knees buckle and I let him fall back in my arms. I picked him up like a baby and placed him on the couch. I'm fighting the urge to feel, anything, for this human. Although he doesn't deserve any of this, I cannot think of it. I watch him as he closes his teary eyes. I gently rub his sweaty forehead and place a cold, tender kiss on it. He opens his eyes, staring at me as I pulled away from him. He looks me in my eyes and says, "I know what you are. You're a demon. That's what your name means. That's all you are.

                    Ashley Lauren Mitchell

Lamia."

It was the first time I'd ever told any human my name and they knew the meaning. I was taken aback. He knew. He was right. That is all I am. A vampire. A demon. That is what my name means. That is what I am.

I looked away from him and stared straight ahead for some time. I wasn't looking at anything in particular. Just looking, wanting to empty my mind. Then I remembered what I must do. I turned back to him and said, "I'm here to end your suffering. I know you feel lost and alone. I know you want your pain to end. I can help you with that. I can send you to be with your family."

The man begins sobbing again. "Dana. Is that what she wanted? An end to her suffering? Did she suffer?" He says as tears stream down the sides of his face.

"No. She did not suffer. And neither will you." I climb on top of him, placing my knees on his arms, restraining them. I grab the back of head and pull it up. His eyes continue watching me. I cannot help but feel pity for this poor, beautiful, innocent human. I rub my hands over his face and through his hair. I rub my thumb across his lips. I lean to him and kiss him. He smells of strong alcohol. His lips are soft and warm. I feel him excite a little beneath me as our tongues

         Ashley Lauren Mitchell

touch. I catch his slippery pink tongue in my sharp teeth and begin sucking. He accepts me. His body quivers for only an instant and then he relaxes. I move my knees to let his hands free. He wraps his arms around me in an embrace and shuts his eyes a final time. When his arms fall from their hold around my body I know that he is close to the end. I slowly pull my teeth from his tongue and lift his limp, almost dead body up to a sitting position. I straddle him and place his head near my heart. I hold him close as I listen to the last beats of his forlorn heart. It stops. I can only hope he finds his family in the afterlife.

When I'm home again and I've taken a shower, I sit at the dressing table in Lily's room to collect my thoughts. That man loved his family. I can feel it coursing through my veins. His memories are in his blood, in my blood. I cannot stop them from running through my mind. I feel him. I feel all of them. Dana, their baby. They're all in me. He was right. I am just a demon. How could I do something like that? A whole family? That must be the explanation. I am death. Evil, incarnate. That poor man wanted to die. He wanted me to kill him. He wanted to be rejoined with his wife and their son. He loved her like...like...like Diamond loved Uncle Tony. A love that you would rather die than live without. I'd never experienced that kind of love. Had I?

Yes. I believe I have. I believe I felt love like that

                    Ashley Lauren Mitchell

for Diamond and Uncle Tony. It didn't matter that they were humans. I'd been with Nathaniel for so long and so often, that I hadn't taken the time to really grieve for my loss. I did love them. And, I lost them. Lately, I haven't given much thought to where Uncle Tony or Diamond could be because of how it might make Nathaniel feel about me. But they won't ever come back to me again, will they? I won't ever see them again, will I? My humans. They taught me how to love. And they, are gone. All I have is Nathaniel. And he isn't even here.

I miss being with Diamond and Uncle Tony, at the club. Existence seemed so much easier with them, at the club. Things made more sense when I was with them, at the club. They made me feel special and important, and like I belonged, at the club. With them at the club. At the club. At the club? That's it! I never went back to the club. This whole time, I hadn't even thought of it again. That's where they became everything to me. Why wouldn't they try going back there? Why hadn't I? It's worth a shot.

I teleported to Désirs Cachés. It's been just over four months since Hurricane Katrina ravaged New Orleans. Most of the city is still abandoned. Bourbon Street is as quiet as it was the days leading up to the storm. The only thing that exists in the club apart from rats and roaches, is the horrendous, moldy smell. Wooden boards are still barred on the doors and

                                        Ashley Lauren Mitchell

thick cardboard covers the mirrors. Debris covers the floors. I step over it and walk up the stairs. I apprehensively step into my old room.

It looks surprisingly intact. My coffin isn't here, but I knew that. Uncle Tony had it taken to a funeral home the night we evacuated to Donaldsonville so that if someone saw it in this room they wouldn't think, whatever they would think from seeing a coffin in this room. The bookshelf is empty. The velvet curtain is tattered and hanging loosely from the rod. The rug is, destroyed. There's no saving the rug this time. Other than this being an expensive rug that cushioned steps and muffled noise, I can't understand why I was so fond of this rug. It is a beautifully designed tapestry. Uncle Tony told me that it belonged to Lily's mother, Nahdia, years ago. I know that can't be the reason I adore it. I don't know if it has sentimental value to me or if it holds some unfathomable message. The last thing I need is another riddle to solve. I walk away from the rug. The shower is covered in mildew and bugs. It wasn't too far from this spot where Sable first caught me naked and off guard. The sneaky little minx.

I crossed the hall to Diamond's office. She'd taken most of the items she had in here back to Donaldsonville with her. One small black and white photograph of Marilyn Monroe lies on the floor under dust and dirt. The last time I was in this room I stomped

                    Ashley Lauren Mitchell

out of here like a spoiled brat because I wanted to feast on...I can't even remember the human's name. I've had so many since then it becomes difficult to remember them all. Oh yes, operation: kill Samuel Hicks. That was his name. Samuel Hicks. The one that got away. I'm sure if he's not dead by now, that he keeps on killing. Why is it easier for humans like him to kill their own kind than it is for me to do it? And I need to do it.

I step out onto the balcony. The cool night air welcomes me. I look up at the dark blue heavens. The sky is cloudy but the stars are still glowing through the gray, billowy clouds. A flood of memories rush through my mind. I close my eyes. A cold breeze whips past my face. At first I think it is just because it is winter in Louisiana. That is the explanation. I close my eyes and I feel it again. I open my eyes. It is. It's Nathaniel. He's standing on the other side of Bourbon Street, staring at me. I take a deep breath. I can feel my nostrils flaring. I don't want to see him tonight, and I definitely didn't want him to see me here. I can't think of an excuse to give him for being here other than the truth; that I wanted to be here because I was looking for my humans. I closed my eyes and opened them, and I was standing in the living room of Lily's house in Donaldsonville. He appears behind me a second later.

"You weren't here," he said.

 Ashley Lauren Mitchell

"You, weren't here," I retorted.

"I thought you'd wait for me. I was preparing to take you somewhere tonight. It took a little longer than expected."

I didn't want to believe him. I didn't want to give in and fall for his charms and then have him blow up in my face during his time of chagrin. "Well, I didn't wait for you."

"I can see that," he said. He was still frigid from hunger, so I know he hasn't been feeding. I can tell that much.

"Where did you go before Désirs Cachés?" He asks.

"To eat," I looked at him sternly, "the same place I ate last night." I let him think about where he'd taken me last night; the house, the woman, the baby. I let it all register before asking him, "How did you know I was at Désirs Cachés?"

He looked away from me. "First I went to the woman's house not far from here. The one you called, Diamond. You used to go there and wait for her. When I didn't find you, I came back here and thought of the only other place you might go. The one place you'd spent more time than anywhere."

I didn't speak. I supposed I was satisfied with his

Ashley Lauren Mitchell

answer, but he still didn't give an explanation for where he'd been. I didn't want to have to verbalize the reasons why I didn't wait for him or why I was at Désirs Cachés. I didn't want him to hear from my lips how much those two humans had meant to me. How much they still mean to me. I could say that I went back for some other reason, but I was tired of lying. Would he know I'd be lying? Did he already know I'd been lying, keeping my feelings for them to myself? I don't want him to lash out at me for my foibles as a vampire; and then disappear without giving me a chance to speak. So, I just, didn't speak.

"Lamia, I haven't been honest with you?" He said.

This sparked my interest. I had to speak. "Oh, really? About what exactly?" I asked curiously, and not putting much effort in disguising my vexed attitude.

"About, hardly anything. Especially about who and what you are." He moved to sit on the couch and rubbed his fingers through his hair. He sighed.

I fought the urge to sit next to him. I stared at the back of his head. I arrested my vehemence seeing that he already appeared to be incriminating himself. He was being tormented by his conscience, and he didn't need any reprove from me. "So are you here to tell me?"

     Ashley Lauren Mitchell

"Yes." He answered quietly. "Even though it means that I will lose you."

"Nathaniel," I gave in and sat next to him, "I won't die just because you tell me the truth."

"I didn't say that you would die. I said that I would lose you."

"I don't understand. Why would you lose me?" I asked. He turned away. "Nathaniel, I thought we were supposed to be the same, you and I. You are the only thing I have left in this world. I won't leave you."

"You will Lamia."

"I won't," I put my hand to his chin and turn his face to mine, "I promise."

"I have to tell you the truth first," he said and jerked his face from my hand, "and then you can...decide."

"Nathaniel, I..."

"Do you love me?"

"What?"

"Do you love me?" He repeated.

"I...I don't know. I'm not sure I know what love is,

					

Nathaniel."

He looked at the floor and thought for a moment, "Yes, I agree," he said despondently. "But I do believe I love you."

I looked at him dubiously, "How do you know? I mean, we're vampires. How would we know what love is?"

"When I see you. When I hold you. When I touch you. When I say your name. It makes me feel...something on the inside of me. It has to be love."

I didn't know what to reply to that. How can he be so sure that what he's feeling is love?

He asks, "Do I make you feel differently inside?"

I thought for a moment before looking at him. His dark, deep, black eyes, reflected the confusion on my face. I wanted to describe how I felt for him, but I was uncertain that I could find the words like he'd done. So, I said the first thing that came to my mind. "Nathaniel when I am with you I feel full, satisfied, like I just fed. I don't feel alone, or like I am the only one like...me. I feel...something, something good." I also wanted to tell him that I felt these same feelings when I was with Uncle Tony and Diamond, but he wouldn't understand. They are humans. He is not.

A smile graced his face. His mood lightened

                    Ashley Lauren Mitchell

and he leaned into me, putting his cold lips against my warm ear, "Let me take you to my home," he whispered.

"Your home?"

"Yes. I've never taken you before. But tonight...it is time."

My mind and heart raced. I could feel the excitement stirring in me. He was giving me something I've wanted for so long; to finally go to his house. To finally, after all these months, see, learn, experience more about him. I can hardly contain myself, "Then let's go." I said, happily.

He took my hand and stood, pulling me with him. He whispered, "Close your eyes."

<u>Chapter 20</u>

When I opened my eyes, Nathaniel was standing next to me, holding my hand. He was already looking at me, smiling a delicate smile. I gave a smile back. Then I looked at my surroundings. We were standing in a forest of tall trees. The moon was just above us, shining brightly. Nathaniel began walking, gently pulling me with him. As we walked along the path, he remained silent.

After a few more minutes we came to a clearing with a less traveled road. It led to the steps of an enormous mansion. There were dimly lit lanterns on each side of the large double doors. The pillars were taller than the trees. It was the most beautiful house I'd ever seen.

I looked over at Nathaniel. "This is my home," he said.

"Where are we?"

"Haiti. I've lived here over a hundred and fifty years. When I left Italy, I lived in Africa for a year or so. Then I came here. I travel often, but this for me, is my own corner of the world. This is where I return to.

　　　　　　　　　　

Where I call my home."

"It's beautiful."

"Come. Let me show you inside."

We walked up the steps leading to the doors made for giants. Nathaniel let go of my hand so that he could use both of his to open the doors. As the doors opened we looked at each other. He was giving me a proud, boyish grin. One I could not help but laugh at. Then he said, "Welcome, Lamia, to my home."

The room was glorious. The floor was marble and made an echo as I stepped on it. The designs in the floor were like hand painted tapestries. There was a huge staircase before me with what appeared to be gold hand rails. Smaller pillars with angelic carvings held the room up. The ceiling curved above us with a sparkling chandelier hanging in the center. It looked big enough to stand inside of. It had thousands of crystals glowing in it. Round rainbow orbs covered the walls and floors. The entire room was covered in them. The chandelier was the most astonishing gem I'd ever seen. It looked like a thousand stars gathered in one light fixture. It was the first room in the mansion and I was more than impressed. It was magnificent. To my left was a room with a large fireplace and long, antique sofa and chaise. To my right was a long curved hallway. I

                    Ashley Lauren Mitchell

couldn't wait to see where it led.

He was standing behind me, hands in pockets, watching me revel in his home's splendor. "Do you like it?" He asked.

I turned to face him. I gave him a smirk and squinted my eyes. He knows his home is grandiose, and that it would be hard for anyone to deny its grandeur. He laughed at me, then walked to me taking my face in his hands. "Come on," he began, "this could take all night if I let it. I have so much to show you...before I can enjoy you." Taking my hand in his again, he guided me up the staircase. He was telling me the story of his travels from Italy when I got distracted.

I hadn't noticed before, but there was a man at the top of the staircase, next to the railing. His back was turned to us. He had on a crisp, white collar shirt and black pants. He stood attentive and resolutely still. I tried to get a better glimpse of his face as we passed him but Nathaniel pulled me too quickly. He kept talking. I looked at him and smiled, listening to his voice and watching his dark eyes glisten in the dimly lit mansion.

The floors upstairs had plush carpet. The walls were lined with paintings and sculptures. We passed so many doors, I lost count. Then he paused in front of another set of double doors. He walked in front of me,

            Ashley Lauren Mitchell

putting his back on the doorknobs. He raised his eyebrows and his eyes widened with excitement. "I know you will love this," he said as he turned and opened the doors.

I followed him in the room. Beethoven's Piano Sonata No. 14 in C Sharp Minor was softly playing on a phonograph. I could hear the light crackling sound, giving it a classic, anachronistic sound. Nathaniel spun around, arms stretched to the high, colorful, stained glass ceiling. Books...thousands of books, neatly filled the enormous book shelves that extended all the way around the room. It was stellar. His library seemed to have more books, than I could read in a lifetime. Even my infinite, immortal lifetime.

"This...is..." I was lost for words.

He laughed a gratified laugh. "I knew you would love it. It took many years to collect all these books. Many are the originals." He lifted from the floor and rose to a high shelf. He took one book from the thousands and brought it down to me. "This is Alexandre Dumas's, Le Comte de Monte-Cristo. I stole it. It even has his signature in it." The book's cover was frail, and looked like it would fall to pieces. "I've read this book so many times," Nathaniel said with satisfaction. He hurriedly put it back in place on the case.

I couldn't stop my smile as I walked, then

　　　　　　　　　

floated around the room. After minutes of letting me explore, Nathaniel called my attention. "Let's go. There's more you must see."

As we left out, I saw another man dressed in a white collar shirt and black pants walking down the long hallway. He had dark skin, as did the other. He moved almost like a robot; calculated, mechanical movements. He closed the doors that Nathaniel and I walked out of. Again I tried to see his face, and again I was pulled along to the next destination.

"Nathaniel?" I finally asked, "Who is that?"

"Oh, that's just one of my house attendants."

"House attendants?"

"Yes. Do you see the size of this place? And being that I am hardly here as often, or only here to slumber, the house attendants are responsible for the upkeep. They live here with me."

"So you have slaves?" I asked sarcastically.

He chuckled. "They're not slaves. They're not even... Well, they're not...human."

"What? Are they vampires, like us?

"No. They are, how do I say? Failed experiments."

I raised an eyebrow and leaned my head to the side. I'd never heard something like that before. "So what are they...exactly?"

Nathaniel pressed his lips together. I could still see the tips of his sharp fangs, peeking through the corners of his mouth. He whistled. After a few seconds I heard footsteps coming toward us. They were hard, heavy, like that of a vampire.

"Lamia, this is Jacque."

The footsteps were upon us. The man turned the corner of the hallway. He was a massive black man with an even blacker tuxedo. He moved as the other did, mechanically, only this one had authority. He stepped to us like a soldier, ready for war. The closer he came, I saw that his eyes were white, almost completely white. He said nothing. He just walked up to us and stopped. With him being this close I could see the thin blue veins across the white of his bulging eyes. His face was sunken in, just a thin layer of skin covered him. His hands were large and strong, with long, blackened nails. He didn't look directly at us. Instead his head was held high and his eyes were directed to just above our heads. He looked like a moving corpse. A well-manicured, moving corpse. He could have been a statue the way he was standing, but his breath was so heavy. He groaned with each one. They were hollow, deep breaths that sent chills through me.

 Ashley Lauren Mitchell

"Jacque is the head house attendant. He runs this place. He was here long before I got here."

"But if you've been here for over a hundred and fifty years..."

"Yes. He's also, one of my experiments. Failed experiments. I wanted to make him a vampire, it just, didn't work out for him. Or for the others."

"Others? How many do you have?"

"I would say at least twenty."

"Twenty? And they all look like him?"

"Some are female. But, yes. They all had the same kind of reaction to the experiments, so they all are like...this."

"They're undead?"

"Yes. They're undead. They can perform only simple, menial functions. They're shells. Controllable, empty shells. It wasn't my intention to make them as such, but once it happened I figured I'd find use for them."

It was one of the eeriest things I'd ever heard, or seen. I did my best to hide my stupefaction. I, at that moment, could not understand the abomination in front of me. I refused to look at Nathaniel. I believe he wanted me to be impressed, but I...wasn't. If anything, I was confused. I continued looking at the zombie-like creature in front of me.

Nathaniel kept talking about his conquests, "They can live a very long time. But they can be killed. They are frail. One crack on the head and their done. They must be taken care of. I take care of them. Or, rather, allow them the freedom to take care of themselves."

"What do they eat?" I found myself asking.

"I'm glad you asked. It is time to make our way to the dining area. It's time for us to eat." He grabbed my hand. "Come along Jacque." He called.

I looked back. Jacque was slowly pacing behind us, as if he could only go one speed. I shook my head in bewilderment. As we made our way to the dining area we passed a door under the stairwell. I paused, and broke my hand from Nathaniel's grasp. I felt something deep inside of me. Something I haven't felt in nearly a year. Nostalgia. I know because I hate the yearning feeling, the longing for times past. Times that one cannot get back. I stared at the door, transfixed. What is it? What is it about this door? What is it?

"Lamia?"

"What's behind this door?" I asked, immediately.

Nathaniel took a deep breath. He hesitantly walked to me. "It's just a coat closet. See." He said as he opened the door. Inside were a few boxes on the floor along with a few hanging coats and jackets, including Nathaniel's leather jacket. "Are you okay? What's wrong?" He asked.

"I just, I had the weirdest feeling, like I could feel..." I realized what I was about to say sounded ridiculous, so I didn't say it. But I felt a presence. A presence I haven't experienced in such a long time. But that's impossible. What I'm thinking. What I'm feeling. My mind and body are confused. My humans can't be here. That is the most absurd thought. But why am I thinking it? Why? Why do I feel this? And why do I feel it here and now?"

"Lamia?" Nathaniel said, "Hey? C'mon," he said, almost in a whisper, and closed the door to the mysterious coat closet.

He tenderly, but almost apprehensively, took my hand, leading me away from the door. I saw him look back at it himself. Did he feel it? Something? Anything? What did I feel? What was that? This trip to Nathaniel's home is becoming more confusing than I imagined. Is that why he never wanted to bring me? Because I'd be like this? Perhaps he didn't think I could handle it. I think I'm proving him right. I do my best to ignore the feeling, whatever it was, that I just felt and keep pace with Nathaniel.

                    Ashley Lauren Mitchell

In the luxurious dining room two regal thrones had been set before a table. It resembled some French monarch setting. The great chairs faced toward the dining area with the backs to the walls. Nathaniel and I walked to them. He acted as a gentleman and led me to my seat first. After I sat, he seated himself in the other seat and called for the house attendants. Two white eyed creatures brought four naked, bound, blindfolded and gagged humans in front of us.

They shivered as they huddled together, sniffling, and sobbing. One by one the house attendants removed the blindfolds. Two men. Two women. They turned to face Nathaniel and me. They all froze. These were not just some innocent humans. No. They were murderers and thieves. A sudden relief and desire surged through me. It seemed so familiar. The sinful receiving justice. My hunger peaked. I need this. I stood, unwittingly and walked to them. Nathaniel watched me. I walked closer to them. The house attendants backed away as fast as their defunct bodies could take them. I walked in front of each one of the humans, looking into their eyes. I wanted to see their evil deeds. I wanted to see them committing their sins. One of the couples murdered their own baby. The other couple, robbed a drug store, killing the clerk in the process. I wanted the couple who heinously killed their own child. "These two are mine," I called to Nathaniel.

Ashley Lauren Mitchell

"As you wish."

I untied each of them and sent Nathaniel the two that I didn't care to have. I looked at my couple. I wanted to be disgusted by their act, but how could I be? Only nights ago I'd murdered a baby, the most innocent of all things. I put my hands on one of their heads. Then I trailed my hand down to their heart. How could they do such a thing? Their own flesh and blood. Their own innocent child. I'm certain the rage that began rising inside of me was directed at my own action. But these were my scapegoats, my whipping boys. I will punish them for all of our transgressions. I wanted to reach in their weakling bodies and rip out their hearts but I chose the cleaner, traditional way, and simply drained them from their necks as the other watched.

Once they were both sprawled on the floor, dead, I looked back at Nathaniel. He was a warm, rosy hue. I know I have the same glow to my skin. I walked back to him and took my seat.

"Now for entertainment." He said and called for his house attendants again. They came to remove the bodies and to pull back a theater-like curtain. It reminded me of my curtain at the club.

There was a long dining table, covered with an even longer blue table cloth. Nathaniel motioned a finger, and the submissive attendants pulled the

                    Ashley Lauren Mitchell

lengthy material, revealing a number of human bodies lining the table. They were all face down and nude, wrapped in chains, and gagged. They weren't squirming or writhing to free themselves. They were either drugged or had reached the point where the body stops fighting and succumbs to the fact that resistance to death is futile.

Nathaniel yelled something in a language I couldn't understand. A loud, low grumble vibrated throughout the house. He looked at me and smiled. I heard a rumble of heavy footsteps. The house attendants were all running to where we were sitting in the dining room. There were at least twenty of them. And apparently they can move faster, when coerced by Nathaniel. All of them had wide white eyes, with small blue veins running through them, glowing against their dark skin. They all groaned when they exhaled. The room was filled with their heavy noises, vibrating against the walls. They stood attentively, waiting for Nathaniel to give his command. He was staring at me. At that moment I wasn't sure what he was going to do or what was about to happen. He said, "I enjoy watching them eat. It reminds me of animals." With a simple snap of his fingers the feeding frenzy began.

Like a pride of hungry lions, the soulless creatures gathered around the ten bodies on the table. I could see tear drops falling from the terrified

                    Ashley Lauren Mitchell

humans to the floor, along with other bodily fluids. In an instant the creatures were devouring the entangled bodies. The humans were squirming and trying to scream as they were being ripped apart. I watched the house attendants eat ravenously, like hungry beasts. Blood, limbs, organs, and entrails flew into the air and splattered on the table and floor. Two of the creatures snarled at each other showing their sharpened black and bloodied teeth, quarrelling for the human flesh. Then one moved to a different human, ending their feud. The white shirts they each had on, were soaked in blood. The horrendous sight held my gaze, I wasn't disgusted. On the contrary, I believe I felt aroused. When I could look away, I glanced at Nathaniel. He was smiling and breathing heavily. He looked at me.

Although his eyes were completely black, I saw the intensity in them. It looked like a trigger had been pulled inside of him. He rose from his chair and stood over me with his hand under my chin. He leaned down to kiss me. Then his hand stroked my breast. He pulled me up to him and kissed me again. This time I felt the warmth and yearning from his body. He started kissing on my neck and chest. I stole a look at the massacre across the room. Nathaniel pulled my head back to him and kissed me again.

He led me to an upstairs bedroom. It had no windows. There was only a large bed. Large enough to fill the room. Our eyes adjusted to the darkness. Then he took me. I felt my clothes being ripped from my body. I felt his hands groping, massaging, and squeezing me. His warm, wet lips and tongue explored me. His teeth sank into arbitrary nooks and curves of my aching body. He nursed from me again. He had me orally please him, and bite down into his erection, sucking the blood from him. Mimicking the humans' sexual act. I felt no shame in it. I only felt pleasure. While lying on top of me I could feel him trying to insert himself inside me. We both wanted it, more than anything we wanted it. I know that we both envied humans at that moment. He tried over and over, but he could not go inside. He stroked anyway. We both were frustrated, exhilarated, but frustrated. Jealous that humans could have intercourse and we, the dead, could not. We continued drinking from one another. It's all we could do.

Once we'd had our fill of the frustrating-satisfaction, we walked, naked, to his sleeping chamber. A coffin, nearly the size of the bed we were just in, was open, waiting for us to climb in and settle for our slumber. I feel like I am levitating, but both feet are touching the ground. The night turned into an experience like no other. I want more. I want every night to be like this with him. We have all eternity to imbibe each other. All eternity together. I laid with my back to him. He had his arms around me, holding me

                    Ashley Lauren Mitchell

close to his warm body. His warm erection rested between my thighs, throbbing to go inside. Nathaniel sniffed me and kissed me softly on my neck as he whispered, "This Lamia. This is what I love. I love you. I love this. I only want you."

His words sang over and over in my head. It was a beautiful song. I let it sing me to sleep, wrapped tightly in Nathaniel arms.

***

Nathaniel had his arms wrapped tightly around his beloved. He whispered in her ear as she fell asleep. He nuzzled and sniffed her neck, reveling in her bloody scent. He wanted it to last forever. He tried staying awake as long as he could, devising a plan to keep her there with him. He listened to Lamia's breathing while she was sound asleep. What was he to do? How can he break the deal with Onaya and get away with it? He realized he was willing to sacrifice the truth about his father to keep Lamia. He only wanted her. He couldn't resist any longer. He drifted to sleep without an answer.

The next night, as the sun descended into the earth, Nathaniel and Lamia lay curled together, locked in Nathaniel's large coffin. Nathaniel lingered

          Ashley Lauren Mitchell

in the darkness of his mind, while his body rested. He thought of so many things, but only one mattered. Lamia. Keeping Lamia. As he forced himself to come up with new ideas, his mind wandered to a place it hadn't been in two centuries. It wandered into a dream.

As his body lay still, his closed eyes began twitching. His mind was falling, deep into the abyss. He saw her, his Lamia. She was gloriously adorned in a flowing white gown. She looked angelic. The stars, the moons, and the sun were behind her. Her light outshone them all. She was reaching for him. She spoke, "Nathaniel? Why did you curse me?"

"What? What do you mean? I'd never curse you. I love you."

"You broke your promise. You promised to bring me to her. Because of you I am trapped forever. Why did you break your promise? Why? Why?"

As she spoke, her glowing white light became red. Flames shot up behind her. Her eyes turned red, her hair turned red, her skin became pale. Then he heard the laugh. The deep, menacing laugh. It was familiar, but it was not Lamia's laughter. Onaya. Her voice was loud and threatening as she exclaimed, "You broke your promise Nathaniel! Do you think you will get away with it? Don't try to get any bright ideas. Bring her to me! Bring me my daughter!"

                              Ashley Lauren Mitchell

With a start, and beads of sweat on his nose and forehead, Nathaniel forced open the coffin lid. He wanted to scream. He panted, attempting to catch his breath. She knew. Onaya knew he was trying to plot against her. The first dream he'd had since becoming a vampire, was no dream at all. It was a nightmare, a warning. She knew how to find him. She had a hold of him. It was no point in trying to outsmart her. He felt defeated. He put his face in his hands and ran them through his hair. He entwined his fingers and rested the palms of his hands on the back of his neck.

He felt small, chilly fingers on his back. It made him feel hopeful and even more defeated at the same time. There was no way around it. He hoped that maybe once the meeting with Onaya was complete, he could have Lamia back. Hopeful. But what if the meeting meant he'd never see her again? Defeated.

He looked out into the darkness of the room, then to Lamia. "Lamia, I have to tell you something."

She looked back at him, "Yes. I know." She said, with regret in her voice.

***

 Ashley Lauren Mitchell

She called me Lamia.

I still heard Nathaniel's voice. His sweet words chiming in my ears. And for some time all I saw was darkness. A darkness so blinding that I wasn't sure if I was really there at all. Then there was light. The sun shining through my eyelids. The sun. My dream. I am having my dream.

I was in the garden with Nathaniel again. Naked and human. He and the animals were sleeping next to me while I watched. Then I heard the voice of the woman and got up to follow it. It all started coming back to me. The details of the trees, the grass, the animals, the sun...the voice. I kept in the direction of the mysterious female voice.

I came upon the colossal, sky darkening tree. As I walked under its overhanging branches, and looked up, the colorful fruit sparkled against the darkness. They were like jewels in the heavens. One of the gems fell from the tree. The voice again; enticing me, luring me to take a bite.

"It's alright, my Lamia. Take a bite."

Who is she? Why do I want to listen to her? To hearken to her voice?

I take a bite. The fruit. It is delicious! It tastes so...familiar. My eyes close, as I delight in the sensation. The succulent juice travels down my

                    Ashley Lauren Mitchell

esophagus. I chew the pulp. It is so soft, yet crisp. I sigh. I open my eyes and look at the fruit, ready to take another bite when I see the thick red liquid oozing from it. Blood. It is not juice, it is blood. I drop it. The deliciousness turns bitter. I feel an aching in my abdomen and I fall to the cool, damp grass. I began writhing in pain. I let out a terrible scream as my body began transforming. Transforming. A white and red light forming in front of me. A face. It speaks. "It is time Lamia." The light fuses into a face, one that I can barely make out, but I know that it is the woman that lured me. Her hauntingly familiar voice. "Nathaniel must bring you to me! It is time! If he does not bring you to me, it will be you that will suffer for it!"

She disappears in a flash, a burst of light. My eyes closed. My body stopped moving. I was numb, completely numb. Everything was quiet. Dark. Still. Suddenly, I felt something. I could move my arms again. I touched my hand to my mouth. Fangs. I have my sharp fangs again. A vampire? I tried sitting up but I couldn't. My feet. I couldn't feel my feet, I couldn't feel my toes. I couldn't move my legs. Eyes closed. I moved my hand down my body. Once I reach my hips, I feel...what is that? My...legs? Where are my legs? What are these? Scales?

"Time to wake up Lamia," she said. "Nathaniel must bring you to me. It is your destiny."

When I woke, Nathaniel was sitting up in the

          Ashley Lauren Mitchell

coffin next to me with his hands on his neck. I could tell he was distressed by something. Did she speak to him? What is happening?

I tenderly place my hand on his back. He turns to me and says, "Lamia, I have to tell you something."

From his tone, I knew. I knew she had spoken to him during the night. Whoever she is, she is in both of our heads. I looked at him regretfully and said, "Yes. I know."

<u>Chapter 21</u>

"We don't have much time." He said. "She expects me to bring you to her tonight."

"Who is she? What's going on?"

"I don't know why I thought I could keep this from you. Keep you from her. Keep you for myself."

"Nathaniel?" He was pacing the room, rummaging for garments. He seemed to be talking to himself, not to me. I called to him again. "Nathaniel?" He stopped pacing.

He took a deep breath. "Her name is Onaya. She told me she's your mother." He started laughing. But it was an eerie laugh of disbelief. It was on the verge of sounding delusional.

"My mother? Did she tell you that during your slumber last night?"

"No," he huffed. "I've known her since before I became immortal. She is the reason I'm like this. She is...is..."

"Is what?"

　　　　　　　　Ashley Lauren Mitchell

"I don't know what she is. And I don't know what she wants with you or why, now, she's chosen to come for you."

"I'm so confused."

"I have to take you to her. I'm not sure what she will do if I don't. But I don't trust her. Not for a second."

"You've known about this all this time and never told me? This is the first I'm hearing of her? And now I must go to her?"

"Lamia?"

"No. I will not. I will not go to her."

"Lamia. Please. You don't understand. I made a deal with her."

"You're right. I don't understand. Why would you make a deal with her for me? What do you get out of this?"

"She was just using me to get to you."

"So all of this? The time we've spent together? It was all because of her?"

"No." He said. His voice was quivering. I'd never seen or heard him so uneasy. He paused from getting dressed and came to me. He took my face in his hands and leaned his forehead against mine. "No.

Lamia. I want you more than she does. But I know she is more powerful than I am. I don't know what she wants with you, but I don't want to provoke her anger. She says she's your mother. I don't believe her. But I don't have a choice. We don't have a choice. We can go to her together. I won't leave you. I promise." I'd never seen him so scared, so desperate. "Lamia. I've done some truly unforgivable things to you for her. For all the wrong I've done, for all the affliction I've caused, I, I'm..."

"Stop. It's okay," I silence him. His uneasy demeanor unsettled me. I didn't want him to feel that way. Who was this woman? What right had she to do this to us? "I had my dream again. I know she is the one who beguiled me to taste the fruit. You are right. We must go to her...together."

We dressed. As we passed the dining area downstairs, I saw that the house attendants had cleaned every drop of blood from last night's entertainment feast. Jacque languidly followed us to the front door, groaning heavily behind us. Nathaniel grasped my hand. "I want to look out at the night sky with you one last time before we go." He said. Two zombie-like creatures opened the doors. The warm night air. I breathed it in. The stars, the full, speckled moon. It all looked as if it were the last time I'd ever see them.

As we walked out the doors and took the first

step down the stairs, I felt that nostalgic feeling again. The one I'd felt when I was in front of Nathaniel's coat closet. It was pulling me back by my left hand. I felt it pulling harder. I turned my head. I may have been mistaken but I thought I saw one of the female house attendants pointing to the coat closet. Her mouth was open like she was trying to speak. Her dead, white eyes glared at me.

Nathaniel tugged on me, breaking me free of the invisible hold. I turned to face him as he spun me to him, putting his arm around my waist. I tried getting one last look at the house. The doors were shutting. The dark-skinned, white-eyed vision vanished. I looked back at Nathaniel. His pitch black eyes stared into me. My reflection, one of confusion, and concern. The expressions that were on both of our faces.

What happens now?

Nathaniel kisses me one last time. Passionately. We relish in each other one last time. I leaned my head back and looked at the moon. It is shining so ominously. Nathaniel punctured my neck with his teeth. I felt him softly sucking and kissing, moving down my chest. He stopped. He breathed a deep, fearful breath. He stood up and pulled my eyes away from the hypnotizing moon to his gleaming dark eyes again. Our faces were solemn, and full of regret and longing for times we would not see together. Is it over for us? Will he be another of those that only makes

                    Ashley Lauren Mitchell

me feel the dread of nostalgia? My lost.

As he caresses my hair he says, "Close your eyes."

Slowly, hesitantly, while holding on tightly to one another, we both closed our eyes.

***

When I opened my eyes I was standing in the middle of a tall building. It felt familiar. All along the walls were angelic nude bodies, seraphs, and other heavenly figures. I let go of Nathaniel's hand and I began walking the length of the nave. I knew this work. This magnificent, profound creation. I know I know this.

"Lamia?"

I heard his voice echo off the walls but I didn't respond. I was entranced. I felt, light, airy. I felt...dizzy.

"Lamia?" I heard him say again. I felt my body swoon as he rushed to catch me from hitting the ground.

"What was that?" I ask, perplexed. I felt as weak as did that time I hadn't fed in days many

 Ashley Lauren Mitchell

months ago.

A loud, thundering noise struck the ceiling. Bright red light shone through the windows at the top of the building. There was a heavy rumble beneath our feet. We balanced each other. Then the knock. It was the doors, someone, something was attempting to burst through the entrance of the building. Black smoke fumed through the cracks. A white light, like sunlight broke through. I squinted my eyes from the glare as the doors swung open. A figure appeared in the middle of the light. It started moving gracefully toward us. As it got closer I could tell from the silhouette that it was a woman. I saw the long, flowing red hair, whipping like a flag in the wind. I couldn't see the bottom half of the woman because of all the black smoke. I squinted harder. She kept moving closer. She moved toward us with such ease and elegance, as if she were simply gliding. When she was close enough to see in detail, I saw that she had long, wavy, red hair. She wore sparkling jewels, and a dress so dark purple, it looked black. She looked like a queen from some medieval time. Majestic. Enchanting. And at the same time, demanding of attention.

Nathaniel stepped in front of me, shielding me from her. She laughed. Her laughter filled the span of the large room. It made the walls tremble. Nathaniel was right. She was, she is, powerful. Just her laughter

                          Ashley Lauren Mitchell

could make the whole structure quake.

"You always make me laugh." She looked at me as if she were seeing a ghost. She smiled at me then looked back at Nathaniel and said, "You've done well." She tossed a small black book to him. He almost fumbled it as he grabbed at it and clutched it in his fist. "Now, tell Lamia that that is all you really wanted. Tell her that you gave her up for that insignificant piece of writing.

"It isn't true," Nathaniel protested.

"But of course it is. That's your mother's diary. All of her secrets. Your father's secrets. And even some of your own secrets, all in that one little book. And to you it's worth getting rid of my precious Lamia?"

"Stop it! You're lying."

"Oh Nathaniel. Am I? Am I lying or perhaps just exaggerating? And I'm sure you have some lies of your own you wouldn't want revealed. Am I right?"

"I didn't know her then. When you came to me. I didn't know I would fall..." Nathaniel turned to me. "Lamia, there's something I need to tell you." His face was sorrowful. "The night of the hurricane months ago, I..."

Before he could finish, some invisible force jerked him away from me. He hit the wall, bounced

                              Ashley Lauren Mitchell

off and landed, hard against the floor. I looked at the woman. She was looking at Nathaniel with fury and vexation. "That is enough! You've served your purpose." She yelled. "You've had your opportunity to come clean and say your truths. Now it's time to say your goodbyes. You have your stupid book. It is time for you to go now Nathaniel."

"No! Wait. Please." He said reaching for me.

"Nathaniel?" I whispered.

The woman looked at me sharply. Her eyes were glowing bright red. Her teeth. She had teeth like mine. The longer she looked at me, her glowing eyes started to dim. They changed. They looked like, mine. The colored orbs gave me pause. Her countenance softened. She...smiled, a very slight smile. "Oh, my dear girl. I do apologize. I forgot you feel something for this, being. But he must go. He was only meant to lead you to me. Your destiny is just beginning. His has come to an end."

Nathaniel and I looked at each other from across the room. I wanted to run to him. To embrace him. I wanted to be next to him. To relive everything we've been through together. He tried getting up to run to me but she was holding him there across the room. I didn't want her to hurt him. I felt myself becoming angry but I knew neither Nathaniel nor I could best this creature.

                    Ashley Lauren Mitchell

"Lamia!" He shouted. His voice strained with desperation.

"Goodbye Nathaniel," she said. And with a swift wave of her hand, Nathaniel disappeared.

"Nathaniel." I whispered again.

"Don't worry, my dear. He's home. Safe and sound. He, is supposed to be there," she came closer to me, "And you are supposed to be here."

I closed my eyes. I tried teleporting to Nathaniel's house. I couldn't. I tried teleporting anywhere but there with her. I opened and closed my eyes repeatedly, trying to get away. Every time I opened my eyes, I was in a different spot in that same building. I was trapped. I couldn't escape.

She laughed. "Where are trying to go?" She began walking toward me. I backed away. "Do I frighten you?" She asked mockingly. I didn't answer. Before my eyes she vanished. In a split second she was behind me, whispering in my ear, "Don't be afraid of me, my daughter."

I turned. It was the first time in...ever, that I'd been...afraid. This is what fear is. This uncomfortable, heart surge. The discomfort in my bowels. I turned quickly and backed away from her.

"Lamia. Please." She said, circling me. "Look

around you. Look at all the beautiful sights before you. Do you even know where you are?"

The question distracted me. I had forgotten that I was standing in the middle of an architectural piece like no other. I took my gaze from her and looked around me. As much as I wanted her to tell me where I was, I wanted to know something else more, "Who are you? What do you want from me? Why am I here?"

"I am called, Onaya. But I'd prefer it if you called me Mother."

"Mother?" I said with disbelief.

"Yes. Lamia. I am your mother."

She looked at me as if she were waiting for me to be thrilled with the fact. "And you," she began again, "are so much more than you realize. Have you never felt you were meant for more than what this world has to offer you?"

I didn't answer her, but in my head I was screaming, 'Yes!'

She smiled at me as if she knew what I was thinking, then said, "The time has come. You are needed now."

"Time for what? Needed for what?"

"Lamia, you were created for a special purpose. You're more than just a killer. You are an angel. An angel of death."

"What are you talking about?"

"You do know what 'The Great Unveiling' is? Don't you? He did tell you of this, didn't he?"

"What? The Great Unveiling?"

"The Revelation? The Apocalypse?"

"No. I...," I was so lost. I had no idea what she meant.

"He didn't give you the right book."

"Book? What book?" I ask bewildered.

"Come." She commanded as she ascended to the ceiling. Before I could tell myself to rise, I was already lifting to the ceiling next to her. It was not by my own will. She was pulling me to her. When we were only feet away from the top, she stopped me. She turned me to her. I could not help but feel some strange connection to her as I looked into her eyes. Her colorful eyes, like mine. It must be like looking into a mirror. She smiled a fond smile at me. She lifted her hand to my face. I flinched and recoiled, holding my head back from her. But she, by her unseen might, brought it closer. She was restraining me, with her invisible force. Her hand touched my face. She sighed. "My beautiful girl. It is I that has waited so long to see you. To touch you." She slowly took her hand away. Her eyes fluttered as if she were blinking a tear away. "Look at this painting," she said as she looked again at the ceiling.

The hands. I've seen this before. The picture that marked the page in the poetry book from Lily's house. The hands that do not touch. "I've seen this before," I announced unwittingly.

"Yes," she snorted. "Such an iconic piece. The hands of God and his creation, Adam." She said it with mild contempt in her voice, as if having to say it angered her. I glanced at her as she looked at the painting. Her eyes glowed red for a couple of seconds before she closed them and shook her head; perhaps shaking away a memory. "And this one?" She said as she moved away from me. This time I followed of my own autonomy.

This one I had never seen before, but there was something about it. Something so familiar. Something so... Then it hit me. The naked bodies of a male and female. The enormous tree. My dream. The painting reminded me of my dream.

But the one in the middle? The one wrapped around the tree. I've never seen before. It was some sort of half-human. I couldn't figure out when or if I had ever

   Ashley Lauren Mitchell

seen it before. I was entranced. I stared harder. It was the creature's eyes that began to glow first. Her head turned to me. Colorful eyes...like mine! She started moving, animated, brought to life, from her place in the painting. Her outstretched arm reaching for me. I gasped and backed away, toward the ground. My eyes were wide with astonishment. Her serpentine body unraveled from the tree trunk. Suddenly, she had me. I struggled with her, but she had me. Her hand grasped my neck. "No!" I shouted, to no avail. Onaya watched from where she floated nearby, and refused to help me. "No!" I screamed again. Both of the half-human's hands were at my throat, strangling me. Once my mouth was open she sucked herself inside, like a vacuum. I grabbed my chest. I could feel her moving inside me. Squirming and suffocating me. Then everything went black. I could feel myself falling to the floor of the building. Further and further I fell. Finally, before I hit the cold hard ground beneath me, there she was to catch me. The woman who called herself my mother. Onaya. She was under me, holding me like an infant. I heard her speak through the constraining darkness I was in.

"Yes, my daughter. It is time to dream. All will be revealed. Tonight, you will know your destiny. Sleep, my princess. Gain your rest and wisdom, for our time has come."

She stopped speaking, but I felt her warm

Ashley Lauren Mitchell

hand against my cold skin. Then I felt, nothing. I was drifting into slumber. A slumber I could not fight. A slumber I could not wake from. A slumber.

<u>Chapter 22</u>

Nathaniel was groggy when he woke on the marble floor of his plantation home. He pushed himself up on his knees. He steadied himself against the floor. Once he'd gained full consciousness, he tried teleporting back to the Sistine Chapel. Each time he tried he ended up in a different room of his mansion. He let out a defeated cry and punched a hole in a wall. He paced the floor before falling again to his knees.

After a few moments Jacque walked up, stood over him, and grumbled. Nathaniel looked up at him. Jacque was holding the black book that Nathaniel was sent back with. It looked even smaller in Jacque's large hand. Nathaniel reached up and took the book. He put his back against the wall and stretched out his legs. He leaned his head back and started banging it gently against the wall. "Lamia..." he whispered. He looked down at the book in his hands and wondered if anything written in it was true, and if so, how would it appease his curiosity now? He was alone, again. How could reading this now, make him feel any better? He sighed.

He thought for another minute before opening it. If it is true, and this is his mother's diary, he needed to prepare his mind to accept whatever was written in it, not that anything could be changed.

Midnight. He had hours of time left of the darkness. He would be with Lamia right now, hunting, exploring. Anything with her was better than anything without her. If it weren't for Onaya, would he have ever even met Lamia? Was his purpose really served and he was never to see her again? Questions loomed in his head. All he could do was think in his loneliness. He hadn't felt this lonely in so long, he found it hard to mentally adjust to the stillness of it.

He flipped through the pages of the diary. His mother's handwriting. He closed the book. He realized he hadn't eaten all night. Although he didn't much feel like feeding. He stood. Jacque followed him to his coffin. When he reached it, he stared at it. Not even four hours ago he and Lamia had shared his sleeping chamber. He started wishing he had brought her sooner, then they would have had many more nights here. He decided to retire early that night, considering he would not be much entertained with the world. He removed his shoes and stepped into his coffin. Jacque, waiting patiently, took his master's clothes, exited the room, and closed the door behind him.

Nathaniel was left with himself and his mother's book of secrets and hopefully, truths. He closed the lid of his coffin, allowed his eyes time to adapt to the darkness, and opened the book again. He flipped until he saw a word that apprehended his interest. The word, lonely. He began reading there.

Isabella Jones' Diary

1805, October 1

I am so lonely. I haven't seen William in nearly a week. He is still out with his comrades celebrating. Although I admire him for his diligence, I'm left alone, with only my parrot, my books and my thoughts to keep me company all day. I wish Mother wouldn't have forced me into being with him. He's an intelligent man but he lacks romance. His words are callous and rehearsed. It makes me uncomfortable. I'm tired of being blamed for us not having any children, when I don't really believe it is all my fault. I cannot talk to him anymore. When we married, I was so young, and he was so, interested. Time has not been kind to us. He used to talk to me. He used to tell me his dreams and aspirations. Now, he barely speaks to me at all. I have tried many times to seduce him. Perhaps then we may have a child. But he turns away. I am lost. I am lonely. I long to go home, but William will not allow it. He wants to keep up this

　　　　　　　　Ashley Lauren Mitchell

facade of a loving obedient wife, and a hardworking, doting husband. I must, as his wife, submit to his wishes. We smile in front of others, and make merry company, but it is so silent in this house when it is just the two of us. I can hear the echo of our footsteps. When he looks at me, it is as if he is looking past me or through me. I do not know who or what we are anymore. And I do not know what to do.

1805, October 5

Last night, William stumbled into the house. How he made it home, I can only imagine. He was mumbling tales of going to war. I know that he had been training for this, but now, to have him leaving? I am not sure how I feel about it. He is hardly ever home anyway. He doesn't talk to me. The people that he wants me to associate with, invite me places, but he gets angry when I go. Am I wrong for only feeling slightly saddened by his imminent departure? In a way, I want him to go?

What am I saying? He is my husband. Of course I don't want him to have to risk his life. Even if it is his choice. William is not a bad man. I believe I am bad for him. If I had to choose, knowing then, what I know now, I would not marry him. Or any man for that matter. I am useless to a man that wants a family and children of his own. Instead, I would travel, socialize,

                    Ashley Lauren Mitchell

and learn. There are so many things I want to do and I feel I never will.

William would not miss me, not like I will miss him. If anything, I believe he feels the way I feel. Trapped. Confused. Cheated. And perhaps even angry. I cannot blame him. I can only hope that he will say goodbye to me before he leaves.

1805, October 16

William has not written to me. He, just as I thought, left when I was sleeping. Without a goodbye. Without a kiss, or a hug. We have grown so distant, having the span of the oceans between us. Why would I expect him to write? I cannot give him what he wants most on earth. A son to carry on his name and legacy. He needs to be away from me. Even so, I wish him safe travels, and slow returns. A few of the other soldiers' wives are having a dinner so that we may 'grieve' together. I am not sure I will be able to empathize. However, I should go. What would they think if I didn't? What will they think if I am not sad enough? Time to switch from having a false smile in front of them when William was here to having a false frown now that he is gone.

 Ashley Lauren Mitchell

1805, October 29

I received a letter announcing William's death today. The printing was so official looking, as if it's looking that way would make the news irrefutable. I will admit, days ago I felt something, a pang perhaps. I knew something had happened. Something terrible. I would not have imagined he would be dead. When I was reading the letter, I felt the same pang in my stomach. He is gone. He will not be returning to me. He didn't deserve death, and at such a young age. I regret so many things now. But mostly, I never got the chance to tell him that I loved him. Despite all the things we'd been through, I still loved him. He was my husband. I cared for him, even though he might have stopped caring for me long ago. Now, I must decide if I will return home. Rudolph and Mother know nothing of this yet. Mother will want me to go back to Italy. However, I think, for a little while, I will stay here and make sure all of William's things are taken care of. I look at them differently now. They hold such sentimental value, that to simply leave them or discard them would be cruel. I need time to process all of this. And it is something I will do alone.

1805, November 3

Today was the ceremony for our fallen soldiers. It was such a bittersweet occasion. It was hard not to

                Ashley Lauren Mitchell

shed tears. There were many wives, most with children, that also fell victim to this tragic fate. What is to become of them now? Some will return home with their parents. Some will stay and remarry. But as for me...I am still undecided. I wrote to Mother. I am awaiting her letter. I just do not know if I want to return to Italy. There is so much that I haven't seen here. Colonel Green and his wife gave their condolences at the funeral. They are very genuine. It is hard to find people like them. They have invited me to dinner almost every night this past week. They told me that if there were anything I needed, to let them know. I have also dined with some of William's comrades. We reminisced, and for the first time ever, I was able to talk with them at leisure, not as William's wife. We laughed. We cried. We all miss William. But as bad as it sounds, I am glad that he was only there in spirit. One of the men had lost his left leg in the war. Others had some less serious injuries. They talked of their war wounds. They were all so kind. I believe I will stay a while longer in London.

1805, November 11

Mother's letter has arrived. I failed at my attempt to persuade her that I want to live my own life for a while. She says I am only twenty-six, still young enough that although I did not have children for William, I still may be able to for someone else.

                                    Ashley Lauren Mitchell

Mother, I know, has my best interest at heart, but I cannot suffer through the heartache of not giving another man a child. I will stay here, in London and continue to make friends, and go places, and learn things. I feel...free, now. I must hold on to it. William's stipend is substantial. And it should last me for a while. I will take advantage of this freedom, to Mother's disappointment. But after all these years, my life is my own now and I will live it as I please.

***

1815, July 31

I am at Clifden house with Lady Eleanor. She and her husband, Baron Cornelius, have invited me to a private, social gathering. It has been rumored that Donal, Cornelius's older brother, has set his eyes upon me, since his last romantic affair did not work out of course. In all the ten years since I've had my freedom, I have yet to find a man that I would spend the rest of my life with. I have become irritated with the acquaintances I've acquired. They all drool and swoon over me. Enraptured by my wit in conversation, and enthralled by my beauty. I feel this, Donal, may be no different. Honorable? Yes. A gentleman? Yes. But I know they are only after one

                    Ashley Lauren Mitchell

thing, to use me for their physical pleasure. It is usually the portly or homely ones that are more confident and aggressive. I grow weary of these associations. Mother too has grown weary. She is still angry with me for not returning home. And for not giving her any grandchildren. Rudolph never married. I assumed as much. He was always so timid with women. And he's so fond of his work, I doubt he would let a woman distract him from it. I miss them, Mother and Rudolph. It is well passed time for a visit. But what will I have to go back to? To go back for? If not only for a visit? I have done so many things and have met so many people. I live such a pampered and lavish life, that I feel guilty for not really having done anything but become William's widow. Is it wrong that I live so well? I am usually surrounded by people, but even then, I feel alone. I have not found a compatible companion. One that sparks my interest and imagination. And when I think I have, his affinity is for other men, and we are only friends. I suppose I'd never start feeling like this again. Trapped. Trapped by this lifestyle. And perhaps maybe, just maybe, I want something more. Perhaps, even, someone, more.

***

1817, May 9

Today I became so frustrated with Donal and his jokes, that I excused myself from his group of friends at the breakfast table. I needed fresh air. I needed to get away from the madness of the crowd. I was in the woods, collecting my thoughts, when I saw a young man lying on the ground. He was the only other person out there. When I called to him, he sat right up, nervously. I believe I disrupted his alone time. His eyes and face were red from crying. I, being the curious, social butterfly that I am, asked him what was wrong. After some gentle coaxing, he told me that he was a poet and that his first publication had done poorly. He told me that a man called Lockhart had essentially behooved him to stick with his day job of being an apothecary and surgeon's assistant. The young man began weeping again. I haven't seen a man cry since I saw Rudolph cry at Father's funeral decades ago. I told the young man, 'If he really loved writing poetry, he should keep at it. Things could only get better with time and practice.' I sat next to him while he shared with me, the story of his life.

The young aspiring poet told me to call him John Keats. He is twenty-one years old. He told me that his father loved horses and had owned a stable. When John was only eight years old his father was tragically thrown from a horse and died. He said that

Ashley Lauren Mitchell

as a result of his father's death, he became angry and aggressive, and he began taking his anger out on other children by picking fights. His mother remarried only two months later to an awful man that took John's father's stable as his own. Eventually, John's mother left the man, but she began drinking heavily. When John was fourteen, his mother died of tuberculosis. He dropped out of school to become an apprentice to a surgeon and apothecary by the name of Thomas Hammond. John told me he enjoyed it but that after his mother died, he found a new way to cope. Instead of using his fists, he used his mind. He began expressing himself through poetry. He said he felt peaceful when he was writing. By the time he was twenty years old he was already a licensed surgeon and apothecary. He said the work was so morbid and that he felt like he had been surrounded by death for most of his life.

John is such a profound individual. I feel such sympathy for him. Perhaps even empathy. I lost my father at a young age as well. But I had my mother. I still have my mother. And he lost both of his parents. Oh, all the things he must have in his head. To say that his life seems so dark, something about him is so bright, like a star, twinkling in the night. He seemed to feel better after talking with me, and in a way I felt honored for it. He told me his friend Benjamin, recommended he stay here in Hastings with him for the summer. He thinks it will be good for John. A way

 Ashley Lauren Mitchell

to get his mind off of things. I told him that while he is here, we would more than likely see each other again.

After leaving him though, I found myself wondering about him. How he would fare. And if I really would see him again.

1817, May 20

I saw John this morning while I was walking with Donal and his circle of friends along the shore. John was walking alone. I felt something inside of me, jump. I was happy to see him. And he seemed in better spirits. I moved away from Donal and closer to Frances, so that he would not think I was attached to a man. We smiled and nodded to each other as we passed. I looked back, brushing my blue scarf from my vision, and he was still looking back at me. It made me feel, warm. I had to hurry and turn back so that no one would catch the blush, that I am certain had rouged my cheeks. I wanted badly to stop and talk to him, but I did not. I wish that I had. A conversation with him would have been much more intriguing than anything the people I was with were discussing. Whig party this and Whig party that. I wanted to know about John's poem. The one he said had caused his sadness. I hope that I will see him again. Next time I see him, I will not let a chance to

 Ashley Lauren Mitchell

converse with him elude me.

1817, May 31

Last night a small gathering was held at Wentworth Place. John was there with a group of his friends. When we first saw each other, I saw the smile on his face. I tried my best not to smile back. I turned from him briefly, attempting to control my eagerness. When I made eye contact with him again, I signaled to a quiet corner. We met there and I told him that we should rendezvous at the spot where we first met in the woods. We discreetly parted and I saw him excuse himself from the party. His friends, took it better than mine. I was bombarded with questions. I told them that I wasn't feeling well. Donal wanted to see me home, but I told him that I would be fine.

I raced through the trees, hiking my dress up with my gloved hands. There he was, standing alone in the moonlight, waiting for me. We embraced as if we hadn't seen each other in years. Then we walked and talked. I asked him about his poems. He spoke at length about nature and mythical creatures. When he speaks, it is like he is speaking in rhyme. He is so talented. But I believe he is misunderstood. He seemed to enjoy telling me about his work. And I enjoyed listening. He walked me to my doorstep and kissed my hand. We said our farewells and I watched

     Ashley Lauren Mitchell

as he walked away. He has awakened something in me. Something I thought was dead and gone. It has been so many years since I've felt blissful and imaginative. This, John Keats, is something special.

1817, June 16

John makes me feel so young. Tonight we saw each other again. And again we snuck away to our spot in the woods. He brought some of his poems with him. We laid in the grass and stared at the moon as he read them to me. He told me he had an idea for another poem he is going to call Endymion. I cannot wait to have him read it to me when it is ready. He loves being outdoors. He says it calms him. He told me he does not believe in any gods; instead he believes in nature, the earth, the moon, the sun. I know his faith was broken because of all he has suffered through. I loved being out there with him as he found a moment of peace from this worldly suffering. I have faith in God. I know there is something greater, more powerful than me. Life, death, and all the things that John puts his faith in, I know there is more to it. There has to be. I will admit, not being able to have children put a strain on my faith, but once I found a freedom and peace within myself, I realized something. There is, there has to be someone, or something controlling all the things I cannot. I will never have children, but I am content with the life I have lived. I know no other.

                                    Ashley Lauren Mitchell

Just as John knows no other. Who would I be to judge or condemn him for his beliefs? We all have our differences. It's just...life.

1817, July 1

I love listening to John's poems. Artists have such vast imaginations. I could listen to him read for hours. It feels so nice to be with someone who thinks deeper than most of the people I associate with. John is so young and has so much potential. I feel this is the beginning of a beautiful friendship. I can only imagine that this is what having a son must feel like. The pride. The wonder. The amusement. He reminds me of Rudolph when he was a young boy. He talks of dreams and his future. He sees life and the world as an enigma and is eager to solve it. I love hearing it all. It reminds me of how I used to be. Curious. Adventurous. Hopeful. I only want the best for this young man. I want him to succeed and excel. I want him to write his poems and feel just as proud of himself as I feel for him.

1817, July 12

John is leaving today with his friends. I saw them early this morning. John had a glimmering smile on his face. It, in turn, made me smile.

     Ashley Lauren Mitchell

He spotted me and boldly ran up to me. He said they were leaving and that he didn't know how long they would be gone. He said he would like to keep in touch with me. I was elated. I told him to write me whenever he could and that we would see each other again one day. He lifted my hand to his mouth and kissed it. He held it there for a while and breathed. When he opened his eyes and looked at me I wanted to cry. He was leaving. I would miss him. I didn't know if I really would see him again. I can only hope now.

***

1817, September 6

It has been so long since I've seen or spoken to John. It was so refreshing to have him read his poems to me. I have yet to have a more interesting conversation with anyone here. I think Donal is understanding how disinterested I've become with him and has finally stopped trying to be intimate with me. He is so much older than I am. I know he wants to be with me, but I just cannot see myself spending the rest of...his life with him. We can continue to remain friends. We have already been associated for some time. I don't mind spending a little time with him. Besides, we have many of the same acquaintances, so I cannot completely avoid him. I care for him, just not how he wants me to care for him.

                                    Ashley Lauren Mitchell

Mother writes that Rudolph is taking very good care of her and the house. She doesn't know where he gets all the money to take care of everything. I send her some when I can, but Rudolph is doing most of the work. Mother never forced him to marry and move away, like she did to me. And it is not my fault that I had already fallen in love with my freedom after William died. I am glad she has Rudolph. And I guess in a selfish way, I am glad he never moved on. Mother needs him. They became so much closer after father died. I think when father told Rudolph to look after Mother and be the man of the house, he really took it to heart. I am glad they are together and doing just fine.

1818, October 6

John has finally written to me. In his letter he writes that he is still working on Endymion and will send a copy to me upon completion. I cannot wait to read his poem. He is also still studying Shakespeare as much as possible. His friends Charles and Richard have him traveling a bit. He sent me a short poem he calls, On the sea. I read it over and over. When I read, or listen to him read his work, I realize how disconnected with reality he must feel when he writes. He hates the rules of the world. And his poems take the reader to another place and time. Somewhere peaceful. When he escapes, the reader escapes with

                                    Ashley Lauren Mitchell

him. He reminds me of how I used to be. Carefree and seeing places and things that inspire me. But now what inspires me? I am nearly forty years old and although I've done quite a few things, I do not feel as if I have accomplished my greatest achievement. I do not even know what it is. I wish I could go back to John's age and not be afraid to let my imagination run wild. With the noble crowds I am affiliated with, I doubt they could understand the talent someone like John possesses. I think it may take a while for his work to truly be appreciated.

***

1818, January 14

I have finally received John's poem. I opened the letter like a child opening a gift on Christmas morning. It is much longer than I anticipated, but I devoured it in one sitting. His first line...

"A thing of beauty is a joy forever, its loveliness increases; it will never pass into nothingness..."

...for some reason, brought a smile to my face as if it had been written for me. As I read of Endymion and Cynthia's love, I could not help but feel lost in it. Lost in the love that was so pure and deep.

                          Ashley Lauren Mitchell

A love you can only dream about. I wondered how John can write of such love at such a young age. He has gone through so much in his life already. His soul is so pure, yet troubled.

1818, April 9

John writes that his poem, Endymion, is being published. I am so happy for him. He says he is also working on a poem that he knows I will love. I am beyond anxious and excited to read it. His friend Benjamin had a dinner at which John was able to meet and converse with some other bright and creative minds. He says it was a meeting that invoked his thoughts. He says Benjamin called it the, Immortal dinner, because the ideas shared at that dinner table will live on forever.

Now, John is in Teignmouth nursing his brother Tom, who has become as ill as he was before. Since he is in Teignmouth, I will go next week and visit him. I will bring his brother some soup, something to warm his soul.

1818, May 25

Yesterday, I saw John in Teignmouth. He looked lively, and was just as excited to see me as I

     Ashley Lauren Mitchell

was to see him. He was with his friend Charles, and his brother George. When we went to the house to see Tom, I met George's fiancée Georgiana. She is beautiful, and I can tell that John has an attraction to her. I feel it is only natural. His brother has great taste.

Tom is so small and I can tell he is in pain. He has this cough that seems to shake his entire small frame. John is taking it, I guess, as well as he takes any situation like this. He is so strong. He took me to his room and read a few of the lines from the poem he is working on. He won't tell me the name of it, but I know I will love it. We talked in his room for a while, and again, I felt honored to hear him tell his life stories and fantasies with me. He knows I do not judge him, or criticize him. Hurting him is something I never want to do. He kissed me on the cheek as he walked me to my door. I know we may not see each other again for some time, but I cannot help but feel a deep affinity for this young man.

1818, July 31

John writes that his brother George has gotten married to Georgiana and that they are moving to America. He revealed to me that he feels saddened by their leaving. He thought he was in love with Georgiana. Poor John. And poor Tom, who only seems to worsen in health. John is on a tour of Lake

Ashley Lauren Mitchell

District and Scotland with Charles. He says it will help clear his mind and also help 'get wisdom.' He says that he feels a sore in his throat that comes and goes, but he forces himself to keep going. He says it is something he feels he needs to do. It is like John to find a way to escape. And who better to tell that to, than a person who loves to escape themselves. I sympathize for John, for all of his loses; yet I envy him for his youth and talent. He says he wants to travel as much as he can, before he must return to Tom. The poem he is working on is almost finished.

1818, October 31

Today is John's birthday. He is twenty-four years old, and more brilliant than half of my acquaintances. We met for lunch today. I gave him a golden laurel crown from Rome that I had Rudolph send to me months ago. John was so happy. I could tell he loved it. In return he gave to me the poem he had been working on. It is called, Isabella. My heart soared as I read it. But after I finished reading it I realized that John was sending a message to me. Is John in love with me? Loves me, surely. But "in love" with me? I am old enough to be his mother. I have great love and admiration for John, but I never thought of him as anything more than a beautiful friend. The son I never had. The lost boy that I only want to help. With each line I read I felt a shiver in my heart. I cried as soon as I finished reading the last line. Oh, John. My head is spinning. I cannot think. I want to hold John close to me and at the same time, keep him far away from me. Have I misled him? Have I shown that I love him differently than a friend? But John is always falling in and out of love with women. I do not want to be one of those frivolous loves to him, for him. I want our love to last beyond what he feels for the other women in his life. I will tell him how much I love the poem, but I will not say much more than that. And I truly do love the poem.

1818, December 13

Today I saw Charles, John's friend, in passing and he revealed the news to me that Tom, John's younger brother has died from the tuberculosis that had been plaguing him. My heart and soul weeps for John. I want to be there with him, and for him, so badly. He was so good in caring for his brother. I cannot imagine what he must be feeling right now. I was torn between going to him or not, but Charles told me that he invited John to stay with him here in Hampstead for a while. It has been a long time since John and I have seen or heard from each other. And after reading, Isabella, I just am not sure of my feelings for him anymore. I feel it wise to stay away from him while he grieves, and is possibly just confused by his all of his emotions.

                    Ashley Lauren Mitchell

1819, January 4

The sky has been ominous and grey for weeks. It's as if the clouds want to burst but simply won't. Then, yesterday, a small drizzle turned into a downpour unlike I'd seen in years. I thought it would flood. I'd just snuggled up in my chair with a book and tea when I heard a soft knock at the door. I stared in disbelief for a time. Then the knock came again. This time a little louder. The wind and rain blew against the windows. I began to get scared and then I heard the voice of him, calling my name. "Isabella. Isabella!" He called. It was John. I ran to the door and swung it open. He stood there drenched and shivering. So many things were running through my mind. He looked...more tormented and beautiful than I'd ever seen him. His eyes were shining and his pupils were large. He almost didn't look like himself. Suddenly, his wet body was fixed to mine and his lips were upon me. I felt my body relax and all inhibition cease for a few seconds. Then I pushed him away from me. I told him that we couldn't. I couldn't. I felt horrible for having to do it. But I knew he was only hurting from the death of his brother. We sat on the couch and he put his head in my lap. I sang to him and rubbed his head until he fell asleep. I watched him as he slept. He was not the same young man I met years ago. Something about him appealed to

  Ashley Lauren Mitchell

me in a way I know it shouldn't. I put his head on a pillow and went to my room.

1819, January 6

When I woke the next morning, John was already gone. He left a note on the pillow thanking me for my company. The rain had stopped. The sun was breaking through the clouds. My mind was racing with thoughts of him. Thoughts of the kiss. Thoughts of him that I've never had. His features seem different to me somehow. He seems as if he's aged more in two years than I have in forty. But I can see the innocence in his eyes. He knows and doesn't know at the same time. And I, I thought I knew. But now I am not sure how I feel anymore.

1819, January 9

Two days ago John came back to my door. Again I noticed he looked different. His pupils were so large. They looked as if they covered his entire iris. He was jumpy and discursive. He was rambling about politics and religion. I couldn't keep up. I'd never seen him like that. I stopped him in his pacing track and stared at him. I knew from seeing Rudolph on drugs, that John had taken something. He told me that he'd gotten a bottle of laudanum from a friend he'd met

                    Ashley Lauren Mitchell

during his apothecary apprenticeship years ago. He said it helped with his cough and sore throat. I knew only a little about the pills and potions. Rudolph used to constantly talk of such things at the dinner table when we were younger; and according to Mother, that is all he still ever talks about. John told me that being an apothecary gives you access to many drugs and that many of his artistic friends admit that it makes them more creative and uninhibited when it comes to their artful expressions.

In all my forty years, I've never taken any drugs. I know that Rudolph has. Mother has written to me on a number of occasions saying that Rudolph had taken something, and that he either would not stop talking or slept for so long she would have to make sure he was still breathing. He calls it an experimental phase, where he uses himself to test his experiments. I do not understand it. But what would I expect from a young apothecary/artist like John? Especially when he experiences death so much. It all seems so strange to me. I'm not sure I've ever even wanted to try something like that. I've been past my limit in spirits many times, but never have I had laudanum or anything of the sort. However, I am not getting any younger. And I have no children or husband.

Before John could finish telling me about what he was feeling from the substance he'd taken, I told him that I wanted to try it. I figured it would help me understand more about my brother, Rudolph, and even more about John. The only deaths I'd ever really experienced was Father's and William's. I was too young to remember Father, but Rudolph was deeply affected. He and Father were together a lot, working in the basement laboratory. After Father's death, Rudolph became more and more distant every day. One day he'd be happy and talkative, and the next he'd be sad and uncommunicative. Could it have been the pills and potions? John seems to never escape his thoughts and memories of death. I can only imagine that that is why he and Rudolph use themselves as experiments. To help ignore the pain that death and loss brings with it.

John pulled a small vial with a brownish liquid in it from his waistcoat. He poured a little in a spoon and quickly took it. In seconds he was smiling and gazing at me, numb. Then he handed the spoon to me as he made his way to the couch. I didn't know how much to take, but I figured less would be better.

After the horrid taste dissipated, and the pungent liquid passed my throat, I felt...it. Everything, the colors, the sounds, the feelings, every sense was heightened. It felt like I knew everything and could do anything. It was the greatest feeling of euphoria I'd ever experienced. It felt like I was floating in thin air. When I breathed, I could feel the cool air fill my lungs and blow from my nostrils. My heartbeat was so strong

　　　　　　　　　　　Ashley Lauren Mitchell

and loud. John and I laid on each other and listened to each other's heartbeats, then he read his poems to me. I felt like I was in another world. A world with only John's voice and our hearts.

When he started reading a poem called To Mary Frogley, the woman he claimed to have once loved, he could hardly finish because I kept laughing at her name; 'Frogley'. Even now it makes me laugh. John stood to his feet and recited his poem, Women, Wine, and Snuff. We laughed at his foolish dramatic act and nonsensical lyrics. We both laughed for hours at anything, and everything, even when they weren't funny. I was so relaxed and happy. We both slept the next day. I in my bed and he on the couch. We slept the whole day and didn't rise until that night. We ate and took another spoonful of the laudanum. We laughed and laughed some more. Although I know he is only doing this to mask his pain, I'm still glad I had this experience with John.

1819, January 12

This morning something happened that perhaps should not have, amongst other things that should not have happened. John was lying in the bed next to me when I woke. I don't remember falling asleep with him next to me. He is usually on the couch. I looked at his young, angelic face as he slept. He must have felt me staring somehow because he smiled and opened his eyes. When I tried to get up, embarrassed, he grabbed my hand and pulled me to him. Out of respect for everything he is going through, I never brought up the kiss that happened nights ago. I know he was just reacting without thinking. But I also know my feelings for him have grown since then.

He brushed my hair from my face and kissed my cheek. Then he kissed the corner of my mouth. I should have stopped him there but I didn't. He placed a gentle kiss on my lips. I, we, felt something else because we kissed again, with longing and passion. Before I knew it, he was pulling my gown over my head. I sat up to pull away. He looked at me with begging eyes and said, "Please Isabella." My heart stopped. I wanted him so badly, as I knew he wanted me. I slowly lifted my arms. While the gown was covering my face and holding my arms up, John began caressing my body. I felt his soft, warm, wet lips kiss my stomach and hips. His hands grabbed my breasts, as his mouth found one of my nipples. My body retaliated in a way it hasn't in...ever. Once he'd finished removing my gown, I pulled his mouth back to mine. Every thought I had left my mind. All I could do was, feel. Feel him. I felt his pain and anger as he thrust himself inside of me. I cried out as his lips and tongue roamed my body. I wasn't sure how much time had passed. We became enraptured with each other.

                    Ashley Lauren Mitchell

Our bodies pleasing one another. I wanted it, and didn't want it. I needed it, and didn't need it. But then I thought, right now, we both want and need each other.

When we were finished, he admitted to me that I was his first. How could I not have known? I could not control my gasp. I'm so much older, and much more experienced than he is. Hearing him say that I was the one to take his virginity made me feel, I don't know, feel like I had stolen it. He did his best to reassure me that it was what he wanted and even admitted that he should have told me before, but that it was too late and he wouldn't change what happened for the world. He says he feels, "Happy in beauty, life, and love, and everything."

Oh, my, John. My young lover. This is all moving so quickly. I know he cannot stay. I know that we cannot be together. What am I doing? I feel young and irresponsible, but also uninhibited and happy. Am I allowed to feel all of these things at once? And, when will it end? As I feel all good things must.

1819, January 17

He came to me that next evening. Spirits high. He is making me behave as I never have before. He brought whiskey and laudanum. We reveled in the effects, and each other. Sweat beading off our bodies as we danced in front of the fireplace. He spoke quietly to me, a whisper in my ear. I felt things I've never felt before with John. He hasn't talked much of Tom or of George and Georgianna. He hasn't spoken of any of them in weeks. At least not with me. Perhaps he just doesn't want to think of it. I like thinking that I am helping John, by being another escape for him. And he is an escape for me. I am finally escaping with John. My body in euphoric bliss. My mind in a fantasy with him. I can see his poems come to life when he reads them now. Some frighten me. Others entrance me. But all of them take me some place else, deep in the mind of John Keats. My young poet. My young lover.

1819, January 21

Last night John and I were lying in the bed. Our naked bodies glistening and panting from our just finished activities. My hands were behind my pillow as I was looked up at the ceiling. It was the twentieth of January. The twentieth. The Eve of St. Agnes. I remembered the story my mother used to tell me when I was young. I told it to John. If a virgin says this prayer on the night of January 20,"Agnes sweet, and Agnes fair, Hither, hither, now repair; Bonny Agnes, let me see, the lad who is to marry me," her true love will be revealed to her. He asked me if I'd ever had a true

                    Ashley Lauren Mitchell

love. I told him that love is a very bittersweet concept. It can make you merry and light, or it can leave you forlorn and lost. Sometimes, love, is just never enough. Then he turned to me and asked if I was in love with him. I wish he wouldn't have asked. I love him. I truly do. But I am so much older than he is. And I feel guilty for having been the one to take his innocence. But to be in love with him?

What was I supposed to do? Lie? Tell him that I am, when I cannot be? No. I couldn't. I told him the truth. I told him, that the feelings I had for him are indescribable. To tell him that I was in love with him, would mean that I want to spend the rest of my life with him. He is so young and has so many more years of this life left. He should not waste them on an old woman that would never be able to give him children. His eyes grew dim with solace. I felt a distance instantly grow between us. I hadn't felt anything like it since William and I lived together. I almost wished I could have taken my words back. But why let him waste his life and love on me? He is so talented. The world will be his love, he just doesn't understand it yet. I took him in my arms and held him. I know he doesn't understand now, but in time, he will. I hope.

 Ashley Lauren Mitchell

1819, January 22

When I woke this morning John was gone. I walked in the front room and on the table was one of John's poems.

Fill for me a brimming bowl,

And let me in it drown my soul;

But put therein some drug, designed

To banish Woman from my mind...

By the time I'd finished reading it, my heart ached. It seemed a cry for...something. Had I broken his heart? I dropped the pages, dressed, and went searching after him. I saw his friend Charles and asked if John had made it back. He said that he hadn't seen John in days. Which made sense to me because John was with me for days. But no one knew that.

Then I ran to our secret meeting place in the woods. As I approached, I saw John standing there with a woman. A woman that appeared around my age. She was tall and had long, fiery red hair. She had a long, dark purple cloak, and dazzling gold jewelry. She was beautiful. I paused, my breath left me. I saw her hand something to John. I put my hand to my heart. John. It was then that I realized how much I did truly love him. I took a step backwards to leave.

                              Ashley Lauren Mitchell

They heard me. I saw her face turn to me. Her eyes were like none I'd ever seen before. They looked like rainbows. Brilliant. Colorful. She smiled a devilish smile and turned to leave. John stood there motionless. I rushed to him. I shook him and repeated his name over and over. He only stared ahead, as if he didn't see me there. When I turned to see where the woman had gone all I saw was a puff of black smoke. I felt fear rising within me. John felt cold when I touched his face. His hand was clasped tightly around something. Something that she had given him. I shook him again. Then I grabbed him, hugging him tightly to me, and fighting my tears. Suddenly, I felt his arms around me, hugging me back. I pulled away to look at him. His eyes still had a distant look in them, as if he were really not there with me at all.

I asked him who the woman was and he said, "What woman?"

"The woman with the red hair. She was just here with you."

He eyes looked angry as he said, "No one," and began walking away.

The impudence. "What did she just hand you?" I said as I stepped in front of him and lifted his coiled fist. When he opened it, I saw that it was a vial. My eyes grew wide. I stepped back. "Is she the one that has been giving you...? You said it was from a friend

                    Ashley Lauren Mitchell

from your time as an apprentice."

"Isabella, stop."

I blinked. "John, what's going on? Please, talk to me. Who was that woman? And how did she...disappear, like that?" Because that is in fact what she'd done. The red headed vixen had disappeared into thin air. But I felt foolish just saying it. I was confused. I was hurt. I was lost.

"You're imagining things."

"No I am not."

He stopped walking, turned to me, took my face in his hands and said, "Isabella, I don't want to talk about it."

We returned to my loft, walking in silence. My head in a whirlwind. When we were inside, he pulled out the vial. I started feeling nauseous. I told him I didn't want to take the drugs anymore. Then, I told him that he should leave. Although, I really didn't want him to go, I thought it would be the best thing for us. He sadly left. I cried for I knew what we shared had come to an end. I was sending my young lover back to the dreadful world. We couldn't stay like that forever, in a drug-induced bliss for eternity. And after seeing him with another woman, as innocent as it

Ashley Lauren Mitchell

was, I know if I hold on to him any longer it would only hurt us more when it is time to say goodbye. My heart is heavy. I picked up some of his poems, and read them to quiet my thoughts. As I read, however, my unease only worsened. My poor John. The angel of death all around him, constantly knocking at his door and taking his cherished loved ones, one by one. I will only die, long before him. Why should he stay with me? Why should he love me? I have to, I must, let him go.

1819, February 3

John has left to go to Chichester. I have the feeling I won't ever see him again. I know it is only for the best. And I only want what is best for him.

Yesterday, I received a letter from Rudolph saying that Mother is in bad health. It has been a long time since I've wanted to go home so badly. I feel it is time now. My life in England has come to an end. I am making plans to leave. I feel I need to leave this place, if not forever, then for a very long time. I feel there is nothing left for me here. I only hope Mother will last long enough for me to get to her. Rudolph is an excellent care taker. He is doing the task I've neglected. But now, it is time. Time to go home.

1819, March 4

I arrived in Italy a week ago. Rudolph looks well. But Mother on the other hand? I fear I will not have much time to spend with her. I've come too late. She cannot rise from the bed. Rudolph makes sure she has the proper medication, but I feel her age is upon her and she may not make it much longer. I sat next to her bed and held her hand close to my face. She felt so cold. She could barely speak, so I did. I told her things I'd never tell another living soul. She smiled and tried her best to laugh when I attempted a joke. It has been so long. I'd almost forgotten about the life I had here with her many decades ago. I was just a young girl, sent off to start a life and family of my own. Something I never did. I start to feel an ache in my stomach. I start feeling that I've let her down for never giving her a grandchild. I never came back, until now, when it is too late. I retreat to my room. Rudolph brings something to help me sleep. I did sleep, for a few hours, then I was awakened by another sharp pain in my stomach. I felt nauseous and I rushed to the latrine. It felt as if I were going to purge every fluid in my body after an hour of running back and forth. I found the strength to go to Rudolph's room, but of course he was down stairs, in his laboratory. I crawled to Mother's room on my hands and knees. I knew Rudolph would be in to check on her soon and I was too weak to go to him. My body was so hot. I laid down in the bed next to

                    Ashley Lauren Mitchell

Mother. I was so warm against her cool flesh. I heard her whispering, but I could not make out the words. It sounded like a prayer. I leaned in to hear her better. "Name him Nathaniel, after your father." I had no idea what she was talking about. I thought she was sleeping, but I asked her anyway, "Mother? Mother?" I called, "Name who Nathaniel?" After a few moments, she opened her eyes and smiled. Tears began streaming down her face. She looked at me, touched my face with her soft hand, and said, "Your son." I blinked in amazement. She closed her eyes. She stopped moving. She still had a smile on her face. I looked away. It was a dream. She was dreaming. I was dreaming. Then I felt it. Her body went completely limp, lifeless. She stopped breathing. My eyes and hands searched for a sign of life before I screamed for Rudolph.

We buried Mother next to Father. There were so few people in attendance at the funeral. It might as well have only been Rudolph and I. We watched our Mother lowered into the ground. This feeling is surreal, almost indescribable. Only now, have I a glimpse of understanding of what John must have felt, losing both of his parents, and his young brother. The world feels smaller and at the same time, vastly larger and overwhelming. My heart is strained, confused. This consuming, crushing feeling overtaking me. My Mother is gone. There was so much time that we didn't have together. That we will never have

                    Ashley Lauren Mitchell

together. My Mother.

When we returned home, I couldn't eat or sleep. I felt sick, weak, depressed. Rudolph gave me something to numb all the pain I was feeling, inside and out. He too had taken a dose. For a while I was able to sleep, then I felt the sharp pain in my abdomen again. I rushed downstairs for more of whatever Rudolph had given me, before the pain became too much to bear. When I opened the door, I saw Rudolph speaking with some man I'd never seen before. Then, I blacked out. I woke in my bed. Rudolph was standing over me. He looked so happy. Then he said, "Isabella, you're pregnant." I closed my eyes and drifted back to sleep.

***

1819, June 25

My heart still aches as my belly gets bigger. I feel the child growing inside me. I can feel its little body squirming beneath my skin. It's the only thing that keeps me from my depression. I cannot stop thinking about John and how he is doing. I do not know how he is and it worries me. I cannot stop loving him. This child I carry is for us, conceived in...love. I should be glad to have a piece of him with me forever. But I cannot tell him about this child. He

                    Ashley Lauren Mitchell

would alter his whole life. I do not want to rob John of his future, but I do not want to rob my child of a father either. I wish Mother was here. I cry constantly. I feel so much sadness. How can I have a child? How can this be happening? Why can I not feel joy from this? Rudolph and I are the only ones who know of my condition. He says I am not eating enough. He has gone from taking care of Mother, to now taking care of me. I am glad I have him. What would I do without my brother? He hides his pain of losing Mother better than I can. I know what he is feeling, but he wouldn't dare let it show. Instead he talks of this child I carry. I envy him. I wish I were as excited about this child as Rudolph is. He asks no questions of who the father of the child is. He says he believes Mother was right and that it will be a boy that we should name after Father. And I promise, if it is a boy, his name will be called Nathaniel. Nathaniel Volta.

***

1819, November 19

Last week I gave birth to my son Nathaniel. It feels odd even saying it. My son. He is healthy and beautiful. His dark eyes remind me of John's. I feel like this is what I have been waiting for my entire life. Raising this child is my destiny. Rudolph is overjoyed that he has a nephew. He's always holding the baby

                    Ashley Lauren Mitchell

and talking to him. He says that he has great plans for little Nathaniel. I'm so happy that Rudolph is here. I'm so happy that Nathaniel is now here. It feels like a family lives in this house again. I wish Mother were here to meet her grandchild. I wish John was here to see his beautiful son. But I cannot. No. I cannot reveal who his father is. John is too young. This would destroy him. It would destroy me. It would destroy us and everything we had. No, I must keep this a secret. A beautiful, beautiful secret.

***

1820, November 11

Nathaniel is one year old today. This has been an unforgettable year. I am so in love with my son. And I know Rudolph loves him just as much. I had no idea this is what it would be like, having a child. Nathaniel is growing stronger and smarter every day. Rudolph and I must keep ourselves from holding him and spoiling him too much, but neither of us can help it.

Last night I had a dream unlike any I've had before. The woman that I saw with John that day in Wentworth, the one with the red eyes and hair, was in my dream. The whole scene played out like it had that day, starting from when I read John's poem and then going to search for him. When I found him and saw him with that woman, she had vanished so quickly. I hadn't given much thought to her since I left England. But last night she was so vivid in my dream. I still have no clue who she is. I remember feeling a mild feeling of trepidation when she disappeared, but in my dream, when I turned to look back at John it was her that was standing in front of me. Her eyes were glowing like two red fireballs. Her hair and cape were flowing behind her. She smiled at me. I asked her what she had been giving to John and she told me that whatever she had given to him, I'd taken as well. She told me it was present in my blood when Nathaniel was conceived. I woke from the dream instantly. I was sweating but I was freezing cold. I rushed to Nathaniel's crib. I panicked when he wasn't there. I ran to Rudolph's room, then his laboratory. He was there with Nathaniel in his arms. He was shaking hands with another man I've never seen before. I told Rudolph I wanted to sleep with my baby. I took Nathaniel back to my bed and tried to forget about the dream. And to forget about that woman for the second time.

I've been thinking about John so much lately. It is difficult not having anyone to talk to about what I am going through. I see more and more of John in Nathaniel every day. It tortures me that things are like this, but what else am I to do? I cannot tell Rudolph. Sometimes I feel he gets too preoccupied with work.

Ashley Lauren Mitchell

He is always up all hours of the night. I have a feeling he is selling some of the drugs he's been concocting. He provides Nathaniel and me with everything we need. He is a great provider so I don't question his actions. It may end up being something else I just want to forget.

***

1821, February 25

Today is one of the saddest days of my life. I haven't felt this feeling since Mother died. The crushing, consuming feeling that Death brings with it. I am still shocked and in disbelief. John. Oh, John. I received a letter today saying that John has died from Tuberculosis. The same thing that took his brother, Tom's, life. My friend, Taylor, sent me a letter a while ago telling me that my once, young lover had fallen ill. It was the only time, in all these years, that I had word of my son's father. But death? Death? How can it be so unforgiving? Oh my John. I outlived him. I never thought I would. How could this have happened? He was so young. Now, when I look at my son I feel regret. I will forever be haunted by the ghost of his father. Nathaniel will never meet John. What will I tell him? Why is this life so unfair? I cannot stop crying.

 Ashley Lauren Mitchell

Taylor sent me a few of John's poems that I read in silence. Tears clouded my eyes. I locked myself in my room. Rudolph must have sensed I did not want to be bothered because he took Nathaniel and left for the day. I wanted to lie in my bed all day and night. It is even more devastating to know that John was in Italy when he died. Rome. Not very far from me. He came here with his friend Joseph Severn, a painter. The warmer climate was supposed to be better for him. He was staying at the Piazza di Spagna. I could have gone to him. I would have if I would have known he was here. Rudolph more than likely could have helped him. Now, it is too late. He is buried and his tombstone doesn't even have his name on it. Why? Why this? Why now? Our son is not yet old enough to talk, and his young father is gone. I cannot stop crying.

***

1832, November 12

Yesterday was Nathaniel's thirteenth birthday. He is so wonderful. He is getting so tall. And every day more and more handsome. I took him to Rome yesterday. I thought it was time to tell him who is father is, after all these years. We went to many places in Rome. Nathaniel was able to explore and discover things about the ancient city that he'd never

          Ashley Lauren Mitchell

seen before. We went to the Sistine Chapel and I took him to the Piazza di Spagna, the death place of his father. That is where I told him what happened. Then, we went to visit John's grave.

Nathaniel was solemn, as I expected him to be. I watched him approach the tombstone with caution and stare at it. Then something caught my eye. A red light dashed through the darkness. When I looked over, in the distance I saw...her. The woman with the red hair. I felt my stomach rise and my heart quicken. She was standing a ways away, looking at me, looking at Nathaniel. I felt something, a mother's instinct to protect her young, even if Nathaniel is just as big as I am. She smiled an almost, reassuring smile, as I stood and walked to Nathaniel. She held up something, a book, that she sat on a bench, and began walking away. When she was out of sight, I walked to the bench. She had placed a small black book there. I picked it up and leafed through the pages. I felt my stomach rise and my heart quicken again. I knew this writing style. It has been many years, but I will never forget the way John writes, or his handwriting. That woman left a poem written by John. Who is she? How did she find me? What does she want?

When we returned home, I read the poem over and over again. It is called Lamia. I know John wrote it. He had to have written it. It could only come

                    Ashley Lauren Mitchell

from a mind like his. It wasn't like the Greek tale I'd heard before. This was his own version, written with another muse in mind. John's poem is about the spirit of Lamia trapped in a beautiful serpent body. She grants the god Hermes the power to see a beautiful nymph for which he is to love forever. In return Lamia asks Hermes to give to her the form of a human woman. When Hermes gives her the womanly figure, Lamia finds the man called Lycius. They fall in love and Lycius wants to marry her, but Lamia only wants to stay locked away with him and their new found love, for fear of her true form being revealed. She finally gives in and lets Lycius have his wedding ceremony. Lycius's instructor, Apollonius, invites himself to the celebration. At the banquet Apollonius reveals what Lamia really is and she vanishes into thin air. Lycius dies from the loss of his beloved.

The poem was without a doubt John's. Another of his tragic love stories that I loved so dearly. Lamia. What a beautiful name.

How did that woman get this? Why did she bring this to me? I need someone to talk to about this. Anyone.

***

1840, September 13

Nathaniel is away at the hospital during the week. He rents a small apartment close to his work, but comes home on the weekends. He tells me of all the women in his life now. I tried telling him, it is not right to play with the hearts of these women. He laughs it away. My handsome son could have any woman he chooses. And he has so many choices, I suppose. He reminds me of his amorous father. John was twenty-one when I met him, as Nathaniel nearly is. I've felt for a few years now, that Nathaniel is, perhaps, a bit different from his peers. I cannot explain it. He is kind and friendly, but still reserved and detached. Rudolph was that way. John was that way. Maybe it's in his nature. Could it be because he does not have a father, as his peers do? He has Rudolph, but he never was able to even meet his father. My poor son. He still spends a good bit of time with Rudolph in the laboratory when he can. I know they are both in on the goings and comings of all those men that buy whatever they buy. I still refuse to ask, and they refuse to mention it.

I have gone to visit London twice. Nothing feels the same there. It feels so haunted. I walked the path that John and I walked together. I visited the house that William and I shared. I found the more painful thoughts to be the ones I remember the most. The ones that clouded my, one time great love for this place. I came back to Italy both times, regretting ever leaving. I hate feelings of nostalgia. The pain my heart feels when I think of what can never be again. It becomes so great, so overwhelming sometimes, I just want to shut myself away in my room. But even here I miss Mother. I miss John. I miss times past that will never be again. I feel things are going to change soon. I don't know what. I don't know why. And I don't know when. But I can feel it deep inside of me. Something is going to happen. I felt it each time I lost someone close to me. I hate this eerie feeling, but all I can do is...feel it.

***

1842, December 3

My life is cursed. My whole world has changed in a night, so unexpectedly. When Nathaniel came home for the weekend from working at the hospital, he was very uneasy. He rushed past Rudolph and I, and locked himself in the laboratory all day. We tried going down there, but he never answered the door. We heard him rummaging around. Rudolph waved it off and went to his bedroom. I came to my room to lie down. Around one o'clock in the morning I heard a scream. It was a fatal cry that woke me instantly and shook my very soul. It sounded like Nathaniel. I sat up in the bed, shaking and listening for the sound again. I didn't hear anything. Was it a dream? Was I still dreaming? I found the courage to get up and go downstairs. I put on my robe and slowly walked to exit my bedroom. When I was standing at my door, I thought I heard someone just on the other side. I touched the doorknob, and immediately pulled my hand away. It was freezing. I heard what sounded like heavy breathing. I put my ear against it. The whole door was cold. I was so afraid. I grabbed my lamp to use as a weapon, and slowly opened the door, but no one was standing there.

I went to the basement. Glass covered the floor. There was a bloody rodent, which looked like it had been smashed, twitching on the table where Rudolph and Nathaniel had worked so assiduously over the years. Then I saw Rudolph. He was lying on the ground. He wasn't breathing. There was blood on his neck. When I wiped it away I saw that he had two tiny holes in it. Nathaniel was nowhere to be found. That mouse couldn't have been what did that to Rudolph. Could it? I rushed to get help.

When I returned, I was shocked to find that the mouse, that should have died long ago, was gone. I followed the trail of blood it left, but could not find it. My head felt like it was spinning. I couldn't figure anything out. After my brother's body was taken away I went to lie down. I tried crying myself to sleep grieving for Rudolph's tragic death and Nathaniel's sudden disappearance. Hours later, I still couldn't fall asleep. I walked the lonely, silent floors of the house.

                    Ashley Lauren Mitchell

Once again in my life, I felt trapped. I needed to get out. I opened the front door and felt the cool breeze against my face. Then I felt my warm tears. I walked slowly into the night air. And there she was. Glowing like a lantern in the distance. I ran to her. Finally, I was able to ask her who she was. She looked at me with her colorful eyes and said, "Call me Onaya. I am an angel of death." I was taken aback. She could not have been serious. I asked her why she was haunting me and she said, "I was not haunting you. I was watching over John's son. I need him for a very important task." I told her to stay away from Nathaniel and she simply laughed. She said, "I am more powerful than you can imagine. I will have what I desire. You will never see your son again. And if you try anything, even so much as speak of me, I will kill you." She disappeared right in front of my eyes. I ran back to the house as fast as I could. I was shaking uncontrollably. I felt I was going to pass out as I stumbled to my bed. When I woke early this morning the house was still lonely and silent. I began making arrangements for Rudolph's funeral.

***

1843, January 19

It has been almost eight weeks since I lost the two most important people in my life. My son and my

 Ashley Lauren Mitchell

brother gone in one fateful night. I can feel myself disappearing from this life. Wanting to simply fade from existence. My spirit grows weaker every day. I have no knowledge of Nathaniel's whereabouts or if he is even alive. I can sense my sanity leaving me. I cannot handle this devastation. I want to know. I need to know about my son. And there is only one person that can give me the answers I need. Tonight, I will go back to the last place I saw her. Onaya. I will call for her. I will wait for her. I will threaten her if I must. But, I must get my answers, even if she kills me.

***

Nathaniel dropped his mother's diary. He was certain what he'd read was all true. He felt so many things. But the one that kindled more than any, was rage. Onaya. She'd known his father and his mother. She had a hand in keeping them all apart. And now, she was keeping him and Lamia apart. "Who is she? What does she want? Why is she doing this? Why did she want me to know all of this?" He asked quietly to the silence. He rested his arms on his knees and bowed his head. He sat there thinking, regretting.

He felt the morning coming. His body became weaker by the minute. He stood and went to a window. He thought about standing there until the sun broke through night. The sky was a pale grey and growing lighter with each passing second. He felt himself becoming dry. His skin began to crack and flake. His body tried to slump over but he fought it. He watched the yellow rays from the sun, light the sky. His skin began to sizzle and smoke oozed out of his crackling flesh. He felt as if he'd just burst into flames. He let out a terrible scream.

Jacque closed the curtains and pushed Nathaniel into the darkness of the hallway. He picked Nathaniel up and with abnormal speed and ability, rushed him to his coffin. He closed it just as the tip of the sun appeared above the horizon. As Nathaniel's body convalesced, his mind began to form an idea. After a few moments he realized what he had to do. He only hoped Lamia would find a way to forgive him for it.

Chapter 23

Call me Lamia.

When I opened my eyes I knew I was in a dream. A misty haze rose from the grass under my feet. I began walking, slowly forward. I heard animals in the distance. My dream. I took a deep breath. I didn't see Nathaniel, or anything other than the enormous tree, with colorful fruit, on the path in front of me. I kept walking to it, gazing at it. It was beautiful, beautiful and grand. I circled it, stepping on its large roots, outstretched and raised on the ground. I climbed a branch and picked one of the curious looking fruits it produced.

Then there was her voice, "Take a bite," she said.

I jumped from the branch to the ground. I looked for her. "Where are you?" I asked, annoyed.

After a few seconds I heard her coming from behind the tree. "I am here my Lamia."

"Why do I dream of this place?"

                    Ashley Lauren Mitchell

"You don't know where you are?"

This is the second time she's asked me this question. And for the second time, I did not know the answer. But I did know that I was, "In my dream."

"Yes, this is your dream. I'm going to explain everything to you here, in your dream."

"Why?" I asked perplexed.

"Dreams are the connection, the gateway, to the unknown, and unseen. Things that normally wouldn't make sense, make perfect sense in a dream. Great ideas and revelations happen in dreams."

"So what is this place that I dream of?"

"This place. This land. This pasture, is called, The Garden of Eden."

"The Garden of Eden?"

"Yes. Your mind travels here because this is where you were...born. Where you became, what you are?"

"And what am I?"

"Your father once held the highest honor any creature can have. He was God's right hand, the most prestigious and envied of all places in heaven and earth. They called him, Lucifer. It means, Morning

Ashley Lauren Mitchell

star. He was the only one able to look upon the countenance of God, and not die. He was magnificent, powerful. He was, I guess, the apprentice to God."

"God would create heavenly bodies, in many forms, all to glorify himself. He gave each of his creations certain powers and purposes. And all of them had souls. He gave Lucifer the power of light. He could expel a bright light from his mouth. He would open his lips and darkness would cease. God only spoke to and through Lucifer. God loved him, and he loved God."

"Lucifer, as a gift to God, one day created beasts in images of his own. They were giant monsters. For many years they roamed the land on earth, existing. They were mindless, brute creatures with no emotions or thoughts. God became bored with the beasts. Lucifer sensed this. He asked God to give them souls, like creatures in heaven, so they could think, feel, know. God refused. No one really knows what happened, or what was said between them, but one day the beasts that Lucifer created began killing each other. God commanded Lucifer to kill all of them with the light that expelled from his mouth. And it was so. Only remnants of that time remain."

"Then one day God had the idea to create something different from anything he'd ever created.

　　　　　Ashley Lauren Mitchell

He didn't tell Lucifer what it was. And although he didn't have to, Lucifer felt, in a way, hurt, for not knowing. All he said to Lucifer was, "Let there be light." Lucifer opened his mouth. Over the course of 700 years, God carefully, and with much detail, created what is called today, earth. He broke apart the continents that the beasts before had roamed. He stretched the lands across the waters. He created many humans. But they were not given the special gifts that the angels received. They were like the soulless, mindless beasts Lucifer created, only, they were made in God's image."

"Your father and I had a special bond in heaven. As do all of the creatures there. God made everything to have a companion. Lucifer was my companion. When he wasn't with God, he would spend time with me. I loved him. And I know he loved me. But there was someone else he loved more than me. Someone he loved even more than God. He loved...himself. He thought himself the most beautiful and important of all God's creations. At times he was arrogant and bragged of his position. But never in front of God. It never bothered me that my companion was the highest of all angels. If anything, it made me a bit arrogant perhaps too. But Lucifer was haunted with the fact he was not able to give souls to his creations. Only God had the power to do such a thing. Lucifer wanted a creation of his own with a soul. He convinced me that we should create

                    Ashley Lauren Mitchell

something. It was the first time two creatures, without the consent of God, created a life, with a soul. God was angry and decided to punish Lucifer and me. I was sent away as you slowly grew inside me. Our creation."

"Afterwards, God did the unthinkable. We all know why he did it. He was so angry with Lucifer. He felt betrayed and saddened with the change in his and Lucifer's relationship. So he decided to make another creation to enjoy. Only a handful of angels knew what God was up to. But were forbidden from telling. One day, God descended from his heavenly throne and stepped onto earth. He knelt to the barren ground and touched it. The Garden sprang forth. Then he took a handful of the dirt in his hand and formed and shaped it into a human. He breathed life into the creature and gave it a soul. He called him, Adam. God would go to earth to be close with this...human. A human. But a human unlike any other. He gave him powers like angels have, and freedom to reign over all the earth."

"Lucifer and I were no longer allowed to be together. My purity was gone. I was cast to earth, in the Garden on the west. I was guarded there by several grotesque, scarlet beasts. They blocked the entrance and exit so that I couldn't leave. It was there in the small corner of the garden that I gave birth to a daughter. You. You were everything that was important to me, and the only thing I had. But once God saw you, he fell in love with you and decided to give you as a gift to Adam. You see? He took you from me."

"Years passed. I was able to see you, watch you grow, but God warned me not to reach out to you. So, all I could do was watch you. God tried to make Lucifer bow down to Adam, the human; because Adam had surpassed him in rank. Adam was pure, Lucifer was not, and could no longer be God's right hand. Lucifer's pride would not allow him to reverence a human. Foolishly, Lucifer once again disobeyed God, and instead, tried to get Adam to bow to him. Lucifer was cast from heaven, along with his angels God knew had been corrupted. They became Lucifer's followers. His demons. God took his power from him and surrounded him by fire that he cannot escape. He dwells below the heavens and earth. He is banished, locked away. All he can do is plan and await the day that he will be released from the prison he is in."

I listened to her tell the story. She was right, in my dream it all made sense. I wasn't sure how I understood, but I did, as if she were telling me something I already knew. But something I didn't understand, was what all of this had to do with me. "What does this have to do with me?"

She looked away from me, as if she were

Ashley Lauren Mitchell

ashamed of what she was about to say. "We cannot always help who we love or are connected to. Lucifer and I were companions. Are companions, still. Even though we cannot see each other, we have a special bond that cannot be broken. We can communicate with each other through different media. And we both still have the most important thing in common. You. You connect us even more."

"You see, your father loved you. You were his only child. You were created by him. You have a soul. But you would spend so much time with the human, Adam, that it enraged your father. He knew you would fall in love with the human and you wouldn't know the truth of who you really were. Who you are really for."

"A fallen angel is one that makes the choice to turn against God and heaven. Your father, Lucifer, was the first fallen angel. I am not a fallen angel, but I am banished from heaven forever. I know things, and have done things, that beings in heaven are not supposed to know or do. I was a bookkeeper in heaven. I loved to write. I recorded things for God, and wrote him many books and poems. It was my handwriting in the Book of Life and the Book of the Knowledge of Good and Evil. They were his notes, but he loved the way I would write for him. Because of this I knew how God created humans, and how humans created other humans. It was in their blood.

                                    Ashley Lauren Mitchell

Ethereal beings do not have blood. They are immortal. But there were vials of the life juice kept locked away for the creation of humans. Ethereal beings were to handle blood with great care and precaution. It was God's special elixir. He created it."

"Lucifer and I both made the decision to create you. We drank the blood. Then we felt something. Perhaps, lust. A fleshly desire. Our bodies, our skin became hot. Then, I remember I felt like I was flying. You see not all angels can fly. Not all angels have wings. We...they...each have a special task, as humans do on earth. That day your father and I knew each other in ways we'd never known each other before. It was beautiful, frightening, and wonderful. It was like we were actually one being, inside of each other. Knowing each other."

"We didn't realize how angry it would make God. I suppose, I thought God would be...proud, in a way. How foolish I was for thinking that. We'd debased ourselves in his eyes. Gave away our purity. He took both of our powers. I was no longer able to write. My task. My gift. Something I loved doing. Every time I'd simply try to put a pen in my hand and put it to paper, it wouldn't move. Like it was just, stuck. I cannot even use a stick to write in the dirt. So, I had to find other ways."

She picked a ripe, colorful fruit from the tree. "This tree is called the Tree of the Knowledge of Good

                    Ashley Lauren Mitchell

and Evil. It is a very sacred tree. After what we'd done, God turned the Book of the Knowledge of Good and Evil into a tree and placed it on earth so no other heavenly creature could read from it, and know the secret of the life giving blood."

"One day while you were with Adam, he fell asleep. You knew I was close. You felt me. I was able to train the scarlet beasts by watching how Adam trained animals. One of my pets brought me to the east side of the garden; where you were. I saw you. I yearned to hold you. Touch you. Embrace you. Tell you, you are my daughter. But I knew you wouldn't understand. I thought if you just took one bite of the fruit, I wouldn't have to explain anything. You would just...know. I called to you. I offered it to you. You were so innocent. So beautiful."

She walked to one of the raised roots of the tree and sat on it. She took a deep breath. Her voice was soft and shaky when she spoke again. It made me see her as vulnerable, less threatening. She did not look at me as she said, "After you took a bite of the fruit...," she paused. She took another deep breath, "you passed out. You were breathing but...barely. In my panic, I called out to God; something I hadn't done since he took you from me. He said that you were supposed to die because you ate of the fruit. I pleaded, I entreated, I begged, for him to have mercy on you. It was my fault you ate it.

Ashley Lauren Mitchell

He cast me from the east side of the garden forever. And he did have mercy on you. He let you live. But...he changed you. You no longer had your human form. He fused your legs together and made you, different. You hated your new appearance. You hid in the branches of the Tree. Adam looked for you but, like God told him not to, he never went near the Tree, where you clandestinely concealed yourself. Time passed. You became bored over the years. You began luring lost animals to the Tree, and tricked them into eating the fruit. The blood of the fruit changed the animals. They became aggressive and started killing and eating other animals. It was the blood. The ferocious animals would stay near the Tree and attack other animals that wandered too close."

"One day, a human came to the Tree. A woman. You were curious and told the flesh eating animals to let her pass. You started talking to her. She said her name was Eve. It wasn't long before, I guess, you figured out she was Adam's new companion. Something came over you, jealousy, more than likely. You tried to get her to eat a piece of the fruit, when she said, "God said, ye shall not eat of it, neither shall ye touch it, lest you die."

"And you cleverly responded," "But you are sitting on its roots right now. That is touching it. Ye shall not surely die. For you see God knows that when you do eat of this fruit, your eyes shall be opened, and ye

                         Ashley Lauren Mitchell

shall be as gods, knowing good and evil."

"Oh Lamia, you were so enticing. The human couldn't resist you. You handed her the fruit. She took it and bit into it. But unlike you, she didn't pass out. You didn't know she was created from Adam's own flesh, so she was just as powerful as he was. Eve took another bite, and another. You watched, appalled, concealing your anger. She thanked you for convincing her to try it. As she walked away with the fruit, she went on and on about how everything looked brighter, more colorful; and how she felt a tingle throughout her body. Then you heard Adam. You panicked at the thought of him eating the fruit. You knew they weren't supposed to eat it, and God would be angry with him if he did. But you still loved him, and didn't want anything bad to happen to him. You only wanted Eve to eat of the fruit."

"There was a low thundering sound that seemed to come from everywhere. You knew it was God. You heard the voice calling for Adam. After some time had passed, all three of them, God, Adam, and Eve, came to the Tree. You knew God was going to question you about the fruit. You hadn't seen Adam in a long time, but when he saw you, the look that he gave you broke your heart. It was a look of disgust, disappointment, hatred. God loved Adam too much to let him die. He allowed both he and the woman to live, but banished them from The Garden

                    Ashley Lauren Mitchell

of Eden."

"For your punishment, you were forced to crawl on your belly and be abused and feared for the rest of your life. You were so disappointed in yourself for Adam's having tasted the fruit, you did what no creature had ever done before. You took your own life. You hung yourself from the Tree that caused you so much grief. But you only succeeded in killing your body. You didn't know your soul would still linger on. It wandered, looking, searching for a new human body, so you could be with Adam again."

"I tried finding you my daughter. I feel it, every time your soul moves on. But finding you proved to be difficult, nearly impossible. Mostly because, you did not want to be found. And every time you'd find another body to possess, you would forget who you are, and what you were searching for. You would get so depressed at not knowing that you would kill yourself, every single time. This last time I knew the time was too close, so I had to do something to keep you from being able to kill yourself again."

She turned to me, "Your father and I have been finding ways to communicate. I use writers, poets, musicians; artists, to convey my abstract messages to him. It is the only way I can...write. Lucifer uses humans by possession, sending one of his demons to do what he cannot. You see? He is like you. You are like him. I can only possess the minds of

                    Ashley Lauren Mitchell

these people. You and your Father possess the entire human body. Taking it for your own. You have done this for thousands of years."

"But now we have decided it is time for your Father to be released from the prison he is trapped in. It is time for both of us, all of us to be restored to our rightful powers. And it is time for you to stop running. We all must be together. If we put all of our powers together, we can be just as powerful as God. We can have and be anything we want. And even better, we can be together. You can have a real family. Somewhere where you belong. Somewhere where you know who you are. Don't you want that?"

I was still processing all she had told me. And there was so much to process. Somehow I felt there was more I needed to hear. I wasn't even sure if I believed her so far. But a family? Somewhere I belonged? Those are things I do want. Then I think about, at what cost? What's the catch? What would I have to do? Nathaniel said that she used him. That he made a deal with her. Is that what I would have to do? Make a deal with her for something? "Nathaniel said you used him to get to me. Is that true?"

"Out of everything I've told you, your concern is for Nathaniel?" She said with disdain in her voice. When I didn't answer, she sighed, "Yes. I did use Nathaniel to help find you for me. But it was his father that I used first. Nathaniel's father was such a

                    Ashley Lauren Mitchell

talented poet. John was so accepting of me. He had experienced so much loss in his life that he was a perfect conduit to work through. He didn't believe in any god; just nature, the earth, the sky, the universe. He had so much potential. I gave him small, diluted doses of this fruit's juice. He saw visions of you after I told him of you. He wrote a poem for you."

My mind went to the poem John Keats wrote. It was for me.

"I enjoyed using John," she continued. "And after he died, I used his son to create a potion that would hold your soul in one human body. That way you couldn't kill yourself again, and I wouldn't have to search for your soul anymore. But Nathaniel, somehow, accidentally infected himself. Once he'd tasted the blood, he changed. And his soul was trapped in his body. It wasn't supposed to happen that way. But once it was done, I decided to continue using him. I used Nathaniel to find you, and prepare you for what lies ahead."

"Prepare me for what lies ahead?"

"Yes?"

"How did Nathaniel find me? And how did he prepare me?"

"Don't you see how corrupt you've become? You are corrupted. You have killed so many innocent

                    Ashley Lauren Mitchell

people, God will never forgive you. You killed the most precious of all living things, a human child, still in the womb. That makes you capable of killing God's son. The child born of a virgin. You are untrustworthy. You have no choice but to join with your Father and me." She came close to me and tried touching my face. I pulled back. She laughed a small, hushed laugh, and said, "And since you have already killed one innocent baby, the act you need to perform should be simple. Then you will be...perfect. A perfect killer. Because, that's what you are my Lamia. A killer."

A killer. That is all I am. The words rang in my ears. I remembered killing the pregnant woman, and her son. My whole body ached. My heart ached. My head ached. I ached for all the pain I'd caused so many innocent people. I once killed humans for doing the things, I'd done. I'd become what I was supposed to hate.

"Lamia?"

I looked at her but I didn't want to. I wanted to...die.

"Lamia, you cannot run from your destiny. You are needed. Your father and I need you. You don't have to feel what you are feeling. Lost. Confused. You are supposed to be with us." She reached to touch my cheek again. I let her. Her hand was warm and gentle.

                    Ashley Lauren Mitchell

"Sweet daughter, all you have to do is take a bite of this fruit, and everything will begin." I stared at the fruit she almost magically produced in the palm of her hand. "It's okay now my Lamia. I've found you. But you are the key. And you are the only one who can do this."

I looked at her and reluctantly asked, "I will have to kill again? Won't I?" She didn't answer. But from the way she looked at me, I knew the answer was yes. "I'm tired of killing. I don't want to kill anymore."

"But that is what you are supposed to do." She huffed at my stubbornness. "I'll promise you this," she began again, "once your father is free and we all have our powers back, you will never have to kill again. Not even to feed. You can do and be anything you want. If you want to be human and be with Nathaniel, you can be. But we have to free your father." She paused. "Please, Lamia. My daughter. We must."

"I need time. Time to think this all through."

"We don't have time, Lamia. Your father has been trapped for millions of years. Millions. I want to see him again. Don't you understand? You are not the only one who is suffering. You are not the only one who has to be alone. I am tired too. I am tired of being alone. I don't want to be alone anymore."

I could hear the sadness in her voice. Or was it aggravation? Perhaps it was both. I understood her loneliness. I understood her suffering. But what she was asking of me? Was I ready for all of it? "I just need some time." I repeated.

After a pause, she looked at me sternly and said, "No."

"No?"

"Lamia. I am your mother. I know you don't believe that, but I am. And, I am asking you to do this. However, if you refuse, I can, make you do it. I will make you do it. I wanted you to make the decision on your own. Out of love. Out of respect. I thought you would be persuaded by my words. I thought you would be happy to finally have a place where you wouldn't feel the need to run away all the time."

"You're right. I don't believe you."

She laughed. "You don't have to. All you have to do is take a bite of this fruit and the truth will be revealed. Just one bite."

I laughed back and said, "No."

"No?" She looked at me first with incredulity, then scorn, and then, she laughed again. It was a contemptuous laugh, and very unpleasant. "Fine Lamia. If you will not do this my way, we can do it

     Ashley Lauren Mitchell

your way. I won't allow you to ruin this for all of us. You are the only one that can release your father and you're saying, 'No?'

"Yes."

"I have been patient with you long enough. I have searched for you. I have watched over you and cared for you. And this is the thanks I get?" She stood to her feet, and stepped away from me. She bowed her head and said, "You leave me no choice."

She raised her hands high above her head, summoning something. The sky grew dark. Black clouds blocked the sunlight. I felt the ground quaking beneath my feet, like a rumbling herd. Then, I saw four giant red beasts running toward us. The looked like lions. They had full red manes, sharp teeth, and stripes on their bodies that alternated from bright red to a dark, deep, sanguine color. They're eyes were a blinding yellow that pierced through the darkness. When they were close enough to reach out and touch, they stopped. I felt their hot breath fuming all around me. Onaya looked at them and smiled, pleased with their presence. She walked up to one of the beasts. It bowed itself and she climbed on top of it, like she were mounting a horse. She looked down from her pedestal and stared at me, with her colorful eyes like mine.

"My beautiful daughter. It is such a shame it has to be like this." She said sarcastically.

She took the piece of fruit she was holding and broke it in half. Bloody juices spilled out and dropped to the ground. The beast she was sitting on, walked up to me. It knocked me off my feet with one swing. It was so strong. Its massive paw held me there, pinned to the ground. Onaya placed the fruit above my mouth and let the juices drip on my face and lips. I tried with all my might to fight it. I turned my head and she followed. I kept my lips pressed together as tightly as I could. My fangs were piercing through my bottom lip, but I kept the liquid from entering my mouth. Onaya gave a command and the monstrous beast, began pressing harder on my stomach. He was suffocating me, crushing me. I tried. I tried. I couldn't take it anymore. It felt like I was going to be pulverized by this...thing. I let out a terrible scream, opening my mouth wide. Onaya seized the opportunity and dripped the juice into my mouth. I felt it hit my tongue and slide down to my throat. I was drowning in it. The beast lifted its paw. I swallowed the liquid and gasped for air. I laid on the ground, shaking, with anger, pain, confusion. What happens now?

At first the fruit was sweet. Suddenly, it became bitter and I began feeling like my stomach was on fire. I writhed and squirmed, pulling myself into the fetal position. My eyes shut tightly. The pain was so

                    Ashley Lauren Mitchell

great! I hadn't felt pain like that since the night I came to be. I hated her for causing this pain. I hated her for doing this to me. The torment continued for what seemed like forever. Then, everything went silent. The pain ceased. And I couldn't see or hear anything.

Ashley Lauren Mitchell

<u>Chapter 24</u>

Nathaniel woke to the darkness of his coffin. He saw a flash of light and remembered what he'd tried to do, and how Jacque had saved him. His body was healed from the sun's menacing rays. Then, he remembered why he'd done it. Why he tried to kill himself. He dreaded having to rise from the safety and comfort of his coffin to face the truth of what he'd been used to do. His mind traveled back to that fateful night.

***

August, 2005

He saw Lamia in the sugarcane field in Donaldsonville. She was in a warm embrace with Anthony, tears streaming down his face. Anthony held her like he knew he would never see her again. Nathaniel watched as Anthony finally got into to his car and drove away, waving farewell to Lamia. Nathaniel watched her, and waited until Anthony's car was out of Lamia's view. Then he made his move.

                    Ashley Lauren Mitchell

Those green eyes. They were wide with shock, as Nathaniel appeared in the passenger seat of the NOPD police car. Anthony was not afraid of Nathaniel, but it took him a few seconds to right the car after almost swerving off the road. The two of them looked at each other, neither wanting to say anything. Anthony tried going for his gun. Nathaniel grabbed it and broke it in pieces. He told Anthony to pull the car over. Then he said, "Close your eyes." With much hesitation, and another failed attempt to escape, Anthony knew he could not fight this being. He closed his eyes. Nathaniel touched Anthony's arm, and the two of them teleported to Nathaniel's home.

***

Then Nathaniel thought of the night he took the woman.

***

Diamond was walking back to her mother's home after a brief visit with Lamia. She was sniffling and fighting tears. Slowly, she ambled in the middle of the street. Nathaniel appeared in front of her. When she looked at him, she didn't show fear, or confusion, only sadness. Nathaniel sensed that whatever he would do to her, she would welcome. Death even being preferable. Nathaniel began feeling, almost sorry for her. She didn't care what happened to her. Nathaniel held out his hand to Diamond. She looked at it, then at Nathaniel's pitch black eyes.

"You are like Lamia? Aren't you?" She asked.

He was surprised by her candor and decided to be just as frank. "Yes."

"Are you going to kill me?"

"Is that what you want?"

She looked at him for only a second before tears broke from her eyes. "I don't know." She answered, as the streams flowed freely down her face. It was an honest answer. A foolish and honest answer. He wasted no more time. He took her hand and they left Donaldsonville.

***

January, 2006

Nathaniel opened his eyes, took a deep breath, and lifted the lid of his coffin. Jacque was

 Ashley Lauren Mitchell

waiting patiently, as his master stepped from his sleeping chamber. Nathaniel nodded to him, thanking him for saving his life. Jacque groaned.

Nathaniel changed out of his burned and tattered clothes from the previous night. He had a feeling that Onaya had already taken Lamia away from the Sistine Chapel, but he teleported there anyway. The building was quiet, and occupied by only a few scattered humans. He was cold and hungry, but he wasn't in the mood to feed. He left the chapel before the humans saw him. He returned home.

His mind raced with anguish. He, reluctantly, made his way down the stairs of his enormous house. He opened the door of the coat closet. And then, he opened the door to the secret passageway, leading to the basement. His...laboratory.

It had been months since he'd traveled down those creaking steps. He didn't want to face the three people at the bottom of the staircase. The three humans that he'd been a nightmare to. They won't forgive him, he knew that. But that didn't matter. The one thing they all had in common was Lamia. And they all wanted what was best for her. He would have to find a way to convey his remorse, and get them to trust him.

'Impossible,' he thought.

As he descended the steps he heard the beeping noises coming from the heart monitors. There were two white-eyed, house attendants, caring for the comatose...captives. He dismissed the low moaning, zombie-like, meandering creatures. He looked at all three of the human bodies before him. All helpless in their beds. Nathaniel thought about how he was once going to, supposed to, kill all of them, but instead gave them a thing like death. They would live, but not live. They would only breathe and not move. Not see. Not hear. One of them had been this way for nearly forty years. He felt something he hadn't felt in a long time. Guilt. How could he be holding these innocent people like this? What had been his purpose for such a cruel thing?

He walked up to the one he needed more than any of them right now. The one he would have the most difficulty with. Nathaniel watched the man breathing for a minute longer. With great ease, he pulled a needle from Anthony's arm; for the second time his life. He waited.

It took only another minute for Anthony's eyes to open. Those dazzling green eyes. They stared at Nathaniel with confusion, and then, realization. As if he'd been waiting to do it the entire time he was sleeping, Anthony's hands darted to Nathaniel's neck. He squeezed as tightly as he could, using the small amount of strength he had. Nathaniel knew Anthony wanted him dead, but would never be able to kill him. It didn't stop Anthony from trying. Nathaniel let him try as hard and as long, as he could. Nathaniel stood there and looked at Anthony's eyes, almost wishing he could feel even a little pain from the attack, for what he'd done.

After Anthony came to the disappointing conclusion that he couldn't hurt Nathaniel, he dropped his hands back on the bed. He looked around and saw the two women lying in beds adjacent to his. He then used his hands to cover his face. He tried his best not to let tears of anger and helplessness trickle from his eyes.

Nathaniel began, "Anthony, I know it will be hard for you to forgive me for what I've done. And perhaps, you never will. I am not in need of your forgiveness right now. It was me, who once saved your life when you were very young. It does not excuse this, but just know that I don't want you dead. I never have. I was supposed to kill you, but I couldn't bring myself to do it."

"Where is she?" Said Anthony.

"That is the problem. I don't know. I need you to help me find her. I think she may be in danger."

"What kind of danger? Who are you? And what have done with Lamia?"

"I've only done what I was instructed to do. I was, I was, possessed."

"Possessed?"

"Yes."

Anthony looked incredulously at Nathaniel. He'd never heard such a thing. Nathaniel knew Anthony couldn't understand it. Humans cannot comprehend happenings in another realm. He tried to explain.

"Internally, I fought with the spirit for years. I kept it from completely controlling my mind. Somehow, I maintained the capacity to remember who I was. When it came time to kill you, I knew I had a connection with you. I knew, I didn't want to kill you. And I knew, how much Lamia cares for you. For the two of you, deeply," he said looking at Diamond. "I don't really know why all of this is happening. I wasn't always this way. I was, of course, once human. But when I changed, I was hardly in control of certain circumstances. I don't expect you accept or believe anything I am telling you. But I know you will help me. I know it, because it is not for me. It is for Lamia."

Although Anthony's body had been resting for months, the strength came back to him almost immediately. He slowly got to his feet. He walked up to Nathaniel. He swung at him and connected with his face. Anthony pulled his hand back, massaging the pain in his knuckles away. Once again disappointed, and somewhat embarrassed, that the hit, did not exact pain to the right person.

"I am sorry you cannot hurt me physically Anthony. I know that you want to. Badly. But I am like Lamia. And you know, as well as I do, Lamia is strong, powerful. You cannot hurt me." They stood for a moment looking at each other as the tension lessened. "Come. We must wake the others. I don't know how much time we have."

"How much time we have for what?"

"I don't know."

Anthony was there to embrace Diamond, when she came to. He held her until she calmed from her hysteria. She was ecstatic to see the man she loved again. She remembered Nathaniel. She wasn't angry with him like Anthony was. If anything, she was grateful Nathaniel didn't take her life when she begged for it. They tried explaining everything to her, even though she too, couldn't understand any of it.

Then, there was the third person. Anthony walked with Nathaniel to the woman's bed. He didn't recognize her, but thought she looked familiar. Almost like Nahdia. Then he realized who he was looking at.

"This is my Aunt Antoinette?"

                    Ashley Lauren Mitchell

"Yes."

"Why is she here?"

"When you and your sister left this place, your Aunt went into an unshakeable depression. She wouldn't eat. She only cried and slept. She even begged for death. But I wanted to preserve her. She was the first human that I put my blood in, and didn't die. My first, successful experiment. She began aging faster after you and Nahdia left her. I put her in this sleep to stop her aging, and her sadness." Nathaniel removed the needle from Antoinette's arm.

Her bright hazel eyes opened and saw Nathaniel. She smiled and said, "Did you find them? Did you find Nahdia and Anthony? Were they in New Orleans like I said?" Nathaniel smiled back, and looked at Anthony. Antoinette turned her head and looked at Anthony as well. After only a moment she recognized his green eyes. "Anthony!" She exclaimed as she sat up. "I thought I'd never see you again. Look at how much you've grown." She opened her arms wide, and even though Anthony barely remembered her, he embraced her like the family she was. He could tell from the way she looked at him, held him, that she had loved him, all his life. When she could finally bring herself to release him she asked, "Where is Nahdia?"

                    Ashley Lauren Mitchell

Anthony looked at her and wanted to cry. "She died. Many years ago."

"No." Antoinette whispered. She laid back down in her bed and began to weep.

"Aunt Nette," Anthony said, as if he'd called her that every day of his life, "Nahdia had a daughter."

"A daughter?"

"Yes."

"Oh my god. Well, where is she? Did she...did she, die too?"

Anthony looked at Nathaniel. He was looking for an answer. He didn't know if Lamia was dead. He knew Lily was, but he couldn't tell that to his long lost aunt right now. He couldn't tell anything to her. At that moment, he felt he didn't know anything to tell.

Nathaniel spoke, "No, Antoinette. She is not dead." He moved to sit next to her. "Remember how you and Anthony were never to taste blood?"

"Yes. I remember."

"Nahdia's daughter was like you and Anthony. When she was a baby Anthony helped her by making her, like you two. He didn't understand the severity of your condition. Through a procedure, Anthony's blood was passed to the baby. Unfortunately when she was older, she did taste blood. And, it changed her."

"Changed her how?" Antoinette asked cautiously.

Nathaniel, Anthony, and Celeste looked at each other. They knew explaining it wouldn't be easy. For nearly two hours they talked about what had happened, and was happening, with Lamia. Nathaniel also told them about his parents, John and Isabella. And then, he told them about Onaya.

"She has Lamia. She claims to be her mother. I don't know what she wants with her, but I don't trust her. What I do know, is that we need to get Lamia away from her."

"And how do you propose we do that?" Asked Anthony.

"Well, first, we need to find her."

The four beings thought about where Onaya had taken Lamia. A plethora of different emotions in the atmosphere. It was hard for each of them to think, to figure out an answer.

After a sudden synaptic surge in Anthony's brain, he said, "I know where she is."

Nathaniel looked at him with disbelief, but then

realized, Anthony really did know. It was Anthony all along. It was Anthony, who always knew, who always had the connection with Lamia. Anthony, somehow had the ability to communicate with Lamia when they weren't together, and he always knew how to find her. Staring at Anthony, Nathaniel tried to fight his jealousy, his disappointment, his hurt, at knowing, Lamia could never be for him. Her heart belonged to Anthony.

Anthony gave the order, he said, "We need to get to New Orleans. Now!"

Chapter 25

She called me Lamia.

When I woke this time, I was back in the large, intricately painted building. Onaya was still holding my head in her lap, as my body laid on the ground. I was not in pain. In fact, I couldn't feel anything. I was completely numb. The only things I could move on my entire body, were my eyes. I stared at her.

"You don't have to do anything anymore," she said.

I felt myself rising. She was controlling me. She stood me upright and I floated behind her as she walked the length of the building. When she came to the back wall she spoke, "This," she hissed, "Is called, the Last Judgment." She ran her finger over the entire darkened length of the wall. She laughed and turned to face me. She walked up to me and asked, "Do you know why I wanted you to stay in this body?" I couldn't answer her. I couldn't move my lips. She knew it. She was taunting me. "I wanted you to stay in this body because of Lily. Yes. Lily. Do you know what was so special about Lily? No, of course you don't, because you didn't really care to get to know who

Lily was. But Lily Leduff was special. Not only did Lily have traces of the fruit in her, thanks to Nathaniel. And not only did you live somewhere dark and cryptic inside her, just like you've always thought. But, what was most important about her, what made her so useful, was the fact that Lily, was a virgin. She was never known by a man. She was so pure. So perfect. And you found her. Your blood is mixed with the blood of a virgin. And now, with more of the potent fruit in you, all I need from you, is your blood." She sighed. "I tried to get you to cooperate. But like I said, you leave me no choice."

She lifted my hand to her mouth. When she opened her lips I saw her sharp dagger-like teeth grow longer. She took my index finger and pressed it hard against one of them. I couldn't feel it, but I watched the blood trickle out my finger. She held my finger there as she closed her eyes and licked her lips. She smiled. When she opened her eyes, they were shining bright red and glowing marvelously. Her face began to change as well. It became wrinkled, but tight. Then two small, curved horns began to break through her forehead.

She put my bloody finger on the wall of the building and slid it across the painting as she did with her own finger only minutes ago. The streak of blood sizzled and disappeared into the wall. Onaya walked to the middle of the building, bringing me with her.

   Ashley Lauren Mitchell

She turned to face the back wall again and yelled, "Arise!"

Ghastly, ghoulish creatures in the painting lit up. Their eyes all turned red, like hers. They all started moving. The figures began pulling themselves out of the wall, letting out painful, screeching howls as they did. I watched one emerge from a boat and onto the floor of the building. It stood nearly ten feet tall. Its skin was as black as Nathaniel's eyes. It had long, pointed ears that protruded from the sides of its head. It was a horrible sight. Another had sharp teeth like mine, but it had wings that spanned out wide from its body. It had pale skin, furry legs, and talons on its hideous feet. Another was a large skeleton. Another, a howling goblin, dressed in all black. Another had a hunched, crouching form. It looked like a deformed animal and human that was somehow fused or morphed together. And the last was a spirit, a dark ghost with a suspicious grin. All of the demons were large, daunting beasts. There were six of them. They walked toward us, groaning like Nathaniel's house attendants.

Onaya held me suspended in mid-air, as the demons came closer. They gathered in a circle around us. All of them just as horrendous as the next. Onaya had a look of pride on her face as she turned to me. "These are your father's most prized demons. They...we," she said with a large, evil smile, "are going to free him tonight!" The demons let out a loud, earth quaking scream of satisfaction.

Once they'd quieted, Onaya said, "But first we must have a little fun. We need one hundred and forty-four thousand souls. And not just any souls. We need wayward souls." She looked away from me and began talking to each of the demons, as if giving a speech would rouse them even more. They looked ready to do whatever she demanded. "We need the blood of thieves, rapists, and murderers. Their wretched blood will soak the ground. Once it's evaporated into the earth, Lucifer will be released! It is time!" Again the demons let out a trembling cry. Onaya walked back in front of me, her eyes glowing, her horns protruding, "And I know just the place to start. My darling daughter, are you feeling hungry?" She mocked, smiling, gratified. "I think it is time to take you back to a place you once called...home."

***

The city of New Orleans. A city that never sleeps. There is always some event, festival, or something, that brings with it large crowds of people. And what lingers in large crowds waiting to strike? Predators. Why did the city of New Orleans, a city whose scent, atmosphere, vibrations, I'd come to enjoy, have to be so damned...cursed? It could be called a sin city. A city of sin. A city whose beautiful scenery, architecture, and culture, brings with it death, disaster, and mayhem. And why tonight, of all nights, did the city have to be swarming with humans?

The lights from the city, blocked all light from any heavenly bodies. The Superdome, a massively round structure, had green, gold, and purple lights all around it. It was breathtaking. It was the first time I'd ever seen it like that. If only I could revel in it. But instead, I am floating above it, paralyzed by Onaya. All of us floated above the city. Watching it.

I could smell them. All of them. Humans everywhere! Yes. I was hungry. And their aroma was filling my senses. Their heartbeats, a rhythm beating in my ears. We stood atop the Superdome. Watching. For minutes, just watching. Some of the humans started noticing us. I could hear their whispers from my place in the sky. They thought it all a grand act done by some production. They howled and cheered. Then they watched and waited for our next move. They were just as anxious to know what would happen next as I was.

Onaya moved first; closer to me. "Do you see all these people?" I stared at her with apprehension, trying to turn away from her. I had an idea what was

                    Ashley Lauren Mitchell

going to happen next. "Lamia, we need your eyes. Just look out into the crowd." The demons started squirming with anticipation. "You won't even have to kill anyone," she said as she moved some hair from my face, as Diamond had done long ago. She kept going, "I'm sure they can handle it," her eyes looking over the demons. They were ready to attack. "But when you can't handle the scent of blood anymore, you will do, what you do best."

I knew she was right. I was hungry, and there were so...many...humans. I looked at the crowd again, and I saw, the first one. He wasn't a serial killer, but he was a killer. He had taken a few lives with his handgun; the one situated in the small of his back, that only he, some of the men with him, and now, I, knew about. I looked at them. A couple of them froze, like the first one I'd stunned. All...killers. Onaya looked at them. They began to glow, distinguishing them from the crowd around them. I looked over the mass of people again. One by one, more and more began to freeze and glow. They, were the souls needed. They were the ones whose blood was soon to spill on the ground.

The demons slid down the roof of the Superdome from where they had been perched like gargoyles. As I kept looking at all of the humans, something began to stir in me. Something more than hunger. Something like, disappointment, maybe, that

                    Ashley Lauren Mitchell

there were so many more people lighting up as I kept scanning. Then I started to feel...anger, rage. My cold skin began to tingle. My breathing became heavier. I felt Onaya watching me. She knew. She knew what was happening to me. She knew the longer I looked at them, the more I would want to kill them. All the sinister souls. And it was in my nature. I couldn't stop it. I couldn't.

I started to see panic rise in the crowd. Some of the innocents were trying to wake the corrupt from their frozen spell, but their actions were futile. Many began swiftly walking away from the Superdome. More panic. Then, they started running.

That was the cue. The demons, one by one, pounced from the ledge of the Superdome. Each landing with a powerful thud onto the ground. They walked up to the humans that had been immobilized, and still gazing at me. I watched as one of the demons ripped the head off of a human. Blood spurted from the neck and spilled to the ground. With a gratified scream I saw the demon devour the head, and with another scream move to the next. All of the demons did the same. One by one, killing the humans.

Onaya watched with delight before turning back to me. "At this rate, it won't be long before your father is released and you will see the magnificent, glorious splendor of the greatest creation of all time. I

                    Ashley Lauren Mitchell

am going to release my hold on you now. Go, kill, feed, and join in on all of the action. It will only get better."

As soon as she freed me from her invisible grasp, I felt it hit me like a wave. Hunger. An overwhelming hunger. An inescapable hunger. The dire need to feed. Blood. The scent of blood was, everywhere, controlling my senses. Now, my self-restraint was loosening its grip on me. One. I'll just kill one, to subdue my hunger. I don't want to be a part of this, mass destruction. Screams, cries, madness grew louder throughout the city of New Orleans. I looked back and saw Onaya still hovering right above the center of the Superdome. Watching, waiting. I jumped onto the concrete into a puddle of blood. Dead bodies, even innocents, were like rubble in the streets. Collateral damage. People were leaving their cars running, as they, ran from the massacre.

I made my way up Poydras St. I kept my eyes down, trying not to make eye contact with anyone. Only looking up to see the street signs. I took a left on Carondelet St. Then, as I crossed over Canal, I realized I was being drawn to Bourbon St. One of the most sinful streets in all the world. Sex, drugs, alcohol, murder, so much sin all on one street. I heard them before I looked up to see hundreds of them swarming before me. They were unaware of what was happening only blocks away. I felt the hunger taking over. I'd held it off too long. There were too many of them. Their blood, hot. The smell, inviting.

One of them accidentally stumbled into me. My hard body knocked him to the ground. When he looked up, I looked down. We made eye contact. He was innocent, but, he...was... right...here. I reached down to help him up. Before I knew it, I had pulled his body to mine. We looked as if we were in a warm embrace, and I was just nuzzling his neck. I don't know why I couldn't help myself, but I drained him. His delicious blood. I felt it filling my body. It was warm. I was warm. I felt...good. I let him slip to the ground as I leaned my head back, allowing the blood to quench my thirst.

Suddenly, I heard a woman scream. She saw what happened. I wasn't careful. I wasn't...I didn't care. I wiped the blood from my mouth as other nosey citizens started gathering. They were getting too close. Too close. Closer. My heart started beating faster. I heard their voices. I heard their heartbeats. I heard sirens in the background, getting closer. Screaming. Closer. Two horse-mounted police officers rode in my direction. Closer. Everything was getting...closer. I couldn't take it anymore!

I looked into the horses eyes. "Up!" I yelled. The gigantic horses reared back, rising on their hind legs, and knocking their riders to the ground. More

                    Ashley Lauren Mitchell

screams. The horses came to me. They were the same two from many months ago. They stood calmly by my sides as people rushed, excitedly away from me. I smiled, as I felt myself becoming more powerful. I rose from the ground and floated across the trolley tracks. The people in their cars stared in disbelief, as some of them rolled up their windows. I was at the very edge of Bourbon Street. Entertainers dropped their instruments. As more people began to notice me, and caught a glimpse of my eyes, many of them froze. The wicked. The innocents, again, tried shaking them, waking them in futility, before they gave up and ran away.

I clapped my hands in front of me. The sound was so loud and thunderous. They all froze. All of them. I opened my arms. Magically, beautifully, a path was cleared before me. Two long rows of humans lined the street, waiting to be mauled, decapitated, or eaten. I smiled at my power. My abilities. I was getting stronger. The blood. It was because of the blood. The more blood I consumed, the more powerful I would become. I wanted more power. I needed more blood.

I floated up to one of the humans. She was trembling, shaking...innocent. Tears streaming down her disconcerted face. But, her innocent blood, will taste just as wonderful as a killers' blood. I rubbed her cheek and moved her hair from her neck. I leaned in to smell her. Oh, she smelled wonderful! I gently tilted her head to the side. I felt her tepid tears gliding down my hand. Her heart was racing, pounding. I closed my eyes and opened my mouth...

"Lamia!"

I heard a voice scream my name. I thought I was hearing things. I paused. Then, I heard it again.

"Lamia! Don't do it!"

Nathaniel! It was Nathaniel's voice! I thought I'd never hear it again! I let go of the frightened woman and floated back to the center of Bourbon Street.

There he was.

It felt as if I hadn't seen him in years; when it had only been one night. I let my feet touch the ground. I ran to him. We hugged each other so tightly. He was cold. He hadn't fed. He pulled me from him.

"What is going on? How are you doing all this?" He asked, looking at the entranced humans.

"It's Onaya. She's done something to me. She's trying to wake Lucifer."

"Lucifer?"

"Yes. She says he's my father."

"Lamia?"

"I know. I don't believe any of this either. But, I can't stop her. I don't know how. You were right Nathaniel. She is too powerful. We have to get out of here."

"Lamia?"

"We need to get away from here. Let's teleport somewhere. Anywhere. We need to go."

"Lamia!" Nathaniel yelled, and shook me from my hostility.

My eyes shot to his. The longer I looked at him, the more my confusion and concern grew. "What?"

"There's something I have to tell you."

"What?"

Before he could open his mouth I heard her. Onaya. She was staring at us with amused suspicion. She touched her feet to the ground. She was yards away from us, but her voice was so loud, it was as if she were right next to us. I'm certain the living, for miles around, could hear her, even above the chaos.

She raised her arms, "Come to me!" She yelled. All six of the demons, ran to her and stood behind her, ready for her every command. She spoke again, "Nathaniel? You clever little devil. How did you know

                    Ashley Lauren Mitchell

we'd be here?"

"Stop this Onaya! No more people need to die," he said.

She laughed, "And this coming from who? You? Just who do you think you are?"

"Onaya, I know it was you who killed my mother and father. I know it was you."

She laughed again, "Your mother, yes. She was only a burden. She had to go. But not your father? It wasn't me that killed him. It was his illness. If it were up to me, he'd still be alive today; instead of you."

She's so...evil. She killed Nathaniel's mother? What kind of a monster is she? "Leave him alone!" I yelled at her. I was boiling with anger.

"Lamia, stay out of this. This has nothing to do with you."

"Onaya, we are leaving this place. You stay away from us. I want nothing to do with you."

"Daughter! Do not test me!"

"I am not afraid of you!"

"Dammit Lamia!" She screamed. She raised her arms in the air, making an 'X' with her wrists. With one, swift, downward motion of her arms, all the heads of

                    Ashley Lauren Mitchell

the humans lining the streets, flew off. They hit the ground with a thump. Blood sprayed everywhere. The bodies looked like sprinklers. Then, they dropped. Covering the street, flooding it with their blood.

Suddenly, beneath our feet, the ground began to glow. The lake of blood, bubbled and started evaporating, disappearing into the ground as if the earth were drinking it in. The black concrete became lighter and lighter until it was nearly transparent. Then, I saw...him! Swimming like a shark, circling in water. But he wasn't a shark. He wasn't a shark at all. He looked like, a...dragon! An enormous, intimidating, ghastly red dragon! He might have been, the most beautiful, and the most frightening thing I had ever seen. He toiled beneath us, slithering his body, and whipping his long, spiked tail.

"Lamia," called Onaya, "This is your father!" Pride and excitement ringing in her voice. Her hair became as fire. It flamed all around her. "We need more!" She yelled. Like lightening, the six demons ran, on to gather more human souls. She looked at Nathaniel and me. Her eyes, emblazoned with fury. "Nathaniel," she spoke menacingly, "You have become to me as your mother. A burden! You attempt to stand in my way! So, I will give you, your mother's fate!"

Onaya stretched her arm toward Nathaniel. She started spinning her hand, as if she were turning a

                    Ashley Lauren Mitchell

door knob, or the dial of a lock. Once her hand could spin no more, she opened her fingers, like releasing a bird. Nathaniel grabbed at his neck. He turned to me. His black eyes, wide, glimmering my reflection. His hands began grasping his shirt, pulling it away. He was breathing heavily, gasping for air. His skin started steaming. Then I saw, his heart, glowing in his chest. He staggered backward. I stepped away from him. I didn't know what to do. I watched, in confusion, and helplessness.

His heart started glowing brighter. His whole body began glowing like a lantern, and his heart, the flame.

"Aaaahhhh!!!" I'd never heard Nathaniel scream like that before. It took me by surprise. I felt my eyes growing wider with astonishment, disbelief. I finally found the will the go to him. I put my hands on his chest, his head, his arms. I didn't know where to put my hands. I turned to Onaya, "Stop this! Now!"

"It's too late! This is his fate! This is his destiny!"

I turned back to Nathaniel. I wanted to cry. I wanted to cry! He was burning, dying, in front of me, and I couldn't stop it. Everything seemed to be happening in slow motion.

The giant, slithering, red dragon beneath our feet was growing more impatient. He started hitting

                    Ashley Lauren Mitchell

his body against the ground, attempting to break free. Small cracks began to form in the pavement. Small burst of fire shot up all around us.

Nathaniel grabbed me. He was so hot. His insides were getting brighter. He fell to his knees. I was brought with him. His body kept falling. I knelt on the ground and put his head on my lap. Onaya laughed. She started blasting buildings with fire from her hands, destroying the city.

Nathaniel pulled me closer to him. He spoke, "Lamia," he strained. I could almost feel the pain he was in. I wanted to. I wanted to take it away from him. "Your uncle," he gasped.

"My uncle? What about my uncle?" I couldn't believe he was talking about my Uncle Tony at a time like this. He was dying. Why is my uncle in his last thoughts?

"He's," he gasped, "he's,"

"He's what? He's what, Nathaniel? What about my uncle?"

"Alive." He whispered, then let out a terrible scream, as his body burst into flames. In a matter of seconds he was ashes in my hands.

Nathaniel was gone? I couldn't move. I could only shake my head in disbelief. Nathaniel, dead?

                    Ashley Lauren Mitchell

And, my Uncle Tony is, alive? I was trembling. I didn't know what to do with myself. I continued to sit there in bewilderment as Onaya laughed loudly.

"His soul is mine now!" she cried, still blasting windows, cars, and any stray human she saw.

It all felt like a dream. A terrible dream. No. This is a nightmare. I sat, watching. All I could do was sit there. Motionless. Powerless. Useless, while she destroyed...everything. So many sounds. Screaming. Sirens. Car alarms. Diminishing heartbeats. I felt like I was spinning. Lucifer's pounding became harder beneath me. We were all here. All three of us. My alleged parents and I. The six minions ran to us and gathered for the moment they've all waited so long for.

In the distance I heard a voice calling my name. It was yet another voice I hadn't heard in a very long time. Calling to me, "Lamia!" It shouted. "Lamia!"

I turned my head. Running up Bourbon Street, like a brave soldier, was my Uncle Tony! "Lamia!" He kept shouting.

I couldn't believe it.

"You!" Onaya yelled. She said it with recognition and aggravation. He stopped in his tracks. "Nathaniel was supposed to get rid of you. You

                                    Ashley Lauren Mitchell

are supposed to be dead!"

I felt that feeling again. The feeling that I only get from her. Fear. I knew from the tone of her voice. I knew. I knew she was going to kill my Uncle Tony. And I was afraid.

"This, is the last time you will stand in my way!"

I felt the milliseconds slowing. Everything was so...slow. So slow, I thought the earth had stopped, and I, was the only thing that could move. Onaya's arm unfolded and stretched toward Uncle Tony. I put my hands on the ground and pushed myself up. I saw an eye in the palm of Onaya's hand. I hadn't noticed it before. But then again, time had made it so that I could see every detail around me. A spark began to kindle in the eye. With a thundering blast, the flame shot out toward Uncle Tony. With every ounce of strength in me, I ran. My feet hitting the transparent ground, one by one. My arms swinging back and forth, pushing me harder and harder, faster and faster. I looked back and saw the ball of fire getting closer to Uncle Tony. He raised his arms, shielding himself from the imminent attack. I jumped.

I felt it hit me. It jetted my chest forward and my arms back. I didn't feel myself scream, but I knew it was my voice, crying out. I hit the ground; my chest first, and my face immediately following. After a brief

                    Ashley Lauren Mitchell

surge of pain, I was completely numb. Again, I couldn't move. I could hear and see, but I couldn't move anything. I thought I heard Onaya gasp, 'No.'

"Oh God! No!" Uncle Tony exclaimed, as he knelt down and turned me over in his arms. I saw him. Tears billowing from his gorgeous green eyes. "Lamia?" He called to me. "Baby Girl? Oh, Baby Girl." I heard him call me Baby Girl. I tried to...I hoped, I was smiling. At the sight of his face. At the sound of his voice. His tears falling on my cheek. Or was it my tears? Did I finally, was I finally...crying? He wiped them away. "Lamia. I'm so sorry Baby Girl." He pulled me to him and hugged me tightly. I smelled him. He smelled, amazing. "I love you Baby Girl," he sobbed. "Do you hear me? I love you Lamia!"

He was so close to me. I closed my eyes and opened my mouth, "I love you too...Uncle Tony." It was the first time I had ever told those words to anyone. But I knew I meant it. I knew saying them to Uncle Tony was what I wanted to do. What I should have done a long time ago. He held me in his arms, looking at me. Rocking me, as I felt my body get warmer and warmer. I felt a burning in my chest. My heart. She'd hit my heart.

I heard Onaya cry out again, "No!" I saw her come to us, pushing Uncle Tony away from me. She looked at me with doubt and...fear. I saw fear in her eyes; eyes that were no longer red and emblazoned,

                    Ashley Lauren Mitchell

but again colorful and sparkled like mine. The ground quaked beneath us. Fire died out as black smoke filled the atmosphere. I saw her eyes again. She looked like she was watching her well-planned operation, dying in front of her. "Lucifer? Don't go!" She cried. She shook me. "Lamia? Don't die. I'm sorry. Don't die. I didn't mean to hit you. I was trying to hit him. Lamia? Lamia?"

Her face became cloudy, fading from my view. Her voice became distant. Everything became distant. My eyes felt so heavy. I couldn't. I couldn't keep them open any longer. I thought I heard her scream. Or was it my Uncle Tony? My Uncle Tony. He lives. I felt my body go completely limp and sag in her arms. My head fell back. I only saw darkness. I only heard my dying heartbeat. I listened for the final one. Then it stopped.

Ashley Lauren Mitchell

<u>Chapter 26</u>

Onaya let out a bone chilling scream as she watched Lucifer struggle to break free. The earth trembled as the transparent ground became translucent, then opaque. The six demons were sucked down through the disappearing cracks in the concrete. Onaya looked at Lamia's body lying limply in her hands. She let out a breath. "Lamia?" Onaya felt her body becoming lighter. She stood to her feet as she began to disintegrate. Her skin became sparkles of small orange flames. As they broke apart, and drifted into the air, Onaya let out one final scream.

Corpses lined the streets. Anthony rose from the ground and slowly walked to Lamia. He rubbed his hands down his face, wiping away his tears. He knelt down beside her, then sat down on the bloody ground. He lifted her head and put it in his lap. He tried putting some of his blood on her tongue. A futile attempt to revive her. Then he let go. He let his defeated tears fall once again.

"Tony?" Diamond screamed, emerging from the balcony doors of Désirs Cachés. He took his eyes from Lamia and looked at her. He shook his head.

                    Ashley Lauren Mitchell

Diamond let out a whimper. "No." She sat down and looked at them, tears streaming from her eyes and dripping from her chin. They were the only people on Bourbon Street. The only people alive for miles. The earth was quiet. Diamond pulled her knees to her chest and continued crying.

The sky opened up. Small drops of water began to fall. Within minutes the rain started to pour. Lamia's body was light, almost weightless to Anthony, as he picked her up and moved her inside Désirs Cachés. Diamond ran down the stairs to meet him. They put Lamia's body on the stage. Diamond tore off a piece of her shirt and started wiping dirt and blood from Lamia's face. Anthony sat in a chair and looked at her. He couldn't stop his tears. He didn't know what else to do. He put his head down and did something he thought he'd never do. He prayed.

"God, or whoever is up there. I need help. I don't know what to do. I am so lost."

***

Am I really dead? Could I really be dead? I felt myself rising, unlike other times where I'd felt like I was falling. I was steadily being lifted higher and higher. My eyes closed. My body weightless. I saw light shining all around me. A very bright light. When I

Ashley Lauren Mitchell

opened my eyes, everything was white and hazy. It was an encompassing haze. It wrapped around me, hugging me, then fell away. I squinted my eyes. I thought I heard something. Movement. Shifting. What was it?

"Lamia?"

A voice. One I'd never heard before. Or had I? I squinted harder. A figure began to appear. Figures. I turned around. I was standing in the middle of a circle. Not people. Not all of them. Some of them looked like a grotesque combination of human and animal, man and beast.

The voice spoke again, a woman, "Lamia, you sacrificed yourself for another?" The way she'd said it, was as though she never thought she'd ever say it. "That is the most selfless thing you can do for anyone. You found your...love. You know and understand what love is. The giving of yourself, disregarding your own wants and needs. Even your own life. You, have done that."

Another voice. It was the voice of a man. I turned to face it. "Lamia, your actions put an end to what would have been one of the greatest disasters of all time. There would have been near human extinction if not for you."

I didn't feel like I deserved the homage they

were bestowing upon me. "Are you... God?"

"No," came another voice. "We are servants of God. He speaks through us. And he is well pleased with you."

"He is?"

"Yes," said yet another voice.

I felt like I was spinning in circles, trying to keep up with the directions from which the voices were coming.

"Not everything Onaya has told you has been a lie," came another voice.

Deep down, I knew Onaya was lying about something. Perhaps everything. But to think that some of it was actually true?

"Onaya really is your mother, and Lucifer is your father. They both once held seats in this circle. They were companions. Lucifer was God's right hand and God would only speak to us through him. After many years, Lucifer began thinking too much of himself. He began thinking he should be as God. Onaya was the one who wrote in the Book of Life and in the Book of the Knowledge of Good and Evil. She had restricted, esoteric knowledge. Lucifer and Onaya believed they were better than us. The two of them came to think of themselves as a king and queen.

They felt they deserved more than we did. God sensed their growing egos, he stopped talking just through Lucifer and started using all of us. It was Onaya who told Lucifer he would become more like a god if he made creature with a soul. She was the one who persuaded Lucifer to help her conceive. They were both cast out of heaven. You were born in the Garden. You have never been here before. You were never supposed to be here. It was believed to be in your nature to be like the ones who created you, Lucifer and Onaya, but you have..."

Silence. The voice stopped. Everything was quiet again. The only thing I could hear was footsteps, echoing up a pathway. They came closer. Soon, I saw a young boy walking to me. He had hazel eyes that matched his curly hair. When he was standing directly in front of me, he took his index finger and curled it, silently asking me to bend closer to him. I did. He didn't speak. Instead, he touched my forehead. I felt something so powerful rush through me. I closed my eyes and saw every celestial being flashing in my mind. I felt like I was traveling, at light speed, through space. I came to a halt and opened my eyes. We had teleported. The young boy and I were standing in...The Garden of Eden.

He spoke. It was the soft, sweet, innocent, voice of a child. "Father wanted me to get you away from them so that I may speak freely with you."

I watched him moving around the garden. He walked up to the animals and pet them. He touched the trees, their leaves, and their fruit. All with curiosity and joy. Seeing someone so young made me feel very unintimidated. Very...at ease.

"Who are you?" I asked.

"They were right. Father says, you have done well," he said ignoring my question.

"Your father?"

"Yes."

"Who is your father?"

He kept walking around the Garden, "This is where you were born?"

Again, he ignored my question. "That is what I am told. Yes." I huffed. "You said you wanted to speak to me?"

"Where is the...Tree?"

"The Tree?" The Tree. He was speaking of the Tree of the Knowledge of Good and Evil. I looked around. I didn't see it. How odd. It is so large that it can be seen from anywhere in the Garden, by just looking up. Like a mountain, or rather an ominous, dormant volcano. But the Tree wasn't there. "I don't know." I admitted.

He laughed.

"What's so funny?" I asked.

"You don't see the Tree because I am the Tree."

"What?"

"I...am...the...Tree."

"I don't understand."

He started jumping all around. Skipping. Doing cartwheels. I'd never been around someone so young. It was kind of...annoying.

"Father says that I am the Tree."

"How are you the Tree?"

"Father says, that some people couldn't be trusted with the fruit of the Tree, so he put the Tree of Life and the Tree of the Knowledge of Good and Evil, in me. Father says, I am his human son, his, blood. Beings in heaven don't have blood. I'm the only one. Father says I am special."

"Wait a minute. You are the Tree?"

"Yes." He said, poking his head from around a tree trunk. I wanted him to be still and talk to me. He was moving around so much. It felt like I was chasing him to get the information I was seeking. He moved back behind the tree again. I heard him say, "Watch this." With one swipe of his hand, he pushed the entire tree over, revealing himself. He giggled, "I see you." He was so strong! And so innocent. I smiled. Surprisingly enough, he made me smile. "Father says, you can't be in heaven. You weren't supposed to ever go to heaven. You have to stay here."

"Why?"

"He says you did some bad things. Did you do bad things?"

I thought about all the innocent lives I'd taken, especially the baby. I let out a deep breath. It was one I felt from deep inside me. I turned my head from him. "Yes." I answered. "I've done some bad things."

"Why did you do them?"

"I," I needed to think about that question. Why did I do those bad things? Was it because of Nathaniel? Was it because of my nature? "I don't know." I answered.

"Do you feel bad about doing those things?"

I thought for only a moment, "Yes," I said. It was the truth. "At the time I was doing them, I didn't think about how bad it would make me feel at a time like this. But, yes, I do regret doing them. I do...feel bad

                    Ashley Lauren Mitchell

for doing them."

The boy came up to me and took my hand. He walked with me and talked to me. "Father says, you were born here in this Garden. He says you weren't like the other creatures in heaven he created. He says you are more like me. You have blood like me. And you and I have free will like humans. Father says he gave humans the gift of free will. That is the difference between beings in heaven and humans. Humans can choose to obey Father or not. They can choose to believe in Father or not. Ethereal beings do not have a choice. They do not have free will. They were made to have only one companion, and both were made to only serve Father. They cannot choose who they love. Father says, Lucifer, your father, wanted free will, like the humans. He wanted the power to choose. He wanted to make his own decisions and be more like...Father. Lucifer knew that Father was going to create me one day; an ethereal, and a human; even more perfect than Adam. So, Lucifer created you first. Father was angry. But, he says you were just too beautiful to destroy. So, he let you live. Although, he wouldn't allow you access to heaven, like I have, Father says, when I am old enough, I will go to earth. He says I will perform miracles and try to get other humans to believe in him. He says I will try to be good, but that humans will try to make me be bad. He says they will doubt me, condemn me. That's why you have to help me. Since you are immortal, you can be there

                                    Ashley Lauren Mitchell

when it is my time to go to earth. And you will help me. Won't you?"

He was so beautiful. His innocence was beautiful. Everything in him. Everything about him, was simply beautiful. I looked at him and told him, "I wish I could help you, but I am dead. Remember? Onaya killed me. That's why I am here?"

"You are not dead. You are dreaming. You cannot die Lamia."

I'm still alive? I'm just dreaming? "Does that mean I will go back to earth?"

"Yes," he answered too enthusiastically.

"And does that mean I will still have to kill humans, and drink their blood for sustenance?"

The young boy's smile went away. He was still when he finally spoke again. "No, you don't understand," he responded. "Father says, you are cursed to be a weapon. One of his weapons of judgment. You see, Father is not always very nice when it comes to punishment. He says some humans, and even some heavenly beings, don't deserve his kindness. They deserve to suffer. I am trying to teach Father to be gentler with the humans, and all his creations, but, he just gets angry when they do bad things. I don't know why they keep doing horrible things to themselves and to each other. It just makes

Father angry. He said he gave everyone and everything a purpose on earth, even though many of them never live to fulfill their purpose. Your purpose is to kill. As his weapon, you must use your powers to help Father. It is the only way. You must kill to live, and you must, live. Humans don't need the blood like you do. They just kill, for all the wrong reasons."

"Why am I cursed? Why must I be the one that keeps killing?"

"Father says...he says...he says, you were the first being to take your own life. And that is a sin."

"But I don't remember doing that. I don't remember any of the things I've been told about myself. I don't remember!" I was so irritated and upset by everything. All the things I've been told that I've done, and all the things I've been doing.

"Father says I was on earth once before. I don't remember it either. He said the same thing that happened the first time, will happen again. He said they killed me. The humans killed me. And in a very mean way. But I am not afraid Lamia. It is my destiny, and it will lead me back here. You must not be afraid. Even though what you did long ago still haunts you, you must be strong, and accept your fate. We all must. Father says you would take your life again if it were not trapped inside the human body."

                    Ashley Lauren Mitchell

I looked at the ground. I felt so empty. I couldn't believe I was that person. I fell to my knees. The boy came to me. He knelt down with me and took my hand. "Lamia," he said, "You have to use the love that you've finally found. It will keep you grounded. It will make you strong. You've finally found each other again."

"What do you mean, 'found each other again?' Who?"

"Adam."

"What?"

"Adam. The one who raised you in the Garden. The one you've always and only loved. Father says that you killed yourself because you lost Adam. Father says, for years after Adam was banished from the Garden, he felt shame and regret for the way he deserted you. It was the look he gave you that caused you to end your life. Adam's soul has been searching for you for all this time."

"But who? Where? Where is Adam's soul?"

"In the one you love the most. In the one you love enough to sacrifice yourself for."

It only took a second to know, "He's in my Uncle Tony?"

                    Ashley Lauren Mitchell

"Yes. When Adam discovered you were going to possess Lily's body, he hid in someone close to her, so that he could be close to you. He wanted to be the one to love you, to protect you, to teach you, like he did in the Garden. Adam wasn't your companion. Adam was your guardian. Your protector. He loved you like a father, and he felt he abandoned you. But, he's found you now. And you have to continue to allow yourself to love again, Lamia. You must take care of each other until it is time for Anthony's body to die, and Adam's soul to move on. It is the only way he will be satisfied; if he can take care of you again."

"He doesn't know who he really is?"

"No. He won't know that until he dies."

Uncle Tony? Dying? I couldn't bring myself to think of it. I'd die a thousand deaths to protect my Uncle Tony. "And when my Uncle Tony does die, will Adam's soul find me again?"

"Yes. It may take many years. Hundreds. Thousands, possibly. But once a soul has a mission, a purpose, it has it for all eternity. Souls are immortal. They never die. They only, reincarnate, relocate, to a different body. They just, have different ways of finding a new host. As I will, one day."

I began to feel like I'd known him before. This young boy. He seemed to be wiser than anyone I'd

                    Ashley Lauren Mitchell

ever met. He seemed to have all the answers. Or, at least, his Father did.

"Aww man," the little boy pouted.

"What? What is it?"

"Father says it's time for you to wake up."

"Your Father is speaking to you now?"

He laughed. "He's been speaking to me. Father always speaks to me. He was giving me the words to say to you. He speaks through me, because I am the only one in heaven and earth that can see him. But he will speak to you, if you speak to him first. And, you must listen carefully. He doesn't always answer you right away. And his response may not be in the form of words. But you will always get your answer. Father just has a creative way of answering when people speak to him. He's funny that way."

"But how do I speak to him? How will I know what to say?"

"You should say, say, whatever you want. Father just likes when you, when anyone, speaks to him, acknowledges him, loves him. Remember. Love, Lamia. Love. You must allow yourself to love. It is the greatest gift in life." He stood from his knees and put his hand on my head. I looked up at the beautiful young boy. "Don't forget the things that I've told you."

He said. "One day we will meet again. Now close your eyes."

I closed my eyes.

 Ashley Lauren Mitchell

<u>Chapter 27</u>

I smelled them. I knew they were close to me, even before I opened my eyes. Humans. Familiar humans. My eyes slowly blinked open. I was in Désirs Cachés, staring at the ceiling. I turned my head and saw Diamond. Her back was to me. She was sitting on the stage, head down, and tears flowing. Then, I saw, him. My Uncle Tony. He was sitting in a chair with his head resting on his thumbs, fists clenched tightly. He appeared to be talking to someone, but no sounds were escaping his lips. I couldn't stand to see either of them like this. Mourning. Me. I sat up. I watched them a moment longer. My humans.

"Hey there," I said. They looked at me at the same time and gasped.

Uncle Tony rushed to me. I could tell he wanted to grab me, hold me. But he restrained himself. He was staring at me with hesitation and confusion. "Lamia?" He asked, doubtfully.

I smiled. Knowing what I know about him now, makes him that much more precious and sacred to me. "It's me Uncle Tony."

                    Ashley Lauren Mitchell

He hugged me so tightly, that if I were a human, it would probably have crushed me. I hugged him back, just not as tightly.

"Oh my God! Lamia," said Diamond "Look." She was speaking to me but her gaze was directed at something behind me.

Uncle Tony looked at her then to what she was looking at. "Oh my God!" He exclaimed.

I looked at them with concern, then slowly I turned my head around. Behind us were mirrors lining the stage. "Oh, my, God!" Uncle Tony backed away as I stood up. I kept staring as I walked toward the mirrors. I put my hand up to touch it. I couldn't believe it. It was me. It was my reflection. I had a reflection! I looked at the glass and knew it was a gift. I closed my eyes and whispered, "Thank you," to whoever gave it to me.

***

It's been three months since that terrible day. As though time had been reversed, Bourbon Street in New Orleans looked like nothing had ever happened.

                          Ashley Lauren Mitchell

All the souls had been returned to their bodies; even the wicked. I didn't know if that was a good thing or a bad thing. It would be bad for the innocent people of this city, but good for my appetite. I remember all those faces in the crowd that were frozen in shock from seeing me. I remember them all. I know they are out there. I know that they are still doing all those terrible things I saw them doing in their eyes. I try to block it out.

I've searched for Nathaniel. I even went to Africa, to the Serengeti, to look for him, but I have not found him. Not even a trace. I try not to think about the last time I saw him. I try not to think about the fact that this curse of mine, is mine only to endure. Not his. He was never meant to be a vampire. He was never meant to have immortality. He was never meant to be, like me. I try not to think about the fact that I will never see him again. Or that all I have of him now are memories. Bittersweet memories.

Uncle Tony and Diamond have reopened Désirs Cachés. Diamond thought it should have a facelift. A facelift that took two months to complete. During that time Uncle Tony and Diamond found a new form of transportation. Me. I would teleport them any and everywhere in the world they wanted to go. As long as they are holding on to me when I teleport, they can come with. The travel makes Diamond nauseous, and it takes her a few minutes to recover once we've

          Ashley Lauren Mitchell

reached our destination. They trust me not to do anything...vampire-like when we are sightseeing in a foreign land.

The first place we teleported, was to Nathaniel's home in Haiti. Uncle Tony told me how Nathaniel had taken he and Diamond there. I know now it wasn't Nathaniel's wish to take them. He was doing what he was made to do. And it was never his intention to hurt them. Uncle Tony told me there was someone he wanted me to meet at Nathaniel's house. We went to the mansion and I met a woman, who, at first glance, looked vaguely familiar. Uncle Tony says she is my great-aunt Antoinette. Or, rather, was Lily's great-aunt. I saw her age in her eyes, but it wasn't present anywhere else on her. She was nearly ninety years old, but looked not much older than Uncle Tony. She was so kind. She hugged me like she'd always known me. She spent hours talking about Uncle Tony, who she still called Anthony, Nahdia, and the family Uncle Tony never met.

Antoinette is living in the mansion that used to belong to Nathaniel. She has developed a bond with the creatures of the house. As if they've known each other for years as well. They serve her now. She looks like she ages a little every time I see her. Like time is trying to catch up with her. Uncle Tony is afraid that she may not live for many years if that continues. She says, that she doesn't want to live forever. That perplexed me. I thought immortality was something that most, if not all, humans wanted. What they wished for. Everlasting life.

She said, "Life is precious, but sometimes it can be so much to bear. I have shed my fair share of tears, and known my fair share of pain. I want to face death with bravery and acceptance when it finally comes for me."

One night we were visiting her, and she told me that in a dream she'd had, something told her to give me a book. She went in the library and picked out a thick book, with a hard covering.

"This one," said Antoinette, handing the book to me.

"What is it?" I asked.

"This is called, the Bible. While I was dreaming, I was instructed to give it to you."

"By who?" I asked curiously.

"By God," she replied.

I took the heavy book and turned its thin, frail pages. After reading the first chapter, I knew why she was supposed to give me the book. I told Uncle Tony and Diamond that I was going to go away for a few nights so that I could read it alone. I went to Africa. I found a cave and hid myself in it. It was there, that I read the book. I studied the book. It was there, that I understood what the young boy was talking about. There were many stories. So many deaths. But there was one message. God is everywhere. He is in everything.

Once I realized who the young boy was that was talking to me in my dream, I felt...honored. And perhaps, even a little frightened. I had the chance to talk directly with God's son. The only one allowed to look upon the creator's countenance, and not die. I thought about when he would come to earth again, and realized, Uncle Tony and Diamond would be long gone by that time. I would be here however. I would always be here. Waiting for him. Waiting for what will happen when he comes to earth. Will it be like the book of Revelations? Will it really be like what the book of Amos, says it will be like? A day of darkness, and not light? A dark day with no brightness? This book puzzles me. The future puzzles me.

Mardi Gras is around the corner, and New Orleans is teeming with life. Good and bad, all here, mingling with each other. I'm sitting at my dressing table in Désirs Cachés. I have so many thoughts going through my head. I stare at my reflection. I find myself doing that a lot. I feel I am learning more about myself just by staring at the mirror. I even talk to myself

                                    Ashley Lauren Mitchell

when I'm looking at it. I wonder sometimes, if humans find it as helpful and entertaining as I do. But, they are probably used to it, and take something like having a reflection for granted.

I see Diamond appear behind me in the mirror. She is standing in the doorway, staring at me with pity.

"You know I hate when you look at me like that." I tell her.

"I know. I can't help it. You look so sad sometimes."

"Diamond, I have you and my Uncle Tony again. I am not sad. I'm just...thinking."

"Well, what are you thinking about all the time?" She asks as she makes her way toward me, and fiddles with my hair.

"About...so many things."

She looks at me through the mirror and says, "The things you must feel. The things you must know. It's more than a human like me can understand. I cannot begin to imagine what your thoughts must be like. But I can tell you this. I'm sure you have the most interesting, profound thoughts. You are so reserved, so trapped by yourself, that no one will ever truly understand you. Your uncle and I love you with all our hearts, and we know you love us. But long after we

                    Ashley Lauren Mitchell

are gone, and you are still here; something we've both come to accept; you cannot forget us. You cannot forget anything that has happened to you."

"How Diamond? How do I remember things hundreds of years from now? Thousands of years from now? Even a million years from now? What if I forget? How will I remember?"

"Lamia," she shrugged her shoulders, "You have to write it down. I'm not much of a reader. I don't have the patience for it. But you? You love to read. You've read hundreds of books. And how do you think history is passed down? Through books."

I looked at John Keats' book on my dressing table. I looked at the Bible in my chair. I looked at the bookshelf in the corner. Diamond was right. It was how humans' ideas, philosophies, theories, and even entertainment, became immortal. Through books. The written word. Knowledge passed down from generation to generation. Reading what happened in the past. Reading the things that went on in others' lives and minds. It was how humans know there is a God, a higher power. Or whatever name they give to the being. The being more powerful than they are; than we are. The being that created us. Created us to be different from all the other creatures of the earth. And in heaven.

Diamond bent over and wrapped her arms

around me. "Maybe tomorrow night you and I can go to Paris again. I really love that city."

We both smiled. I'm so glad to have her back in my life. As she pulled her arms away, her diamond bracelet caught a thread on my robe.

"Whoops," she said. "Oh, well, we'll just get you another one tomorrow. In Paris." She laughed. We laughed. "I'm gonna head downstairs before Tony comes up here asking why I'm taking so long. I swear, that man can still irk the hell outta me." She laughs, but behind her laughter I know, nothing about Uncle Tony irks her. Nothing at all. Not one bit.

Heartbeats pound loudly through the floorboards and above the music. But then, the music gets louder, even louder than the heartbeats. It is time. I look at my reflection and smile. I put the mask over my iridescent eyes. I must admit, I enjoy this operation more now, than I ever did before.

Their footsteps are climbing the stairs to my room. I go behind the curtain. The door opens, and then closes. I hear Diamond laughing on the other side of the door as she turns the key to lock my guest in. She is hilarious. The man looks around the room. He is still, quiet. He holds his breath. The only thing moving is his heart. He listens. He waits.

"Bonjour Monsieur." French. It makes me think of

Diamond. I think I will take her to Paris tomorrow night. She does love it there. I appear before him. Nude. "I remember you." I did remember him. He was one of the pernicious humans I saw that night atop the Superdome. "Yes, and I think you remember me too."

"Nah. I don't remember you." He says as he rubs his hands together menacingly.

"Of course you do." I don't toil with him for long before I take off the mask. He remembers me.

Blood is still as delicious to me as it always has been. I believe that will never change. Sometimes, I feel I cannot get enough. But there are times, like when I was in the cave that, I don't feel like feeding at all. The blood, the taste, it can cloud my mind. It can be the only thing I want and desire. So, sometimes I go a night without feeding. I even do as Nathaniel and I did that night in Las Vegas. I walk amongst the humans, watching them, learning them, smelling them, wanting them; but restraining myself and my hunger. Since everything happened, I feel I have gained more control of myself. I feel like I can control my hunger more, my actions more.

I pick up my dinner guests' body and teleport to the middle of the Pacific Ocean. I drop the body in. It makes a small splash. The moon is so beautiful, big and round. The stars, so bright. The reflection on

　　　　　　　　　　　Ashley Lauren Mitchell

the calm water is like thousands of jewels sprinkled across the ocean. It is quiet out here. I look at the water, stretching miles and miles into nothing. Only the water below me, and the moon and stars above me. Peace. But I cannot stay. I have to get back.

I walk out the back door of Désirs Cachés. Uncle Tony throws his hands up. "What happened to the body?" He asks.

"I took care of it Uncle Tony."

"You took care of it? That's supposed to be my job." He laughed. The New Orleans Police Department was so glad to have Uncle Tony back. They gave him a new car, a Dodge Charger. Although, I think Uncle Tony only cares about the size of the trunk. A trunk that I don't let him get to use as often anymore. My way of getting rid of the bodies is better than his. It's safer than his. It poses less risk of discovery. Not for me. For him. He knows it. "Thank you Baby Girl." He says and rubs my cheek.

I love when he calls me that. We laugh and I give him a hug. I missed him so much when he was away. I missed this, so much. I had no idea how much, until now. I heard his quickened heartbeat. He loves me. He kisses me on the top of my head.

"I'll be back. He says. "When Diamond comes to your room, cuz you know she is, tell her I'm moving the

                    Ashley Lauren Mitchell

car."

"Okay," I answer as I watch him drive away. I look up at the night sky. Then, I close my eyes. I wait for it. I wait for the cold breeze to blow across my face. But it doesn't. I go back to my room.

After Diamond and Uncle Tony leave me for the night, I am again left alone with my thoughts. I look at my room. It's different now. Diamond redecorated it. She chose black and purple for the color scheme this time. It is charming, quaint. Black candelabras and plush, purple furniture. A large chandelier with black jewels. A dark purple curtain. Diamond calls it, eggplant. It reminds me of Onaya's cloak. The dark, deep purple color. Onaya. My mother? What's become of her, I do not know. If I will ever see her again, I do not know. I'd rather not. But sometimes, I still wonder, about, my mother. About my father. About myself.

I sit and look at my reflection again. I remembered Onaya said I'd soul travelled many times before. How many times? And the humans that I possessed? What were they like? Why did I choose them? Or were they chosen for me, like Lily was? Lily. I know I'm so different from that girl, that poor girl, who didn't get to live out the rest of her life. Although, I know she is happy in heaven with her mother, I owe it to Lily to make sure her family and friends on earth are safe. Are loved.

My eyes wander and land on the bookshelf. Lily's books. She loved to read too. I wish she would have kept a diary, so that I could know more about her. More about her thoughts, her dreams, her aspirations. More about the person whose body is now my own. Then I think about what Diamond said. Words. A way to keep a soul immortal. Through art, through music, through literature. But I don't write. I do not do any of those things. Although it's true I have quite the affinity for reading. But writing? Art? Music? Onaya was the one with the power of the pen. She was the one who had the gift of...but she lost it. She lost her gift. And the need was so strong, she was forced to find other ways. Conduits. Ways to get her thoughts, feelings, emotions, ideas, messages, through to Lucifer. I looked at the Bible sitting in my chair. I looked at the poetry book next to me. The people that wrote those books, still live on in a way. Their stories, still being read and shared. Their souls, will live on into eternity, with me. With my soul. But, I am no author, nor poet. I am not like them.

I rise from my dressing table and make my way to my coffin. My mind is still racing with thoughts, thoughts, and more thoughts. I can control my hunger and my actions. But how do I control my thoughts? My never-ending thoughts. My all-consuming thoughts. I am back to that. I am back to not having any being, like me, to talk to. To understand me.

                        Ashley Lauren Mitchell

Except for him. The young boy. The boy that told me that no one would ever understand us, he and I. Or why we were really sent to earth. "But how can we make them understand?" I asked aloud to no one. My thoughts giving itself voice. Then, I heard something. Above the heartbeats and music, I heard something.

A voice? I opened my coffin. It was dark in my room. A candle was lit on my dressing table, but, I had blown all of them out before stepping into my coffin.

I looked around suspiciously, before making my way toward the light. The candle gave my warm skin a fantastic glow. I saw it in the mirror. I looked harder. Then I noticed, standing behind my reflection, was the young boy. He was smiling like he was happy to see me. I turned around. He wasn't there. I turned back. He was in the mirror, but he wasn't in the room with me. Only in the mirror.

"Lamia. We cannot make them understand. We can give them the knowledge they need, but their understanding must come from within. First, they must want to understand. And then, they must accept it."

"Accept what?"

"Accept the fact that they, as humans, will never truly know everything. They will never truly

                    Ashley Lauren Mitchell

understand everything. The fact that the universe, and their history is way more complex than they could ever imagine. The fact that their lives are on borrowed time. The fact that there is something more to the earthly life that has been given to them. The fact that there is something greater than they are. The fact that many of them spend their entire lives searching for answers they were never meant to know, when the greatest and most powerful thing in their world, is love. It is the only answer. The only thing that can save them. Love."

"But how do I let them know that? How do I get them to understand that?"

He lifted his arm and pointed to the dressing table in front of me. There was a black ink pen and a small tablet that wasn't there before. I stared at it as I heard him say, "Write it down."

By the time I looked back up, the young boy was gone. I looked at the supplies again. I was skeptical. I didn't know if I even knew how to write, let alone, knew what to write. I picked up the pen. It felt awkward in my hand. I let my fingers grip the instrument. I stabbed at the air with it like it was a knife. No. That's definitely not what I'll use it for. I don't know what to write. How am I supposed to get my message across to humans? How is the dead, supposed to communicate theories of life to the living? What to write?

I put the pen to the paper and scribbled on it. It works. I can make marks on the paper. Okay. Now make a letter. I wrote the letter, 'I'. Simple enough. Now write, 'am.' Okay, so I can write, 'I am.' 'I...am...I...am...I am not a monster.' No. No. That's not right. I scratch through it. My first line to humans cannot be 'I am not a monster.' They might think I'm some sort of monster or something. No. I need another line, something else. Maybe I should just introduce myself. Yes. I need to let them know who I am, not what I am not. They need to know what I know. And what I know is...who I am. And...what I've been through. Yes. I am Lamia. That's it. I am Lamia.

Call me Lamia.

At least that is what I tell people to call me. However, many of them don't last long enough after hearing it to repeat it. I live at Désirs Cachés...

　　　　　　　　Ashley Lauren Mitchell